A Voice in the Dark

A Voice in the Dark

The Philharmonia Years

by
Alexander Kok

Emerson Edition
E414

First published in Great Britain in 2002 by Emerson Edition Ltd.
Windmill Farm, Ampleforth, York YO62 4HF

The author and the publishers have made every reasonable effort to contact all
copyright holders. Any errors that may have occurred are inadvertent and
anyone who for any reason has not been contacted is invited to write to the
publishers so that a full acknowledgement may be made in subsequent
editions of this work.

ISBN 0 95062 096 3

Cover: Alexander Kok aged nineteen (always known as 'Bobby')
Photograph by John Vickers, London

Typeset in 12pt Gill Perpetua

Designed by Sandra Oakins

Printed by Panda Press of Haverhill, Suffolk.

Dedication

This book is dedicated to my close relations and also to friends in Cheltenham who, for the past thirty years, have supported the work of the Cheltenham Music Centre. Also to Walter Legge who, more than anyone else, encouraged me in my search for an understanding of what 'Life on Earth' could reveal through the medium of music.

Contents

Acknowledgements

I want to thank my brother Myron for his patient editorial help, Virginia Fortescue for her painstaking attention to detail and Katharine Prynne for her support from the time I began to assemble and order memories of my career. Thanks are also due to Martyn Jones, the archivist of the Philharmonia Orchestra, for his generosity in providing material from the archives. I am grateful to Alan Sanders for his sensitive words of criticism and advice, and even more to June Emerson for her determination to prevent faulty intonation. Finally, my thanks to Ken Day, Charles Mackonochie and Dave Culshaw for their help in tracing the whereabouts of some of the Alvis cars I have had the privilege to own since 1950.

CHAPTER ONE

Beginner's Overture

In 1938, entirely against my father's wishes, my mother left South Africa and brought her four sons to London to complete their education.

By the end of 1942 my eldest brother Darrell, having qualified as a doctor at the age of 21, was working at Friern Barnet Hospital in London. Felix was studying the violin at the Royal Academy of Music, and Myron, the youngest, was at St George's Chapel, Windsor.

Officially I was studying the cello at the Royal Academy of Music, having, together with Denis Vigay, been awarded the Ada Lewis Scholarship. Unofficially I was deputising, usually at short notice, in the Jacques String Orchestra, the Boyd Neel Orchestra, the Leslie Bridgewater Theatre Band at the Haymarket Theatre and whatever else came my way. Most weeks I would work in Fred Alexander's radio orchestra in the mornings and for Izzy Geiger in the afternoons in a tearoom ensemble in the Strand. In addition to all this, Felix, the pianist Virginia Fortescue and I broadcast a piano trio from Bush House for the BBC World Service every month.

With little time left for private practice, I trudged around wartime London carrying the cello, either because there were no buses, or because an over-worked conductor wouldn't allow me to board an crowded bus with my 'great fiddle'.

At the Academy on Tuesday afternoons Sir Henry Wood conducted the Senior Orchestra. This was the high point during my first year, which ended abruptly in my second with his death in 1944. His wisdom, generosity, and humour endeared him to all those students learning to walk the tight-rope of the orchestral repertoire.

On alternate Thursday afternoons there was a chamber concert for which rehearsals took priority. Chamber music presented the greatest challenge of all for me, so I took every opportunity to participate. Benjamin Dale, the Warden of the Academy, was always there to assist and instilled in us the essential rules of ensemble playing: unselfishness, and the ability to listen. I also played sonatas every week with Joyce Hedges who was not only an exceptionally fine performer but also gifted as a sight-reader. Nothing seemed too difficult for her and I felt completely outclassed by her technical ability and stage presence.

Until Mother decided to move us to Belsize Park we were renting a small, semi-detached house in Hendon belonging to Douglas Cameron, a cello teacher at the Royal Academy. A pupil of his, playing in the ship's band on the *Arundel Castle* when we travelled to England in 1938, had advised Mother to send me to him for lessons. The war intervened, Douglas Cameron left London, and it was not until late 1941 that Mother was able to establish contact again. It was a pretty little house, and although it was on the small side for the five of us it was nevertheless a happy time, in spite of air raids and straitened circumstances. Mother was working at South Africa House, Darrell was working at various hospitals, Felix was still at the Academy, and Myron at St George's, Windsor.

Eighteen months later, Mr and Mrs Cameron wanted to return to their home and suggested we ask Emmy Bass of Ibbs & Tillett, Concert Agents, if Mother could rent a large furnished flat near Chalk Farm which had been vacated by the Griller String Quartet soon after the war started. The flat, situated on the top two floors of a large house, had been more or less abandoned after the war began. Mother was naturally very grateful when the owners agreed to a lease that she could afford. We loved the extra space, but as all the household provisions had to be carried to the top floor Mother had the worst of the bargain.

Germany's latest invention, the 'doodle-bug' (the V1 rocket), kept us awake for most of the night before Felix was to play Vaughan Williams's *The Lark Ascending* at the Academy in June 1942. The noise of anti-aircraft guns at the top of Primrose Hill had interrupted our practice that night. There was so much commotion that we failed at first to notice the far more ominous sound of exploding bombs and to wonder why we hadn't heard any sound of aircraft engines. Felix and I climbed out on the flat roof and watched the searchlights playing criss-cross against the clouds. Searing flashes of exploding gunfire lit up the skyline and the noise was so deafening that we were forced to cover our ears. Mother begged us to join her in the basement but watching the enemy was too much of a temptation. The lethal implications only occurred to us when a large object veered in our direction. Somewhere in the vicinity of Chalk Farm it plunged into the earth in a giant flash followed by an enormous explosion.

For the rest of that night, and for the years that followed, many 'doodle-bugs' flew over our house. We learned to calculate the distance by the noise of its engine and hoped that they would pass us by.

The next day Felix and I went to the Academy as usual. With Sir Henry Wood conducting we rehearsed in the morning and gave the end-of-term concert in the afternoon. Felix played his piece as if nothing had disturbed his rest the previous night.

It was in July 1943, with the death of Benjamin Dale, that the character of the Academy suddenly changed. The students missed his informal, but always instructive, chats and began to rebel against the schoolroom atmosphere that the 'new broom' had brought to the post of Warden. Within a few months the feeling of fellowship and fun, at least such fun as was possible in time of war, seemed to have disappeared. His successor Dr Thatcher appeared to us more of an administrator than a teacher, who appeared to create rules simply to make his own job easier. I was probably

Sir Henry Wood

working too hard outside Academy hours, and the wartime diet didn't help either, but I began to be irritated by the routine jobs Dr Thatcher allocated to me merely because I was a scholarship holder.

That year I had my first attack of tenosynovitis, and had to spend hours waiting around at the rheumatism clinic near Great Portland Street; this didn't help either. When I explained to Dr Thatcher that rheumatic fever (which I had contracted in 1941) had left me with severe muscular problems, and that if I practised for more than an hour or so I was left with an arm that ached, and noticeably swollen fingers, he merely shrugged his shoulders and mumbled something about 'growing pains'.

To make matters worse, on Tuesday afternoons Sir Henry Wood's successor Clarence Raybould seemed to guarantee the onset of either the one or the other disability, and often both at the same time. As all string players were required to play in the orchestra, this weekly dose of muscle-pain, coupled with the humourless drudgery that he managed to bring to the occasion, became irksome. I was also having to refuse lucrative offers of work that clashed with Academy obligations. It was strange that, in those earlier heady student days when playing professionally, I never had aches and pains.

Dr Thatcher did not seem able, or willing, to accept that I tried to play the cello as I had learnt to sing as a chorister at St Mary's Cathedral, Johannesburg. He seemed more concerned with pure academic learning than the development of any performing talent I may have been born with. Years later Casals was to tell me 'You must always make the music sing, my boy, always sing!'

William Alwyn struggled hard to teach me harmony and counterpoint, and also tried to temper my 'certainties' about Dr Thatcher with some sense of proportion.

'You cannot fight shadows,' Alwyn continually reminded me; advice I was to be given by several other mentors in the years that were to follow. William Alwyn never talked down to his pupils, and always managed to impart scholarship without pedantry; altogether the best guide anyone could have had in studying musical analysis and performance. He more than anyone, in my two years at the Academy, helped me to find a balance between being *outside* a performance and yet at the same time, *inside* the actual notes. He agreed that although academic study may help to give validity to the style of a piece, knowledge alone did not necessarily elevate performance. The ability to phrase, regardless of the instrument, was what elevated instinctive awareness beyond the limitations imposed by intellect and discipline.

Later on, in 1949 during my very first lesson with Pablo Casals (*Le Maître* to his pupils), I tried to explain my version of this performer's ethic. Casals summed up my confused rhetoric.

'Yes, my boy, but you must understand first with the heart, then with the head. But, when you play, you always must play from the heart. Yes,' he repeated, as if to himself, 'always from the heart'.

Because the war had virtually halved the student intake at the Academy, I was able to participate in many more concerts than would normally have been the case, which brought useful benefits. Performance nerves were gradually brought under control and I had many opportunities to experiment with phrasing and dynamic contrast. I learned to ignore mistakes during performance because an odd slip could easily become a future memory hazard. Facial contortions, and self-indulgence too, had to be avoided, being embarrassing to watch and irritating to listen to.

One morning Joyce Hedges and I were told we had to perform the Rachmaninov Sonata at a Thursday Concert. Dr Thatcher entered the room while we were rehearsing and listened for a while. He then proceeded to deliver a lecture on accent and rhythm. It is true that we had been experimenting with the main theme in the first movement by widening the dynamic range, lengthening some notes and shortening others. I wasn't sure that I was justified in what I was doing but Joyce, as usual, was accurate and totally convincing. What seemed logical to us appeared to irritate Dr Thatcher profoundly. He advised me to read a book called *Rhythm, Structure and Purpose of Music*, which I dutifully did, but was more convinced than ever that he and I would always be irretrievably at cross-purposes.

Many years later a BBC producer told me that, when judging radio performances, BBC listening panels take into serious consideration what they call 'the tingle quotient'. I knew at once what he meant. I had felt it in the Mozart *Ave Verum*, and later when hearing Casals play the *Sarabande* from the Bach Suite in C minor as an encore at the Royal Albert Hall.

It was on the day that I collected a Betts cello that the Trustees of the Academy had agreed to lend me that I first met Fred Alexander. I was just about to cross Marylebone Road when a small wiry figure in baggy trousers and a sweater stepped out and gripped my arm.

'You're Bobby Kok, aren't you? Henry Elman told me that you might be at the Academy today.' (Henry was the freelance contact who had been offering me dates from my first year at the Academy.)

'Glad to meet you,' I said.

'Henry told me that the Academy was going to lend you the Betts cello,' he continued. Before I had time to comment Fred went on to ask whether I would consider lending him my own cello.

'What has happened to yours?' I asked guardedly. I had heard about Fred and his accident-prone life.

'The strap broke as I was cycling to Maida Vale Studios this morning,' he replied. 'The neck and belly have been damaged and it's going to take about two months before I can get it back from Hill's.'

'When do you need it?' I asked.

'This afternoon, 2.30 at BBC Maida Vale,' he answered promptly.

Realising that I was being emotionally blackmailed I began to feel slightly churlish. What he was *really* saying was 'can I have the Betts until mine has been repaired?'

'You had better use the Betts for today' I said grudgingly, 'but as it is still early, shall we go and see whether we can persuade Mr Whalenn to lend you one of his cellos for the next few weeks?'

There was little that Fred could do but agree. On the way he talked about his theatre work in the West End, studio broadcasts in several small BBC studios dotted around London, film sessions at Pinewood and Elstree, occasional work in the Palm Court Trio and innumerable other entr'acte bands. It was clear that he was a very busy man.

On arrival at 34 Nottingham Place we found my teacher talking to Paul Hill, of Hill and Sons. Paul was taking a cello from its wooden case and was about to hand it to Mr Whalenn. We watched as he examined the beautiful golden varnish and then Paul Hill turned and asked me if I would play the instrument he was holding, and then the other one still in its case, so that he and my teacher could hear what they both sounded like. He made me sit down before he handed it to me.

'If you trip and fall, I shall be responsible,' he explained. 'You are holding a very rare instrument. Have you heard of Stradivarius? You have? Good, because you are going to play us a little bit of the Romberg C major Concerto on a fine example of his work.'

It was the first time I had ever played a Strad, but I didn't enjoy the experience at all. Certainly, compared with my cello, there was a difference of touch. When I played my own cello I could hear the noise I was making right under my ear, but the sound of the Strad seemed to begin its life at the other end of the room.

'The bigger the room, the better the cello will sound,' Paul said, responding immediately to my puzzled reaction.

Fred then took up the challenge, and within a few minutes, the cello was speaking in that mysterious way that Italian instruments have. You first have to find that voice, then have the talent to project it. To do that you had to be the player of the quality Fred was. We then played the other cello and I was told subsequently that Amaryllis Fleming had bought one and William de Mont the other.

Some time later that day Fred rang to invite me to do a series of broadcasts with him in a recently formed light orchestra at the BBC. Very soon I was playing for him at least twice a week, and was his first call or 'Deputy Sub-Principal' as he called me.

One morning, at rehearsal, I couldn't help noticing that Fred didn't seem to be his usual cheerful self. The conductor that day was a European refugee who was beginning to make a niche for himself in London. His energy was so overwhelming that we were soon gasping for a breather. The 'carver', as this calibre of conductor was usually called in orchestral parlance, had the makings of a bully. He wanted more tone, and in the dry acoustic of Maida Vale Studio Two the sound of the orchestra was admittedly dead. He kept demanding more sound from the strings and the more we remonstrated that we couldn't play louder, the angrier he became. Finally we gave up trying to explain and resorted to watching the second-hand of the BBC wall clock, creeping towards the statutory tea-break.

The second half of the rehearsal began with the overture *Morning, Noon and Night in Vienna*, by Suppé. This piece has a lovely cello solo, which Fred began to play in his usual impeccable way. It was, of course, beautifully in tune and immensely enjoyable but the sound was definitely on the soft side.

'Very good,' said the conductor, after the first run through. 'But,' he added, 'please, try to play a little louder.'

Fred said he would try and we started from the beginning again. He had hardly finished the first phrase when the conductor stopped again.

'Please!' he said. 'Please play a little louder—it is not strong enough.' He then tried to ingratiate himself by saying 'You make it sound like it is all night and no morning.'

Nobody laughed. We started again. This time there was no sound from Fred, who was looking a picture of abject misery.

'Why don't you play?'

'I can't,' said Fred. 'I've tried very hard but I can't afford a really good cello—not just at present.'

'Don't waste any more time. Play!'

'It's no good,' said Fred. 'I need a better cello for my new job at the BBC, but they pay so little that I can't afford to buy a complete one. This one has a lovely belly, a very good scroll, and it is exactly the right size for me. The trouble is,' and he turned the instrument round for us all to see, 'that I haven't been able to afford a back for it yet.'

With one accord the orchestra collapsed, and nobody, not even the humourless 'carver', could possibly continue with the rehearsal. He called another break.

During this second interval I saw Fred take out the cello I had helped him choose from Mr Whalenn two months before. Exactly when he had persuaded Paul to lend him a back-less cello I was never able to discover. Knowing Fred as I did, I am certain he had become dissatisfied with his own instrument after playing on the two Stradivarius cellos.

Soon after my first experience of Fred's histrionic talents, Dr Bischop, an elderly Hollander and a Rhodes Scholarship Trustee who had got to know Mother while she was working at South Africa House, introduced me to two fellow Afrikaners, Etienne Amiot and Arnold van Wyk. Both worked in the Overseas Service of the BBC at Bush House. Mr Amiot suggested that I and my two elder brothers should broadcast a piano trio to South Africa once a month, but early in 1944 Darrell, the eldest, qualified as a doctor, and, as his post-graduate work took him away from home so often, we were eventually obliged to work with another pianist.

Letter-writing has always been difficult for me, so these broadcasts gave Father a direct, if somewhat tenuous, link with three of his four sons. It was difficult to maintain contact with him during these war years, and atmospherics made our broadcasts almost impossible to hear properly (something I was glad I didn't know at the time).

At that time the history of relations between Britain and South Africa were unknown to me. Only later did I learn of my father's deep anger about our new home. He wrote to us as often as circumstances permitted, but it was often very difficult to read his letters because, in the interests of wartime economy, the volume of mail had to be limited. Private letters were photographed and reduced to about the size of a post card and much of what had been written was illegible.

I asked him once why he refused to remain in England after his one visit in 1939. His reply was that I should read an entertaining, if biased, biography of Rhodes by Sarah Gertrude Millin. At the time, her sins of omission were more obvious to him than to me, and it never occurred to me that Mother's decision to separate the family was a cause of grief to him. He never allowed his private sorrow to burden the tone of what he wrote, so for the last seven years of my father's life, I lived and worked in total ignorance of his loneliness, final illness, and the manner of his death.

In October 1947 he died, and within a few weeks of his death our house in Notting Hill Gate was burgled. A suitcase was stolen containing a recording of the Schubert Trio in B flat that my two brothers and I had made in Johannesburg in 1939, a few family heirlooms and souvenirs, and Father's letters to me. Although I never re-read them, I nevertheless have some recollection of what he wrote and I still have the two books he sent me.

Although I was escaping the moribund atmosphere of the Academy more often perhaps than I should have done, for Joyce Hedges daily existence was very different. She lived about thirty miles from the Academy, had nowhere to stay in London and no transport of her own. As pianists were more plentiful than string players, the more I succeeded in finding work, the more depressed and defeated she became.

One day a friend told me that ENSA (Entertainments National Services Association), had formed a new classical music section, having decided that music should not only soothe but also serve to inspire. Apparently not all service personnel were content with *Roll out the Barrel* or yet another performance of *The White Cliffs of Dover*. I persuaded Joyce that it might be worth our while applying for an audition as a duo. Even if we failed no possible harm would be done, and there was a chance of raising the stakes for both of us. We sent off our application and received a request to audition at Drury Lane Theatre.

CHAPTER TWO
A voice in the dark

Joyce's teacher, Vivian Langrish, agreed that we should audition for ENSA, and although I had had doubts about my abilities as a soloist, I felt reasonably confident about playing as a sonata duo. Joyce had, earlier that year, won a prize entitling her to play Rachmaninov's *Variations on a Theme of Paganini* at the next season's Promenade Concerts. I was her junior by several years, and consoled myself that there would be time for me to try again if she was successful and I wasn't.

The disparity in available work for cellists and pianists has always been a problem for the latter. Although I needed more time to practise than she did, Joyce had the time but I did not. Early on the day of the audition we played through my cello solos, and, although conscious that the Brahms Sonata had perhaps not been rehearsed as much as it might have been, we left for the Theatre Royal, Drury Lane, full of the optimism of the young.

The first shock for me was the enormous sloping stage of the theatre. Confronted by the vast, dark, silent auditorium a feeling of panic swept over me. Outside the streets had been full of bustling porters shouting cheerful obscenities to each other and carrying piles of wicker baskets filled with market produce on their heads. Inside the theatre was depressing, dreary, cold and remote. My second shock was the discovery that my part of the Brahms Sonata was missing.

'Don't fret,' said Joyce. 'Play as much as you can remember and save the explanation for later.' It didn't appear to be an insurmountable problem while off-stage, but her easy solution suddenly seemed far from simple on-stage. Before I had the time to whisper to Joyce that I had lost my nerve, someone in the dark auditorium asked for the names of the pieces we were proposing to play. In a barely audible croak I named the pieces we had prepared, but put them in reverse order. If the Brahms was at the end we might not have to play it at all.

'Brahms,' said the voice from the darkness. 'Let's hear the Brahms.'

I sat down and looked despairingly at Joyce, but I needn't have worried. After only a few bars of the first movement the voice interrupted and asked whether I played the Haydn Cello Concerto. The question seemed inappropriate as I was supposed to be the cellist in a sonata duo.

'Yes,' I replied, without thinking.

'Good.' The voice in the dark was authoritative. 'Come and play it to me next week. Next please.'

It was true that I had played the concerto in the privacy of my own room, but would I be able to perform it to that 'someone' in a week's time? As we were leaving the stage the full extent of what I had let myself in for began to dawn on me. Joyce and I had agreed to audition as a duo. For that I was prepared and would have enjoyed the opportunity of playing sonatas very much. Now I would have to face another audition, this time as a soloist. In 1943 there was only one Haydn cello concerto, the D major, since the easier work in C major had not yet been discovered. It would therefore be impossible to pretend, at the last moment, that I had learnt the wrong concerto. Nothing had been confirmed in writing, so I could perhaps have been able to gain a little more time. It never occurred to me that anyone would fail to be impressed by Joyce's performance. It seemed obvious to me that even though we were auditioning as a sonata duo, her contribution would be the one to be selected.

We left the theatre and went to the little Italian café I frequented whenever I was working in the vicinity. How could I hope to learn the Haydn in a week? We ordered our coffee and sat in silence for a while, each waiting for the other to make the first comment. There were several implications in the current development and I could see that Joyce was upset.

'I've not been asked to return for another audition,' she said glumly, 'but you have.'

'Don't be silly,' I replied. 'You've obviously passed but they are not sure about me.' Nevertheless the chaos of the morning's events could not easily be ignored and I began to consider whether anything could be done to salvage matters. While we were sitting immersed in our thoughts the café gradually filled up with tough-looking porters whose work-technique I had been admiring so much earlier that morning. I felt myself drawn to them, drawn also to this great Metropolis with its millions of inhabitants all striving for - what? Certainly not the opportunity to hear Alexander Kok play the Haydn Cello Concerto, of that I was sure.

The nearest person, a burly but kind-looking man, suggested it was a 'great fiddle' when I asked him if he could tell me what he thought my cello was. Then the thought struck me. All these people must also have had challenges to overcome. I wasn't alone. The longer I sat there, listening to their talk about war, shortages, relatives in trouble or away in the Armed Forces, the more I felt that I should at least try to think of my challenge as an opportunity presented by that voice in the dark. Slowly I began to warm to the idea and, by the time I reached home, I had made up my mind to learn the concerto.

A week later Joyce and I were back in Drury Lane, but this time before we had even reached the artists' room, Joyce was asked to wait in the wings while I was taken to a small office. There I was introduced to Mr Montague, a kind looking man who placed a tick beside my name on a typed list in front of him. After shuffling some papers and various forms he produced a new file and asked the usual questions about name, nationality, liability for military service, date of birth, and so on. As he talked I was becoming increasingly agitated. Why was I not playing before having to complete the paperwork? What must Joyce be thinking? I asked Mr Montague if we would have any opportunity to rehearse a little before we played.

'We?' he asked.

I explained about Joyce patiently waiting for me in the wings. Without responding, he pulled out a contract for me to sign, saying that I had been accepted as a cellist in the Classical Section of ENSA. He then went on to ask me to reserve several dates, including some for a tour of the UK. He also wanted to know whether I would tour abroad, explaining that if I were to be captured I would have the rank of a Junior Officer.

As he rambled on I began to come to my senses. This was absolute madness. The whole idea had been to help Joyce find some work so that she could afford to live in London and build a career, and for us to gain a little more platform experience. The Haydn was a side issue. I had assumed, wrongly, that the panel wanted to hear me play a more demanding piece. Now, here I was in ENSA, with an offer of concerts while Joyce had not been offered anything. I asked Mr Montague when I was to play the Haydn.

'What Haydn?' he asked.

'You surely must remember. When I was here last week I was asked by someone in the stalls to come back and play the Haydn Concerto.'

Mr Montague glanced at a large desk-diary.

'Oh yes. I do remember now,' he said. ' But don't worry about it,' he added with a smile. 'If you had said you couldn't play it you wouldn't be here today.'

I was both relieved and disappointed. Relieved because I didn't have to play. Disappointed because I had never before worked so intensively on one piece and was almost looking forward to the challenge. I still think it might have been a better test of my ability if I had been called to account that morning. One way or another my career might have had more direction, even if the audition had only resulted in my having to go back to the practice room. On the other hand it is just possible that the owner of that voice in the dark knew best.

In the months that followed I travelled extensively for ENSA in England, Scotland and Wales both as soloist and as a member of several other concert parties. I shall never forget a concert in Southampton on Good Friday 1944. The programme included the Beethoven A major Sonata, some cello solos including *The Swan* by Saint-Saëns and an arrangement of Franck's *Panis Angelicus* with cello obligato. It was to be given for about 600 troops who had just arrived back in the UK after having been incarcerated aboard a troopship for several weeks. Their disembarkation had been scheduled to enable them to come to the concert before returning to the transit camp.

It is always difficult to please all tastes at all times, but on an occasion like this the attempt was verging on the impossible. What sort of entertainment would be suitable for men who had been on active service for years, who had been cooped up in cramped conditions for weeks and who wanted above all to forget about army discipline for a few hours. There had only been two choices available to them: further incarceration in the transit camp, or Beethoven, *Panis Angelicus*, and *The Swan*. They turned out for the concert to a man.

A printed programme with the usual brief music analysis and short biographies of the artists was available, and this should have provided the audience with a hint of what was to come. Perhaps, in mitigation of their subsequent behaviour, they should have been given an opportunity to leave before the concert began. Previous ENSA concerts had passed without too many mishaps and I was expecting the normal restrained but polite applause.

The tenor, a Norwegian called Eskil Arse, decided to introduce a chummy note into the proceedings by describing each item in fuller detail, 'Just to help create the right mood,' he explained. When this tall, thin, and terribly sincere man gave phonetic certitude to what could previously have been thought to be no more than a rather mischievous printer's error, the whole audience erupted.

My Dutch name *Kok* means *Cook* in English. However, for healthy young troops, brought up in a society where homosexuality was rarely referred to publicly, except in terms of extreme disapprobation, the prospect of being entertained by Messrs Arse and Kok was more than mortal man could bear. If this were not enough, the tenor's pronunciation of the word *Panis* was ambiguous in the extreme.

For some minutes it was impossible to make a start, but with the appearance of two military policemen the furore finally subsided. It was obvious however that the troops were in no mood to take the players, their music-making or the concert very seriously. At every pause or interval a few would slip quietly away, and by the time we had finished there were only about ten people left, and that included the performers, the officer in charge and a fire officer.

I once read that the Marx Brothers, on their first visit to the Mid-west, were not going down very well with a rough audience. Suddenly the hall began to empty as word got around that there was a fight going on outside. After the fight was over everyone trooped back expecting that the show would be resumed. When the Brothers refused to continue the audience became a threatening mob. This so enraged Groucho that he strode on to the platform and berated the audience. Thinking that this was part of the show the audience responded in kind. As a consequence, a routine was created that was first developed into a review and finally into the unforgettable Marx Brothers films.

I wish that I had had the presence of mind to turn that good-humoured laughter to such profit. Instead I just became annoyed. The whole set-up had a touch of the ridiculous about it and they were simply passing judgment in the only way they knew. In due course I was asked to explain what had happened at the concert in Southampton. I talked about music, musicians and the phonetic implication of my surname. It was suggested that I might use a stage name in future but, after consideration, I decided that Kok, apart from being palindromic, has the advantage of being concise.

Shortly before the war ended there was talk of a possible tour to the Far East. Extreme climatic variations can cause havoc with instruments and at supper after an ENSA concert at an army-training centre in Wiltshire, one of the officers suggested I should use a copper cello. I had never heard of such a thing and I asked him to tell me more. The officer, a Kentish man, explained that his village church had just such an instrument.

Apparently during the Civil War a platoon of Cromwell's Roundheads, in a burst of puritanical zeal, had smashed and burned the church organ. Thereafter vicars had to rely on an odd assortment of instruments to lead the singing. As time passed this support changed from serpents and sackbuts to the more malleable tones of a string quartet.

With the arrival of coal mining there were further changes to the life of the village. The local cellist began playing on Saturday nights in a newly established mining community hall in the next village. To begin with all went well. He borrowed the cello on Saturday night and returned it the next day, providing a bass line for both spiritual and secular needs. Soon, however, the cellist began to find that the walk on Saturday night, followed by an early rise on the following Sunday morning, was more than he could manage.

The priest was a forgiving man. He understood only too well how after the week's labour, and then more hard work on Saturday night, the over-worked cellist would succumb to the attractions of another village's nightlife. To counteract the tensions that were threatening to divide the congregation, the vicar persuaded a coppersmith to make a copy of the community cello. The copper cello would remain in the church in case of emergencies while the wooden one could still be used for important services.

When the church organ was eventually reinstated neither instrument was required. Saved from the melting pot by an amateur musician, the copper cello was suspended in a corner near the altar where it had remained ever since, serving both as a decoration and a souvenir of things past.

I was intrigued by this story and so one morning in May 1945 I travelled down to Kent and introduced myself to the vicar. I had taken some used strings and a bow with me and soon had the instrument working. It had very little dynamic range and the notes boomed in such a way that a change of pitch necessitated exaggerated articulation by the left hand. There was also a time-lag between the stroke of the bow and the sound, making it rather difficult to play fast. Nevertheless it would do. How it was to be transported was a problem for another day. I returned to London, wrote my report and waited for official reaction. Two months later the United States exploded the first atomic bomb over Japan, and by the time the second one was dropped, it was obvious that the war in the Far East would no longer require the use of a copper cello.

CHAPTER THREE
Hampton Court

It was while playing with the Jacques String Orchestra in 1944 that I took part in a series of concerts at Hampton Court. Initially I was intrigued by the building's historical associations and its architectural changes over many centuries, but I gradually found myself becoming more interested in the craftsmanship of the anonymous workers than in the posturings of the Palace's former occupants, particularly in the matter of the politico-religious conflict between Cardinal Wolsey and Henry VIII.

From the craftsmen who built this wonderful example of Tudor architecture I was eventually led back to the composers and the music of the time. *Dum Transsiset Subatum*, written by John Taverner, while holding a position in a society dominated by Catholic values, spoke directly to my heart and mind. It was inconceivable that this same man, having converted to Protestantism, helped to destroy beautiful Dutch church organs and thereafter chose to write music that was as arid as the desert from which his new-found Biblical inspiration had its written source.

Three centuries of polyphony, anchored in buildings of immense acoustic satisfaction *ad maiorem Dei gloriam* came to be supplanted by secular offerings to the Greater Glory of Man. There can be no justification for vandalism that attacks the essence of creative works of art that reach beyond the gratification of a personal ego.

I thought about the generations of skilled workmen who had, over the years, made their individual or collective contributions to the complicated mosaic of the Palace—building, inventing, creating works of art in stone, wood and textile. I imagined them eating, arguing, plotting, grieving, listening to and making music. How fortunate it is for us that Hampton Court escaped the fate of so many other fine buildings, destroyed during the years of Reformation and Counter-Reformation that followed in the next two centuries.

The orchestra was rehearsing for an evening concert when suddenly our efforts were interrupted by the sound of an enormous explosion. There had been no prior warning so we concluded that it must have been a land mine. We were later told that an unexploded bomb had been detonated near the local gas works and that both bomb and gas container had exploded. A few months later the unofficial grapevine provided the information that the 'doodle-bug' had been superseded by the V2 rocket. The explosion at Hampton Court had in fact been a V2.

London was definitely not a very healthy place in which to live and work. Officially everything was fine and concerts would take place as planned. Fairly heavy bombing by enemy aircraft in the early part of the year was followed in the course of the summer by more rocket attacks. First came the Vl followed a year later by the V2 but nevertheless, in this period of great uncertainty and with the possibility of sudden death at any moment (especially for Londoners), Mother borrowed two hundred pounds from her elder sister for the deposit on a house just off Finchley Road.

When the house was vaporised by a V2 rocket a week before completion, Mother bought another further along the same road, but a little nearer Golders Green. At a time when anxious parents tried to have their children evacuated for their safety to Canada and South Africa or to country areas in Britain, she chose to keep hers in London, apart from the youngest son who was at school in Windsor.

During her last illness I asked her how she managed to control her fear during the period of the rocket attacks. She reminded me what Luther had said: 'Even if I were to be told that the world would perish tomorrow, I would nevertheless go out and plant an apple tree today.' This was part of her background, and coupled to her innate spirit made her the woman she was.

Through the good offices of Sir Sidney Clive, my elderly mentor at the Royal Academy, I was fortunate enough to meet Major and Mrs Cecil Wills, two of the kindest people I have ever met. They both loved music enough to help the next generation of young artists overcome some of the profession's early hazards. Major Wills included me in visits to various museums and auction rooms to see examples of Chinese and Japanese pottery and porcelain in which I was beginning to take an interest. This led me on to the Victoria and Albert Museum and a study of period furniture in period settings. Little by little I learned how houses were built and about the people who built and lived in them. I was curious to know who served in them, who played music in them, what sort of music was played, who paid for the events, who made the instruments, the strings, the bows. I learnt about preparing surfaces prior to painting, about coping with damp, woodworm and fungus. It began to dawn on me that, as far as repairing houses was concerned, there is usually an answer for everything, even if finding it requires a great deal of physical and mental effort.

The social life to which the Wills introduced me was very gratifying, but the atmosphere at work was completely different. The dislike of the upper classes was almost more threatening than the bombing. I was sitting in a Lyons tearoom one day, talking about the war and what should be done to rebuild bombed cities and to raise the general standard of living and education. An elderly woman sitting at the next table interrupted our conversation and gave me a sharp reminder that the class struggle in England, although temporarily submerged by the war, had resurfaced but with added venom as a result of the landslide victory of the Labour Party.

'The upper classes must be destroyed, and until that happens, there will be no lasting peace in the world,' she said.

Over the next few years I was to see countless lovely houses demolished because their owners were denied the funds to maintain them. Beautiful two-and-a-half-inch thick mahogany doors, complete with door furniture, were torn off solid brass hinges and thrown on rubbish heaps to feed the fires of envy. This then was the real cancer that had emerged from the war: an all-consuming, envy-ridden iconoclastic desire to destroy the old values so as to implement new ones. During the six long years of the war people appeared to be united in their support of the war effort. Even before the war was over I sensed that this apparent solidarity had been a mirage that was fast evaporating.

The Greeks taught that civil war is the greatest evil in politics, and that the wise politician should conveniently direct the people's passions outwards. The bitterness I encountered in England during the latter part of the war, especially in the industrial north, reminded me of the very real poverty I had witnessed as a young boy coming to London in 1938. World War Two certainly solved the unemployment problem for politicians of the day, and the destruction of vast areas of Europe would keep workers busy for many years to come.

In the winter of 1949 I was returning home on a late train to Waterloo from a recital in Southampton. My hostess in Southampton had kindly provided me with some sandwiches and a flask of coffee for a journey that would probably take several hours. I had hardly settled down to enjoy them when the door opened and two men entered the compartment. They sat down opposite and eyed my provisions.

'You gonna give us some of that bread?' said the smaller one, wedging me into the corner of the compartment. I had four sandwiches so I offered two.

'What about the other two?'

I replied that I was hoping to eat them myself.

'You ain't as hungry as we are,' said the other, paring his fingernails with a flick knife. Before handing over the coffee I swallowed a cup and handed them the rest. The gesture seemed to please.

'We just jumped ship,' the one man said in between mouthfuls, still holding the open knife in his hand as he ate. 'We ain't had no food for a long time and we got no money.' The point was easily taken so I handed over my last pound note to the man with the flick knife.

'Thanks, mate.'

When we were nearing London, I was asked to point out Clapham Junction and when the train stopped the two men disappeared. As we pulled away from the station they came back.

'When we get to Waterloo, you just tell the ticket collector we got on at Clapham Junction.' The flick knife re-appeared but he could see that I didn't need any persuading.

As it happened there was no problem at Waterloo. The ticket collector accepted the men's story and they disappeared into the night. I reported what had happened and asked whether this sort of robbery by blackmail was commonplace. The ticket collector shrugged.

'It's too late to argue,' he said. 'Anyway, we've been told to lay off and not to ask these recent arrivals too many questions.'

I now had only some loose change left, so I found a taxi and explained the situation to the driver. He was sympathetic but it was very late and he was tired. He took me as far as my money permitted and then set me down with a cheery goodnight.

Carrying the suitcase in one hand and the cello in the other, I began the long walk from Baker Street. I had just passed Finchley Road Station when a police car stopped. I was asked by the sergeant to open the suitcase, and after satisfying himself about the contents, he wanted to know why I was walking. I explained the happenings of the night and told how I had been left with no money. It was all fairly comical and I was not really annoyed, but he was.

'Ever since the end of the war,' he said, 'we can't keep track. We used to know the regulars but it's anybody's game now. Jump in and we'll give you a lift home.'

CHAPTER FOUR
A Slow Trill in a German Dance

Travelling around London on public transport gave me plenty of time for reading. My first attack of rheumatic fever in 1941 confined me to bed for over six weeks and Mother, ever solicitous, had provided me with a selection of books. Her theory was that I should take the opportunity to read each book five times rather than five books once. Her reading schedule included a complete volume of Shakespeare, the King James Bible, Trechmann's translation of Montaigne's Essays and, as a concession, some historical novels by Jeffery Farnol, Zane Gray, and other examples of what Balzac would probably have described as 'the Opium of the West'. Most of the books in my sickbed library were not exactly easy going, but with nothing else to do I found myself at first interested, and then absorbed. What stimulated me more than the wisdom and speculation of the Bible and the Bard was the compelling range and insight of Montaigne's non-proselytising humour.

As the years pass I discover new Montaigne truths again and again in the endlessly inquisitive narrative of his writing. He has provided many trains of thought that have kept company with me during boring recording sessions, especially those in which pop singers were guided a hundred times through areas of uncertainty before achieving a possibly saleable product.

My daily merry-go-round was made even more complicated when I fell in love with a beautiful girl called Gillian Lightfoot. Unfortunately I found that quoting Shakespeare's sonnets is one thing, but success with the opposite sex is another. My calf-love's attempts to express the Bard's flights of fancy died as they were uttered. My brother Felix got there first.

I worked with Fred Alexander and Henry Elman on the basis that sometimes 'sudden illness' would cause one of them to call me in at the last minute. Conductors knew very well that these recurring maladies were either an early-morning broadcast followed by another broadcast, or a film recording. Within this flexible arrangement the three of us were able to operate a mutually satisfactory strategy. It provided 'fixers' (the middlemen who booked freelance players) with a cellist's 'bum on a seat'. Band-leaders and conductors never had to worry because a player's primary duty was to mark the parts correctly for whoever would be playing at the performance. In this way evening concerts, late or early-morning broadcasts, 'Come Dancing' or whatever, were provided with a vital safety-net should some special 'gig' (i.e. the one that paid the most) be offered at the last moment. Sometimes the entr'acte dates required me to do either the rehearsal or the concert, but whatever suited the fixer suited me.

James Whitehead, an extremely talented cellist I had met while working in the Boyd Neel Orchestra, asked me to play in a performance and recording of Benjamin Britten's *Serenade* for tenor, horn and strings. Some months later he invited me to play in the first-ever concert of the Philharmonia Orchestra, recently founded by Walter Legge. The inaugural concert was to be conducted by Sir Thomas Beecham, and

The Maharajah of Mysore, whose financial support enabled Walter Legge to launch the Philharmonia

Walter Legge

Photograph Douglas Glass

the first rehearsal was to be at the Kingsway Hall on October 27th 1945. In the preceding eighteen months I had gained valuable platform experience which I put to good use at that concert. There were four cellists in the section and I was the fourth.

As soon as I arrived for that first rehearsal I realised that there were not going to be any 'rehearsal deputies' here. I had moved into a different field. The leader of the orchestra on that never-to-be-forgotten occasion was Leonard Hirsch. Looking round I recognised many colleagues with whom I had worked before. The principal cellist, Anthony Pini (Charlie) I knew of but had never met. He was a fine instrumentalist, and his honest and poetic recording of the Elgar Cello Concerto exactly illustrated the character of the man. No nonsense, no pretence at emotion, perfect intonation and rhythm and a beautiful tone. Without doubt the most distinguished principal I have been privileged to share a desk with. In the few months of Charlie's association with the orchestra I was educated to a degree that was only equalled, although in an entirely different way, by his successor Raymond Clark, whose playing became as legendary as the Philharmonia Orchestra itself. Jimmy Whitehead was sub-principal, James Harvey-Phillips was number three, and I was number four. Nineteen years old and tall, I felt acutely self-conscious, having been introduced to Charlie by Jimmy as 'the baby' in an orchestra of star-ranking hardened professionals.

The orchestra assembled and I sat down on the last chair in the cello section, frighteningly aware that there were only four of us. I remembered Fred's rule of thumb for string players in an orchestra: 'He who is heard is lost'. In other words, you ensure that you play in tune with everyone around you, you don't hang on to notes, you begin and end with the section, keep an eye on the bow speed of the principal, and always play, within the pulse of the beat, with the rest of the orchestra. Tuition in the art of orchestral playing under Fred's watchful but kindly eyes and ears had been a pleasure and a privilege I have never forgotten. Nevertheless, sitting that morning on the platform of the Kingsway Hall, I felt wholly unprepared.

Before I had time to dwell on all this everyone stood up (this is something that rarely happens in the difficult business of shared artistic creation) and Sir Thomas Beecham walked slowly towards the podium. He seemed to know everyone, stopping to have a word with those nearest to him as he crossed the platform. He greeted Charlie and Jimmy and then stopped in front of me.

'I don't think we have met before,' he said a deliberate manner that completely unnerved me.

'No, Sir Thomas,' I replied. 'We haven't.'

'What is your name, my boy?'

'Kok, Sir Thomas.'

With a wicked twinkle in his eyes, he looked for a moment at Henry Ball, one of the second violins.

'Kok,' he repeated. 'Hmm, Mr Kok. And here we have Mr Ball. How singular!'

There was absolutely no mockery in his voice, it was just an example of the endless delight Sir Thomas took in word play.

Years later, while having one of those farcical medical examinations that insurance companies insist on, the examining doctor was interested to learn that I was a professional musician. He asked me if I had ever played under Beecham and I described the events on that morning in 1945. The doctor then told me that as a newly qualified practitioner, anxious to establish himself with the more affluent members of London society, he had been called on to attend Sir Thomas. Delighted as he was to have such a distinguished patient, he soon came to realise that this would be no easy brief. It was evident that his duties were not going to be confined to medical care alone. His elderly patient intended to extract as much pleasure as possible from this coda to his richly varied life.

Sir Thomas was obviously lonely, and must have found a sympathetic listener in the young doctor. He invariably insisted that they should both smoke a very large cigar with their morning coffee. This became a regular occurrence and as a result the routine medical examinations took up a great deal more time than the young doctor's practice could afford. One day however Sir

Thomas explained that he was having what he described as the 'Marks and Spencer' of the profession to lunch, so the medical examination would have to be conducted without the customary cigar and chat. The young doctor was not at all sorry as strong coffee and a cigar before lunch had never really appealed to him. As he was being shown out of the sickroom Sir Malcolm Sargent was ushered in.

In the years that followed I became impervious to jokes about my name, but on that morning at the Kingsway Hall I felt embarrassed and humiliated. However, Sir Thomas's little joke did not cause me any lasting damage. On the contrary it brought me, or rather my name, to my new colleagues' attention.

Sir Thomas asked us to look at the German Dances by Mozart. It was soon obvious that there were several mistakes in the orchestral parts and although they were mostly minor ones, precious rehearsal-time was wasted in putting them right. The resulting discord between librarian, players and conductor became so acrimonious that Sir Thomas suddenly slammed down his baton. He turned to the stalls, empty except for his wife, the management, and members of the orchestra not required in Mozart's German Dances.

'Who has been tampering with my parts?' he thundered.

Then, in his inimitable way and looking in the direction of Lady Humby (as he called his wife) he added 'My private parts.'

As he spoke the word 'private' he turned round very slowly and faced the orchestra with an ingenuous expression on his face. The wicked glint in his eyes caused enthusiastic approval at the new tone of the rehearsal.

Leonard Hirsch, on that memorable morning, was having some trouble with his trill. Most string players have little difficulty in acquiring the technique of trilling, but some have to employ what is called in the trade a 'hand-wobble' and Leonard Hirsch was of these. The trill used as a bridge between several of the movements

Artur Schnabel with Leonard Hirsch

was to be his personal hiccup that morning. The conductor wanted him to trill as fast as possible. As leader of the orchestra, he had to play these links but, unfortunately for him, they consisted almost entirely of sustained trills, not simply the occasional decoration. After playing the link for the first time, Leonard looked up at Sir Thomas, who had stopped the orchestra.

'Mr Hirsch,' said Sir Thomas, 'do you think you could extend the length of the trill a little?'

Leonard said he would.

'Good,' Sir Thomas drawled amiably, stroking his goatee beard. 'Then let us try once more.'

Once again Leonard embarked on his solo. In a desperate effort to generate every ounce of trilling-speed he launched himself at the link. The sight of his anxious, perspiring face just topping the music stand, attached to an invisible body, was an invitation to laugh that everyone had trouble in resisting. It was evident that he was straining every nerve, but it was becoming equally evident that although the length of his trill was acceptable, the speed still did not match Sir Thomas's artistic conscience. Once again Sir Thomas stopped the orchestra.

'Mr Hirsch,' he said, with just a slight edge to his voice, 'at least two minutes on that last trill. Please.'

Leonard had already picked up the early-warning signal and his facial contortions reflected the painful dichotomy of good intention thwarted by technical limitation. He further intensified the speed of the hand-wobble and at last Sir Thomas appeared to be satisfied.

This was my introduction to the tight-rope that every musician must walk. The ever-present hazard in his professional life. The rope that spans promise, expectation and performance.

CHAPTER FIVE

Ginette Neveu and the first of many firsts

In November 1945, only a month after the Philharmonia concert, I was astonished to find myself sitting next to Charlie Pini on the front desk of the Philharmonia's cello section in EMI's Studio One at Abbey Road.

Since I had begun to work for the orchestra, every event had been a 'first' including one of London's life-threatening fogs. On the day of the recording the fog was so thick that the engineers in the recording room had difficulty seeing the orchestra at the far end of the studio. We in turn found it hard to see the soloist and, given the choice, would have preferred to have her playing where the conductor was standing. It would have been easier to follow her tempo changes because then we could at least hear her.

The Philharmonia had been booked to record the Sibelius Violin Concerto with Ginette Neveu, one of many young soloists whose careers had been interrupted by the war. Together with Pierre Fournier and Gyula Bustabo, she had not only survived the war, but was already one of Europe's most promising young soloists.

Her appearance was as striking as her playing was passionate and beautiful. Even the gloomy lighting in the studio failed to dispel the magic of that occasion. She projected a unique intensity of concentrated sound which was catapulted into the lives of all who sensed the pulsating energy she produced from her Stradivarius. Her neck and shoulders looked like those of an athlete trained as a javelin thrower. Her strong fingers sped over the fingerboard with a sustained mastery that was spellbinding. Even if her eyes did protrude slightly, none of these larger than life characteristics detracted from a presence that was transformed the moment that the fingers of her left hand added their intensity of expression to that of her wonderfully controlled bowing arm.

The afternoon recording began at 2.30 and the evening session at 7.30. It was the orchestra's first major recording since its inaugural concert at the Kingsway Hall in October and it was the first time I had worked at the famous studios in Abbey Road. It was also the first time I was to sit as sub-principal cello in the Philharmonia. In three hours we had completed the recording of the first movement under the expert guidance of Walter Susskind.

At the end of the first session I was so entranced by the occasion that I felt unwilling to leave the murky studio that had just provided me with such a wonderful example of the generosity of the truly talented. Just as I was putting my cello away I heard once again the unmistakable sound of Neveu's Stradivarius and decided to stay out of sight and listen.

She was practising the Walton concerto with the same extraordinary passion and vitality she had invested in the first movement of the Sibelius for the past three hours, and goodness only knows for how many hours before. Peering round from behind the orchestral platform, I was reminded of a painting by Van Dyck of a magnificent white horse. There was an amazing similarity between the neck of this noble animal and that of the lady I could just see in the shadow of the dimmed lights. The wonderfully proportioned contours of the neck that dominates the entire painting seemed to parallel the classical boldness of her profile.

Before the evening session began, players had already conceded her pride of place. In the afternoon, there had been the usual noise and chatter but in the evening whatever little conversation there had to be, was conducted in whispers.

At that time Sibelius was enjoying cult status at the Royal Academy of Music, led by Ronald Smith, one of our leading piano students. He never stopped praising the work of Finland's hero in his stand against Russia's dominating oligarchy. He could quote endlessly from obscure works that are now a well-known part of the century's heritage. The Violin Concerto had not been well received in Berlin before World War One and its full power only emerged when Heifetz recorded it in 1935. Neveu, however, added a certain 'something' that lifted her playing above the masterful, but somewhat detached execution of the Heifetz recording.

During the afternoon session I had sat on the second desk as number four with James Harvey-Phillips as number three. Five minutes before the start of the evening session, Joan Ingpen (the orchestral manager) asked me to sit on the first desk as number two because Jimmy Whitehead was ill and unable to play. I was absolutely dumbfounded. Why wasn't Harvey-Phillips told to sit with Charlie Pini? However nothing more was said and a substitute, called in at short notice, took my place at number four.

There was a lot I still had to learn about the politics of orchestral playing, especially the problems of personality clashes. Harvey-Phillips had declined to move up to number two because, as the saying in the orchestral profession has it, 'there are those who can play themselves into an orchestra as easily as they can play themselves out'. As a freelance player, one had always to be especially vigilant.

Although I had been sight-reading quite happily that afternoon, it was quite another matter to sit next to the most accomplished cellist in London.

We began the evening session punctually and with Charlie's generous and reliable support I was soon floating in a new orchestral experience. In between takes and playbacks we got to know each other and established a relationship that survived the initial hesitancy I had felt because of the disparity in the standards of our cello playing, and because I was nineteen and he was over forty.

By the interval I was so relaxed that I felt able to mention a catastrophe that had taken place at the Academy the day before. I had been the soloist in Dvořák's Cello Concerto, with Clarence Raybould as conductor. For some reason his beat was never where the sound suggested it should have been, and vice versa. The ultimate humiliation had been the 'Clarence Raybould capitulation signal'—a large white handkerchief he waved around to indicate that a truce was necessary. When the orchestra finally ground to a halt, Mr Raybould stepped off the rostrum and made me begin the slow movement again, this time accompanying me on the piano. He was a fine pianist and accompanist and there was no ensemble problem, but his control vanished completely as soon as he returned to the baton. The rehearsal was a disaster.

To my surprise Charlie just laughed.

'Come and play it to me tomorrow,' he said. The next day I spent the whole afternoon with him, and nobody could have been kinder or more helpful.

'Go and practise,' he advised. 'And another thing. Insist that Clarry allows you to play it again if it goes wrong, but make sure he rehearses the orchestra on its own before you play it.'

Ginette Neveu's recording of the Sibelius has become a legend. The experience of working with this remarkable woman that day has remained vibrant in my memory. It was not just the power, control and intensity of her playing that fascinated me, it was also the opportunity I was given to join with others in appreciating her formidable talent.

Without Walter Legge's judgement and energy Ginette Neveu would not have been there that day and generations of music-lovers would have been the poorer. For me there was also the awakening of a love for music written by a genius whose works are one of the few twentieth-century legacies that can be cherished without apology. Last, but by no means least, the day's work provided me with an insight into the self-disciplined precision insisted on by Charlie in his cello playing and team leadership. Every note and every dynamic in every bar of the music we played mattered to him, and he made sure it mattered to us.

Ginette Neveu had the same passion for detail as Charlie, but expressed it on an infinitely wider canvas and at a much higher level. She was able to hold in the reins of her emotions until the moment came when the music required her to free herself from that edge of restraint and elevate her playing to a higher concord. Her death in an aeroplane crash on 28th October 1949 was an appalling example of fate's indifference. One cannot reconcile oneself to such an event.

In 1993, during a lecture given in Cordes near Albi by an eminent instrument maker from Paris, I heard an incredible tale. The lecturer told of an amateur violinist who was on a walking tour in a mountainous region of France when he heard a beautifully toned violin being played. On enquiry it transpired that, many years before, the owner had found a battered oblong metal box. When he opened it, he found a violin. It was the very same instrument, played by Ginette Neveu, to which I had listened with such rapture in November 1945 at Abbey Road Studios, London.

CHAPTER SIX
Lipatti

Dinu Lipatti looked up at me and smiled. We were alone in Studio One, Abbey Road and I was in a dream.

We had been recording the Grieg Piano Concerto with Alceo Galliera conducting. The rest of the orchestra had left the studio in search of more material nourishment while I had remained, listening to a pianist making beautiful sounds. In this concerto, which I had heard *ad nauseam* during and after the war, I had been transported into another world by the tone Lipatti produced in the very first bar.

My first Lipatti-revelation had been at a Walthamstow Town Hall concert in November 1946, when he played Mozart in a way I had never heard before. The sounds he made possessed a life and form that was an inspiration. Now, less than a year later, in September 1947, he looked frail and vulnerable—that is until he started to play. Suddenly, it was as if there was another presence, some hidden source or guiding force that helped him to sense overtones and subtleties of nuance that I could never have perceived.

Dennis Brain had told me that Lipatti was suffering from lymphatic leukaemia and, as it was my eldest brother's special subject, I had an idea of the debilitating effect of this malignant disease. From the dynamic, almost startling energy of the opening phrase of the concerto it was difficult to imagine that he was in anything but robust health. From his early twenties, in addition to the stress caused by his flight from Rumania in 1943, he had had to contend with the encroaching effects of this bone-marrow malfunction that was to end his life at the age of thirty-three.

From the orchestral player's point of view, the measurement of an artist's worth is an unspoken recognition of the mood or integrity of the occasion. That morning, the orchestra's behaviour was impeccable. More often than not, soloists and conductors have to contend with blatant bad manners from certain players, whose lack of attention and unrestrained conversation during rehearsals and recording sessions are often the cause of tension. Especially irritating, from EMI's point of view, were late arrivals at the beginning of a session, and a lack of attention when wax record 'takes' had been started, and there was little or no margin to play with. There were always a few members of the orchestra who remained oblivious to the irritation their lack of consideration and responsibility created. The fact that the recording company was paying their fees never seemed to matter to them.

That morning it was different, as it always is in the presence of true genius. Even the most belligerent players were silenced by Lipatti's playing that created, in turn, a unique empathy between orchestra, soloist, and conductor that remains vivid in my memory as I write over fifty years later. Lipatti's limpid, fluent, seemingly effortless playing captivated the hearts of all those present.

It is probably difficult for non-orchestral players and audiences to understand the complex emotions attached to being the 'fall guys' for soloists, and especially for conductors who, even when not up to the mark, are paid vast and unrealistic fees. Both sides of the divide have to earn a living but 'market forces' deem it necessary that soloists and conductors receive the accolades while the players, on whose musicianship they have to rely, receive paltry financial rewards.

That is one side of the coin. On the other hand, there is the camaraderie that exists between players who, in order to achieve their own standards, must depend on similar standards of performance by colleagues sitting around them. To achieve an overall pattern of excellence requires so much more than merely to act as a messenger, standing in front of the orchestra, and waving a baton.

The Philharmonia had already had several tussles with Galliera, especially when he was trying to teach us to play Strauss's *Don Juan*. For my part, I managed (as did every other member of the cello section) to survive having to play the two famous tricky passages at the beginning and middle of the work on my own in front of an embarrassed orchestra, but the aftermath of antipathy against the conductor was difficult to cope with. Hardened as most of us were by the war and by post-war gloom, cold and privation, it was asking too much to carry the burden of conductors and soloists who failed to cope, as we had to, with the exigencies of the moment.

On this occasion, however, the whole orchestra recognised the genius of Lipatti. We assembled in the studio. Nobody was late. We were introduced and there was little conversation, even when the oboist was given the piano A to tune to. Those nearest to Lipatti could hear immediately that even the sound of the octave A he struck, had a sonority we had not heard before in that somewhat unsympathetic studio. Walter Legge wrote in his tribute in *The Gramophone*, February 1951, that the 'softness' of Lipatti's sound came through strength.

Our previous concert with him in 1945 had been equally special, but from where I had been sitting I had been unable to see him. On the day of the Grieg recording I could see and marvel at this frail little figure. Supported by broad shoulders, his large head and pale face with its philosopher's brow was deep in concentration. His disproportionately large hands and fingers ranged over the keyboard giving life to each note. Every phrase was alive and every note significant.

Before he felt able to focus on a performance, Lipatti had to feel confident that he had achieved his ultimate in the physical and technical aspect of the work. Total economy of movement left him free to follow the dictates of a sensitive aristocrat of the highest calibre, never hindered by uncertainty.

By the time Lipatti returned two years later to record the Schumann concerto in April 1948, the Philharmonia had undergone several changes of personnel, and was beginning to achieve a sound of its own. The arrival of friends and colleagues such as Manoug Parikian, Sidney 'Jock' Sutcliffe, Dennis Brain, and Neill Sanders meant that I was no longer feeling isolated as the youngest player in the orchestra.

The orchestra had made an earlier recording of the Schumann with Schnabel as soloist. Alec Whittaker was first oboe at the time and the recording did not go at all well. Schnabel insisted that Alec should imitate his interpretation of the first subject. Alec couldn't, or wouldn't. Disagreement led to acrimony and, before long, some members of the orchestra were involved in a manner that was unnecessary and embarrassing.

I had got to know Schnabel through Sir Robert and Lady Mayer and therefore chose to opt out of the argument. I did feel that the fracas became unnecessarily offensive on our side, when a little flexibility would have been all that was required. Although I loved Schnabel's kindness and sense of humour, I found myself drawn toLipatti and his playing of the Schumann in a way that is difficult to describe.

Schnabel was wise and paternalistic, a man of immense insight and limitless generosity as regards sharing his love of music with me during later years when I was associated with The Edinburgh Piano Quartet. He had a lovely sense of fun and I found him a joy to be with. On the other hand I felt Lipatti possessed a greater sense of responsibility and urgency in his love of music, possibly because of his irreversible affliction. He too had a sense of the lasting joy to be found in the art of performance, but he never, to my knowledge, lectured his audience.

I doubt whether Lipatti would ever, under any circumstance,

have entrapped members of the audience as Schnabel did at the last concert of an annual Beethoven sonata series he gave in New York. Schnabel disliked playing encores. Some members of the audience resented this apparent lack of appreciation and vociferous clappers closed in on the edge of the platform making his escape impossible. He took a bow, seated himself to tumultuous applause, and proceeded to play an entire Schubert Sonata. The clappers were now in the way of the audience that had remained seated, and very soon the atmosphere changed, with predictable murmurs from those who wanted to see and hear. Schnabel's justification was that to play an encore not connected in any way with what had just been performed trivialised the entire occasion.

He encouraged Lipatti to work on the Beethoven repertoire at a time when Lipatti was still hesitating. The fact that he performed the *Waldstein* Sonata in the last two years of his life was entirely due to Schnabel's influence. However, in comparing Lipatti's performance of the Schumann Concerto with that of Schnabel, I still feel that Lipatti was altogether more at ease and, dare I say it, more technically assured.

Similar thoughts were coursing through my mind as I sat listening to Lipatti practising in the studio. Why was the Schumann so difficult to perform convincingly? Then the penny dropped. When it was being played by a talent such as Lipatti's, it looked and sounded as if there were no problems to solve.

Before the interval I had been intrigued by his keyboard stance and now had a half-profile of the man as he played the second Etude of Chopin. I was fascinated by the grace with which the left-hand chord sequences appeared to be singing a song I had never heard sung in that way before, although it was a piece I knew well. I had so often heard my erstwhile girl-friend practise and perform this work but it had always sounded difficult, looked impossible and did not seem to make much musical sense anyway.

Somehow I must have disturbed him. He stopped for a moment, as if he was expecting me to say something. Overcome with embarrassment I mumbled an apology.

'Do you want to practise?' he asked.

The question was so unexpected that I almost joked that I certainly needed to if I was to keep up with the music he was making. Fortunately I thought better of it, apologised again and began to leave. Turning round, I saw that he was still looking at me. I explained that I had been particularly fascinated by the liquidity of movement in his left hand in the Chopin Study, adding that I had never realised it could sound like that. He looked at me for a second and then began to play the left hand on its own.

'You see,' Lipatti said, 'the movement of the wrist, hand, and lower arm must move as if they are making a circle, or rather an oblong that is slightly curved. Also the speed of the movement must be consistent,' he continued. 'In this way you can make the chords sound like a melody. The notes played by the right hand are the accompaniment.'

I asked Lipatti if I could stay and listen.

'But of course!' he replied.

CHAPTER SEVEN

Some Knitters and a Rolling-pin

Dame Myra Hess's lunchtime concerts at the National Gallery fulfilled a great need in the British psyche during the war. It still puzzles me that those wonderful concerts, and the hundreds of small music clubs established all over the United Kingdom, were allowed to become nothing more than a memory a few years after the end of the conflict.

Jimmy Blades (playing four notes on two drums from a symphony written by Beethoven) provided a spiritual message of solace to some and, at the same time, a warning of impending retribution to others. Like the concerts at the National Gallery, these four notes, broadcast at intervals all over the world during the day and night, helped to sustain a nation in its time of isolation.

The destruction of the Queen's Hall, the birthplace of Sir Henry Wood's popular classical concerts, was one of the war's tragic legacies. The Royal Albert Hall was the only alternative venue available to Sir Henry as a temporary home for these Promenade Concerts. The BBC presumably thought that performers, audience and 'Promenaders' would agree to extend this option in perpetuity. Although all three essential elements for concert giving (composer, performer and listener) would be enclosed in an acoustic nightmare, these facts were either overlooked, or conveniently ignored.

Looking on the bright side, the Albert Hall's generous echo extended the length of the musical message. Jimmy's four notes became eight notes and, in certain weather conditions, twelve. 'Three times four notes for the price of one' as Jimmy once remarked with an impish look. Sir Henry Wood's Promenade

Concerts were a wartime bonanza which has gone from strength to strength ever since. The 'Britain can take it' message meant that summer concerts, as a wartime therapy, would not be put into cold storage until the Queen's Hall was rebuilt. That was the promise, and the Promenade Concerts would henceforth take place in one of a great German prince's many contributions to England's cultural heritage in the nineteenth century.

Standing in the top gallery, I heard my first concert in this vast building a few weeks before World War Two, or perhaps I should say, I heard everything twice. The echo made nonsense of what was happening seventy or eighty feet below.

In the summer of 1944 I worked for a week as a deputy with the London Philharmonic, but unfortunately Sir Henry spotted me sitting at the back of the cello section and told the Warden of the Academy. The opportunity of earning a little extra cash ended abruptly. Later that same year (but now as a spectator) I was at a rehearsal with John Kennedy, whose extremely talented son Nigel has achieved an acclaim that his father and grandfather (the first principal cellist of the BBC Symphony Orchestra) deserved but were never to attain. John and I wanted to hear two works Sir Henry had rehearsed the day before with the senior orchestra at the Academy, but particularly the slow movement of Beethoven's Fifth Symphony.

It was soon clear that this movement's technical difficulties, which had caused Sir Henry to spend more time than he wanted rehearsing the cello section of the Academy orchestra the day before, were also giving the cellists in the London Philharmonic a few headaches. (Incidentally, the third variation of this movement is often used as a sight-reading test because it contains several typically *Beethovenesque* problem-phrases that are surprisingly difficult to play convincingly.) A great deal depends on exactly how well the cello section interprets the conductor's upbeat to the first bar if the theme is to sound convincing. Similar uncertainties about how the conductor means to convey his tempo changes throughout the symphony require, particularly from the orchestral soloists, the utmost concentration.

Sir Henry was rehearsing Sir Thomas Beecham's famous orchestra for a concert that night, and it was very gratifying to discover that the three variations on which the movement is based were being played only marginally better than our student efforts the day before.

At the concert we managed to find a spot in the audience near Sir Henry and, by the time the orchestra began the long repetitive *pianissimo* section in the coda that precedes the last movement, we had already noticed several minor hiccups. From here on it should be more or less plain sailing, or so we thought. Sir Henry brought his baton down with an audible swish to begin the last movement. A bar too soon and, unmistakably, very much on his own.

In the way miracles work the orchestra must, at that particular moment, have been playing on automatic pilot. Nobody played the triumphant opening chord of the last movement as conducted, and the audience was none the wiser. Shortly afterwards a member of the orchestra told me that at the rehearsal the following morning, Sir Henry had apologised.

'Gentlemen,' he said, 'I am sorry about last night. But,' he added rather sheepishly, 'even in the best families accidents can happen.' What an honest contrast to the brazen attitude of those conductors who receive accolades merited by performers in the orchestra.

There was a great deal of work for musicians in post-war Britain, especially for those who were prepared to travel. One great advantage we had, compared with the opportunities available for young students today, was that the Arts Council was still providing buffer finance to music clubs. There were therefore thousands of concert venues for ensembles, where today there are probably only hundreds.

Our first tour under the auspices of CEMA (the Arts Council's version of ENSA) began in Wales and ended in Shropshire. Feeling adventurous, we decided to include the Schubert Trio in B flat major as the main work in the programme, with two other less ambitious pieces in support.

The first concert was to take place in a small village in North Wales. On arrival we learnt with some dismay that we were not to play in the School Hall but in a small room that housed the local Women's Guild. The reception committee was very friendly and spoke about the evening's concert with such enthusiasm that we assumed that most of the inhabitants of this remote little village would be coming to hear us play.

The CEMA representative explained that during the previous weekend the piano in the School Hall had been vandalised and the only alternative was to use the piano in the Women's Guild. The piano had been tuned especially for the occasion.

'You must not be misled by its appearance,' she went on. 'Of its class, it really is a tip-top instrument.'

It was therefore a little disconcerting to discover that only eight fervent members of the local Guild of Knitters had decided to attend the first public appearance of the Beaufort Piano Trio in Wales. (The trio was so named because Daphne Ibbott, the pianist, lived in Beaufort Mansions.)

At one end of the room stood the tired-looking upright piano while at the other, hissing quietly to itself, was a large urn. It was damp outside and, with the help of the urn, the atmosphere inside was becoming equally damp. The three of us bowed to the well-intentioned but muted applause of eight elderly ladies.

Looking at our audience, the drab hall and particularly the urn, I wondered whether all the hours of preparation had been really appropriate. Due to a mechanical fault in the car we had arrived with just enough time to wash and change but with no opportunity to have even a seating rehearsal. Daphne had therefore not been able to try the piano, find an adjustable chair or arrange for some generous music lover to turn the pages for her.

Even under the best conditions, and with players of proven ability, a satisfactory performance of the Schubert can be depressingly elusive. However, with the optimism of youth we decided that, come what may, we would rise to the challenge.

We sat down and Felix and I attempted to tune. The piano was of variable pitch: flat in the bass, sharp in the treble, and had a few indeterminates in the middle. We watched for a few moments while two ladies checked the boiling water and then began to play in the hope that Schubert might still the Welsh chatter.

In a piano trio performance the string players sit in such a way that the piano keyboard is visible to them as well as to the audience. On this occasion, after the loud and dramatic opening passage, I noticed that the angle of the keyboard seemed to have altered. I was now unable to see Daphne give a pre-arranged signal where the cello begins a phrase that leads into a slightly slower second subject. We had agreed that it was much easier if Daphne were to give me a nod to achieve that slight alteration of tempo, and we had spent many hours rehearsing it.

By the end of the first movement the distance between us was quite considerable and Felix was forced to move nearer to the audience. The audience, all eight of them, had already edged their chairs to within a few feet of us, perhaps trying to get further away from the urn, which had begun to hiss more loudly. I prayed that the magic of the music would rescue the occasion, but it was already quite obvious that something was drastically wrong. Every time Daphne played loudly, the piano moved.

I had just played the cello solo that begins the slow movement, a particularly beautiful and poignant piece of music, when I noticed that the entire audience was knitting. That they were bored with our playing was certainly possible, but how could they ignore such wonderful music?

With a sense of mounting outrage I also realised that two ladies had gone over to the urn and were making preparations for the interval tea. I felt deeply hurt. We had worked extremely hard and yet we had failed to get through to our audience. It was all terribly depressing.

It wasn't until we were well into the fourth movement that I realised what had been happening right through the entire performance. One of the casters on the piano was missing. As Daphne played the last chord of the trio the piano lurched to one side and collapsed with a loud crash.

The faces of the audience expressed mingled irritation and compassion. Irritation because we had caused their piano to move out of its place by playing too loudly, and compassion because we were young. Nevertheless they were willing to forgive, because we had tried so hard, and hoped we would all feel better after a cup of tea.

We found out after the concert that, many years before, one of the local ladies had kindly offered the Women's Guild the use of her rolling-pin to effect a temporary repair to their piano and there it had remained ever since. This was their first CEMA concert, and as the instrument in question had never previously been subjected to such a sustained attack, perhaps it was not surprising that the rolling pin had become dislodged.

Some conductors are called 'knitters' in the cruel parlance of orchestral players, and Rudolf Schwarz was one such. When he allowed passion to supersede prudence during performance his stick technique was usually the first sacrificial offering. Both his elbows would gradually cross over each other in a movement that made him look like a determined cardigan-creator. I'm sure he was aware that this technique could be distracting, but nerves or artistic temperament, or perhaps both, made him impervious to any criticism.

Schwarz had been a viola player in his youth in Vienna. Because of the role violas fulfill in the modern symphony orchestra it is possible that composers sometimes demand more than the instrument can be expected to give, because of the way it is built. As a result of this in-built hazard viola players, like cellists, have become a breed apart, and Schwarz was well aware of this.

In the 1960s he was conducting Strauss's Don Quixote with the BBC orchestra in Ireland and I had played the solo cello part in the first of three performances. At the next rehearsal we were discussing the lack of balance at one point and I suggested that if a fingering could be agreed for a tutti viola and cello phrase, it might sound better. Rudy (as he was affectionately called) laughed.

'You should know by now, Mr Kok, that you can never hope to persuade another string player to finger and bow a *tutti* passage in a way that will satisfy your own artistic aspirations. You are a romantic cellist. You should remember that when you link the sound of the cellos with the sound of the violas, you create a problem. We all know that one of the coldest elements in the world of music is a viola solo.'

I reminded him that there were exceptions, and mentioned William Primrose. He recorded the Walton Viola Concerto at Abbey Road in 1946 with the Philharmonia with the composer conducting. I had the good fortune to be asked to a party afterwards where I heard him dominate the performance of a Mozart quartet in a way that was both irritating and yet, at the same time, utterly convincing.

'The trouble is,' I told Mr Schwarz, 'few viola players have managed to achieve the exuberance that flowed from his playing. I don't think I have ever heard such a vibrant, expressive viola tone.'

I went on to ask about a section in the Strauss where the aspiring Don (cello) is being brought down to the level of the perspiring Sancho (viola). I wanted to know whether the viola player has to imagine he is at all times a leaden-footed valet, or should he try to match the rich, vibrant sound of the cello (Don). Primrose, being the talented viola player he was, would obviously

Walter Primrose

dominate a performance. He could make it extremely difficult for the cellist to let the audience hear Don Quixote in perspective, as it were. Unless, of course, the cellist

happened to be a Feuermann, which would create even more problems.

In the performance we were giving in Ireland the viola being used was a Richardson (one of Lionel Tertis's less inspired visions), while I was playing on an Italian cello. The two sounds just didn't gel.

'Perhaps this is what Strauss intended,' I suggested jokingly. Schwarz was silent. 'Are you thinking what I'm thinking?' I asked. 'Perhaps there are two cold things in the world: a viola and a cello trying to play in unison?' He smiled endearingly.

'I think we'd better find a bowing for the section before we talk ourselves into re-writing the parts,' he said, waving his pointed cigarette holder at me.

CHAPTER EIGHT

The need for an 'A'

I have often wondered what decided Walter Legge to engage Reginald Kell, rather than Frederick 'Jack' Thurston, to play Mozart's Clarinet Concerto at the Philharmonia Orchestra's first concert on 27th October 1945. The ravishingly beautiful tone quality Jack could produce, when in the mood, would often remind me of Einstein's reported comment after hearing Menuhin play for the first time. 'Perhaps, after all, there is a God.'

I had a similar revelation when I first heard the orchestra's principal woodwind and brass soloists. In all the years I spent in their company their instinct for music-making, combined with rare talent, would sometimes be enough to make me lose my place during the performance.

Nevertheless Walter Legge's choice on this occasion was the brilliant and naturally extrovert Reginald Kell. His performance of the Mozart concerto that night provided me with the first 'tingle quotient' I was to experience as an orchestral player. During those first few years the Philharmonia benefited from the playing of both of these superb clarinettists who contributed a stature to orchestral woodwind sound that is hard to describe without exaggeration, except to say that it provided evidence that magic does exist in music. (Bernard Walton, who took Jack's place in November 1953, added a different but equally unique lustre to the halo created by his predecessors. His early death in 1972 robbed music lovers of a truly great player and a superb orchestral musician.)

Sir Thomas Beecham's disagreement with Walter Legge about artistic control of the Philharmonia after the first concert makes clear that, in the view of the conductor, creating a new orchestra would be doomed from the start unless his (Beecham's) guidelines were adopted.

'The new orchestra will bear the name of the Beecham Symphony Orchestra....'

'The name of *Philharmonia*, or any similar title, has been flatly rejected as signifying nothing. It is capable of causing much confusion, as well as sounding slightly preposterous.'[1]

Nothing daunted, Walter Legge named his orchestra Philharmonia. Although a great deal has been written about Sir Thomas and his devotion to music, we read and hear very little about Walter Legge. His contribution to improving the quality of recordings and raising the standard of music performance at concerts, his love and knowledge of music in the professional world he helped to create about him, and the ideals that had inspired him seem to be generally ignored or even contested.

Both men were endowed with great talents, but whereas Legge's efforts have received very little recognition, the Philharmonia, in spite of Sir Thomas's gloomy prediction, has gone from strength to strength. Sir Thomas did conduct the orchestra again many years later, but his absence from the rostrum in those early years demonstrates another axiom of the performing world: 'Nobody is indispensable.'

Within the first year of its inauguration the orchestra established, and has maintained to this day, a wide range of concert giving and recording activities performed to a very high standard. First at Friends' House, then at Abbey Road, Kingsway Hall, Walthamstow Town Hall, Watford Town Hall—in fact in any hall where both the acoustic and the external noise level were acceptable.

---

[1] Sir Thomas Beecham's letter to Walter Legge dated 30th January 1945
Walter Legge: Words and Music (Edited by Alan Sanders), p. 97
Gerald Duckworth & Co. Ltd. 1998

I was still a student at the Academy when I joined the Philharmonia in 1945, but it was clear that further academic study was becoming irrelevant. It seemed more appropriate to play in the real professional world than in a student setting at the Academy where the successor to Sir Henry Wood failed to achieve much more than student standards. Funnily enough, this did not seem to apply in Sir Henry Wood's time. His attitude was based on economy: economy of time, effort and rhetoric; his own as well as that of the orchestra. The disciplines he asked of his students he applied equally to himself. Ten minutes before the rehearsal started Sir Henry, already on the platform with his tuning plate, would stand in front of each student in turn and sound an A, not moving on to the next until he was satisfied that he had achieved the pitch he wanted. Consequently, by the time the rehearsal was due to start, there was a good chance that the whole orchestra was in tune with a standard pitch. Any uncertainty thereafter was more likely to be due to student error.

Sir Henry would have remembered a disaster that, a century before, had led to the creation of The Royal Military School of Music at Kneller Hall. The story was that Queen Victoria ordained that all regiments should participate in a giant 'Empire Spectacle'. Many hundreds of representatives from her dominions were gathered in a vast parade to pay homage to the great Queen. In due course she arrived with her Consort and the moment came to play the National Anthem. The first chord reduced participants and non-participants alike to a state of shock followed immediately by tears of laughter. Until that moment every band in the British Armed Forces had played at the pitch (as Tovey once said) of its grandmother's piano.

A second attack of rheumatic fever slowed everything down just at a time when my duties, as a senior student in my last year at the Academy, required me to participate in the many activities Dr Thatcher had planned for 1946. My illness only served to exacerbate his hostility to everything and anything I was trying to do. It was time, like the Arab in Mark Twain's book, to 'pack my tent and silently steal away'.

Meanwhile Walter Legge was searching for a principal to replace Anthony Pini and then, to make matters worse, Jimmy Whitehead decided that he wanted to teach and play concertos rather than record orchestral music. I was encouraged in my decision because, quite apart from the benefit of being involved in a wide musical canvas, there was also the practical help Walter Legge's orchestra was giving my family. We were able at last to afford a few of life's luxuries that had been denied for more years than I could remember. I was now earning enough to buy a better cello, help the family budget, and keep up appearances on important social occasions without having to borrow clothes from my brothers.

Those were still the days when recording depended more directly on the ability of the player than the engineer. Today, technology allows the player to correct mistakes at will. Until 1949 an average four-and-a-half minute recording would be indented on to a wax master, and a mistake meant having to repeat the entire section all over again. This inevitably produced its own category of possible disasters and resultant tensions between player, management, conductor, and soloist.

As can be imagined it was very much more frightening as we neared the end of a take. Walter Legge's solution for the problem of recording nerves was 'rehearse-record'. By adhering strictly to a strategy of rehearsing, recording and then finally performing works at a concert, the Philharmonia, under his artistic direction, managed to acquire a reputation within the next few years which was described as being 'second to none in the world'. Colleagues like Dennis Brain (also ex-Academy) created, with other members of the brass and woodwind sections, standards of performance in the orchestra that may subsequently have been equalled elsewhere but surely never surpassed.

The next major events in my life were my meeting with Pierre
Fournier and the appearance of Herbert von Karajan. Fournier's
playing completely silenced any criticism from the know-alls of
the cello section, always a factor to be taken into account. Nobody
failed to be moved by the ravishingly beautiful and sensitive
performances with which he made his post-war début in England.

Karajan also made an immediate impression. During rehearsals
and performance he was extremely well behaved and, as a
conductor, had his emotions under control to an astonishing

Above *Pierre Fournier*
Right *Pierre Fournier in Broadcasting House, London*

degree. More important was the clarity and 'language' of his beat. With Karajan I felt secure because there was no risk when you needed assurance. When his baton came down, you knew there could be no misunderstanding.

To play exactly on the beat and to accent the first beat in every bar (a *sine qua non* of Sir Malcolm Sargent's music philosophy, for example) was now a thing of the past. Furthermore, Karajan was

Photograph Alexander Kok

willing to be enlightened if we had not understood his direction, unlike many conductors. During performance his beat was consistent with what had been agreed at rehearsal, and at concerts he never took anything away from the well-contoured phrases we had taken such pains to achieve in preparation. His intelligence and his iron self-control, at rehearsal and on the rostrum, were key factors in the immediate psychological success he enjoyed.

In the slow movement of Tchaikowsky's Fifth Symphony, for example, Karajan had a way of suspending his body on the rostrum that reminded me of photographs I had seen of Nijinsky. Karajan's insistence on an accent-less preparation to Dennis Brain's haunting horn solo, followed in turn by the tutti celli, achieved moments of real magic. The dreamlike quality of Strauss's Don Juan illustrates Karajan's ideal of trying to balance the instruments of the orchestra so that they can respond to any nuance required by the score.

For Karajan to have succeeded in creating an orchestral style in a foreign orchestra was, in itself, an achievement; to have done so in England was indeed a triumph. Here there are few, if any, buildings that lend themselves to the creation of a traditional sound. There is no permanent 'spiritual home' for music, no British equivalent to the Musikvereinsaal in Vienna, or the old Berlin Philharmonic Hall. In London, where permanent homes for opera, ballet, and orchestra simply are not supported on the same scale as in Russia and Germany, musicians have to adapt.

On the positive side, lack of funds for rehearsal time has created special talents in sight-reading in this country, qualities that remain of considerable worth at a time when commercial music entrepreneurs attach great importance to music yet remain unwilling to pay for it. In the case of the Philharmonia there was a vast amount of prestige work available. Music written for films like *Henry V, Richard III, Hamlet* and many others all provided scores that are now part of the repertoire of the concert hall. Those recordings relied to a large extent on an expertise in sight-reading that was not easily matched in Europe or America.

It is to Karajan's credit that, in spite of the lack of a spiritual home for his English orchestra, he nevertheless achieved what became known as the 'Philharmonia Sound'. A sound that was not the product of one particular concert hall, but of the players and their conductor performing in any hall or, indeed, despite the hall.

Another of the many problems Walter Legge had to contend with was that of the 'deputy' system. Most orchestral players of the time were not contracted in precise legal terms. There were many historical reasons for this, but the end result was that no major orchestra, apart from the BBC Symphony Orchestra, had its own base. Most players took whatever jobs were offered and then farmed them out when better-paid or more interesting ones became available.

In spite of all these problems, together with other problems of post-war London and anxieties caused by the Cold War, Walter Legge and Karajan were able to create an orchestra and a sound that became as legendary as the men themselves.

There were also problems of temperament and sentiment. There were internal conflicts between players at a personal level. As the ambitions of Walter Legge and Karajan were translated into international achievement, so too did the disciplines of their vision begin to affect the relationship of players to both management and conductor. Lesser talents were anxious to use the orchestra as a means of advancing their careers. Everyone wanted to benefit from the genius of the record producer who had put the orchestra together, and of the conductor who was teaching the players how it was to be used.

Mounting pressures caused new hostilities between those players who accepted Walter Legge's dream of creating a musical instrument which would do justice to the orchestral repertoire, and those who preferred the comfortable *status quo*, and who could not, or perhaps would not, respond to the high standards now demanded of them. Some, on whom the evils of wartime propaganda had had a particularly destructive effect, found themselves unable to overcome their latent hostility to foreigners —especially Germans.

'These bloody Germans,' said Alec Whittaker one cold winter's day at the Albert Hall. 'They're either at your throat or at your feet.' Alec was a morose Mancunian whose oboe playing could create calm amidst the worst furies of a tempest. I understood his words but failed to see how someone, whose oboe playing could still the air, divined so quickly that Karajan's nature was foreign to his craft. I was still under the illusion, in those far off days, that the power of music was essentially its ability to elevate man away from his baser self.

'Just you look that bugger straight in the eyes and tell me what you see,' said Alec on the way to a rehearsal for a bread-and-butter Sunday concert at Southend.

This was difficult for me as a rank and file cellist. There were no solos for me to play that would require me to discuss, face to face, what Karajan was seeking to achieve at rehearsals. Whereas in Strauss's *Death and Transfiguration* the few bars of solo oboe near the beginning of the work could dominate the mood of the whole orchestra and, in turn, create magic for the entire performance, Karajan's gift was that he allowed Alec the scope to achieve this bit of heaven. Why then was there this antagonism between the player and the conductor?

Karajan was a self-contained man who did not encourage casual conversation. Furthermore, he had committed himself to a gimmick at the time that was both original and interesting. He believed that the power of his concentration should flow into our collective psyche during performance, and that this could only be achieved if he kept his eyes shut from start to finish. He would walk on to the platform, bow with courteous reticence to his audience, look briefly at us, close his eyes, and we would then be off on a new musical experience. It was a novel approach and I suppose, given a perfect world, could even have contained an element of logic, but there were obvious problems. If Karajan had to keep his eyes shut during the entire work, how would he know when to start each successive movement? He cheated. I noticed that his eyes would open slightly and, in those few silent moments between movements, they would dart from one side of the orchestra to the other. Compromise number one.

Disaster struck during a performance of *Don Juan* at the Albert Hall. Karajan's insistence on a wide variety of colour from the players had, within a few months, transformed the texture of the orchestral tone to such an extent that it could on occasion heighten one's sensual awareness to an almost unbearable degree. We were getting near to the end and to judge from the expression on his face, Karajan was in some distant world. I was floating along on a cloud of new sensations when there was a loud crash.

In an attempt to accommodate Karajan's unusually wide range of tone colour, the timpani player had been forced to dampen his drums with some dusters. With the grand climax approaching, he was trying to remove them with one hand while continuing the *diminuendo* with the other. Bending down, with an extended arm, he was unlucky enough to have edged a set of cymbals off their stand. In the stillness that had been achieved the effect was deafening. Without waiting, Karajan brought his arms down for the explosion of sound that was to provide the contrast to the *pianissimo*. The orchestra responded nobly, with the exception of the timpanist. By the time he had collected his wits and joined in with his drum roll at full power we were already half way into our *decrescendo*.

There were post-mortems, accusations and counter-accusations.

'If he had kept his bloody eyes open, he would have seen I wasn't ready to play,' said Jimmy Bradshaw.

Karajan said nothing, but had got the message. From then on there was a compromise between his inward-looking approach and the practicalities needed for the proper management of the vehicle that was to transport us all to higher realms. The timpanist was shortly afterwards transported into retirement.

I never found Karajan to be capable of displaying much humour, but in this instance I would love to have been the proverbial fly on the dressing-room wall later that evening. On the other hand, his ability to distance himself was an advantage when orchestral tensions were running high.

Suppose an oboist had crossed swords with a horn player. If the latter wanted to make life difficult for the oboist, he could play so softly that it would be virtually impossible for the oboist to match him. The conductor would then have to determine what the levels of technical possibilities were when insisting on a *pianissimo* entry. I have witnessed many unhappy scenes where the conductor simply did not have the necessary orchestral training and experience to understand how to resolve such matters.

On the many occasions I played under Karajan I always felt that he would take trouble to understand the nature of any technical problem a player had to deal with and the possible solutions, but if he didn't know he was not ashamed to admit it.

Remote as he was, there was one subject where I found him very accessible. He was interested in motor cars. Dennis Brain and I used to spend many hours looking at the glossy car magazines that were beginning to appear in the shops and it was not long before this hobby of ours caught the attention of the Maestro. In the years that were to follow it was our joint interest in car technology that enabled us, in some small way, to bridge the gap with which Karajan kept most people at bay.

By the late 1940s London was having to cope with its greatest post-war plague, the militant union. Not content with the Labour government's high-level endeavours to impose a legally enforced

Robin Hood policy, the unions had decided that the time was ripe for confrontation at the lower level as well. Over the next thirty years strikes were to become the strategic weapon of groups of union leaders who were determined to keep memories of industrial exploitation in the nineteenth and early twentieth centuries at white heat.

Dennis Brain and Denis Matthews at the end of the war,
broadcasting in their RAF uniforms

I was as irritated as anyone else when the lights kept going out and the trains wouldn't run, although I never doubted that these men had just cause for their anger. Their fathers and their fathers' fathers had been the victims of international finance capitalism just as my father had been. Touring around wartime and post-war Britain, I had seen slums of indescribable squalor. How could the greatest World Power of the day tolerate such conditions? They were not the result of two world wars. The wars had in fact stimulated economic growth to such a degree that many people, servicemen and civilians alike, had ended up with bigger bank balances in 1945 than when hostilities had started in 1939. In the years that followed I had to admit, in moments of sober reflection, that even though I could never really trust the motives of the strike leaders, my sympathies were usually with workers struggling to survive in a fast changing world.

Meanwhile, in his office at EMI, Walter Legge must have had food for thought as a result of the zeal of militant union leaders. Efforts to make a master disc on wax with an electrical current fluctuation liable to occur at any moment, occasioned many laughs for the orchestra, but it spelt possible ruin for him and for some of the orchestra's financial backers.

In some ways it was a horribly bleak time but it was also a period of great excitement with recordings at Denham Film Studios, Abbey Road, Watford and Walthamstow keeping the orchestra on its toes.

CHAPTER NINE

Pierre and Lydia Fournier

On that lovely morning in the spring of 1947 everything went wrong that could go wrong. I awoke late, totally confused by a very realistic and disturbing dream. By the time I finally left Mother's latest acquisition (in Dawson Place, Notting Hill Gate) to find a taxi to take me to Victoria Station, there were none to be had. After carrying my suitcase and cello for what seemed to be an eternity, the driver of an old battered high-loader stopped in front of me and I offered silent thanks to the Almighty.

Once inside the taxi panic set in as I remembered my dream. I dreamt I had lost my position in the orchestra and became convinced that my trip to Paris would cost me my job. I knew that as an orchestral cellist I could always find work in London, but it would mean that the study-in-Paris and work-in-London project would have to be abandoned. I knew that many cellists wanted my job. Why should Walter Legge keep my place for me? Would a month's study with Pierre Fournier really help me to acquire the mastery that his playing had revealed?

An old-time Southern Railways breakfast revived my spirits and by the time the train arrived at Newhaven I was in a far better frame of mind. Pierre Fournier had agreed to teach me and Walter Legge had given me his blessing. A friend had found me a room in Paris where I could practise all day and, if I had the energy, I could attend French lessons at the Sorbonne in the evening. I remembered the time in Johannesburg I had won a tap-dancing prize using the Gershwin *An American in Paris*. I already felt drawn to a city I had only read and thought about—a city immortalised in such lovely and descriptive music.

My address for the next month was to be 229 rue de Tolbiac, Paris 13. Doubts began to awaken nameless fears. Number 13 was a Pagan number, but why be afraid of a number? My thoughts began to chase shadows.

On arrival at Dieppe I told a solemn-faced customs official that there was only a cello in the wooden case. Just as I did so I remembered the bars of chocolate Joyce's father had given me at the last moment, which I had stowed amongst some socks, underwear and handkerchiefs. Predictably the lid of the case swung open and the entire assortment of goodies tumbled out on the counter and then on to the floor. I was too frightened even to look up, but if I had, I would probably have seen him doing his best not to laugh at the sight of a large man, dressed like a rabbi, frantically gathering up bars of melting chocolate with large sweaty hands. Fortunately he was a forgiving soul and let me through without comment.

Still shaking, I boarded the train to Paris and managed to find a seat in a compartment that had room for me, my suitcase, and the Zanoli cello that Walter Legge's orchestra had enabled me to buy. The third class railway carriage was crowded, the slatted wooden seats were hard, the compartment was full, it was hot and I was very uncomfortable, but I was in France and for the time being that was good enough.

On arrival in Paris I was to meet M Lavaillotte, a teacher at the Conservatoire, principal flautist of the Paris Opéra Orchestra, and the son-in-law of my landlady-to-be. He had suggested that I wait near the central ticket office at St Lazare. It was rather unfortunate that this happened to be near the entrance to the main lavatory. I stood there wondering why men seemed either to resent or to shrug off my appeals for recognition. The hours passed and I began to question whether this was the right day—or week. With a sense of growing panic I realised that I had bought a single ticket and that I would not have enough money to pay for the journey home.

M Lavaillotte was supposed to provide me with French money. Number 13 was definitely not my lucky number.

Just as I began to walk towards the station superintendent's office, a little Frenchman complete with beret approached me and asked in fairly good English what the problem was. He had noticed me waiting and assumed that I was in trouble. I told him my story and showed him my friend's letter of introduction to Madame Loquet.

'*Bien*,' he said. 'Follow me.'

He bought two métro tickets and guided me all the way to Madame Loquet's apartment in Paris 13 where, refusing to accept any money or even to have a drink with me, he vanished round the corner and I never saw him again.

Madame Loquet said she was delighted to see me but unable to house me. M Lavaillotte was on holiday and would not be returning for at least another ten days. She had already explained this to her son-in-law, who had nevertheless managed to forget about me.

Nothing daunted, she contacted an English-speaking friend of her late husband who obligingly found me a very pleasant room in a hotel in Montparnasse. He must have assumed that I was a man of the world, to judge by the accommodation he arranged for me. My room had a small, south-facing balcony on the first floor of a little hotel called the Hotel d' Or. It was comfortably furnished and had mirrors everywhere. I had absolutely no idea why beds were being made at all hours of the day and night and why men and women seemed to be constantly in need of so much rest.

The noise I made as I prepared for my first lesson must surely have destroyed anyone's hope of achieving a blissful escape from the trials of daily life. Scales, arpeggios, studies, Bach Suites and the Schumann Cello Concerto may have served some purpose I suppose, for when I was involved in my search for human happiness they were free to articulate their concupiscence.

These very natural activities were later to be officially forbidden by order of the *Assemblée Nationale* and at the instigation and insistence of Mme Simone de Beauvoir.

'Sin must cease so that France might live.'

Nevertheless, everyone at the Hotel d'Or appeared to be contented and happy. The chambermaid who brought me my *petit déjeuner* would sometimes plead for 'a tune' instead of the unending scales and exercises. It was a lovely way to start each day. While this cheerful servant of the oldest profession freshened up my room I would sit on the balcony in the spring sunshine, eating my freshly cooked rolls and drinking my first cup of coffee.

I finally moved to 229 rue Tolbiac, Paris 13. John Hedges, Joyce's uncle, arranged with M Lavaillotte to pay the bill and I was able to settle into my room at last. The street was long and rambling, with tall shuttered houses on each side, creating a permanent atmosphere of gloom. The houses were sited without any attempt to benefit from an occasional ray of sunshine and almost all were sorely in need of attention. But it was a street in a Paris still free from the dubious benefits of the motor industry. My room was dark, over-furnished and hideously depressing, but there were compensations. It was the smell of Paris that I still remember, that lovely mixture of the Gauloise cigarette and garlic.

There were the ubiquitous *Saurnier* buses with their drivers and ticket-collectors each playing his part with nonchalant skill in those endearing but unlovely passenger transporters. There were the *deux-chevaux*, Citroën's great challenge to the recently state-pirated Renault product. What Citroën could make for $100 could not be matched by the Renault car industry, so Citroën was forced to sell for $300. There were also the old chain-driven *Berliot* lorries that looked and sounded as if they had seen service in World War One. There were few motor cars but many thousands of bicycles and taxis.

Finally there was Mme Loquet. A living example of the shadowy ladies who glided past my window, she nevertheless had an endless fund of love and motherly concern that was never withheld.

Probably because of an inactive liver, I was never really able to shake off a feeling of depression during the time I studied in Europe's 'City of Romance'. Gershwin's *American in Paris* had portrayed an exuberant, extrovert reaction to the city. Perhaps things had been different when he had visited Europe between the wars, but the mood of the Paris I knew was never matched by the sense of tingling expectation his music had aroused in me. Probably his liver had been more efficient.

I had agreed with Walter Legge to return to London to play in important concerts and recordings. Many rising stars were attracting his attention in Europe and he was keen that his orchestra should be well represented. It was therefore while studying in Paris that I first began to work seriously with Karajan.

An extremely talented pre-war graduate of music, Karajan, like so many of his generation, had his career blighted by the war. He was able to pick up the threads once more in that same year that I began to study with Fournier. In fact we were both beneficiaries of the same mentor, Walter Legge.

Paris, in that winter of 1947, with 'Ol' Blue Eyes', Frank Sinatra, singing *Strangers in the Night* and evoking memories of rain glistening in the reflected light of picturesque lamps and shadowy figures silently crossing deserted roads, remains vivid in my mind. London's favourite song at that time was much more robust, with street musicians, barrel organs and pub pianists singing the praises of a '*luvverly bunch o' cokernuts*'. But however pleasurable the British pub and the French café, neither offered me anything that could compare with the feeling of being inspired by another cluster of Walter Legge's discoveries.

I had already been made aware, as a chorister, that some music can generate an ethereal happiness, an illusion of levitation that is quite beyond analysis or description. In the second year of the

Philharmonia concert series I experienced a level of music-making that opened up completely new vistas for me. I learned to recognise, in Beethoven's music, a power that can transcend mere pleasure. In the concerts that we gave with Artur Schnabel there were moments when even to attempt to analyse what had occurred seems frivolous. There is nothing that I can explain, except perhaps my conscious recognition of his use of precise 'philosophic' timing where, to heighten his audience's awareness of emotion, he suspended sound. Imitating Beethoven's 'silent' bars, Schnabel enhanced the actual moment of silence by making his audience acutely conscious of the exact but inaudible 'pulse' of the music. In the slow movement of Beethoven's Fourth Piano Concerto this magic, created by silence, was evoked for me for the first time at the Albert Hall.

'Regard each day as if it were thy last, the next day's joyful light thine eyes shall see'. I found this advice to be totally acceptable in itself. The only problem was that my study of Montaigne had awakened various desires that didn't seem to fit into the religious tone of the advice I was trying to follow from the other Book, the one my grandmother had wanted me to consult each day. A thought, condemned in the context of the Bible, seemed to provoke disturbingly fresh signals of appeal as expressed by Montaigne. As a young man with normal healthy inclinations I had no desire to hold myself in a state of academic suspense when all around me there was incontrovertible evidence of a compromise that appeared to be producing an atmosphere of much greater contentment.

Friends in England seemed to be so positive, so certain, and I alone, it seemed, remained full of doubt. Never more so than when the implications of my stay in the Hotel d'Or began to sink in. Trying to survive professionally while at the same time accepting the challenges and tribulations that affairs of the heart create, appears to be a continuing problem.

My interest in the opposite sex was directed towards those ladies in whose company I could experience the joys of Montaigne's Heaven, tempered by an acute awareness of the proximity of the Bible's Hell. My early loves were all sustained by a magical belief that mutual recognition and joint acceptance of a particular situation inevitably meant dedication, love, marriage, children, responsibility—in that order.

Obviously I was confused then as to what love is, and remain even more so now. I believed that there were barriers between the sexes that had to be understood and resolved with care and discretion, so that no aspect of acquaintanceship and growing familiarity should ever develop into mutual distaste and aversion. These problems had to be solved in order and in truth. But isn't the very act of loving a denial of truth? Mother had spoken very scathingly about 'Love'. In her opinion the word was a much-misused term for self-gratification. Love, she believed, was to trust that a favour would be returned, but not that it had to be discharged. To love a flower was, in her opinion, a much more exact application of the meaning of the word. I have found that loving was, and remains, almost as painful as it is rewarding, and that length of life is of less importance than intensity and quality of life.

Mother was certainly very reticent about discussing relationships and my brothers and I were never encouraged to bring girl-friends home. When we nevertheless did so, she placed them in two easily distinguishable categories: those that could be heard practising a musical instrument and those that could not. Girls in the second category seldom came again, even if they were score-readers or musicologists. Consequently our knowledge of the moods and caprices of the opposite sex was limited to a respect for virginity protected from insensitive male assertion by a halo of assumed chastity by us boys and presumably by the girls. In other words a halo had become a noose, and it was only later that I came to understand Mother's oft-quoted advice: 'For every bad man there is a worse woman'.

I had worked in most of London's theatres by the time I arrived in Paris, and was aware of the delights of the outward form of the female nude. Nevertheless of 'woman', either in a physical or emotional sense, I had no knowledge at all. I had not yet turned the corner of erotic libido, nor faced the dichotomy referred to in Ovid's amusing comment concerning problems inherent in the pursuit of passion: 'Full oft the man who viewed the secret parts was stayed in full career and, gazing, felt his passions cool'.

Working to a strict routine in order to maximise the benefit of each lesson with Pierre, my only outing was to meet my eldest brother for lunch at a house owned by the Rothschilds in the Rue St Honoré, but used temporarily by the Royal Army Medical Corps.

There are two memories of that first year in Paris that can still raise ripples of embarrassment. I had been invited to the Fourniers' home on 14th July to celebrate the French National Day. Pierre and Lydia Fournier were to give an informal concert that was to include a first performance of the Martinů Second Sonata, with a dinner-dance to follow. I found a seat as far away from the performers as possible and was just beginning to relax into the mood of the second movement when the telephone rang. Nobody moved. Pierre and Lydia went on playing. The bell went on ringing. Eventually, with an audible sigh of impatience, holding his cello in one hand and walking stick in the other, Pierre limped across to answer the call. He was obviously irritated.

'Résidence Fournier. *Qui?*' His voice was tinged with disbelief. To my utter consternation he turned to me.

'Bobby, it is for you.' I picked my way through the audience in total silence and took the phone out of his hand.

'Hya Bobby! It's Pauline. Dad said you were in Paris and I was to be sure to phone you. Can you come to dinner tonight?'

This was surely one of music's silent bars transcribed into real life. I was speechless. How could Pauline possibly have known that I was at the Fourniers' apartment. Aware that everything I was trying not to say was being listened to by Pierre's attentive audience, I mumbled some vague excuses, replaced the receiver and made my apologies. In the embarrassing silence that ensued I returned to my seat as quickly as possible and the first performance of Martinů's Second Sonata continued without further interruption.

My embarrassment was to return soon after. I had intended to escape as quickly as possible, but as I had not yet been introduced to Madame Fournier I realised that I would have to stay put. My hosts were fully occupied with their friends so I was trapped. Soon the opportunity was made for me. Lydia came over to where I was sitting and insisted that I dance a tango with her. She was as beautiful as she was graceful, and as we moved to the rhythm of the music I began to feel what dancing the tango with a beautiful and generous lady actually implied. Up to that moment I had only *seen* the implications of the dance.

The floor space seemed suddenly to become less crowded and for the next few minutes it was just Lydia and I who were dancing alone in some non-material world. I looked down at this fascinating woman and felt, in that single instant, a new physical awareness.

Clasping my right hand, with her body now almost touching the floor, she squeezed my fingers ever so slightly, as if daring me to follow her, as she sank even lower. A non-biblical message about which there could be no mistake, began to make its presence felt. Both now warming to the occasion, Lydia's impromptu movements released in me a libido I had never experienced before as we continued with the dance.

Meanwhile, Pierre's initial good intentions looked as if they could easily vaporise. He was finally prompted to limp across to his wife and whisper to her in French.

'Lydia my dear, he is only a boy.'

She laughed, gave me a hug and a kiss—and Mme Fournier had acquired yet another slave for life.

Shortly after the Fourniers' memorable party I returned to London, to find that there had been changes in the orchestra. The new leader was a young Armenian, Manoug Parikian, and in the cello section an ex-BBC player called Raymond Clark had replaced James Whitehead as number two. Fournier was also in London, participating in a series of concerts at the Central Hall, Westminster, with Szigeti, Schnabel and Primrose, in what was to become a memorable series of chamber music performances. He had suggested to Schnabel that I turn the pages for him, so later in the season when he and Fournier recorded the Beethoven cello sonatas at EMI Studios I was allowed to repeat the honour. It was the opportunity to be a part of this distinguished group of musicians that encouraged me, more than anything else, to try to develop certain tenets of performance, the most fundamental being that of stillness.

Of the four players, Fournier and Schnabel seemed to be the best at concentrating the mind without inhibiting a wider emotional involvement in them, as well as in their audience. When performers indulge in extravagant movements to reinforce what appears to be some mysterious and elusive quality in their musical offering, they merely distract and disturb.

During the following year I was a frequent guest at the home of Pauline's parents, Sir Robert and Lady Mayer. After concerts at either the Central or Albert Hall, I was usually invited to a buffet supper at the Mayers' home near Lancaster Gate. Schnabel would relate fascinating stories about pre-war Berlin when he and his wife devoted Sunday afternoons and evenings to music-making. Artists were able to try a new piece for the first time, knowing for certain that they would have a fine piano and friendly reception, and that any suggestions that might be made would seek to elevate and not denigrate their performance.

Top *Manoug Parikian*
Bottom *Manoug Parikian in his new Riley*

During these exciting and challenging months nagging doubts began to occur in me from time to time. Why was there so much discussion by Sir Robert and Lady Mayer about social evils and the need for change? Schnabel had an Olympian humour, Fournier was capable of adroit answers but the Mayers seemed to be advocates of world revolution. I was caught up in endless political discussions about which I knew nothing. The battle cry was always 'Freedom from Want, Freedom from Oppression'.

I had just read Tom Paine's book The Rights of Man and, coming from a country that had been vandalised and then systematically ruined by the money barons of Europe, I felt I too belonged to a nation that had had its roots destroyed. Nevertheless I had never felt oppressed; quite the contrary. I felt that England had taught me how to value discipline in a free society, how to value the right to independence and the opportunity to remain independent. The supporters that were attracted to the voices of protest, circa 1947, seemed to have come from many different social backgrounds.

That savage indictment of Britain's governing classes by the lady in Lyons Corner House at Marble Arch had cut me down to size. She had heard me talk one afternoon about trying to raise high standards even higher and must have assumed I was advocating a return to happier days in an affluent society.

Aneurin Bevan then caused shock waves in the House of Commons by calling members of the Tory party 'vermin', while every day chauffeur-driven heads of unions, earning large salaries, were trumpeting defiance of the basic laws of economics via the news media. The Mayers seemed to be living in post-war London's art-loving, 'how to be rich and still feel poor,' reform-lobbying, millionaire-fringe. And why shouldn't they? Sir Robert worked hard, he was generous and he loved music. It was a fast-changing world, with some struggling to maintain the status quo and others trying to break into new social and establishment territory.

Britain's Labour government avoided the revolution against class privilege that caused so much bloodshed during the century, but it was from the rich that I heard for the first time about hardship and government mismanagement - the very people whose wealth was under political threat. These wealthy connoisseurs of poverty in others, while deploring the general lowering of standards, seemed unable to grasp that the political reforms that accompanied the Labour party's landslide victory of 1945 were just another variation of the eternally recurring leveller's mentality. Inevitably it would be reflected in art, architecture, painting and music.

At the same time that the devastating effects of Labour's post-war tax on the inheritors of large and beautiful houses were being acknowledged, I was forced to concede that it was nevertheless a Labour government that had initiated music-tuition as part of the school curriculum. I had many discussions with my hosts, who never failed to ridicule my untutored arguments, but nevertheless they did their best to help me balance my intensities as a musician with what they described as the 'realities' of life in the twentieth century.

I can understand Sir Robert and Lady Mayer's point of view now, fifty years later. At the time, I found it very difficult to accept. I was told repeatedly by Lady Mayer that it was absolutely essential to balance judgment. Politics, philosophy and music had to be related to what she considered to be 'reality', yet my attempts to describe the reality of those 'unheard' beats in the slow movement of Beethoven's Fourth Piano Concerto, never failed to amuse her.

Not until I had been reduced to a state of near immobility by one of Schnabel's performances, did I really begin to feel the power of Beethoven's use of contrast as a vehicle to concentrate the mind. At that memorable concert I heard for the first time the statement of opposites being reversed as the music unfolded. The raucous orchestra, subdued into quiet acceptance by the piano, reaches into sublime eloquence but never makes a strident appeal in the process.

I still hear this example as sound, but I instinctively translate what I hear into philosophy, or morality. What ruins this experience for me, however, is that if the pianist doesn't time the entry exactly within the rhythm of the silence that follows the explosive orchestral entry, then, in my opinion, he hasn't got it right.

And if Walter Legge had not 'got it right', the inestimable riches of his 'star' discoveries, with whom I had the privilege of working during those years of pilgrimage to Paris, would never have been mine to treasure: Schwarzkopf, Seefried, Grumiaux, Christoff, Callas, Galliera, Ackermann, Klemperer, Karajan, Lipatti, Fournier, Solomon, Schnabel, Primrose, Kletzki, Krips, Kubelík, Markevitch, Flagstad, Stokowski, Szigeti, Tauber, Cortot, Thibaud, Neveu, Furtwängler, Krips, Fischer, Desormière, Dobrowen, Fischer, Francescatti, Giulini, Cantelli, Hotter, Iturbi, and so on, and on.

CHAPTER TEN

Elisabeth Schwarzkopf and Irmgard Seefried

I met Neill Sanders for lunch on 26th September 1947, the day the orchestra was to record excerpts from *Hansel and Gretel* with Elisabeth Schwarzkopf and Irmgard Seefried. Neill's wife had fallen in love with another horn player and I had done my best to console him about 'love denied'.

Neill was saying that since he was second horn, while Dennis Brain was Number One, his wife's adoration for the Fourth Horn was proof positive that status was not necessarily a factor in a relationship.

'Love is not love which alteration finds.' Neill spoke the words without bitterness. For a while we sat in silence, afraid to cause more hurt to the memory of what had once been so real. It was easy for me to mumble the usual platitudes, that life was too short to hold grudges so make a new start. In the end as long as the magnanimity of the one who is left is recognised and appreciated what else is there to say?

To change the subject he told me that Walter Legge had recently discovered two sopranos in Austria who had raised not only his hopes but also his blood pressure. This reminder that the world still kept on turning changed our mood, and we set off for Abbey Road Studios with lighter hearts.

The orchestra assembled and Walter Legge seemed much happier than usual, which was always a good sign. Two very beautiful young women entered the studio and, looking across at Neill, I realised that we were both back to square one. Long before Walter Legge had introduced them to the orchestra I had fallen in love with both Elisabeth Schwarzkopf and Irmgard Seefried.

Elisabeth Schwarzkopf and Irmgard Seefried

Humperdinck's music was familiar enough to me. It was one of the last student productions at the Academy in which I had played and I had been left with the feeling that the music was rather lightweight, but on that afternoon at EMI Studios I was transported into another world. My first reaction was to thank everyone. Our mediocre student performance had nearly ruined this opera for me, or perhaps these two voices showed what outstanding talent can bring to music, lightweight or not.

Of the two, Seefried's voice and personality were immediately engaging while her companion seemed more reticent, almost unsure of herself. I was not alone in envying Walter Legge that day. To be able to make music the way he wanted was in itself a victory over circumstance, but to do it in the company of such unalloyed beauty was reward bordering on unfair advantage. It is rare to find superlative singers who are also beautiful. To have found two women who were talented, career-minded, conscientious, and utterly professional was indeed manna from heaven not only for Walter Legge but for music lovers, and for those of us in the orchestra who were feeling vulnerable - especially Neill and me that afternoon.

Seefried's career remained rooted in Europe, helped by a long-standing friendship with Karl Böhm and after her marriage, shortly after this recording in London, to Wolfgang Schneiderhan the co-leader of the Vienna Philharmonic Orchestra. When the Philharmonia Orchestra gave a concert the following year at the Musikvereinsaal in which her husband played Mozart's G major Violin Concerto, my abiding memory of this concert is not so much of Schneiderhan's fine performance but of his wife. Sitting with rapt attention to the left of the platform, and apparently oblivious to everything except her husband's playing, she enhanced the entire evening's experience. Dennis Brain and Neill Sanders played a Mozart Divertimento for two horns and strings, and the evening ended with a Mozart symphony. Beautiful music played in the most beautiful of concert halls and a performance that was unblemished from beginning to end. Unforgettable.

Manoug was not quite so enthusiastic and it was not difficult to understand why. He could easily have rivalled Schneiderhan's performance but unfortunately politics had intruded and Manoug had been the loser.

After the concert a few of us went to celebrate in a favourite haunt of Viennese orchestral players. None of us were great drinkers but the occasion seemed to deserve a little more than the usual pint that night. Manoug was still fairly reticent about the evening's concert and although he had perfected a talent for appearing to be detached at all times, he seemed to want to unbend a little. He had worked hard to develop a cool, calm manner, so much so that the orchestral nickname for him was 'Choc-Ice'. His dark complexion certainly added weight to his platform appeal.

We had hardly sat down in an alcove near the usual Viennese Beer Cellar band, when the leader came over and asked Manoug if he would honour them by playing a few pieces with them. Manoug had no option but to oblige, and by the time he had taken his violin out of its case he was being cheered from all sides. He must have felt encouraged by the warmth of the welcome, but after a few minutes we realised that he was definitely not his usual self. By the end of the first selection of waltzes he was visibly ill at ease and covered in perspiration, something we had never seen before.

As soon as the performance was over Manoug got up quickly and thanked the band. To the accompaniment of vociferous applause he returned to our table hot and cross. At first we teased him. Nothing Karajan had asked him to do had ever occasioned such excess of heat. Manoug then revealed that, although the melodies had been familiar, the actual notation had been altered in so many ways that it was almost impossible to read. Generations of leaders had added their own fingerings, one on top of another, and in the poor light he could hardly see what he was supposed to be playing.

Elisabeth Schwarzkopf went on to become one of the twentieth century's incomparable artists. Over the next twenty years I was privileged to hear her work many times, and she never failed to give the utmost dedication to her art. Thanks to Walter Legge she was based for many years in London, singing opera, Lieder and oratorios. Had she remained in Europe, recording schedules could never have been so well planned. Not once did I hear her make any comment on the lack of concentration in other musicians. She invoked an attention to detail that was matched by few instrumentalists.

In 1937 she participated in a recording of *The Magic Flute* in Berlin. As a member of the Opera School, she had been in the chorus of the Favres Solisten Vereinigung, a semi-professional group of music students and serious amateurs that had been invited to provide the chorus in the Beecham/Legge recording of *The Magic Flute*. Almost nine years later, on 3rd March 1946, Walter Legge heard her singing the part of Rosina in *The Barber of Seville* at the Theater an der Wien and by the end of the month he had arranged for her to audition for a recording contract with Columbia.

Having accepted Walter Legge's advice to sing as a lyric soprano, she was soon recording alongside Fischer, Gieseking, Furtwängler and Klemperer.

Irmgard Seefried was probably never driven by the same ambition to overcome challenges as Schwarzkopf. In that recording of *Hansel and Gretel* in 1947 at Abbey Road Studios she appeared to have an engaging, affecting simplicity that contrasted well with her colleague in their two roles. Both were enchanting, making me wish I had studied singing in Vienna.

It is probably not unfair to say that Seefried never achieved the accolades earned by Schwarzkopf, ten years later, singing the part of the Countess in *Figaro*. A critic wrote 'We cannot believe that there is a more perfect presentation of this part on the stage today'. Many thousands of her admirers cherish some particular memory, some gem of a performance of opera or *Lieder*. In her enormous repertoire she demonstrated again and again character, determination, artistic integrity and sympathetic understanding.

Yet there was a darker side which I sensed one dark winter's night when I was walking round the block of Abbey Road Studios. I met Schwarzkopf coming in the opposite direction, and we were both startled. It was misty and there was an understandable reticence before she acknowledged my greeting. In that brief moment I saw, in the expression of her eyes, someone I would never truly know. In her fleeting look of courteous salutation I saw a force of character that gave new dimensions to my regard for this peerless lady.

What music is there that can reflect the dual roles of the chief protagonists in war: Greed and Moneymakers? Walter Legge made me aware of the great German musical tradition. Through the medium of the gramophone record he helped to re-create the magic of a lost generation. Elisabeth Schwarzkopf, later to become his wife, was an essential part of that re-creation. For days after that meeting I wandered about existing on the edge of infinity. There was only one thing to do. I would go back to Paris and learn more about cello playing from Fournier.

I had just bought my first Italian cello, a Paulo Testore. As I began to know more about Pierre Fournier, this supremely eloquent French poet, so did my friendship for him grow. He was a wonderful teacher. I had concertos to learn, his amazing bowing technique to imitate and develop, and books to read. This time I was not as fearful of isolation as I had been on the previous visit to Paris.

In London I hadn't been able to settle. I couldn't bring myself to read and, worst of all, I couldn't practise. Mother's latest house purchase had landed us with tenants. The house was a lovely example of mid-Victorian architecture, connected in some way with Turner, and had a quaint dignity despite its pretence to status. The front porticos would have suited a much larger building, but sash windows and lintels of better proportion in the front elevation helped to offset an architect's error.

The drawback was that the top floor was occupied by a husband-and-wife team whose tenancy rights were protected by the powerful 1917 Tenancy Act. By a strange coincidence the husband was the orchestral librarian to Sir Thomas Beecham's Royal Philharmonic Orchestra while the wife was a medium. He, as librarian, was only working a five-day week, but his wife needed seven to deal with the increased business caused by the aftermath of the war.

If I practised before leaving for Denham Film Studios at six thirty a.m. they both complained, not surprisingly. If I tried again in the evening I was interfering with the medium's work. During the hours of the day that practice was permissible under the law, she would invoke all her powers of persuasion, legal and otherwise, to try to stop me. If I persisted, the police were called.

Each evening, when her assistant had left, she would deposit the day's refuse on the landing. After a few days of decomposition the stench would reach my room and the position was then reversed. I would call in the local Health Department Inspector who would merely suggest that if I didn't like the smell I should empty their rubbish into the outside bin and be a bit more neighbourly. Such was the power of the 1917 Act. Everything I was doing was anti-social, particularly my cello practice, but everything Mr and Mrs Brownfoot did was within the law. In a final attempt to reason with the local arm of the law, I tried to explain the problems of communicating a musical line in a performance, but to the constable a cello was something totally incomprehensible.

I had a similar problem with some of the bread-and-butter conductors who were climbing on to the Philharmonia bandwagon. The success of the orchestra meant that many would-be conductors hired the orchestra hoping to acquire some of the qualities that had established its reputation. This meant that we players had to attempt to educate these conductors, usually with little success. Karajan's ambition had been firmly anchored in Berlin, Vienna, and Salzburg before the war, and rather than accept a post that might compromise his chances when Furtwängler retired, he chose to go to La Scala to await the only three appointments that had value for him.

It seemed to me that the orchestra was being used merely as a training ground for aspiring job-hunters. It was time to ask for another period of leave. I had just read *War and Peace* and had begun to long for a rhythm of existence that would allow more time to read and make notes. The present was my gateway to the past, and I felt unwilling to waste my life playing for conductors who had nothing to say.

On arrival in Paris I went to hear Nathan Milstein at the Salle Pleyel, then found a favourite café in the Champs-Elysées and was content to just sit and watch people. I went to see *Lucrezia Borgia* and saw Martine Carroll emerge in all her pristine elegance from a bath. With France's houses of pleasure now empty and abandoned, such a spectacle was considered to be sailing dangerously close to the newly codified Winds of Change in Simone de Beauvoir's post-Second World War France.

I enrolled as an *étudiant étranger* at the Sorbonne and even began to look for work as a cellist. This would have meant leaving the Philharmonia for a while but it would have been worthwhile just to be able to study with Fournier. There was absolutely no chance. The French Union was as protective of its members as our own.

It was a perfect autumn. Paris was beginning to stir again after the long summer holiday. The streets were still uncluttered by the French equivalent of the 'people's car', and it was a joy just to be alive.

One day Mme Loquet handed me a letter. It was from my father. I opened it while I sipped some coffee at a café near the Place Hugo before going to have my lesson. Father had never expressed much interest in my career and I had the impression that my family was sceptical as to my chances of success as a soloist rather than as a cellist in an orchestra. There was criticism if I did something that was foolish, but anything positive I managed to achieve seemed to pass unnoticed.

'To play in an orchestra is an admission of failure,' Mother would constantly remind me. Even if it was a very fine one it was still just an orchestra.

Father's letter to me made it clear that he was ill, and although I didn't understand the hidden message at the time, he was probably trying to make me aware that the end was near. He wanted me to return to South Africa and help him to start up a business. Twenty-five years earlier he had turned his back on the offer of work of this kind. So what had happened in the meantime?

I suddenly realised that I had grown up without giving consideration to his views about what I was doing with my life. We had grown so far apart that he was totally ignorant of what I had already achieved. As I read his letter I felt drained of all hope, quite unable to absorb the implications of his isolation as well as those of my own.

When I arrived at Fournier's apartment he was still teaching. I listened to him playing the Bach Suite in D minor and gradually began to regain some of the enthusiasm with which I had set out on that day. We decided to continue with the Bach, but as soon as Pierre began to play the Sarabande the floodgates opened. Pierre was nonplussed. He asked me what the trouble was and I showed him Father's letter, which he read.

'My poor boy,' he said.

I felt completely deflated and decided to return to London. Pierre was adamant that I should not make a hasty decision but I felt humiliated. What was the point of struggling against the odds? My family simply did not realise the implication of my having lessons with one of the greatest instrumentalists of the twentieth century, while at the same time holding a position in an orchestra that was already considered to be second to none. I had always assumed that Father understood what Mother had tried to do, and although he and I had never corresponded, she would always keep him informed. I realised that, now the war was over, he assumed that we would return to South Africa.

'Come back to South Africa,' he had written, 'and help me with a project I have in mind.'

My over-reaction was typical and totally unnecessary. I had got to Paris by my own efforts and if I had written to explain I am sure Father would have understood. However common sense did not prevail, and I returned to London with a heavy heart and no plans for the future beyond having to earn a living and help to meet the demands of family life.

When I arrived home the house was empty. Father was dying and Mother had taken the first available boat to Cape Town. My eldest brother Darrell was in Hamburg, Myron the youngest was still at Harrow, and Felix was somewhere in Europe with the Boyd Neel Orchestra.

On the kitchen table were letters to each of us. It was going to be a race against time to reach Father's bedside before he died. Two days earlier his letter to me had destroyed my self-belief. Now I learnt that he was dying of lung cancer.

My eldest brother managed to obtain compassionate leave and intended to travel with Mother but problems with the railways delayed him and he arrived in England too late to make the connection in Southampton. Two days later a telegram arrived informing me that Father had died in the early hours of 28th October 1947.

I find it difficult to remember what passed through my mind during those days. I remember going to Harrow School with Darrell and Felix and waiting in Myron's room, having first informed the House Master why we had come. Darrell, already well trained in the business of the dead and the dying, simply said 'Father died last week on 28th of October.' Myron said nothing and Darrell gave his arm a gentle squeeze.

'Don't feel too bad about it,' he said. 'Dad was in great pain.'

We left and went back to 22 Dawson Place. Darrell went back to Germany. Felix left on another of his tours, and once again I was on my own.

Mother was to be away for six weeks and, just before she was told about Father's condition, had agreed that a major part of the house should be renovated. Gradually the gracious little house took shape, and by the time Mother returned home in early December most of the filth had been cleared away. Although she was glad to be back, I was conscious that she had changed.

When she herself lay dying, she spoke quite often about her

marriage, and about the husband she had probably always respected, although she could not love him. It was only in the last two years of her life that she came to understand his point of view. She had always thought he was weak when he needed to be strong. He seemed unable or unwilling to adjust to the changed criteria imposed on his country by Britain. A situation he made worse by constantly thinking back to a lifestyle that no longer existed. Mother on the contrary, although loving the cultural achievements of the past, was essentially someone who lived in the present. Also, because she was a mother, necessity required her to look to the future.

Father's excessive smoking over many years had aggravated a lung condition caused by exposure to the hot sandstorms of German West Africa during World War One. It was later exacerbated beyond cure by the dust of the copper mines at n'Kana.

I was passing through Bloemfontein on a solo tour of South Africa in 1961 and decided to visit Boshof, the Free State town near Father's place of birth. I was able to meet some of his relatives, in particular the cousins with whom he had stayed towards the end of his life. Their farm was situated in what has become a particularly desolate area of the province. It is dusty and devoid of trees, set in an endless expanse of flat open veld. What water there is comes from boreholes that have to be sunk to very great depths. Life is now indescribably harsh, and yet this was the area to which he had finally returned to prepare himself for the time when he would have to make his own 'next big step'.

I eagerly accepted an invitation to spend the night with relatives I had never met before. After supper, in the fresh coolness of the night, I sat under the same tree that he had sat under and looked out over the same flat empty expanse of veld. What had made him choose this particular place? There must have been something to stimulate him, some high point, during the long hot days before he died, where the only benefit to him was the isolation of the veld. To me it seemed desolate, unyielding, with nothing to alleviate the monotony. What was he thinking about as he sat under the shade of what he used to call an upside-down tree? He had been in constant pain, but rather than return to the Rand, he had chosen to remain near his birthplace.

When Father was a young boy this country was quite different. Where there is now parched land there was water and growth. As I watched the sun sink in the silence of the limitless expanse of sky above the distant horizon I began to understand the quality of peace that Father must have needed in the last few months of his life.

Almost everything during his lifetime had changed for the worse. In 1899 the Orange Free State, in a gesture of extreme gallantry, had gone to the aid of a neighbour. Like the Transvaal, it was defeated, humiliated and destroyed. In the daily ritual of abuse being directed at descendants of people like my father, is any thought ever given to that brave offer of help? If the Orange Free State had simply stood by and watched Britain's Foreign Office, acting on the orders of the élite of London's 'square mile', create artificial circumstances that were deemed necessary to justify the annexation of a Sovereign State, my paternal grandparents might have retained possession of their farm. What they had built up might not have been destroyed by the military arm of the British government.

During my brief stay at the farm I was told about the twenty-five thousand Cape Afrikaners who had fought in British uniforms in a bid to exterminate their Republican brothers. Together with their British and Imperial Allies, they far out-numbered the thirteen or so thousand Cape rebels from the North Eastern districts of the colony, who had joined the defenders of the two Republics. What could have been the motive of men that would kill their own flesh and blood?

I also learnt about Republican burghers who had lost heart as the war dragged on and had deserted their cause. Because their farms had been burnt, their wives and children either killed or imprisoned in concentration camps, why not fight those men who would not see sense and capitulate? The Great Trek of 1836–58 had been a watershed event in Afrikaner history; the Second English War had made that crystal clear. What is not so apparent to the outside world is that it divided the Republican Afrikaner in the North from the colonial Afrikaner of the South. Like the tragedy of England's persecution of the Irish, it aroused sentiments that will probably never be reconciled.

CHAPTER ELEVEN

Gerry-speak and Beethoven's Ninth

The Philharmonia was well on the way to achieving world status which was, in large measure, a consequence of the collaboration between Karajan, and all the other beneficiaries of Walter Legge's talent for artistic direction. However, it was becoming clear to many of his key players that their contribution would continue to be subservient to Karajan's strategy of boosting his own career. Karajan was exploiting not only the orchestra but also the artistic flair of Legge himself, in order to secure the two premier positions in Europe available to a ruthless and ambitious conductor. It was also becoming clear that there was never going to be a spiritual home for the orchestra in London like the Musikvereinsaal in Vienna. The Philharmonia rose to the challenges and gave Karajan his opportunity to achieve international eminence. London's music-lovers contributed their support. It is ironic to reflect that none of this would have happened if it had not been for Walter Legge. As Elisabeth Schwarzkopf told me later, 'Walter was a rare combination of someone with great discernment yet willing to stand in the wings and allow others to take the accolades'.

Few people realise how hard it was for him to achieve his ambition. Without doubt the orchestra could not have survived but for the sheer determination of its founder and artistic director. Only by investigating every avenue did he manage to delay the parting of the ways between the orchestra and its founder.

There were many reasons why the ideals that inspired Walter Legge were never encouraged by the banks that went on to benefit from London's burgeoning pop culture. The Labour Party manifesto of 1997 made clear that music's role has to do with profitability and not artistic achievement. The pop industry makes millions from gullible young minds and that is all that matters, but there is no excuse for the lack of support from the Arts Council.

It is evident that the performance of contemporary music as represented by composers like Boulez, whether esoteric, eclectic, or eccentric, requires patronage. Sir William Glock, the post-war Music Controller of the BBC, considered it his duty to provide the necessary airtime for what apparently has limited appeal, and was once described to me as 'cacophonic' by Casals.

'Nothing is good, or bad, but thinking makes it so.' The pop branch of the music industry makes recordings it sells as 'music', but which I consider to be mere noise. Similarly, the classical section produces recordings of 'authentic music' played according to the rules of 'authentic pitch' but which sound arid and sterile to me. Radio and television channels help to finance these new fashions promulgated by the Music Industry and leave me with little hope for the future of music that is either 'live' or 'alive'–that is until I hear uncorrupted young talent, or old talent that has remained uncorrupted.

One day I arrived early at Abbey Road Studios to mark the cello parts of Beethoven's Choral Symphony in preparation for our first performance with Karajan. I then began speculating about the phenomenon of sound with regard to the acoustic of the concert-halls in England and Europe. Was making music in a hall with an acceptable acoustic the only way to create an ideal sound? Was there such a thing as an ideal sound? If there was, what did it depend on? Was it possible to achieve an ideal sound when recording a live performance?

The only hall available for concerts at that time was the Albert Hall and that, from the point of view of both audience and player, was a recording anachronism. We had been told that Karajan wanted to devote the first half of the rehearsal that afternoon to the cello and bass cadenza that comes just before the last movement. I wondered what his reaction would be to the Hall of Echoes.

A voice at my elbow startled me out of my reverie and asked me to mark the bass part as well. I immediately recognised it as that of the bass player Gerry Brooks. I told him that as I didn't play the bass, I couldn't oblige.

'You know I've often told you that I should have taken up the bass instead of the cello. What would Jim say if Karajan's ideas didn't work? He wouldn't be very happy if he saw me marking a bass part, you know that as well as I do.' (Jim was James Edward Merritt, principal bass.)

'You don't *take up* the bass,' said Gerry, evading my query. 'You descend to it. In any case,' he continued, 'it isn't called a bass. You should know that by now.'

'What do you call it?' I asked.

'A dog house,' Gerry answered.

I hadn't realised that some bass players might feel that they were permanently marooned in some sort of purdah at the bottom of the orchestra. Although Gerry and I had often sparred in a friendly way we had never really discussed the relative merits of our respective instruments.

'Do you ever get any real pleasure from playing the bass in an orchestra?' I asked, 'or do you have a kind of love-hate relationship that is heightened by whoever is conducting?'

Gerry eyed me with an amused look. 'You really are a *barnpot*,' he replied. I had heard him use the word *barnpot* on many occasions. For those within earshot Gerry's verbal contributions to the day's work were a source of unending amusement. His vocabulary, rich and varied in ornamentation, was always delivered with an air of uncompromising disdain.

'What does *barnpot* actually mean?' I asked. 'As a matter of fact, what do those other odd words mean and where did you learn them?'

'I didn't learn them, I invented them,' he replied with evident satisfaction. 'There just aren't any suitable words to describe what I think about conductors, and the way they make us play, so I had to invent my own.' By this time Gerry was sitting on Raymond's chair and lighting his stubby little pipe. 'We won't talk about phrasing just for now,' he continued.

'Why?' I was curious. 'Why exclude phrasing?'

Gerry looked pained. 'Allow me to finish. Phrasing is another area of debate with its own vocabulary. Just stick to my use of the word *barnpot* for the moment.' He pulled hard on his pipe and watched the smoke curl up.

'A conductor draws attention to a mistake for two main reasons,' he began. 'Either because a note is wrong or because it is too loud, too soft, too long, too short etc. Perhaps there is an error in the part or possibly in the conductor's score. In any event the player has to react. He must either correct the part or he must inform the conductor that there is an error in the score. So long as everyone is trying, all will benefit. Do you agree so far?'

I nodded and Gerry continued.

'Let us suppose that the conductor hears a mistake. There are some carvers who seem to take pleasure in making you look a fool—you know the sort I mean.'

I said I knew only too well.

'Well,' said Gerry, 'there is only one answer. You must never admit that *you* are wrong. Either the part is wrong or the *carver* is wrong.'

Gerry stopped for a moment to relight his pipe.

'Let us suppose,' he continued eventually, 'that the conductor's score and the parts, for one reason or another, are all wrong. In that case the situation is *barnpotic*. If the part is right but the score is wrong, then the carver is a *barnpot*. If, and I admit this can happen, the player is wrong (but this is never admitted), then the situation is *pernumerunt*.' Gerry sat back, drawing heavily on his pipe, apparently lost in thought.

Spurred on by this information I asked Gerry if, in his opinion, the Ninth Symphony had been written by a *barnpot* or for *barnpots*? Or adding variation to the theme, could the cadenza of the Ninth Symphony be described as being *pernumerunt*. To my surprise Gerry seemed quite offended.

'You don't use my vocabulary in that context,' he said severely.

'Beethoven is Beethoven.'

I couldn't really argue with him on that point.

'But what does the word mean?' I asked, undeterred.

'*Per*, as in 'pertaining to', *numer*, as in 'numerous', *unt*, as in ...'

Here he paused leaving me to complete the obvious word-picture.

There was a special reason why Gerry considered the rehearsal that afternoon to be *pernumerunt*. It had to do with his position in the bass section. The further a player is seated from the first desk the safer he or she feels when a conductor begins to ask for an unaccustomed attention to detail. On this particular day, due to illness on the first desk, Gerry had to play as sub-principal. Naturally, on the basis of 'He who is heard is lost' Gerry would have to be a little more discreet than usual.

Whenever there was a tricky passage it was a tradition that the more confident players would play a little louder, while the less able would only look as if they were playing. In professional jargon this is called 'feathering' and was a happy arrangement that had endured for generations. With new recording techniques came new problems. It was becoming not unusual to have one microphone per stand. For players who had made a reasonable living by skating on rather thin orchestral ice, the new development was one that needed careful consideration. With the sound being fed into the recording console, for either Walter Legge or Karajan to listen to at their leisure, there appeared to be no escape. With technically-minded conductors it was now more likely going to be 'He who is not heard will most certainly be lost —in respect of future employment.'

We gave the concert and *The Times* described our performance as 'Coherent and convincing.......a memorable performance of the great work which Karajan controlled by remaining firm but modest.'

What critics write and what players can identify with in print the next day will always remain a mystery. This time however a little mystery of my own was clarified. During the performance I could see Schwarzkopf and Christoff quite clearly. Karajan was also watching the two singers, with eyes that were more than half open. As we were nearing one of the defining moments in the last movement Karajan began to tense up in sympathy with the technical problem about to confront the soprano. When a singer is of Schwarzkopf's stature it is absolute magic, as indeed it was that night. It was as if Karajan needed to *see* that corner where the enharmonic change allows the same note to become the 'path to acceptance'. When the singers had returned to less challenging registers his eyes closed again. Karajan had been anything but 'firm', and as far as I could judge, being 'modest' wouldn't have helped at that critical moment. We players, with our hearts, eyes, and ears attuned to the cross-currents without which a performance is lifeless, were obliged to provide the platform on which that subtle transition in the soprano part has to rely. Karajan's musical integrity proscribed his self-imposed rule at that moment. It was not modesty, as stated by the critic, it was artistic unselfishness of the highest order.

CHAPTER TWELVE

Birmingham and the Starlings

A recording of the 'Immolation Scene' from Wagner's *Götterdämmerung* at Abbey Road in March 1948 was to be the occasion of a post-war reunion for some of the older players in the Philharmonia. Most of the members of the orchestra had either heard, or had worked with, Wilhelm Furtwängler, but for younger players like myself, it was to be a first-time introduction to one of the major talents of the twentieth century.

I had often been allowed to leave my cello underneath the platform in the studio at Abbey Road by a sympathetic studio attendant. One day I found him carting a large number of box files he said he'd been told to incinerate. As they were ideally suited for storing music I asked him for a few and he gave me over a dozen. I was surprised, and a little worried, to discover that they contained some letters to, and from, Walter Legge. They were fascinating to read, providing me with an insight into the man's character, and added to the regard I already felt for him. Feeling extremely uneasy, I bundled them all into a suitcase and handed them back to the attendant, who nearly passed out when he realised the mistake he had made.

An example of Walter Legge's capacity for enthusiasm was shown in one of the letters written to a newly knighted friend. My impression remains that he was delighted to learn that his friend's service to music had been recognised. I am in no doubt that the feeling was genuine, but was there maybe a regret that his own not inconsiderable service to music-making hadn't been appreciated in his own country?

Pierre and Lydia Fournier prepared me for the experience of

working with Furtwängler and Flagstad and although I am not sure whether Pierre had actually played concertos with Furtwängler as conductor, his admiration was unstinted. Like Furtwängler, Fournier had also been pilloried simply because he had given concerts in Germany during the war. Poised in 1939 to establish his career as one of the most distinguished cellists of the century, war intervened. The main banks in London, Montreal, New York, Boston and the Far East made sure their buildings and industrial investments in Europe weren't disadvantaged, but nobody has ever pilloried them.

Six years earlier, when Furtwängler was just beginning his long fight against unjust confrontational tactics of organised world-hate, fellow musicians expelled from Germany attacked him for not leaving his country. In 1933 he was a symbol, not only in Germany, but also in the rest of the world—the embodiment of German music. Furtwängler's world-status as a musician with strong principles had been seen by the banking oligarchy as representing a useful cultural weapon against the threat of communist expansion. It was well-known that Furtwängler believed Stalin to be an enormous threat to the peace and stability of Europe's cultural institutions.

When Furtwängler had served his purpose he was unceremoniously dropped. His sole duty as a musician, as critics had been saying since 1933, was not to provide Germany with wonderful concerts in Vienna, Salzburg and Berlin, but to *emigrate*. Pierre Fournier told me about Furtwängler's sense of values and how necessary they had been to people of conscience in Paris at the time when, before the war, he, Pierre, had been my age.

'The leaders and bankers of Europe's democracies negotiated money deals with Hitler, signed treaties and non-aggression pacts,' he told me, 'but only Furtwängler was castigated for trying to lead from within. For that, like so many people, he was persecuted. I played cello music wherever I could because I was and am still grateful to have been given a talent. For that I too was persecuted.'

Furtwängler had wanted to demonstrate that the essential qualities of German music still survived. By 1947 he had sacrificed seventeen years of his career in helpless compassion for his people, and for his art.

Furtwängler and Flagstad entered the studio, the orchestra rose and the artists were introduced. Although we were both tall men Furtwängler towered above me. I looked at him with an inner feeling of helpless rage that politics and politicians should have the power to waste the lives of such people. He climbed on to the rostrum and about five minutes of recording time was lost in offering and returning salutations. Not an economical way to record but that time was, for me, beyond price.

The entire orchestra made certain that its collective will would translate his quivering uncertainty into the positive and unanimous release of the 'Furtwängler sound'—an instantly recognisable, gloriously rich and sonorous bass coupled with a warmth of tone from the upper registers of an orchestra that now glowed. This, in my opinion, was to become the basis of the 'Philharmonia Sound' —from Furtwängler, not Karajan. Walter Legge's use of Furtwängler, Karajan, and Klemperer, three conductors from Germany, must surely have played a major part in creating the present high standards of orchestral playing in Britain.

The very first chord of the Wagner drew a sound from the orchestra I had not heard before. It would have been easier for me if I could have moved back to get a better perspective but the recording engineers were adamant and the section had to stay put. I had to endure discomfort but found that I was able to play even though my view between the music and the conductor was completely out of line.

The conducting techniques of Furtwängler and Karajan could not have been more contrasted. How Furtwängler obtained a cohesive vertical sound using the stick as he did was a mystery. Karajan achieved his results by eradicating doubt, yet they both allowed the orchestra to breathe. Despite completely different methods of controlling the orchestra, both managed to achieve memorable results.

That first concert with Furtwängler, on 22nd May 1950, demonstrated the extraordinary logic of his use of a slightly altered tempo in the giant echoing Albert Hall to achieve a clear aural perception of the notes. The particular problem was the last movement of Beethoven's Seventh Symphony in which the cellos and basses have an awkwardly written passage that rarely sounds convincing. Until then I had failed to grasp the overall majesty of the symphony, largely because previous conductors had not established a tempo that could combine the two opposing ideas with a convincing insistence. Consequently, the work lacked balance and its rhythmic and dynamic impact was weakened.

Furtwängler taught us that for music to 'live' it has to rely on what Casals later described as 'Les accents justes et les accents naturels'. By ensuring that a phrase was supported by accents on pulse beats, rather than on bar lines, it was easier for the orchestra to play as Furtwängler wanted. Without our realising it he convinced us that that was how we wanted to play in the first place. It was a wonderful experience to work with him and to be near enough to share moments of great emotional intensity that his perception re-created from the printed page.

With Karajan it was different. What was fascinating about his stick technique was the inexorable insistence with which the orchestra was trapped into submitting to the force of intellectual analysis before we were asked to implement it physically. Even after he had made his point he would not stop worrying at the problem until he was certain that we understood, not only intellectually but also in a physical and sensual way. He took endless trouble to acquaint himself with the technical difficulties presented by each instrument, and left no stone unturned in his search for the most convincing approach to teaching us to play music the way he wanted to hear it. He would then take us all with him on a communal voyage of discovery.

Rehearsals with him were a painstaking intellectual exercise, an exhausting emotional experience and not infrequently an uninhibited excursion into unrestrained sensuality. Every piece of music we prepared was explored and examined in a 'tactile' fashion. Karajan was like a sculptor chiselling away at a statue.

Both Karajan and Furtwängler were perfectionists and both expected total dedication from their players. Furtwängler seemed to be enjoining us to co-operate with him in a release of sound and energy. He was inviting us to make a joint statement of belief in all the collective crafts that make up the magnificent instrument we call the symphony orchestra.

Karajan not only enjoined us to follow him into his world of music, his force of logic was an added element of persuasion. First he established his credibility, and only after we had accepted it were we invited to follow, but it was definitely a case of the iron hand in the velvet glove. Only when he had finally achieved orchestral discipline did he feel free to concentrate on his main preoccupation of training us to produce the 'Karajan sound'.

Karajan's most effective technique of persuasion was the studied stammer. He often used it when he felt compelled to push, just a little further, the boundaries of reasonable criticism to minimise the risk of injured pride. Raymond Clark tried harder than most to explore all conceivable avenues of interpretation so as to facilitate the task of the conductor. Karajan was well aware of this and always approached him with the utmost circumspection.

For example, we were rehearsing the *tutti celli* solo section at the beginning of the slow movement of the Beethoven Seventh Symphony prior to a recording and subsequent tour of the UK.

'Can you play the first note so that it is not louder than the second?'

Raymond played the phrase.

'That is good. But-but-but-but... the phrase must be without accent. It is one entire beat—every section must sound as if it has only one beat.' The sentence would then be greatly extended by a more liberal use of the stammer-analysis-cajole method, and somehow even the most potentially explosive situations could be defused.

Experienced players could be excused for sometimes feeling irritated at the additional strain caused by Karajan's attention to detail. Old habits die hard, especially when nurtured by other conductors who rarely feel safe on the rostrum unless there is a pounding beat in every bar to guide them through the score. Another of Karajan's idiosyncrasies was to wear his watch on the inside of his wrist, over the inevitable black sweater. In this way he could look at it surreptitiously without giving the impression that he was allowing his concentration to wander.

Both of these two conductors were meticulous in their preparation of the works to be performed. Furtwängler managed to achieve magical moments in rehearsal that carried us on to a heightened awareness in the concert. Karajan, however, never seemed to manage the bridge between rehearsal and concert in quite the same way. He wanted the orchestra to be like a well-constructed wall that he could lean against, but Furtwängler would seek to add dimension to what had already been built.

During the flight to Boston on the last tour I made with the orchestra in 1955 Karajan complimented Dennis Brain and me on the technical efficiency of the orchestra. Nevertheless we had the distinct impression that our concerts seldom improved beyond what had been achieved at rehearsal. He agreed that these extra nuances never seemed to be present at either rehearsals or performances in London. I told him about the cold-douche-acoustic Raymond and I had experienced at the opening concert of the Festival Hall in 1951, and he agreed that if English players had the luxury of concert halls like the Musikvereinsaal this would make a difference. Dennis pointed out that the strings were probably worse off than the brass, but London's new concert hall was a dismal setting in which to give that little extra nuance.

The Philharmonia's first tour of the UK was to include Edinburgh and end at the Birmingham Town Hall. Karajan had

Karajan rehearsing in the Kingsway Hall 1955, his watch on the inside of his wrist.

taken immense trouble to prepare the programme artistically, psychologically and also 'cosmetically'. Nothing was left to chance. Even the seating rehearsals were undertaken with the same meticulous attention that was given to the music. For reasons that I have now forgotten, Rafael Kubelík and Eugène Goossens were also involved. By the last concert of the tour the orchestra was well able to cope with the acoustics of different concert halls. It was assumed by the management that Goossens would take Karajan's view of the Beethoven Seventh Symphony on trust that night in Birmingham, and simply follow us, the players.

The concert began with a well-known overture followed by a concerto. After the interval came the Beethoven. The audience appeared to be enraptured, and the hall had that special quality of stillness that is one of the real joys of performing. Even the usual coughs and sneezes were subdued to acceptable levels. We began the slow movement and the elegiac quality of the opening bars, followed by the haunting celli obligato, had just the sound Karajan would have wished for, the pianissimo being sustained at whisper-level throughout.

We had just begun that well-rehearsed passage when an enormous roar erupted from the roof of the building. Goossens kept going and we tried to follow but the serenely beautiful atmosphere that had been so carefully nurtured was irretrievably shattered. We struggled through to the end and then launched ourselves into the last movement in the hope of blotting out the commotion, but even the startled audience was unable, when the movement was finished, to match the intrusive racket with their applause. It was later discovered that thousands of starlings had chosen that magical moment in Beethoven's Seventh Symphony to come home to roost.

One autumn morning we had been booked to record Beethoven's *Eroica* Symphony. With Karajan as a fellow car-lover we looked forward to the possibility of discussing his most recent purchase in Germany. Dennis had recently acquired an Austin Seven tourer as a second car so as to obtain the maximum amount of petrol coupons while I, with the second largest instrument to move around London, was still car-less.

The scene that morning in the Kingsway Hall was a familiar one. Some members of the orchestra were tuning to the A of the oboe, while the remainder exchanged the daily gossip. The orchestra was ready, but where was the conductor? We knew that Karajan was in the country and since he was a very disciplined man, it was unlikely that his non-arrival could have been the consequence of over-indulgence on the previous evening. When Walter Legge stepped on to the rostrum I thought for a moment that a new dimension was about to be added to our interpretation of the *Eroica*. I had come to respect Walter Legge's knowledge and interest over a wide range of subjects, but the thought that he might be our conductor in a recording of Beethoven's Third Symphony needed some consideration.

'Ladies and gentlemen,' he said, 'we have a problem. Herr von Karajan does not think we can record the *Eroica* today. He says that to play in E Flat major you need to have a dry, clear day in order to capture the real breadth and tonality of the key.'

This piece of information was greeted with understandable scepticism, but then rich possibilities opened up as I began to ponder the implications. Perhaps the all-powerful Hardy Ratcliffe of the Musicians' Union would have to widen his field of negotiation so as to include a weather/humidity clause... However, my speculation was interrupted.

'We are going to record instead the Symphony No.4 in A by Roussel.' Presumably the key of A contained the correct humidity quotient and would therefore be acceptable for the prevailing weather conditions. Or was it that key structure is a more important factor in Beethoven than in Roussel? I shall never know.

'To save time I think we had better take an early break.'

When the orchestra re-assembled it was clear some had fortified the inner man with something stronger than tea or coffee. While we were waiting for habitual stragglers to appear Herr von Karajan descended to the floor level and began, for some reason, to talk about the Vuillaume double-bass.

'This instrument is so large that it requires one who plays the notes and another who uses the bow. In Germany we have such a bass.'

The expression on the face of James Merritt, our genial principal bass, was rather like a St Bernard lost in a snowdrift. The morning's events had left their mark and his face showed without any doubt the contempt he felt for the proceedings and for Karajan's attempt to fraternise.

'In England,' he said, 'we have a bass that needs *three* men to play it.'

'Oh!' Karajan was, to do him justice, instantly suspicious. 'How is that possible?'

'Simple,' says Jim. 'One chap works the notes.'

'Yes,' says Karajan.

'Another chap works the bow,' continues Jim.

Karajan stood silent and waiting in the sudden hush that had descended.

'And what does the third man do?' he asked icily. Jim didn't bat an eyelid.

'Oh, him. He just reads the notes for the other two.'

In the ensuing laughter Jim maintained his stoic St Bernard look while Herr von Karajan seemed completely mystified.

Furtwängler and Karajan in 1948, Cantelli and Klemperer in 1951; each contributed some special quality that players had no alternative but to respond to. The interaction of all these elements contributed to the sound and style of a truly wonderful orchestra that I still relish fifty years later. My lasting impression of Furtwängler was that he made me feel at peace. Karajan aroused emotions that were often contradictory. Cantelli I adored for his unflagging and intense integrity of purpose. That so much talent had already been trained and developed in such a young man was astonishing. Klemperer I felt sorry for but could never take seriously. Yet he extended the orchestra's life in a shared Indian Summer and the legacy of the orchestra's past held sway.

CHAPTER THIRTEEN

Neville, Dawson Place and Fournier

Father died in October 1947. A year later, 22 Dawson Place, Mother's latest acquisition, was beginning to reflect her creative insight into little matters of detail that caused her such endless concern, and her sons even more aggravation. She always took a great deal of trouble, and the end result was inevitably our gain. Cushion covers reflecting dominant colours in curtains, walls painted with slightly different shades of the same colour, all presented a harmonious backcloth to each day's changing light patterns.

One spring afternoon, shortly after Easter, the unexpected cancellation of an afternoon rehearsal enabled me to return home early. Wandering through the completed house I was suddenly made aware of the enormous responsibilities Mother had undertaken in 1938. It was nine years since she had decided to make the move to England. Despite continued and grinding poverty she had acquired, repaired and refurbished this beautiful home. In 1938 there had been nothing. Now there was this lovely house, reputedly once the home of Turner.

During the two sad and confused years that followed Father's death, much happened that was to influence my career. I worked with artists who were already famous and with others who would later become internationally established. I made several trips to Paris, but because Fournier was often on tour, it was now more an escape from orchestral drudge than for serious study of the cello repertoire. My working days were just as full as they had ever been, but the style of my life had changed. In some ways things were never to be the same again.

The monotony of endless rehearsals, recordings, concerts and theatre-work was occasionally broken by autumn broadcasts from King's College Cambridge where I played the cello continuo in performances of magnificent choral works in this unparalleled setting. These performances were never boring but the weather was invariably damp and very cold. The conditions in which the orchestra had to function were generally so appalling that it was sometimes touch-and-go whether a live broadcast could ever emerge from the chaos. (None of our broadcasts from this wonderful Chapel produced the pear-shaped sounds that have become the hallmark of today's 'authentic' performers. Perhaps our playing was not as alive and fresh as it seemed to me at the time, but it certainly never atrophied into stylistic absurdities, as so often happens today.)

These broadcasts were some of the most memorable of my career. Because they ended late, there was always the threat of mist and fog when driving back to London, but this was more than offset by the freshly ground coffee in the Copper Kettle opposite the main gate before the coach left.

Boris Ord, the choirmaster of King's College Chapel, was usually grumpy and always looking for perfection while trying to cope with new recording technology. The visits to Cambridge once again made me realise how indifferent acoustics could affect the quality of the player's tone, inhibit his performance, and spoil the listener's enjoyment. Did I imagine it, or was there a special quality about our broadcasts from King's College, as compared with concerts we were giving in London? Damp and cold as it was, why was the sound of the orchestra in King's so magical, unlike the sound produced in the equally damp Methodist Chapel where we rehearsed in London? I could not explain the almost sensual quality as I played, particularly in works like the St John Passion with its sublime cello solo.

Fifty years ago, orchestral playing was still the top rung of the ladder for most instrumentalists. Today, with no cafés and only a few theatre bands offering employment, and especially since synthesisers have replaced session players in providing pop culture with appropriate noises, playing in an orchestra has become the bread-and-butter of professional musicians.

From 1948 my work with the Philharmonia increased and with it a feeling of becoming trapped into the orchestral player's philosophy of 'survival at all costs'. A mixture of aggression towards imposters, and total submission to real talent whenever it surfaced. Concerts with great musicians were unforgettable but they were not very frequent.

The Philharmonia was becoming increasingly an orchestra whose main function was to record repertoire that could ensure commercial success. This was not unreasonable, but it also meant that most aspiring conductors needed, for commercial reasons, to record the same pieces as their rivals. Inevitably, the same works were repeated over and over again.

My ideal of the perfect life-style would have been to work in the town and have a home in the country, but the main difficulty was the lack of money. Mother was still living on a financial shoestring. Her income was made up exclusively of allowances from her three working sons, but this was not really enough to maintain a home and a public school education for her youngest son. To help balance the family budget it was decided to convert our very elegant dining room and the billiard room into a self-contained maisonette.

At this time I had begun to rehearse with Neville Marriner and Stephen Shingles in a chamber group that called itself the Virtuoso String Trio. When Neville announced his intention to marry Diana Cardew, he asked Mother if they could be the first occupants of the newly converted section of the house. In due course Diana and Neville came to live at 22A Dawson Place and I was given an insight into the life-style of *bons viveurs*.

One of Neville's many talents is an admirable gift for creating an atmosphere in which music can be enjoyed. His tongue-in-cheek attitude to both work and play was in complete contrast to the life I was leading. Battles with Mother were not infrequent because she resented my lack of progress as a soloist while my contemporaries were already achieving recognition. I was only too well aware that I couldn't play the cello, for example, like Alan Loveday could play the violin, but Mother was not convinced. Even so, I was finding myself less and less willing to accept the antics of ambitious conductors who could kill any love of music stone dead before they had even lifted the baton.

Neville however never seemed to have any of these problems or, if he did, he managed to hide them. One of his greatest gifts was an ability to control and disguise insecurity with a puckish humour. Of the three members of the Virtuoso String Trio Stephen Shingles was the one who had his feet most firmly on the ground. I dreamt of France, while Neville (always on the alert for an alternative to spending a lifetime being totally dependent on orchestral playing) had been wise enough to marry where money was. I had begun to miss my trips to Paris and felt an irresistible urge to visit 229 rue de Tolbiac once again just to remind myself of a rhythm of life I was fast losing touch with. During the following three years the trio survived in spite of the logistical difficulties of us all being front desk players in our respective orchestras. As soon as we had acquired a credible repertoire we felt it was time to try for a BBC audition.

Neville was just beginning to experience the truth of one of Montaigne's little quotes: 'Marriage is a good institution. The proof is the few marriages that work'. Never once, however, did he give any hint of the dramas that must have been going on at home. On the day of our audition, we had agreed to meet near Shepherds Bush and travel together to Portland Place, where we were to make a test recording. Neville failed to appear and, after waiting for as long as we dared, Stephen and I took a taxi on our own. In those days, the IRA had not yet extended its long arm of death and destruction to London, so admittance to the BBC was not the problem it is today. Steve and I approached the main enquiry desk, hoping against hope that Neville had already arrived.

'Can I help you?' said the bespectacled, middle-aged lady. Stephen explained who we were and why we had come.

'Can I have your names please?' she asked.

'Marriner, Shingles and Kok,' Steve answered promptly.

I looked at the uncomprehending face of the receptionist and saw a twitch on that of the doorman. I tried to catch Steve's eye but he was far too worried by now. We were only fifteen minutes away from our deadline and technically should already have had a balance test. There was no help for it and uncontrollable laughter enveloped me. The serious urgency with which Steve had pronounced our names was just too much.

Neville finally turned up as cheeky as ever. We passed the audition, but what we played and how we played is something about which I can remember nothing. We were offered several broadcasts and even attempted the Dohnányi Scherzo at a tempo that had been inspired by the Heifetz, Primrose, Feuermann recording.

Towards the end of my very enjoyable association with the trio we were offered an early morning recital of a Beethoven String Trio. In spite of his domestic problems Neville always managed to work as if the imminent break-up of his marriage was never going to happen, and usually had an impeccable grasp of the work in hand. However on this occasion, one and a half days before a broadcast in 1953, we were faced with a crisis. The simple fact was that we had expended a lot of energy rehearsing the Beethoven String Trio Opus 9 in C minor. Neville had indeed remembered that three flats were involved at some point. However we should have prepared the E Flat major Trio.

Fortunately for us, Granville Jones, one of the really bright stars of our generation of Academy students, was staying with Neville. He was far above many of his contemporaries in his grasp of phrasing and nuance, and also had that very rare gift of being able to set a tempo. It was he who helped us to put together an acceptable performance although none of us had ever played it before. Even our visits to Neville's lavatory to gaze on the famously reclining Marilyn were restricted to moments of urgency rather than of prurience.

A few months after this I played with the trio for the last time at a girl's school near Berkhamstead. It was spring, and 'the bird' in the form of an astonishingly photogenic Marilyn Monroe was most definitely 'on the wing'. In conversation during rehearsals the sap was continuing to rise with alarming frequency. There was also the arrival of Molly in Neville's life. She gradually began to take charge, helping to steer him through the break-up and subsequent divorce. The trio knew what to appreciate in this beautiful and remarkable lady and Neville, wise and lucky as usual, managed 'To have by letting go'.

When we arrived at Berkhamstead, Neville was in his usual irreverent mood. After rehearsing we had tea, changed into our tails and in due course mounted the platform of the School Hall. Before us a thousand ostensibly chaste virgins sat, guarded by what appeared to be an equal number of hawk-eyed virginal spinsters. Over recent years Neville had developed a talent for public speaking. Just before we began to play he decided for some reason to say a few words about each item - perhaps for Molly's benefit. It caused a feeling of foreboding in Steve and me as we could never be sure just how far Neville would conflate fact with fiction, or use us as props in his pre-concert chat. Our dread was not without reason for, instead of describing the Lennox Berkeley String Trio as the English equivalent of a lightweight French composer (or something along those lines), Neville looked slowly around the large hall with a completely deadpan expression.

'I don't really know what I can say about the music, from the composer's point of view, but as a performer I can assure you that we shall probably do more than justice to this piece by Bollocks Likely!' He then sat down and began to play. For a moment the penny didn't drop. I had been watching the young audience and was fascinated by the variety of facial expressions that had, only a few minutes before, worn a collective mask of induced boredom. I was so entranced that he and Steve started the piece without me. Neville stopped immediately and gave an audible sigh as if to say 'See what I mean?' And off we started again, but this time to vociferous applause from the girls and stern reprimands from the teachers.

Shortly afterwards, Neville had a serious car accident and was absent from the musical scene for a while. I was becoming less and less willing to face a life of playing and recording orchestral music, but what I wanted to do instead I really couldn't say. The piano trio with Daphne and Felix was becoming fairly well established but I wanted to expand into a musical life that matched, on a different plane, what I had experienced on the orchestral concert platform, and I didn't feel the trio would ever achieve this. I was also beginning to suspect that my talent did not equal my aspirations, and the end result was a lack of conviction.

I loved Dawson Place, especially the friends to whom Neville had introduced me, but in the end decided to move into a flat in Knightsbridge to see if this might ease the tension at home. It did not. Mother was greatly offended by my leaving home and, added to this, there were unexpected complications in my love life.

Whilst studying with Pierre Fournier in Paris, I met Amaryllis Fleming, an auburn-haired cello student of his; easily one of the most beautiful women I had yet encountered. I was told that she was the adopted daughter of Mrs Fleming, sister-in-law of the writer Ian Fleming, and that she was the daughter of Augustus

John, the painter. All this also coincided with a series of important concerts which, in the world of the cinema, would be described as 'star-studded'. It was at one of these concerts that I once again met up with the auburn-haired cellist whose status as a soloist was so much admired by Mother.

Another distraction was the actress Virginia McKenna, who lived two doors away from my little house in Rutland Gate. At Denham Studios, where many of my working days were spent, I gazed in silent admiration at the dancer, Moira Shearer, at Jean Simmons and other Rank Starlets. Then, through Amaryllis, I met Jemima Pitman, who lived in a lovely house in Cheyne Walk, full of the paintings her father had agreed to store for Augustus John during the war. I may have been unsettled before, but now I very nearly became unhinged—the diet was too rich and the courses that made up the banquet were not at all well matched.

Mother's attitude to life was not complicated. She had no time for grey areas. I cannot imagine her accepting the validity of 'it all depends on the way you look at it'. Things were black or white, hot or cold, beautiful or ugly, right or wrong. Whether it was a question of idle bureaucrats, lazy builders, deceitful shopkeepers, or her children's lady friends, one was reminded of the policy favoured by Fisher, Britain's First Sea Lord at the turn of the twentieth century: 'Hit first, hit hard, hit anywhere.' The principles that guided her were instilled into me from a very early age and they certainly left their mark.

I was also bewildered by the increasing disorder I saw all around me at all levels of society. I was associating with wealthy people who, just like the Mayers, were fascinated by the *concept* of socialism. These people lived in beautiful homes, beautifully furnished. They went on expensive holidays and never lacked for money, or so it seemed, and yet they loved to rub shoulders with people who were threatening them with ruin and impoverishment. One evening, at a cocktail party, I expressed surprise at this attitude to a young lecturer in sociology from Cambridge who told me rather grandly that if I were to try going down a coal mine, I might understand. When I told *him* what Sir Sidney Clive and Casals had told *me* about the millions of intellectuals imprisoned or killed by Stalin (quite apart from the ten million Ukrainians who had been deliberately starved to death in the 1930s), it made no impression on him at all. However, I couldn't help wondering what ten years in a Soviet camp of corrective labour might do for his powers of understanding. Some of these latter-day flagellants were obviously seeking to divert divine wrath from themselves by allowing the 'workers' to scourge them till the blood ran, the *vox populi* representing I suppose in this instance, the *vox dei*.

Not all the people I met at these gatherings were so blinkered and platitudinous. There were many honest men and women asking intelligent questions about the anomalous situations politicians were busy creating for the coming generations. For a non-political animal like myself, the only Utopia I recognised seemed to have no meaning or place in the society in which I lived and worked. I was convinced that if Walter Legge had been able to build a Musikvereinsaal I would have found instant anchorage. Meanwhile, my orchestral colleagues were either sceptical about my motives when I defended the rights of the individual, or dismissive when I objected to concepts about World Government and its dubious blessings.

There appeared to be a vast conspiracy of silence by rulers who had already destroyed much that was beautiful in the world and who now threatened everything I had come to love in art, music, and architecture.

Once again I turned to books for an answer and this time I tried the Russian authors. Russia had been our great and gallant ally during the war against National Socialism, and I was anxious to learn something about the men who had paved the way for the twentieth century's experiment with International Socialism. I started off with *War and Peace* and was so mesmerised that I stayed in bed for nearly five days quite unable to put the book down. I had a great deal of work at the time and had to send deputies to play for me at the Albert Hall, Denham Film Studios, and the Globe Theatre, so it proved to be a very expensive read by the end.

I tried other Russian authors and found them equally enthralling. Never before had I encountered such powerful and evocative writing, such perception and such psychological insight. It did not, however, answer any of the questions that were troubling me; on the contrary it raised quite a few more which I am still wrestling with to this day.

As a result of reading these authors I started thinking seriously about the destiny of individuals and of nations. Calvin says that everything in Heaven and on Earth has been pre-ordained since the beginning of time, although this is hotly disputed by Tolstoy in *War and Peace*. He seems to suggest that all events in life are no more than a concentration of minor shambles, eventually adding up to one gigantic shambles. Consequently in any given period of history the Top Dog is the leader who, through lack of opportunity and because of insufficient time, has not yet accumulated quite as much evidence of the shambles as his nearest competitor. The moral of this is, I suppose, that one should take no heed for the morrow. 'Sufficient unto the day is the evil thereof.' Could this be the Russian version of what the English call 'muddling through'?

As the year dragged on I was losing the will to work. To add to my troubles I had another attack of rheumatic fever and by the time I was on my feet again I decided to make a clean break and get out of London.

Without really expecting any response I wrote to Pablo Casals asking him whether he would listen to me play and help me decide what to do. To my utter amazement I received a friendly reply suggesting that I should visit him in Prades.

CHAPTER FOURTEEN

That Tango and Casals

In the early 1970s I was touring South Africa and happened to be staying with friends in Pietermaritzburg for a few days. I was surprised and delighted to hear that Pierre Fournier was to play the Dvořák Cello Concerto that night at the Town Hall. Just after he had played the passionate middle section in the slow movement, there was a dull thud, unmistakably the sound a dead body makes when it hits a hard floor.

Shortly before the concert I had seen a member of the audience give up his seat to an elderly frail-looking man. It was at the end of the row so I couldn't avoid seeing the man fall sideways into the aisle. For a moment I was stunned, unable even to think what should be done. Pierre, the conductor and the orchestra, who had heard the sound but hadn't associated it with death, continued without interruption. For me, watching the removal of the lifeless body, the little cadenza near the end of the movement took on a new and intensely elegiac quality I have never forgotten.

After the concert I met Pierre and we arranged to meet again in Capetown a few days later. With no social duties or concerts to perform we decided to be entertained rather than be the entertainers that night. I had played in the orchestra that provided background music for the film *The Lion in Winter* that was being shown locally that night, so Pierre decided that it would be interesting to see and hear how I earned a living. When it was over we decided to walk and enjoy the cool breeze of a warm, winter's evening.

Speculating about the paradoxes of our profession, I asked him whether the cello had always come first. His studied response made me aware, for the only time in nearly thirty years of friendship, to what extent polio had blighted his professional life. Looking at me with his courteous, endearing smile, his widely spaced dark eyes full of mischief, he reminded me of that fantastic tango I had danced with Lydia on my first visit to Paris in 1947.

'Bobby, when you and Lydia danced that night I was happy for you but I was also envious.' I had obviously got it all wrong that night. Lydia danced because she loved dancing. Body movement was part of self-expression for her and I was the lucky recipient of a favour—nothing more. The point was that I didn't have a paralysed leg. That was something Pierre would always have to live with and it was something I should have realised at the time if I had had any sense. I looked at Pierre and laughed.

'What's so funny?' he wanted to know.

'If you only knew how muddled I was after you came across and told her that I was a little on the young side,' I said. 'I had never before felt quite so adult, and then you come along and remind me that I was still "only a boy!"' Pierre smiled and said nothing.

'Do you remember those suppers we used to have at the Mayers' house?' I went on. 'Lady Mayer always made me feel slightly juvenile because of my inability to understand her insistence that music and morality had about as much in common as a politician's prattle compared with the wisdom of a statesman. I realise now that questions by a twenty year old about the place of music in a philistine society may have sounded a little over-intense, but would you and Schnabel have taken her side at the time?'

'Perhaps she was a little unkind,' Pierre said, touching my hand lightly.

'Why do you say that?' I was curious.

'Well, just think about those wonderful stories Schnabel used to tell. What did they say to you? They made clear that it was possible to live and work, and still remain true to one's art in a society dominated by prattlers and statesmen.' Pierre, as always, had seen the whole picture.

'Survival is what matters,' I said in turn. 'There are no absolute standards. This was the philosophy being advocated, as I remember, by Lady Mayer. Expediency, compromise, turning a blind eye, double-dealing if you have to, and knowing how to manipulate ground rules. This was the message I thought she was trying to teach me. The trouble was that I was too young to understand.'

'Probably,' he said with a smile. 'But I still don't quite understand. What has all that got to do with dancing the tango with Lydia in 1947? How old were you that night?'

'Nearly twenty one,' I replied, feeling slightly uneasy, and wondering what was going to come next.

'Do you know what is implied when a beautiful woman dances the tango with a young man?'

I hesitated. Should I admit to Pierre that by dancing with his wife I had been sexually aroused? The fact that Lydia was older by several years had seemed to give the occasion a veneer of respectability. I had assumed I was on safe ground, until Ivor Newton told me a story about Heifetz and Benno Moiseiwitsch. Before Lydia married Pierre she had been the wife of Gregor Piatigorsky. It seems that Benno had given a superb recital at the Carnegie Hall. At a party given afterwards by Gregor, Benno had celebrated his success by dancing the very adult version of the tango with Lydia. He had left the next day for a tour of Canada, and in conversation with another member of the concert party, happened to mention his erotic experience of the previous evening.

'Heifetz won't like that,' said his companion. 'He's rather possessive, especially when it concerns other people's wives. I wouldn't be at all surprised if you don't get a telegram this week.'

He was right. Benno did receive one, but decided not to open it. Ten years later, at another party, this time in London, Heifetz caught up with Benno.

'Didn't you get a telegram from me after your Carnegie recital?' Benno pretended to look blank.

'No,' he said trying to look as if he was thinking hard. 'No I'm sure I didn't.'

'Pity,' said Heifetz. 'You played marvellously. I was hoping we could have got together for a few concerts and recordings.'

It was a delicious story, but looking at Pierre, I thought better of it. He and Lydia looked happy enough when I first met them in the summer of 1947. Since then his career had gone from strength to strength and mine had—well where had it gone? It had hardly begun.

'Back in 1949,' I told Pierre, 'I used to think all great artists were hard working, serious, creative people, whose greatest gift was their ability to discipline wayward inclinations. As a boy I was never advised about what is, after all, an essential element in our lives. All I was made to understand was that self-management was an essential part of life, particularly in relation to the opposite sex. You and Lydia looked so perfectly matched.'

'Don't you believe it,' said Pierre, amused. 'Lydia and I had our struggles, but the nature of the problem changes with changing fashions. Film producers today, unlike the one who directed the film we saw tonight, seem afraid to trust the imagination of their audience. They leave us with nothing of our own to contribute to the mix; nothing with which to stir our own conscience. I have come to believe that familiarity and being taken for granted are two great impediments to being happily married. The problem is how to balance the two.'

After we said good night I didn't feel like going to my hotel, walking instead to a little Italian café for a last cup of coffee before flying to Johannesburg the next morning. The evening had revived many memories of those early years after the war, one of the most vivid being of Amaryllis Fleming, known to all her admiring friends as Amo. She was totally captivated (just as I was) by

Fournier, the international cellist, and by Pierre, the true and loyal friend. In 1949 I was confined to bed with a second attack of rheumatic fever. Amaryllis had been whisked off by her mother to Kingston, Jamaica 'to protect her from herself', as she explained to me. She had sent me a 'get well' card with a picture of a perplexed-looking cellist using a nude female torso as a cello. On the other side she had written 'You must have had a Victorian upbringing.' Mother brought the card up to my room and as she placed it on the bedside table gave me a sideways look that spoke volumes.

For weeks prior to receiving the card thoughts on 'how to remain sane and be a successful musician' kept going round and round in my head, constantly routed by the memory of Amo's whimsical smile, especially on the occasion of our last meal together.

Having ordered more coffee from the Italian waiter in Capetown I thought again of the Italian café behind Marble Arch where she and I met for the last time. I was enjoying my favourite dish (thinly sliced liver, crisp bacon, white bread and butter, and a cup of strong tea) while at the same time trying to put my emotional entanglements, since joining the Philharmonia in 1945, into some sort of perspective. We had both been taught and inspired by Pierre, but as she had also spent several months studying with Casals and Suggia, there were many things we could happily discuss.

I talked. Amaryllis listened. Did she have regrets, especially about her relationship with Pierre? What was she hoping to achieve, as a cellist of considerable talent, in an incredibly tough and unsympathetic world? Would music, on its own, ever be enough to maintain and sustain her interest? Did other artists have the same difficulty coping with the feeling of emptiness that I felt in my life? A sort of nameless uncertainty and longing haunted me. Did she and Pierre ever feel the void I seemed unable to shake off?

Did she have the same sense of fulfilment playing concertos in public, that she experienced when giving solo recitals? I paused for a moment, anxious to hear her reply.

'Do you believe in contraception?' she said.

There was little room to manoeuvre. Avoiding a direct answer, I tried instead to describe the nature of my long-standing friendship with a girl who lived in Rutland. Once a week during term time she came to London for singing lessons. Our separate existences over a period of several years had become a source of real strength for both of us. Neither ever felt the need to compromise each other's good intentions but, as I was beginning to suspect while eating my liver and bacon that morning in Marble Arch, the reality of the woman sitting in front of me was becoming a problem. I had to ask myself whether perhaps, as Shaw said, my chastity had not merely been denied opportunity. With opportunity available in the person of a beautiful woman sitting at the same table, chastity might well prove to be a formidable opponent.

'All very sad,' she said, 'but you haven't answered my question.'

It was useless to prevaricate any longer. I said that I had not yet been obliged to make the relevant decision. Amaryllis eyed me with mock seriousness. Then, when she said that I still hadn't answered her question, I had to laugh. I told her about the Hotel d'Or in Paris and about the many mirrors in my room.

'Do you really expect me to believe,' she said, and this time mockery had been replaced with serious concern, 'that you could spend a whole week in a place like that and not have the faintest idea of what was going on? What on earth did you think the mirrors were for?'

'I was not really sure at the time,' I replied, 'but they certainly came in very handy. Pierre had suggested some bowing and I found that I could check my wrist and elbow from every angle.'

Amaryllis laughed. It was getting late and she had to go. We said goodbye and she kissed me lightly on the cheek, the only kiss I was ever to have from her.

'I asked you if you believed in contraception,' she said with a twinkle in her eye, 'but I imagine that you probably manage very well without it.'

There had never been any open discussion in the family about sex or its implications. Montaigne has written several times about the function of the male organ and its regrettable unreliability in the sex game. In today's emancipated times, when the male has changed from hunter to hunted, can he still hope to control this unpredictable member in his new role? If *interest* is aroused, is it still an essential part of civilised man's code to maintain control and direct that energy into other areas, such as VAT or his tax returns? There appeared to be no alternative but to adhere to my grandmother's dictum: 'Strait is the Way and Narrow is the Gate'.

Less clear was why my friends managed to treat a problem of great importance to me with such irreverence. Was it a case of my 'needing more than being needed'? It didn't occur to me that everyone has a need and that it was not necessarily a sign of weakness to reciprocate the needs of others in order to lessen one's own. It was also becoming obvious as the weeks of my illness dragged on, that the problem had less to do with my having sex than with my not having sex: I needed to allow myself to respect the benefits of pleasure.

My first attempt did not prove to be a great success. Sex was undeniably exhilarating and went far beyond anything I could have ever imagined, but it was not a path to salvation. Nor was it the slippery slope to a bottomless pit dug by the ever-present Lucifer with the Pointed Tail.

I went to see Walter Legge and asked for leave of absence, this time for three months.

'Where do you want to go this time?' he asked not unkindly.

'I was hoping to spend the time with Casals,' I explained.

'But he can't play in tune,' he responded, amused.

I was rather taken aback and wanted to know more but Walter Legge would not be drawn. I had a feeling that there were other issues involved but could elicit nothing more from him.

My last concert with the Philharmonia before leaving for Prades was as sub-principal. It was to be a live broadcast from Maida Vale studios with Szymon Goldberg directing and playing violin concertos by Bach and Mozart. When I arrived in the studio I found that Mr Goldberg had placed the orchestra in an expanding arc, with the front desks at the hub and the other players radiating outwards. As it was a special occasion, a live broadcast, there was also to be a live audience in the studio.

The co-leader of the cellos at the time was Haydn Rogerson, whom Walter Legge had brought down from the Hallé Orchestra in Manchester to co-lead with Raymond Clark. Haydn had known Casals since before the war, and was kind enough to give me a letter of introduction to present to Le Maître, as he called him, when I arrived in Prades. I was also to give *Le Maître* another letter containing family news. Haydn explained that Casals was godfather to his son. As he spoke, he pulled the letter out of his pocket and, in doing so, he also pulled out a packet of contraceptives. This instantly recognizable commodity slid across the open expanse of floor.

A ripple of amusement spread from the orchestra to the front rows of the audience. Szymon Goldberg had arrived by this time, so I put my foot on the packet and we started the Mozart G major Concerto. During the course of the performance I managed to slip the offending object into my pocket, and Haydn's mishap was soon forgotten.

The next morning I had to be off early, so I asked my brother Felix if he would return Haydn's property to him at their next meeting. He said he would and I left for Prades.

A few weeks later I received a very edgy letter from him describing the events subsequent to my departure. Members of the Boyd Neel Orchestra often played a game as they travelled by train to concerts. When the train was in a tunnel a man's wallet would be filched from his pocket, usually by a member of the opposite sex, and the contents publicly examined when the train finally emerged into the light. Felix had been selected as a victim

Pablo Casals at his villa in Prades

and Haydn Rogerson's little packet was duly displayed for all eyes to see. Understandably he felt he had been placed in an invidious position and on returning home he packed them up ready to send to me with the recommendation that I should look after my own affairs in future. Unfortunately, he left the little parcel at home where Mother discovered it while tidying his room. She opened it and demanded an explanation. Obviously he failed to provide one that satisfied her, and the outcome was that Mother wrote me a very severe letter listing a full range of sins to be avoided in future.

The Grand Hotel in Prades was dingy, unkempt, and favoured nobody. I was at first unable to bring myself to use the 'hole in the floor' and to make matters worse the Public Baths were on the other side of the town.

At dinner a few days later I met other pupils of Casals. One in particular, Rudolf von Tobel, was a German Swiss who had been studying with Casals since before the war. As a Swiss National, Rudolf had been allowed to visit *Le Maître* every year even during the period of hostilities, and Casals was grateful to him not only for his loyalty but, understandably, for the little luxuries that he could bring with him from neutral Switzerland.

With the passage of time, Rudolf had taken it upon himself to create a kind of buffer zone between *Le Maître* and would-be pupils. If you wanted lessons with Casals you went to Rudolf von Tobel first. I was given the impression that Casals knew about this arrangement although he had made no mention of it in our correspondence.

At face value it seemed very reasonable and I liked Herr von Tobel. He had a marvellous sense of humour and a fund of excellent stories. He was a small man with an anatomical structure that displayed a cruel lack of proportion. His head was large, his eyes sad and luminous. From the waist upwards his body was long, but from the waist downwards his legs were short while his feet were enormous. The whole suggested a complete mix-up in the

Stork assembly line. What really surprised me were his hands; they were wonderful, as if made for the cello. Long, supple fingers, well related in size, and with very little web between the third and fourth. I was fascinated to watch Rudolf tuning up the Montagnana cello used by Emanuel Feuermann, whose playing of the *Tango* by Albéniz had inspired me to learn the cello twelve years and one war earlier. The sound of the open strings was breathtaking, and when Rudolf asked me if I wanted to hear him play a movement of a Bach suite, I suppose I was expecting a performance that would certainly not surpass Feuermann, but would nevertheless have had some redeeming features. But the nasal, emasculated sound emanating from this superb instrument was something I wouldn't have believed possible. My own Testore sounded far better.

It was then that I began to have my first misgivings about what I had let myself in for. I told Rudolf that I had fallen in love with the Casals recording of the Boccherini A major Cello Sonata, and wanted to play it to *Le Maître* myself. Rudolf looked dubious. He insisted that before we did anything, we should first learn how to sit, so we studied posture. This proved to be difficult as most of the chairs in that part of France seemed to have been made for short-legged men. Several books and cushions later I managed to achieve a stance that satisfied him.

I was to learn the importance of posture later, after a few more years in the wilderness, but on that day I was impatient to get on with the lesson. Having been told how to sit with my back in one position and my head in another, and many other things besides, I eventually ventured to suggest that the problem of posture could perhaps wait for another day. Although I accepted the reasoning and logic of what Rudolf was trying to instil in me, he was not cheap.

His system of diluted *ersatz* Casals was no doubt intended to stave off time-wasters, but I had already realised that however good Rudolf might be I was better, posture or no posture. When at the end of the lesson I was given a prepared handout and an appointment for another lesson ten days later, I realised that I would have to act quickly.

I returned to my room fuming, but what was I to do? I had given up three months' work in London in order to come and study with Casals. I couldn't afford the time or the money to have endless discussions with Herr von Tobel. I went down to supper in a state of irritation and deep depression.

The following day my despondency was noticed by another pupil of Casals, an American from New York called Madelaine Foley. Before I knew what had happened we were having a heated discussion about British Imperialism, Zionism, Fascism and the joker of the pack, South Africa. By this time, in 1949, I had drifted a long way from my own country and ethnic origins, and if I thought about such things at all, I saw myself as one very small part of the Great British Empire. Madelaine and her American friends attacked England's Imperialist policies in Palestine while Rudolf put the case for the Arabs. I was ridiculed when I quoted Toynbee, who had defined the Anglo-Saxon Empire as 'a noble attempt to link various cultures and ethnic groups within a pool of Nations, agreeing to co-operate when they could, and to differ when they could not. Nevertheless, all were to be bound by ties of loyalty to the British Crown.' My new acquaintances seemed to be speaking from their own experience, and whereas they could back up their statements with a bewildering array of facts and figures, I soon realised that I knew very little about England and its past.

On one point however we were all agreed. Everyone had a sincere veneration for *Le Maître–The Master of the Bow*, as Fritz Kreisler had once called him. We spoke at length about the philosophy of cello playing, and the problems of combining our researches into the language and meaning of art with the necessity of earning a living.

During the next few days this mixture of music and politics (or 'philosophy', as my new acquaintances preferred to call their sustained anti-imperialist rhetoric) took second place to my problem with Rudolf. Madelaine, who was already becoming the proverbial Jewish Momma, took pity on me and arranged matters with Le Maître that very same evening. I was to have my first lesson the following Thursday.

For the next few days I practised all the hours that consideration for others permitted, and when Thursday came I was keyed up to a pitch of expectancy that I had never before experienced. There was a feeling of weightlessness in my movements as if I were treading on air. On only one other occasion can I remember having experienced anything remotely similar. Twenty years later when I had just completed a lecture on the Beethoven A major Cello Sonata, a member of the audience asked me to play the whole work through. Although I was a little taken aback by the unexpected request, I sat down and found to my surprise that I had tapped a new source of energy, a peculiar blend of love for the piece and for Beethoven allied to a complete absence of over-critical self-consciousness. I was like a puppet on strings and the strings were controlled by the hands of *le Maître* who, all those years before, had provided new insight to fingerings and bowings that had added their contribution to the lyricism of the work. In that one performance the sum total of years of work and study came together, and for a few brief moments, I was allowed to experience the joy of playing without fear or inhibition.

My first lesson with Pablo Casals was a somewhat similar experience. I seemed to coast through the Boccherini Sonata with no conscious effort, sustained throughout the performance by a state of euphoria. That is how I remember the afternoon. It is of course possible that Casals judged my performance in a slightly different light, but he was kind enough not to make any discouraging remarks. On the contrary, he gave me three hours of his time and said I must bring the Schumann Concerto for the next lesson.

I left the little house on the Route Nationale, walked along the road under the tall plane trees and reached the hotel. I had a great deal to think about and decided to walk to Eus, an abandoned village about three miles away.

At the end of the previous century, a vine disease had ravaged the vineyards and destroyed the livelihood of a whole generation of people in that region of France. The villagers were forced to leave, the houses fell into decay. Wells and water conduits collapsed and eventually the little hillside town died. I reached Eus in time to see the most spectacular sunset I have ever witnessed. The whole valley, the 'Garden of France', lay before me. Everything was still. It was perfection, trapped for a brief moment but held in the mind for eternity.

It was getting late and even though it was still warm, my hands suddenly felt very cold against the stone parapet of the deserted town square overlooking the valley. I set off down the escarpment in front of the church and began the long walk back to Prades. By the time I reached the road in the floor of the valley, where the heat of the day was trapped by the sinking sun still shimmering in the distance, a sudden change of body temperature made me shiver with an intense cold I had never before experienced. I could hardly climb the four flights of stairs to my little room in the hotel and for the next few days I remained in a state of fever, unable to eat or drink. The rheumatic complaint I had suffered from earlier that year must have weakened me more than I had realised. I now contracted a virus and was not allowed to see anyone. Food was left at my bedroom door and it was several days before I returned to some kind of normality.

I have always wanted to play the cello, and yet most of the time the music I hear in my mind's ear becomes almost unrecognisable when my hands become involved. My first lesson with Casals had proved that it was occasionally possible to be liberated from self-doubt. However a lesson that had promised so much had been followed by this first sign of a blood disorder that has dogged my career ever since.

After a few days I was feeling slightly better and was dozing in bed when a knock on the door followed by the low, plaintive voice of Rudolf, woke me with a start. He was the last person I wanted to see at that particular moment. Apart from the slight feeling of guilt because I hadn't told him that Madelaine had arranged for me to play to Casals, there was still a risk of infection for visitors. I kept quiet hoping he would go away but there was another more audible knock.

'Bobby, I want to talk to you.'

There was nothing I could do but let him in. 'Come in, the door's open,' I called out and lay back in the small room, made even smaller by the presence of a magnificent armoire. Rudolf came in and sat down by the window looking out at Canigou, the thirteen thousand foot mountain with its snowy peaks, the source of abundant water for the beautiful and fertile valley below.

In the awkward silence that followed he occasionally looked accusingly at me, his dark brown eyes full of hurt and sadness. I felt as if I had assassinated a friend and began to hope that my temperature would come to the rescue and envelop my mind once more in the mists of the fever that had confined me to bed in the first place. I decided to resist his attempt at emotional blackmail and talked instead about the walk to Eus. I asked why the village had been abandoned and what was the vine disease that had destroyed the region. I talked about Switzerland, Prades and life in Vichy France. I mentioned Spain, Franco, the British Imperialism referred to by our fellow students. Finally, in desperation, I talked about Lenzerheide, not far from where he lived, and where I had made my first attempts to ski in 1946. All my questions and comments were met with stony silence.

I decided I simply had to get Rudolf out of the room, but before I could summon up the strength to suggest that we should talk when I was feeling a bit better, he spoke again in a voice of doom.

'Bobby. Why did you play to *Le Maître* without telling me?'

I was so enraged that I reacted before there was time to think.

'Rudolf,' I said angrily. 'I had one chance to play to Casals, but there will, I hope, be many opportunities to play to you. My chance came, and I took it.'

'Is that all you have to say?'

I was speechless. How could this man be such a pompous ass? He sat absolutely still, obviously waiting for an explanation.

'Rudolf,' I began, trying to remain as controlled as possible. 'You have known *Le Maître* for many years. I have only three months' grace from the orchestra. A chance to play to *Le Maître* came my way and I took it. I can honestly say that after my lesson I felt as if I was in paradise. Are you saying that it was wrong to enter heaven, given the opportunity? Was it wrong to be listened to and advised by one of the supreme masters of the cello?' I sat up in bed and looked straight at him. 'Well?' I asked, after he had remained silent for some time. 'Please answer me.'

Rudolf began to cry. I had been so wrapped up in my own complexes and lack of confidence, that it had never for a moment crossed my mind that it was he who needed to be thought well of. Tears I was not prepared for. All my anger disappeared and my heart went out to this poor, lonely man. After a long silence he left the room and I never saw him again. I felt as wretched as if I had whipped a chained dog. How is it, I wondered, that good intentions and kind gestures by human beings are so difficult to manage?

But worse was to come. Madelaine told me that Rudolf had become attached to me. He was unmarried, he had no relatives, he was fond of children, and he genuinely wanted to help me choose the right path to cello playing because he thought I needed guidance.

I had to be back in London the following week for rehearsals with the Boyd Neel Orchestra, prior to a tour of Portugal, so I left two days later. Our paths didn't cross again and my meeting that afternoon with Rudolf remains a sad episode of an otherwise unique experience. Because he had effectively wasted two of the three months I had planned to stay in Prades, I asked Walter Legge if I could resume lessons with Casals after the Portuguese tour. This time he had to refuse my request. Instead he invited me to share the front desk of the Philharmonia with Raymond Clark as sub-principal. My professional life in London was to become busier than ever.

I did not to return to Prades until 1955.

CHAPTER FIFTEEN

Suggia

Rehearsals for the Boyd Neel Orchestra's tour of Portugal in 1949 were to take place at the Chelsea Town Hall and were linked to a concert to be conducted by Enesco. While explaining to *Le Maître* why it had been necessary for me to curtail my study in Prades I had jokingly suggested that perhaps it might interest him to conduct a few concerts, either in Prades or London. Casals had the usual twinkle in his eyes as he talked about Enesco, one of the great violinists and musicians of the twentieth century. I tried to paint a rosy picture of the two of them, travelling around the world, enlightening music lovers who had lost out because of World War Two, but *Le Maître* would not be drawn. The answer was a polite but firm 'No'.

On the morning of the first rehearsal I took a number 52 bus from Notting Hill Gate, promising myself that if the day went badly, I would alight at the Royal Albert Hall, walk across the park and spend a little time on the bridge over the Serpentine. Set in the trees and gardens of this most lovely of London's parks, the view from the west side of the bridge is one I have treasured all my working life.

I had not played with the Boyd Neel for nearly four years and looked forward to it with mixed feelings. During World War Two, deputies like myself had to sight-read most of the music at the concert itself because travelling arrangements had usually gone wrong and there was rarely time to rehearse before the concert. It was therefore somewhat unsettling to find, after playing no more than a few bars of Bach's Brandenburg No. 3, that I wasn't able to 'fit' with my colleagues. The harder I tried, the worse matters became. My three months with *Le Maître* had made me develop idiosyncrasies of pitch and rhythm that made it much more difficult to play in an orchestra. Casals had helped me to improve my ear and bow control as part of tone production. In the privacy of my room this was no problem, but playing with a group was requiring adjustments I no longer knew how to make. In just three months I had already forgotten how hard it is to play with one eye on the music, the other on the conductor, and both ears alert to the style of the band. That morning the immediate problem was to know just how to fit with the intonation of my colleagues.

Walter Legge had warned me that by going to Casals I would only be compounding my uncertainties. Hadn't he told me earlier that year that Casals didn't play in tune? I hadn't been sure what he meant at the time but perhaps there was some hidden truth that I needed to learn. I looked around and saw that my good friends were apparently enjoying themselves. It is always extremely difficult to talk about intonation without making it look as if fingers are being pointed. As James Galway explained to Karajan in Berlin some twenty years later, when his intonation was being questioned: 'Herr von Karajan, it is not that '*I*' am out of tune, '*it*' is out of tune.

I had got to know Boyd Neel well during the war. He was a gifted man and a passionate lover of music. I used to envy his ability to combine, even in wartime London, an elegant city life-style with a cottage in the country. Most of all I envied his ability to be successful in all that he undertook.

During the coffee break, I played him some of the passages I was worried about and explained that, on their own, they sounded in tune, but when I played with the rest of the section things were not quite so happy. I was anxious not to lose the benefit of the three months' hard work in Prades, and asked Boyd if he would consider rehearsing sections of the programme solely for intonation. Where was I going wrong, or was it just something one had to accept? Boyd, an unwavering democrat, was dubious.

'It means that everyone would have to agree to give it a try,' he said.

'Poppy Kok,' commented Maurice Clare, the leader who had happened to overhear our conversation. Maurice was talented as a violinist, but totally insecure as a person. He rejected my suggestion immediately, something he no doubt regretted when, a little later, he mis-managed the solo violin arpeggio flourish at the end of the *Capriol Suite* by Peter Warlock.

When the orchestra broke for lunch I remained seated, wondering what to do and convinced that everyone around me was as embarrassed as I was. I decided to practise some of the problem passages, playing them first as I imagined *Le Maître* might have wanted hear them, and then as they had just been performed by the cello section.

I began to speculate about the morality behind my concern. Why worry? I kept asking myself. The others didn't really seem to mind. Everyone is doing their best, why not just leave it at that? 'Don't rock the boat!' as Raymond Clark would have said to anyone trying to find too many answers all at once, but the questions kept coming.

Casals had taught me first to listen with the inner ear by studying the score, then to analyse ideas that came after the heart had provided the emotional need. I realised that analysis will then subconsciously widen the thinking and, with luck, identify a sentiment that, although latent, may not have been recognised.

Looking up I found the penetrating eyes of Enesco fixed on me. His amused smile invited some kind of response so I explained my problem as best I could.

'You are beginning to learn,' he said with a smile.

Picking up my brother's violin, he played me a section of the C major Fugue for unaccompanied violin by Bach. When the difficulties of the work permitted, he would nod his head, as if to say, 'Here's an example of what you are trying to understand!'

Then he began to talk a little about remedies.

'You're fighting problems,' he said. 'Don't! Find answers! But it does not end there. If you feel you are at odds with everyone around you, then you should adopt their intonation, bowing, phrasing. Be as flexible as you can. When you are sure you can fit with everything they do, you are in a better position to select what you like and reject what you don't like.'

Put like that it seemed obvious, but I had needed to be reminded. I recalled my lesson with *Le Maître*. I had been very nervous to begin with but had somehow managed to play through my jitters into some semblance of a standard. Just as I was leaving, I had asked him whether I should give up and go and grow potatoes, or something. Always kind and polite, *Le Maître* just looked at me and smiled.

'Remember,' he said. 'You already play well but you still have much to learn. If you are wise you will always want to learn more. In that way you will be as good a player as you can be.' I told Enesco my little story and he nodded his head in obvious agreement.

'Remember also,' he said, 'the process of *becoming* is part of something else, something wider. What it *will* become. It is a subjective force, and if you are really to deepen your understanding, there must be interplay between one and the other state.'

'But how long does one wait before deciding to make a choice between one and the other?' I asked. 'And when will one know that a choice can be made or that the time is right?'

Enesco smiled. '*Le Maître* told you that you will be as good as you can be. He is right to say that. But to answer your question, I think you must just believe that you will know what to choose and that you will also know when the choice can be made.'

Over fifty years later, I am at last just beginning to understand that making the initial choice of a subject for imitation is only the first step in the process of artistic development. The second is the search for an artistic identity and this development requires further choices and new beginnings.

On that morning in the Chelsea Town Hall I should have played along with everyone else, analysed the results and then used the analysis as a basis for further work. A kind of cellistic *perpetuum mobile*. Art, I now realise, does not materialise fully formed. Like the caterpillar it must pass through many stages before it becomes a butterfly. I decided to 'feather' my way through the remainder of the day's rehearsal so as not to arouse any more irritation.

On the way home my thoughts went back to Prades. Just a few days before I had been given a delicious farewell dinner by the chef at the Grand Hotel. Now I was back in London with the prospect of nothing but orchestral playing ahead of me in a city without a concert hall worthy of the name. Why had I left Prades for this? Was it some sense of family obligation coupled with a never-ending lack of finance, leading to that melancholy, so aptly described by Disraeli as 'the invariable attendant of pecuniary embarrassment'.

Yes and no. There *was* a sense of family obligation, and there *was* a serious lack of money. More worrying was my growing awareness, since the visit to Prades, that my involvement with music was not exclusively limited to playing the cello. There was a newly awakened interest in the role that philosophy must play in trying to attain an ideal without subsequently destroying it. To philosophise about music was not merely a recipe for inertia, it was helping me to appreciate. There were also Montaigne's words of warning: 'Court success, and she will spurn you.'

In due course the day of the orchestra's departure for Portugal arrived. Felix was still fairly cross about the scene at the rehearsal, but willing enough to share the cost of a taxi to Northolt Airport. As soon as we arrived, he went straight to the bar and bought two large brandies. I did not drink or smoke and had assumed that my brothers didn't either. I was therefore shocked to see Felix, cigar in one hand and brandy in the other, obviously intending to get the show on the road.

Here was I, worried and anxious about rhythmic context, pitch variation, bow control, point of contact, rubato, phrasing, and a host of other matters, while Felix was obviously relaxed and happy. I went over and reminded him of his promise to Mother never to touch strong drink. Felix, demonstrating yet again his gift of infinite patience, merely waited until I had finished. Then picking up the brandy he had bought for me he emptied it, assuring me that if I wanted to be a martyr, he didn't. I had wanted to ask Felix whether or not I should accept Walter Legge's offer to join Raymond on the first desk of the Philharmonia Orchestra, but this was clearly not the moment.

During the flight to Lisbon I had time to think. I was twenty-three, still drawn to Paris and Pierre, and there was the whole cello repertoire to learn. There was also the orchestral repertoire. Most of the notes were playable at sight, but that was not what Walter Legge wanted. I felt that he expected from others the same devotion to the disciplines of music that he demanded of himself. Since 1947 he had allowed me time, but now he wanted my time.

I could not ignore the honour. There was a great deal I could learn about orchestral playing from colleagues like Raymond Clark, Manoug Parikian, Jack Thurston, Gareth Morris, Jock Sutcliffe, and Dennis Brain. All in their different ways contributed to the success of the Philharmonia. Nevertheless I was still worried that playing in an orchestra without a spiritual home, like the Musikvereinsaal, would turn me into the sort of cynical, middle-of-the-road player Walter Legge was trying to prevent me from becoming. It was not his fault that none of the new breed of banking aristocrats was prepared to endow London with a worthwhile concert hall. A mere drop from the ocean of mineral wealth inherited from Rhodes and appropriated from the two Republics could easily have created several equivalents of the Musikvereinsaal for London.

We began the tour with two concerts in Lisbon and then travelled by train to Oporto for the rest of our stay. Just as I was about to leave the platform after the first concert, a lady approached me and asked who my teacher was. I explained about Fournier and *Le Maître* and she laughed. 'Predictable,' she said. We talked a little about the music we had played and she asked about my future plans. The odd thing about our conversation was that I kept wondering where I had seen her before. She then told me her name was Madame Suggia, before taking her leave and moving on to talk to Boyd.

I was still wondering where I had seen her before when I suddenly remembered Jemima Pitman. Jemima's father had housed many of Augustus John's pictures at their home in Cheyne Walk, London, and there had been a startling portrait in the collection of a lady in a vivid red dress playing the cello. Standing in front of me was the model.

The next day, Felix, still cross about the brandy incident at Northolt, told me to stop mooching around and behave like a normal human being for once. Feeling sorry for oneself was not only juvenile, it was self-defeating. He had arranged for us to have lunch with the Lyles of Tate and Lyle, and he put me on oath not to discuss anything tendentious that was likely to lead to general embarrassment. I promised that I would try. In addition to my post-Casals depression I was not feeling very well. Two large ulcers had appeared at the back of my throat, making it very painful to swallow or even talk. Even though I had the opportunity to eat the food, I knew that I would not be able to enjoy the occasion. Boyd, a practising doctor at the time, gave me some nice looking tablets, no doubt assuming that I was intelligent enough to read the blurb. They tasted rather nice so I sucked them one after the other like boiled sweets instead of at four-hourly intervals as had been clearly prescribed. By the following day my tongue looked as if it had been pickled and has remained sensitive to penicillin ever since.

There was a wonderful and completely unexpected consolation prize on the day we went to lunch. Seated next to me was Suggia. Quite forgetting my promise to Felix I soon launched into a deep and increasingly animated discussion with her about Casals, Fournier, Feuermann, Piatigorski, cello playing and cellos - as only cellists seem able to do. After we had adjourned to the verandah overlooking the bay, the conversation continued well into the afternoon. Sitting there, in the company of this vivacious, highly intelligent woman, was a truly idyllic and unforgettable experience.

Suggia told me about her own search for identity during the time she had spent with *Le Maître*. She spoke of the courage of her people, and of a country that had been used as a testing ground for the rival ideologies of Falangism, Fascism, Communism and National Socialism, not to mention the individual greed and ambition of politicians, bankers, and the military. As she spoke, I was reminded of a third cellist in my circle of friends. Like Casals, he was also a Catalan and also a victim of the 1936 Civil War. His name was Francesco Gabarro – Gabby, as he was known to colleagues. He had arrived in England in 1947 from India, where he had been playing trombone and cello in the Bombay Symphony Orchestra.

Gabby had been a pupil of Casals, and like Casals had found himself unable to remain in Spain under Franco and the Opus Dei. After the Civil War in Spain and then the war in Europe had ended, well-wishers in Bombay had persuaded him to leave India and look for work in England. I had been able to offer a small token of friendship and respect by proposing him for membership of the Musicians' Union.

Suggia was interested to know about what was happening in England, and I was sorry I couldn't enthuse more about a country that seemed to have lost its soul. Having just spent three months in Prades being lectured by young American Zionists who considered that all the evils of the world stemmed from the selfishness of the British Empire's Anglo-Saxon ruling clique, I was no longer sure whether England had ever had a soul. I mentioned this to Suggia, but she was more inclined to question the role of international banks than that of small-time political opportunists.

Since I had last seen my father in 1940 I had more or less forgotten what he had said about his former employers, the Anglo American Corporation. He had, of course, not talked about 'International Finance Capitalism' but of the acquisition of South Africa's mineral wealth by mine owners and money barons. Suggia's words were like an echo from the past, and for me that past was my father. I remembered his sad farewell and the expression of vague hopelessness on his face. It was just like the expression I had seen only a month before on the face of *Le Maître* during our occasional evening soirées. He had talked about Spain, his reasons for leaving his lovely home near Barcelona, and his decision to live in the little French town of Prades in l936. For him and for Suggia there had been sacrifice, sadness, bereavement, hardship and self-abnegation which, in the end, had driven them both into exile.

I put it to Suggia that in this century music-makers should have ample opportunity to assist in portraying the true role of Man's Conscience in films, television and documentaries. All these need music to enhance their images of fact and fiction, but how often can a music-maker express his *own* belief? He sells his art to the image-maker for a negotiated price and the film industry in turn is controlled by the financial corporations. These play paper games with paper money, while guarding their true wealth behind massive interlocking, international cartels. If Orson Welles had been helped to produce films as he visualised them, instead of being deliberately throttled for having dared to create *Citizen Kane*, how much more could he not have achieved? What could lesser mortals hope to achieve when their views opposed those of banks?

The loss of talent in all the arts has been immeasurable, but it is my belief that musicians have lost more than anyone else. Their role in society has changed drastically since the arrival of the recording industry and more recently of television and pop music.

Since Suggia had never played background music for a film, she was unable to comment, but was obviously sorry that I had lost my way so early in the jungle that is supposed to be paradise.

'The desire to be of service is not necessarily vanity,' she said. 'Helping others—the young, colleagues who have stumbled, the community in which you live and work—it all enables you to escape from self-doubt and from most of the negative forces in life.'

I looked at Suggia—a frail, elderly and diminutive lady—but in my mind's eye I saw again, as in the painting, that glorious splash of colour and the dominating presence of a woman and her cello. Augustus John had touched upon the very limits of awareness. The cello bow was at the tip, the head at an extreme angle, the spike stretched out and exaggerated. The cello was presented in such a way that it would initially capture the eye, which would then travel on into new and deeper mysteries.

There was nothing more to say. We parted, having met only twice, but I have never forgotten this vital personality. I learnt, many years later, that at the time of our meeting, she was nursing a dying husband, while herself coming to terms with the first stages of what she knew was a terminal illness.

I caught my brother's eye. I had broken my promise and had again become involved in a serious discussion at a social function. But I *liked* serious discussions, especially at social functions! For me they were, and still are, the elixir of a life that demands fusion of the various duties, joys, and sorrows that mark the time between birth and death, not isolation into little compartments.

Our last day before returning to England was to be devoted to visiting the famous firm of Blackburn & Cockburn. We were to be initiated into some of those mysteries by which the art and craft of the sherry producer can tickle even the most jaded appetites. Felix was in his element, but for me the occasion was completely alien. Alcohol is an acquired taste and, as Mother never tired of reminding us, a habit not to be encouraged.

Boyd had arranged a farewell party at the hotel that evening to which we were all invited. Blackburn & Cockburn had presented each member of the orchestra with two bottles of sherry, and these had to be consumed before we could face HM Customs the next morning. To my surprise, I found that the gathering was to take place in the room Felix and I were sharing.

The evening started well enough. Boyd made a short speech and Maurice Clare made a long one. For reasons of orchestral diplomacy the tour manager made the shortest speech possible. Toasts were drunk, and counter-toasts proposed. As the evening progressed people gradually either collapsed or disappeared with the most unlikely companions. Those who remained became increasingly boisterous. Peter Mountain obliged with a song and others were encouraged to follow suit.

By this time the room was getting hot and stuffy and, by general consent, it was decided that somebody needed a cold bath. While it was filling up we looked around for a likely candidate and it was Neville Marriner who was eventually selected. Before he could escape, he was dragged to the bath and, after a brief scuffle, pushed into the cold water in full, if by now disordered, evening dress.

Eventually, with forty bottles of sherry disposed of, there was nothing for the rest of the party to do but leave. Felix, oblivious to the world, had collapsed into an armchair, so I asked Boyd and Peter to help heave him on to his bed. It was only after they had left that a question suddenly struck me. I had been the only sober person there, was that conscience—or cowardice?

I stood at the foot of the bed looking at Felix, lying still and at peace with the world. He was, as always, composed and secure in all his dark elegance. He had been drinking wine and I had been drinking grape-juice. He was somewhere far away, but I was definitely in the here-and-now, stone cold sober. I envied him his poise and self-control and longed to achieve the balance he always seemed to achieve between hope and aspiration.

CHAPTER SIXTEEN

Two Lagondas and a Bluebird

During a recording session at Abbey Road, very early in my relationship with Walter Legge, he caught me reading from a book I was trying to hide on the music stand. I realised that I had transgressed but the book was so funny and so apposite I couldn't put it down. Written by Wechsberg, a theatre-player-cum-ship's-musician, the book was called '*Looking for a Bluebird*'. It consists of a series of short stories of a New Yorker about the funnier aspects of an otherwise drab existence in New York. It had come my way the day before and I was instantly hooked.

Leaning over the music stand, Walter Legge picked it up and pointed to a particular page.

'Isn't that marvellous? I've read this book many times, but that section never fails to amuse me.' From then on it became a book we both constantly re-read, each time sharing another of its insights into the fallibility of the human experience.

In my quest for wider learning I never had any interest in Great Ideological Clashes and always tried to avoid being drawn into political discussions. I was therefore most intrigued to learn from Clifford Bax that he and his brother Arnold, the composer, had both taken politics very seriously in their youth. We had met one evening at a party where he made the startling statement that the war had achieved nothing.

'When I was your age,' he said, 'I believed that Lenin had the right answers. Many others of my generation believed it. The politicians believed it too and went to war to prove that their belief was justified. Then, just when the last shot had been fired in 1945 our Prime Minister announced that we had fought the wrong enemy. Today politicians already seem to have forgotten about World War Two and keep talking about World War Three. Frankly,' he said, taking another sip from his glass, 'it's just a bloody mess. Out of the frying pan into the fire, so to speak.'

I never talked politics with Walter Legge as politics simply did not interest him. In his world the search for perfection in the art of music and its performance was much more important, so important that it took on an almost metaphysical dimension.

On that occasion when I heard Schnabel play the Beethoven Fourth Piano Concerto, I was still in a state of shock at the wonderful way in which he had performed when I met him afterwards at the Mayers', I asked him to explain whether one first had to *experience* a deeper awareness before being able to share it with others. I was thinking of the bridge-passage in the slow movement, after the angry orchestral statement. He tried to make me understand that, particularly in Beethoven's music, it was possible to think of the sound as if it were a language. What was important was that sometimes, as in speech, there had to be silence. This was the moment when the intangible becomes a living experience.

Lady Mayer suggested that perhaps we should leave these 'grey areas' to the metaphysical poets. My enthusiasm for the 'language of music' was obviously something she considered to be merely an abstraction. Our disagreement soon degenerated into an argument about opinion and, as Voltaire has so aptly commented, 'In matters of opinion there is no argument.' Nevertheless, I should still like to know why people who were prepared to attend a series of serious celebrity concerts given by Schnabel at the Albert Hall seemed little embarrassed by the vulgarity of the triple 'change-of-dress' show (a different dress for every concerto), given by Eileen Joyce the following Sunday at the same venue. Was it that Schnabel's abstract overview of art might kindle a spark in some young mind that could in time challenge entrenched concepts of an egalitarian society? Was this why it was necessary to discourage talk of higher values?

During the tea-break at the recording with Schnabel a few days later he mentioned our recent discussion with Lady Mayer to Walter Legge who was sitting with us. Walter Legge was obviously not keen to get too involved.

'I agree with you both, but we don't have the time to talk about it now. One thing is certain however. Nothing will ever be the same as it was in 1939.'

I found it difficult to accept that mass-production was the only criterion for a better life, that a factory worker should *not* receive a reward other than money, or that a politician should *only* be concerned with the re-distribution of wealth and not be required to consider how that wealth had first to be created. In any case what was the ultimate purpose of wealth? Since 1945 Europe's wealth has certainly been re-distributed but, as might be expected, not the wealth of the two or three hundred owners of wealth on a global scale. What have been the benefits? 'You've never had it so good' is one oft quoted statement but how do they explain the fact that a large section of the population seems to be so utterly disaffected?

In today's world any aspiring young classical musician has to ignore the image of 'youth' created by the mass-media. Some do succumb to the temptation of drug-taking, but most do not.

Listening to Radio 4 constantly as I do, I seldom hear discussions about a search for beauty. Occasionally critics of local housing departments comment about 'units of accommodation' offered to the disadvantaged and a 'denial of human dignity' to the underprivileged. Form and beauty are seldom referred to. I wonder about our preoccupation with democracy. With its reliance on an arid materialistic basis for existence, can it lead to any degree of higher awareness? It is sad to reflect that the twentieth century appears to have produced so little in terms of beauty and grace that can parallel the eternal elegance of the Spitfire and Concorde—and of course Alvis motor cars.

Since joining the Philharmonia my life-style changed radically from having to share a pair of 'best trousers' with Felix to earning good recording fees at Denham, Abbey Road and the Kingsway Hall. I was touring Europe, going to and playing at Covent Garden with Schwarzkopf and attending cocktail parties in Mayfair given by the musical élite of London. All this was balanced, as I saw it, by abstinence and contemplation in Paris. Earning a living was delayed by the need to learn.

During the summer of 1948 three things happened: I bought my first car, South Africa voted Jan Smuts out of power and I had been noticed by the Inland Revenue.

Suddenly I wanted to know who I was, who my ancestors were and where they had come from. If it had not been for the talent Felix had shown, that had brought the whole family except for Father to England, where would I have grown up? I knew that as a South African I was a citizen of the British Empire, but I knew nothing of the curses spawned by the growth of that Empire. I began to realise that I was using certain terms of common reference every day without properly understanding what they meant.

With cars I was on safer ground. Carrying the cello from studio to studio and from concert hall to concert hall was very tiring. I discussed the problem with Dennis Brain on several occasions. My budget could only stretch to the deposit on a new Ford Popular, with a waiting list of at least two years. That would have been the sensible thing to do, but my ambitions soared much higher.

Quite by chance I discovered a little 1939 Lagonda Rapier, a two-door saloon fitted with a 10hp engine. It had an elegance the Ford did not aspire to but in size it could not measure up to the Lagonda V12 Rapide Saloon which Dennis had been hypnotised into buying. This Lagonda was one of those beautifully exotic motor cars of the late 1930s that defy all logic and fascinate beyond belief. It could pass anything on the roads in its day, except a petrol station. Consequently the greater comfort it provided was cancelled out by time spent in filling and re-filling the tank.

In 1948 the poor design of the suspension on most cars was a matter for serious concern but at least the Rapier had a little bit of glamour to offer. When our respective cars were being discussed our colleagues pointed out, with some amusement, that whereas I was large, but thinking of buying the *smallest* Lagonda ever made, Dennis was on the small side but had bought the *largest* Lagonda ever made. It added a touch of Laurel and Hardy humour to while away the boredom.

I was even able to convince Mother that to buy a Lagonda Rapier for £150 instead of a Ford for £400 was the right path to follow and coaxed her into accompanying me to the garage. I went straight to the bonnet and began to enthuse about engineering and design perfection. Mother went straight to the boot and asked me where I intended to put the cello. I went round to the boot and turned the handle. It came off in my hand and the lid fell to the floor. The salesman hurriedly explained that, in the event of a sale, all these little problems would be put in order. Mother said nothing but began to walk towards the door of the garage. Before leaving she turned and reminded me that I had a concert at 7.30 and that it was already after 6pm. The Lagonda Rapier was never mentioned again, and since that day I have seen very few examples of the model.

My next choice was a Standard Swallow 10hp four-seater tourer. It was light green and had a beautiful air of the countryside in spring about it. With its wire wheels and chrome knock-on hubs it was a delight to behold. In addition, it came from the same stable as the unique pre-war SS Jaguar. This particular car had always held a fascination for me. Like Georgian architecture, it was just right. Everything was in proportion and for what it was intended to achieve, it could not be improved on.

As I had never driven a car before, I persuaded Felix to take it from the garage near Lancaster Gate Station to our home at 22 Dawson Place. Mother, who had agreed to come with us, suggested that a test drive would be advisable.

'Don't you agree?' she asked the salesman. I am sure he didn't, but he lacked the firepower to disagree. The four of us somehow climbed in and managed to negotiate the narrow mews behind Lancaster Gate without mishap. No sooner had Felix turned into the Bayswater Road than a car in front of us stopped without warning. We couldn't. The driver of the vehicle we hit blamed Felix. Felix blamed the brakes. Mother blamed me. I decided that Mr Armstrong Siddeley had been right: if you needed bumpers you shouldn't be driving. Fortunately no serious damage was done but Fate, in the person of Mother, had intervened and a second car salesman bit the dust.

Being noticed by the Inland Revenue re-directed my energies back into the philosophy of study, and I decided that as I was still a part-time student, why not earn as little as possible so as to avoid further investigation. I had been earning since about 1943 and apart from a little pocket money plus travelling expenses, the rest of the money had gone towards the cost of running the family home. All this now had to change. A letter arrived from HM Inspector of Taxes stating that a large sum of money was owed. It was no laughing matter but I was slightly cheered when my brother showed me a report in a daily paper about a Northern Rhodesian first-time taxpayer. He had apparently expressed his concern to the Tax Man as follows:

> 'Sir, I have to reply to the attached form. I regret I am not interested in the Income Service. Could you please cancel my name in your books, as this system has upset my mind and I do not know who registered me as one of your customers.'

Dennis Brain kindly introduced me to Howell Wade & Co, a reputable firm of accountants and the matter was soon settled.

Things did not end quite so happily with Mother. A condition of my new status as a customer of the Tax Man was that I should have my own bank account. Mother refused to accept that this was a legitimate condition, and insisted that it was only a ruse on my part to enable me to buy a motorcar. Since all the money I had earned since 1943 had gone into Mother's account, I would have been able to claim a considerable amount of it back because I had been the principal wage earner. It was simply a question of semantics, but Mother was adamant. The whole thing was a ruse and remained so until her dying day.

To equate money with the rewards that music offered seemed to be an insoluble problem. A great sadness for me now is that, when I decided in 1953 to leave the mantle of artistic security so freely offered by Walter Legge, I betrayed a trust. He had been happy to allow me the opportunity to seek wider horizons since I had first asked him in 1947 if I could study with Pierre. At the time I had no idea just how heavy the financial burden of the orchestra would become, and just how little support he would receive from English patrons. When I resigned from my position as a full-time player in the orchestra (largely as a consequence of my continuing personal quarrel with the poor acoustic of the Festival Hall) it had been an emotional decision. With hindsight I realised that it was the wrong decision—wrong precisely because it had been emotional.

It must have amused Walter Legge to hear me recounting my experiences every time I returned from a self-financed sabbatical in Paris, but friends soon lost patience with my quest for 'deeper understanding'. I had one of the best orchestral jobs in the world and yet I wasn't satisfied. I was also always short of money, but this was because my earnings went into the family purse and into further self-education, although they may not have realised this. I began to understand the real significance of a joke a Jewish friend once told me: 'I haven't got any money because I am too busy earning a living'.

CHAPTER SEVENTEEN

Edinburgh and the Firefly

Finding financial support and creating work for the Philharmonia was a continuing headache for Walter Legge and Joan Ingpen, the orchestral manager. New talent needed to be contracted to boost record sales. A concert platform had to be provided for the orchestra's soloists and above all for Karajan. Legge was forever looking for ways to raise the level of musical awareness in members of his orchestra and, at the same time, determined to reach a wider and more discriminating audience.

Meanwhile, the relevance of 'expressive' intonation, bow speeds and *rubato*, was becoming an increasingly important part of my daily practice routine. Practising scales and exercises was equally important, but this was something I had known nothing about prior to my lessons with Casals. Having become aware of these disciplines had not made playing with the Boyd Neel Orchestra any more enjoyable, while on the tour of Portugal, or in my work with the Philharmonia after my return.

On May 22nd 1950 Kirsten Flagstad gave the first performance of the *Four Last Songs* by Strauss at the Albert Hall. Because of the acoustic Walter Legge was anxious about the orchestral texture. Both the singer and the orchestra would be on the platform, rather than the orchestra being in the pit as in an opera house. He was also worried that, with only one three-hour rehearsal for the Strauss songs and all the other works in the concert, Furtwängler might not be able to achieve his demanding standards. Furtwängler devoted most of the rehearsal to Strauss so there was little time left to rehearse the other pieces. Would the orchestra rise to the occasion?

Lighting in the mornings used to be supplied by the Albert Hall's own generators. Consequently the platform was not so well lit for rehearsals as it was in the evening, which made it difficult for the orchestra to read the notes. One of the songs required Flagstad to sing outside her normal range. Would she be heard? In spite of his anxiety that the *tessitura of Frühling* might prove to be a challenge, it was mastered by Flagstad at both rehearsal and concert.

As if this wasn't enough, the Maharajah of Mysore, the sponsor of the concert, considered that he was entitled to an acetate disc of the songs. The Musicians' Union steward was advised by the Union that a recording fee would have to be paid. Time spent debating the pros and cons of additional financial reward for the orchestra meant that valuable rehearsal time was wasted.

Musicians living and working in Europe were paid royalties at that time; those in England were not. Although the orchestra was paid one extra recording fee, it was only in 1988 that the Musicians' Union would eventually be compelled by the Monopolies and Mergers Commission to inform its members that, since 1946, it had been receiving royalties from broadcasts of recordings, many of which were the consequence of Walter Legge's endeavours, not the Union's. There is still no acceptable explanation as to what has happened to these monies. Between 1946 and 1988 12.5% of the net worldwide annual royalties attached to broadcasts of recordings made in the UK had been paid into the account of the Musicians' Union amounting to many millions of pounds. It would be interesting to know what sums were donated by the Musicians' Union to the Philharmonia prior to the Rome Convention of 1961.

To run an orchestra obviously costs money. When you have a man with a cultural conscience like Walter Legge, it is not surprising that his artistic standards were viewed without interest, with disbelief, or even disapproval by successive governments, and especially by banks. He had obtained promises of financial assistance from such disparate sources as the Maharajah of Mysore, the Philharmonia Concert Society, the Gesellschaft der Musikfreunde of Vienna, and Ibbs & Tillett. The interaction of these and other non-state funding sources had helped to provide London and the record industry with some of the most memorable musical events in the first few years of the orchestra's existence.

In the early 1950s the Maharajah's property was absorbed by Mr Nehru's 'New India' regime, for the greater good of its peoples, or so members of the orchestra were told. For Legge the consequence was an initial reduction of the Maharajah's annual recording subsidy, followed by a total withdrawal of funds within the next three years. Recordings were already planned with Karajan, Galliera, Furtwängler, Paul Kletzki, Albert Schweitzer, Lipatti and others but where was the money to be be found? Today, fifty years later, outrageous amounts are paid to favoured performers, but in 1950 Legge had a struggle to pay even the very modest fees current at the time. Nevertheless, such funding as was still available from the Maharajah made it possible to underpin at least another three years' work for the orchestra. Why did the financiers in London's square mile not step in?

After the Schumann-Karajan recording of April 1948 Lipatti had been too ill to record with the orchestra again. Instead of recording the Chopin Concerto in F minor, Galliera replaced this with Respighi's *Brazilian Impressions*. I had seen the recording-van used to record the Festival Concerts in Prades, and read in Walter Legge's tribute that the same van had travelled to Geneva to capture whatever benevolence cortisone might extend to Lipatti's life expectancy, but my eldest brother had warned me not to expect a miracle. The high hopes that attended his last summer of music-making which began in July 1950 with recordings of Chopin, Bach and Mozart in a house near Geneva, were cut short. Within five months, his treatment having failed, he was dead.

Fate can be so cruel. Ginette Neveu had been killed in 1949 and other deaths in this period included those of Furtwängler, Cantelli and Kathleen Ferrier. All of them were a shattering loss for Walter Legge, the Philharmonia and for music lovers, but for Legge the loss must have been particularly acute, as his tributes to the artists he loved makes abundantly clear.

In 1949 the orchestra had played in Liverpool, and I took the opportunity of paying my respects to the new Cathedral. Every day the press was reporting the despair of dockers forced to witness the destruction of their city and their way of life as a consequence of changing 'market forces'. For the previous two hundred years their labour had played a crucial part in the creation of the greatest empire that had been assembled on this planet. An empire whose slave-cotton-opium trade with India and China had made untold millions for international banks like Rothschild, Baring, Jardine Matheson, Swire, Morgan, Sutherland. Now suddenly there was nothing. Could the moneymen not have given something back to Liverpool? More than thirty years later print workers in London were to experience the same despair in their battle to cling to old traditions and privileges.

Walking up the untidy street that led to the new building I looked with disbelief at the enormity of Scott's masterpiece framed against a background of empty, half-derelict houses. The building is probably a masterpiece but when the business of the Church no longer concerns itself with the day-to-day interaction of the people, was this really the time to be building such a vast meeting place? Was there really any intention to provide a meeting place for the people's spiritual and secular needs? If so, what were these needs thought to be? Chartres was built in one generation, the unskilled labour being contributed by the inhabitants of the town itself. The building was large because it was believed that the business of each day's liturgical and secular activity required magnificent and beautiful precincts. They were beautiful because they had to give substance to the belief that 'man shall not live by bread alone'. In 1949 the City of Liverpool looked to me as if it was dying, spiritually and materially. The huge Cathedral was no more than a mausoleum in a graveyard.

Back in London, during the silent moments of recording and rehearsals, I would often remember those beautiful days in Prades. I was disenchanted with my home life, my work in the orchestra, having to live in London. I was continually reminded that the hatreds generated by class animosities were destroying the last remaining symbols of inherited wealth and social privilege.

At the opening concert of the Royal Festival Hall in 1951, the cello section consisted of the first-desk players of the five permanent London orchestras. Seating positions for leaders of each section were allocated in alphabetical order. Raymond Clark was principal cellist and I, as sub-principal, sat next to him. His right to lead the cello section was undisputed but I became conscious that some of my colleagues resented the fact that a twenty-four-year-old should be allowed to occupy such a privileged position on such an important occasion.

That had been the first shock. The second, which was much more significant, was the sound of my cello in this new hall. It was harsh, remote, and forbidding and flattened out in a most unpleasant way. Having by 1951 performed with the Philharmonia in many European halls with their beautiful acoustic, I was not prepared for the dry, matter-of-fact tone produced in what had been advertised as London's exciting new contribution to the orchestral concert scene.

I was not alone in my disappointment as there was much criticism from other musicians and music critics. All sorts of reasons were given to explain the hall's acoustic by so-called experts who were loud in their own defence. The consultants, in particular, advised at length on materials, design and texture—all hot air as far as the players were concerned. As Raymond said later when we were discussing the problem, they must all have had 'cloth ears'. It is no wonder that the photograph of the orchestra, taken at the opening ceremony and which used to hang in the artists' bar, shows an assembly of such glum faces.

One evening I was in the main foyer bar of the Festival Hall, belatedly enjoying a remedy for the Performance Blues—the one I should perhaps have enjoyed with Felix en route to Portugal in 1949. I was just about to drink my artificial stimulant when a tall bearded man, an English look-alike of Fidel Castro, asked me what I thought of the hall. I told him. For several moments his face registered total disbelief. He was speechless. In fact the poor man looked so dumbfounded that I bought him a drink. In due course we bought each other several drinks, agreed to meet again after the concert, and perhaps have a meal. In the end we spent the entire night arguing about architecture, music, and politics. We were both large men and neither would yield nor be easily intimidated.

The next day we met again at his suggestion but this time in the company of a friend of his called Leo Goldstone. They were both architects and both worked at County Hall planning London's future skyline. Although they claimed to be socialists, they nevertheless managed to give me the feeling that they were, in reality, intelligent and dedicated anarchists. Both had real and special gifts in various fields, but the bearded Castro, whose name was Charles Chase, had one quality that set him apart. He owned, as did his father before him, an Alvis motorcar.

How anyone could have held such views about architecture and yet revere values built into the design, performance and aesthetic of the Alvis motor car, I shall never be able to understand. His love of cars and music was genuine but the very things he loved were the product of a system that depended on loyalty and a sense of service. This the unions, to whom very little appeared to be sacred, were doing their best to disrupt. How, I asked him, could he compare the Alvis TA14, the least expensive post-war Alvis, with a Ford hybrid, bumping along on what usually felt like square wheels?

Since our arguments continued unabated in the context of the tower blocks my two new friends were helping to design for Central London and for urban redevelopment in general, we eventually had to accept that the differences between us were impossible to bridge. For Charles and Leo all architecture had to be of today's world, whereas I wanted to repair and preserve as much as possible of London's beautiful past.

By great good fortune, I had recently discovered the chassis, engine and gearbox of an Alvis Firefly 11.9hp.

Even without its ash-framed Cross & Ellis bodywork, the vehicle fired my imagination. I rented a garage and for over a year applied myself to learning the details of car repair and maintenance. I also found a Sunbeam Speed Twenty Weymouth Saloon body that more or less fitted the Alvis chassis. All that was missing were some front wings. With a little coercion some Citroën Light Fifteen wings were made to fit and the entire front assembly was protected by Standard Swallow bumpers, with two Armstrong Siddeley quarter bumpers guarding the rear.

The car was undoubtedly a hideous hybrid but just as the faces on the north side of Beverley Minster emphasise reality by distortion, so did this little Alvis of my own creation. The tricks that had to be learnt in order to assemble my home-made vehicle were legion and taught me many things I would never have known had I simply purchased a Ford Popular.

Early in the 1950s the orchestra had to give some concerts in Edinburgh. Despite my limited talents as a car mechanic, its stalwart qualities enabled me to make the return journey in my DIY car without mishap. With its crash gearbox and heavy chassis, its acceleration and road-holding were solid rather than sporty. It was delightfully safe to drive and, because of its inherently strong

Top *Alvis Firefly SB 11.9 Cross & Ellis Tourer*
Bottom *Alvis Speed 20 SB Vanden Plas Tourer*

design, could sustain severe damage without exposing its
occupants to the horrors of twisted metal that characterise many
of today's accidents. Later I acquired a Cross & Ellis saloon body
for my Firefly, removed the existing abortion and bolted the new
body-shell to the chassis. After this I had to install an electrical
wiring circuit, correct the front axle tramp, adjust the carburettor,
repair and re-wire the magneto and then repaint the car.

Dominated by accountancy law, superior end-products have
undoubtedly been produced by today's design, manufacture,
marketing and distribution techniques. Nevertheless the thrill of
seeing the twin P1OO head lamps of an Alvis Speed Twenty

reflected in the rear mirrors, followed by that long, beautifully proportioned body, disappearing ahead on the relatively uncluttered roads of the early 1950s takes a lot of beating.

Alvis restoration, especially when carried to extremes, is very time-consuming and left me with little opportunity for much else. Mother became so tired of having oily clothes fouling up her well-ordered home that I decided to move out for the second time and was fortunate enough to find a little house in Knightsbridge where, if I had been blessed with a grain of sense, I should have remained.

The Alvis Owner Club was growing in numbers. Neill Sanders had bought an Alvis Silver Eagle and Dennis Brain was thinking of buying a 4.3 Charlesworth Saloon. One afternoon, taking a short cut to Hyde Park through a mews near my house in Knightsbridge, I found a beautiful 1934 Speed Twenty Vanden Plas Tourer in very good condition. What was better still, the price was only £100.

It took more than a year to complete the work on the Firefly and as the orchestra was again booked to play at the 1952 Edinburgh Festival, I decided to drive up in it. Unknown to me, members of the orchestra had laid odds that I would never reach my destination. Manoug Parikian told me later that apparently Markevitch and Karajan both knew about the flutter and that it is even possible that they themselves may have been invited to paricipate.

Since I had to travel up to Edinburgh on my own, because nobody would trust me or my car, I decided to leave London a day early and was the first to arrive at the hostel where the orchestra was to be housed. As there was nobody about I decided to use the internal roads as a race circuit and fit in a little practice. I soon found that by slipping the clutch in second gear and staying in second and third gear at peak revs, I achieved a fairly rapid lap circuit-time.

A little later Manoug arrived in his new 1.5 Riley Saloon and joined in the fun. We decided to see who could complete three laps in the fastest time. By the next afternoon most of the other car-owners in the orchestra had also become involved, and they gathered at the more interesting corners of the circuit to act as unofficial marshals. The rules were spelt out and there were to be two trials. Each competitor would be allowed to choose either a standing or a flying start and the one with the best time would be the winner.

In the past week the orchestra had been adding to its already considerable prestige on the concert platform but now, whenever time permitted, several key players were devoting every spare moment to racing round this newly established Edinburgh motor circuit. As the number of competitors increased, so did the noise and inevitably our little initiative was cut short. As my 11.9 Cross & Ellis Saloon had clocked up the best time, by the time the dead hand of the law arrived, it was adjudged the winner.

At one time or another I have owned every Alvis model excepting the 1927 forward wheel drive and the 4.3 dry sump model. I was captivated by the sheer elegance of the Charlesworth Speed Twenty Five and also the TC2100 drop head but when I dwell on things past I inevitably return to the Speed Twenty Vanden Plas Tourer. It had elegance, power, good road-holding, extraordinary body comfort and, considering that it was an open car, an amazing silence that made it a pleasure to drive. Charles Chase and I felt that the Club's purpose should be to provide Alvis with a reasonably consistent order-book so that much needed replacements could be readily available. It was evident however that there was another point of view, namely that an alternative manufacturing and marketing facility should be provided. We considered this to be counter-productive and strongly disapproved. Our aim was to encourage the company to produce specialist cars in spite of the hostile climate of post-war Britain's preoccupation with egalitarianism. Just after that first Alvis-hybrid trip to Edinburgh in 1950 matters came to a head in the Alvis Club. Fretwell stepped down and Ken Day accepted the position of Club Secretary, a position he was to hold for many years with great distinction.

Adjustments and maintenance were laborious and time-consuming, but after all the effort there was always the reward—the sheer delight of hearing a well-tuned engine—a sound you could recognise with your eyes closed. I had a variation of Karajan's eyes-shut rule. You heard a car coming, closed your eyes and made your guess. Only when the car had passed were you allowed to open them again. If you cheated you demeaned yourself.

After the final concert at Edinburgh that year there was to be a reception at the Town Hall to which members of the orchestra had been invited. The period of work with Karajan had been exacting and rewarding but there was however still a measure of resentment about his having been a Nazi protégé. Added to this certain players liked to dwell on the fact that Britain and the *Reich* had been at war only seven years before. On the whole the atmosphere was one of goodwill but one member of the orchestra was not prepared to let bygones be bygones and this was Gerry Brooks. Gerry's view of life was in general rather jaundiced, and I don't think I was ever able to establish what he really thought of music or the profession. One thing was certain however: he didn't like the bass and hated having to play it for a living.

Official receptions tend to be tedious affairs made worse by the endless speeches that always accompany such occasions.

'I'm not wasting my time going to the reception,' said Gerry as we were leaving the Usher Hall after the concert. 'Ernie Rutledge and I are going to that fish restaurant near the railway station.'

Towards the end of the evening I was talking about Gerry to Jim Merritt, the principal bass, when Jim said 'Talk of the devil!' I turned round and, to my astonishment saw a rather perplexed Gerry entering the lobby, not at all his usual self.

'Nice of you to show up,' said Jim chattily. 'Did you have a good meal? I hope it didn't cost too much. You've missed some wonderful food here. It really was bloody marvellous.'

It had indeed been 'bloody marvellous'. Post-war austerity restrictions still held the country in thrall but on this occasion nothing had been spared. Jim and I had never before seen such a spread. There were delicacies such as succulent chilled asparagus, salads, meats, pâtés, fruit, cheese and sweets for all tastes. Edinburgh had been more than generous.

Gerry stood stock still looking completely flabbergasted. In stark contrast to his ready wit and free-flowing capacity for comment, he suffered from what the late W C Fields used to call 'an impediment in his reach'. In other words, he was careful with his money to the point of avarice. He and Ernie had decided that they would treat themselves to a really expensive meal, possibly to celebrate having survived a hazardous few weeks. The agony on his face betrayed his realisation that it had been an expensive mistake.

Just at that moment, a lady came towards us offering cigarettes and cigars neatly laid out on a tray. Gerry's eyes suddenly came to life. Not all was lost. He could at least help himself to four large Havanas. Two for Ernie (who was a non-smoker) and two for himself.

'That will be four pounds please,' said the lady. Cigarettes and cigars were the only items the City elders had not felt obliged to provide free of charge.

By the time we had to leave I was in no fit state to drive, so I shared a taxi back to the hostel and relaxed into a deep sleep. The next two days were free and I had planned on making a leisurely trip back to London via Cambridge in order to show the Firefly to my eldest brother. Next morning after breakfast I went to collect the Alvis but couldn't be sure where I had left it. After several hours of fruitless search up and down the streets near the Usher Hall, the inevitable truth began to dawn on me. Having had no key with which to lock the car, I had the previous evening been obliged to risk leaving it open. Normally I would have removed the contact-breaker but on this occasion I had decided not to. I never saw the Firefly again.

Karajan was definitely becoming more friendly. Even the episode of the damp day at the Kingsway Hall appeared to have

PHILHARMONIA ORCHESTRA

1951

FIRST VIOLINS
Manoug Parikian
Max Salpeter
Jack Kessler
Jessie Hinchliffe
William Monro
Marie Wilson
Nathaniel Conras
Hans Geiger
Granville Jones
Peter Mountain
George Laulund
Arthur Davison
Kenneth Moore
Derek Collier
Alfred Davis
Michael Jones

SECOND VIOLINS
Gerald Emms
Ronald Sirrell
James Buyers
Frank Bilbe
Jean Lefevre
Kathleen Sturdy
Stephen Evans
Charles Verney
Ernest Rutledge
Dennis Brown
Pierette Galeone
Michael Freedman
Roland Stanbridge

VIOLAS
Herbert Downes
Maurice Loban
Bernard Davis
Anne Wolfe
Leo Birnbaum
Roy Patten
Muriel Tookey
Sam Rosenheim
Ken Essex
Lance Lange
Michael Mitchell
Andrew Appleton

CELLOS
Raymond Clark
Alexander Kok
David Thomas
John Holmes
Tom Hill
Peter Beavan
Noria Semino
Nelson Cooke
Jack Long
James Marchant

BASSES
J. Edward Merrett
Adrian Beers
Gerald Brooks
Ronald Peters
Desmond Wrench
Sam Stirling
Geoffrey Clarke
John Honeyman

PICCOLO
Arthur Ackroyd

FLUTES
Gareth Morris
Ronald Gillham

OBOES
Sidney Sutcliffe
Stanley Smith

COR ANGLAIS
Peter Newbury

CLARINETS
Frederick Thurston
Archibald Jacobs

BASS CLARINETS
Wilfred Hambleton

BASSOONS
Cecil James
Peter Parry

HORNS
Edmund Chapman
Neil Saunders
Aubrey Thonger
Alfred Cursue

TRUMPETS
Harold Jackson
Dennis Clift
Jack Mackintosh

TROMBONES
Stanley Brown
Arthur Wilson
S. Trottman

TUBA
Arthur Doyle

TIMPANI
James Bradshaw

PERCUSSION
L. Pocock
Harry Eastwood
F. Kennings
Fredrick Bradshaw

HARPS
John Cockerill
Marie Goosens

CELESTE
Richard Johnson

been forgotten. He had recently been appointed musical director at La Scala, Milan, and it was being whispered that he was now planning the assault on Vienna, Salzburg, and Berlin. There were problems in that Böhm, Krips and Krauss would need to be out of the way but Karajan was a patient man. If and when all three prizes were his he would then be in a position to combine them with his work at La Scala.

The Philharmonia's European tour of 1952 was intended to demonstrate not only the general excellence of the orchestra but the virtuoso quality of its key players. That it also provided Karajan with an instrument that would establish beyond doubt his claim to be the only logical contender for the Berlin Philharmonic Orchestra may have been fortuitous, but it certainly helped him to further his plans. The riches of Berlin would have to wait until Furtwängler vacated that particular podium but that was not a problem for Karajan. He was content to wait as he had already, before 1939, clearly recognised the financial advantages in planning well ahead for the interchange of productions and casts between the great opera houses of Europe.

With Schwarzkopf's help he was to put La Scala firmly back on the map as one of the two leading opera houses in Europe. Both had relied on Walter Legge, and without his support I doubt whether either would have succeeded quite so dramatically.

CHAPTER EIGHTEEN

Otto Klemperer

'Vy do you laugh?'

Klemperer had already asked for an explanation in a voice that was not entirely without menace. Speechless with embarrassment I remained rooted to my chair unable to move, or even to think of moving out of harm's way. I looked up as he loomed over me, his gaunt tortured face silhouetted against the dark arena of the Royal Albert Hall, his eyes full of anger and suspicion.

He remained standing in front of me, waiting for an answer. I continued sitting and waited for the next tirade. His speaking voice, never very pleasant at the best of times, sounded even more harsh than before.

'Tell me. Vy do you laugh?'

I now felt completely paralysed, unable to comprehend how, without any warning, my cosy little world had collapsed around me. Why it was that I alone was being questioned in front of the whole orchestra.

This was the first occasion that the renowned Dr Otto Klemperer had conducted the Philharmonia Orchestra and there was no doubt, that afternoon in March 1948, that the orchestra was on its mettle. Klemperer's exploits, especially with the opposite sex, had attracted considerable attention over the years. Although some of the more bizarre elements of his private and public life might have suggested that he was accident prone, there was always the possibility that others were deliberately calculated to stimulate interest.

He suffered a partial paralysis as a result of an operation in 1939 to remove a brain tumour, but in spite of this he managed to achieve considerable international status. His reputation as a conductor of uncertain temperament had preceded him in both the press and on the orchestral grapevine. None of us were sure what to expect, but some of us were more than just a little apprehensive.

At that time Klemperer was over 60 and he continued working with the Philharmonia until he was well into his eighties. He had been well groomed in the traditional German manner, beginning with the piano, followed by training as a chorus master, and then as *Kapellmeister* in smaller opera houses until he was finally appointed as the First Conductor at Cologne. With over half a century's experience in concert and opera performance, and with a special affinity for Beethoven, Bruckner and Mahler, he was a worthy successor to Bruno Walter.

I had arrived early that afternoon to have a look at *Symphony in Three Movements* by Stravinsky, which most of us had not seen before. To sight-read a major symphonic work with such an unpredictable character was definitely going to be a nervy occasion. Many of us, especially those occupying what is known in the profession as the 'hot seat', were very much on edge that afternoon.

Arriving early proved not to be such a good idea. Until I heard the jumbled sounds of what already seemed discordant music, exacerbated by the nervous attempts of a few string players to play unfamiliar notes far too quickly, I hadn't felt any qualms. Nervous anticipation is infectious and soon I began to feel the tell-tale signs of incipient stage fright. The chair suddenly seemed too low, the cello spike needed constant adjustment, there was not enough resin on my bow, the bow itself needed re-hairing. Since the time I had put the cello away the night before everything seemed to have gone wrong, in spite of the fact that yesterday I had used the same chair, the same bow, the same length of cello spike, and was playing in exactly the same spot.

Otto Klemperer and Artur Schnabel on board the Isle de France in 1933

I was bending down to adjust my spike for the umpteenth time when I noticed a pair of wellington boots pass in front of me. I looked up and realised that this must be the man himself. Wearing wellingtons in London, particularly on the platform of the Albert Hall, seemed a little odd. Perhaps some well-wisher had warned him about the English weather. From my lowered position I was able to watch him as he surveyed the orchestra and I was not at all sure that I liked what I saw.

It was nearly time to begin the rehearsal but there was still no sign of the principal cellist, Raymond Clark. Raymond had established a reputation as one of those unfortunates who can never be on time. His superb playing obviously balanced any anxiety the management may have felt but his colleagues were less kind and he was frequently referred to as 'the late Mr Clark'.

Someone introduced the conductor. A few players clapped, others tapped their bows and the cynics, as usual, carried on with what they were doing. Just as Klemperer was about to begin Raymond walked on to the platform. The orchestra gave him their customary greeting but on this occasion there was an extra degree of enthusiasm. Dr Klemperer was not prepared for the rowdy foot-shuffle that heralded the late-comer's entrance. He lowered his arm, no doubt meaning to give Raymond a chance to settle down, but unfortunately some of the more nervy players misunderstood the movement and began to play. The strangulated sounds that emerged were not all that funny, but in the context of the occasion it was the safety-valve that broke the tension.

Those who had played sat red-faced in their chairs. Many of us collapsed with laughter at the strange sounds that floated into the Albert Hall. The humourless ones, of whom there were quite a few, were definitely not amused.

Dr Klemperer had not noticeably reacted to the delay and misunderstanding caused by Raymond's late entry. Neither had he seemed irritated by the laughter and banter, but in some strange way he must have misjudged the mood of the orchestra. Even though there was laughter there was also a sense of discipline. We were not inattentive and would not have allowed our humour to detract from our playing.

As the rehearsal progressed we found that Klemperer's conducting was not as helpful as it might have been. A little laughter at his own mistakes would have helped the atmosphere. As we were sight-reading and using virgin copies of the work there were bound to be mistakes: wrong notes, miscounted bars, wrong entries. Some were due to lack of attention but most were the consequence of printing errors. It was becoming obvious that, whatever mood Klemperer had been in when we started, he was now definitely irritated. The more acid his comments became the more the mood of the orchestra changed. Matters came to a head when we reached a point where the harp was featured in a long solo.

The harpist, Maria Korchinska, was a woman of striking appearance. She was a Russian immigrant and although she had become a British National she nevertheless remained true to her land of birth. As Dr Klemperer had yet to learn, she was not a person who could easily be browbeaten. She was fluent in several European languages and did not hesitate to answer him in his own vernacular when a few well-chosen adjectives were needed to win the argument.

She sight-read her solo, apparently without mistakes, and settled back in her chair, assuming that Dr Klemperer would be continuing with the rehearsal. For some unaccountable reason he asked her to play the solo again. The orchestra, sensing that there was an opportunity to score another point, applauded her sight-reading feat with a combination of shuffling feet, tapping of bows and clapping.

His mask-like face surveyed the orchestra with scarcely concealed contempt.

'It does not take much to get applause in this orchestra,' he said.

Of the many quotes there are about this man, this has always remained in my mind as an indication of his abiding anger at the arbitrary accidents of fate.

If Klemperer was becoming unsettled I, on the other hand, was beginning to relish the way the rehearsal was progressing. With the unflappable talent of Raymond Clark beside me I was able to relax into my chair and occasionally look round to see how other people were getting on. This was when I noticed that both players on the first desk of violas were in trouble. Before they were able to send out a distress signal to colleagues sitting near them, Klemperer stopped. The music stopped. They didn't.

Even under the best conditions the sound of a viola in distress is comical. It has a distinctive voice, usually of protest or pain and sometimes both at once. The noises emanating from the two players made it obvious that not only were they both lost but that they were also a few beats out between each other. There was the sound of violas skidding unevenly to a halt followed by a fruity expletive from Moisha Lobin.

All the changes of mood, from tension to animosity, spilled over into laughter. I got the giggles and, even though my sides were aching, I simply couldn't stop. I was desperately embarrassed, knowing what it feels like to be laughed at, but I was helpless. Trying to hide behind the cello, I hoped that the uncontrollable urges would subside, but it was useless. Every few seconds, back would come another spasm and each time more of my colleagues would be ensnared as well. Soon the whole cello section was convulsed—all except Raymond. He had been deaf in his left ear for years, so hadn't heard either the cause of the mirth or its effect on the rest of us. It was while I was looking at the floor, with my head down as far as possible, that I saw the gumboots again.

'Vy do you laugh? Vy?'

The whole afternoon's pantomime flashed through my mind. How could this be happening to me? It seemed as if some outside element had entered into my normally serious approach to orchestral playing and had opened up new vistas of pleasurable participation.

I stood up. Even standing on my toes I was only just able to look Dr Klemperer in the eye.

'I don't know,' I said, red-faced and confused.

Klemperer looked at me balefully, piercing any mask I might have been trying to assume. He must have realised that I was not really responsible for all the chaos. Giving me one more glare of disapproval he turned on his heel and returned to the rostrum.

I sat down amidst total silence. The orchestra was suddenly one unit, a tightly integrated group of people who realised that any one of them could be the next target. All of them no doubt felt, as I had done that afternoon, that there was never any guarantee that laughter and tears would be far apart. But in my case they were near enough to make me feel that my days in the orchestra were numbered.

Stories about Klemperer are now legendary, but when I first met the great man he had still to create part of that legend. What continues to sadden me however, is that on that afternoon I may have given the impression that I was laughing at him, the man behind the tragic mask which illness had bequeathed to him. It is surely inconceivable that anyone as gifted as Klemperer could have thought for a moment that it was he who was being laughed at.

Nearly twelve years later I realised that I needn't have worried. I was then in the BBC Symphony Orchestra and Klemperer had been engaged to conduct a performance of the *Missa Solemnis* by Beethoven. After I left the Philharmonia, Karajan became totally involved with his work on the Continent and Cantelli was killed in an air crash. Walter Legge helped Klemperer as much as it was possible to help a graceless individual. He devised programmes featuring the major works of Bach, Beethoven, Brahms and Mahler. He arranged concerts and recordings with Schwarzkopf and other great artists in England and Europe, achieving a devoted, almost uncritical following.

On the day of the broadcast we played through the *Missa Solemnis* and then began to repeat various sections. Much to Paul Beard's irritation, Klemperer decided to repeat the entire violin solo. Paul was nearing the end of a long and distinguished career as leader of the orchestra. He was suffering from arthritis and from several other impediments of advancing years. For some reason, he found it easier to play with his legs straight out in front, and with his back bent the wrong way. To the onlooker it looked

Otto Klemperer with his daughter Lotte and Clem Relf,
the orchestral librarian.

almost grotesque. Although the sound he produced was a trifle harsh, the main reason for that was the terrible acoustic in Studio One.

We started the movement and as Paul began the slow descent of the opening phrase, I couldn't help noticing that he seemed to be slipping down the chair even more than usual. Was this a sign of nerves? I hoped it wasn't. Paul was too experienced for that. I looked up at Klemperer and could have sworn he was asleep in his chair. (Because of his state of health Klemperer rehearsed seated in a large chair carried from hall to hall.)

Paul played on. Occasionally, and for no apparent reason, Klemperer would wave a lethargic arm in the direction of the choir and then relapse back into a seeming coma. We arrived at the end of Paul's long solo, and suddenly the great man (he was over six-foot four) got up with a surprising burst of energy.

'Misshshtah Beard!' he said. Paul went on playing.

'Misshshtah Beard,' Klemperer repeated. Paul eventually stopped, his feet stretched out even further. He glanced up at Klemperer, who was now facing Paul, leaning heavily on a walking stick for support.

'Misshshtah Beard. The last note.'

'What about it?' asked Paul.

With an unavoidable shower of saliva Klemperer explained.

'The note, that lassht note—it is sssharp.' I cringed in my seat.

'Sharp?' said Paul.

'Yessh, Misshshtah Beard. Sssharp,' said Klemperer. 'It is sssharp.'

Paul looked at him in genuine astonishment.

'Sharp, you say?'

Before Klemperer could launch into another stuttering attempt, Paul continued with calm candour, that brooked no reply.

'Impossible!'

'Imposshible?' Klemperer looked surprised and slightly at a loss.

'Vy imposshible Misshshtah Beard?'

'I have perfect pitch,' said Paul.

There seemed to be no answer to that. Klemperer looked down at Paul, as if he had been presented with some sort of insoluble riddle.

'Ssho, Misshshtah Beard, you have perfect pitch?' The orchestra waited in hushed expectancy and nobody moved. 'HO! HO! HO!' he gasped and the sound chilled me to the marrow.

Unable to support himself any longer, he collapsed into his chair. Laughing must have been as physically exhausting for Klemperer as embarrassingly painful for Paul. It seems that Dr Tovey's definition of perfect pitch as 'knowing the pitch of your grandmother's piano', hadn't prevented Paul from playing that last note a little on the sharp side that day.

I was certain by now that Klemperer hadn't recognised me although I was within his immediate firing line. I wish that I'd had the courage to ask him: 'And why did you laugh?'

CHAPTER NINETEEN

Toscanini and Cantelli

Mother was not keen to move to France but I couldn't forget my recently discovered bit of domestic paradise, that part of France in the vicinity of Canigou near Prades. Although she agreed that I had benefited from my lessons with *Le Maître* she was adamant that it wasn't remotely feasible to migrate to the Pyrénées Orientales merely to be near Casals. My eulogies of Canigou didn't impress either. She found mountains and hills oppressive and considered that travelling to Perpignan, the nearest large town, would be costly and irksome. In any case, as she never failed to remind me, I had to earn a living. It was quite evident that Paradise for her was to be found in London, and preferably in a part that was reasonably flat.

Mother never discussed her house-buying strategy until it was too late to argue and, while I was in Prades in 1949, she had found a large detached house in Holland Villas Road. She had managed to persuade the manager of Barclays Bank that it was a good investment and scraped together enough money to buy it for £8,000. That was where she had decided the family would live and, by April 1950, her objective had been achieved. When I got back I realised that once again she was right and I too fell in love with the house. She had amalgamated the family's joint investment in 22 Dawson Place, and my share had been automatically transferred to the new family home.

Vivien Leigh, Laurence Olivier, Olive Zorian and her husband, John Amis, Lois Arnell, David Carritt and Percy Cudlipp were among our neighbours in this wide avenue lined with chestnut trees. There were parties at the Amis flat where John Kennedy, cellist and father of the future violin prodigy Nigel, entertained us as a raconteur and amateur guitarist. Further down the road were other friends at whose parties Peter Ustinov and Donald Swann would delight us with endless mimicry and humour. Although Ustinov's play *The Love of Four Colonels* had just achieved great success, searching for the ultimate car seemed to be occupying most of his energy at that time. Anything that took his fancy was usually bought on impulse. The most spectacular was an enormous Mercedes Benz open tourer which he said had once belonged to 'ze butcha of Cracow'. At the other end of the scale was a tiny two-seater Jowett Javelin open tourer. His generous proportions and the car's compact dimensions were a sight to remember.

Mother always seemed so certain, and unable or unwilling to capitulate to fear. What she couldn't understand, in the early years of my career as a professional musician, was that the source of my inspiration was external. It had to do with my work in the orchestra and with advice freely given to me by Legge and Fournier, not forgetting the other wonderful talents my association with both had introduced me to.

During my three months in Prades in 1949 Casals would occasionally invite pupils to spend an evening talking about music and listening to records. It was clear to us that the death of many of his friends all over the world had saddened him, and that he was lonely. It is true that only the Pyrenees separated him from the Spain he loved and from the Catalan friends he had not seen for many years. He was nonetheless a stateless exile. The values to which he had responded as a young aspiring artist, and which had been such a major influence throughout his career, had been almost totally destroyed by the contending political dogmas of the twentieth century. I could not rid myself of the impression that he had already begun to tire of playing in public before the end of the previous century, when ideologues were erecting those barriers between him and his audiences that would eventually alienate him from the outside world. All that would remain for him by 1936 was his inner world and the little oasis in Prades.

On leaving the army Darrell, our eldest brother, returned to St Bartholomew's Hospital in London with the intention of becoming a physician and in 1953 he announced his intention to get married. Nobody who knows him could suspect him of the emotional immaturity that Mother considered to have been such an important factor when *I* told her in 1949 that I wanted to marry Margaret Hooson. Nevertheless Mother's reaction was instantaneous and hostile.

It is possible that her self-imposed exile in England may have had something to do with her attitude to other women. She had welcomed the opportunity to move to England and it was Felix's talent which had made it possible, but her attitude to life in exile was in many ways slightly ambivalent. Her command of English increased as her reading widened, but right up to the end of her life she never stopped speaking Afrikaans. A phrase here and there, or a few apt sentences to add colour to an argument were always produced at the right moment. In South Africa where she grew up her ambitions could only be realised through the medium of the English language, which was the instrument of British domination. Therefore to a large extent she had turned her back on her own Afrikaans culture. Nevertheless every time any of her sons were about to compete for scholarships or prizes she would exhort them not to 'let our country down' and 'show the English what an Afrikaner can do'.

She had a little notebook of favourite sayings collected as a child. One she never tired of quoting to us was a verse from Sir Walter Scott: 'Breathes there the man, with soul so dead, Who never to himself hath said, This is my own, my native land!'

What puzzled me was why she had become so devoted to London. Her instinct for survival in an alien country, one that had taken such extreme measures to ensure the destruction of her own, never failed to amaze me. Was it because London was so cosmopolitan? What would have happened to her if she, as a Voortrekker daughter, had been restricted to the isolation of life in the veld and been deprived of the artistic stimulus of a great capital city?

She had survived an attack of meningitis after her release from the concentration camp in Bloemfontein and, once again, reading was to help her. A hundred years later it is sobering to reflect on the remarks of a very young girl, written in the margins of her Bible and the many books she acquired with the help of cigarette cards obtained from her elder brothers.

With the destruction of her parents' farm her childhood habitat had been destroyed. Though she chose to leave the desolation and sail far away into enemy territory, perhaps in her heart of hearts she wanted to keep hold of her own kind to remind her who and what she was.

The decision Casals made in 1936 to accept the isolation of exile appears to parallel, but for different reasons, that of my mother in 1938 to leave South Africa. It was the British Foreign Office that had helped General Franco conquer Spain, depriving Casals of his beautiful home near Barcelona for the rest of his life. He would never capitulate. He did allow a few people into his inner sanctum in Prades but he never forgave Britain or America. My mother, on the other hand, must have decided to forgive, and above all to forget, the genocide that Britain inflicted on the Afrikaner after 1900. She remained a committed Londoner for nearly fifty years.

In the three years following my return from France in 1949, I had to help supervise builders and decorators, and also assist my brothers in renovating 18 Holland Villas Road. I began to learn at first hand how some architects and developers design and build houses simply to enclose space, while others attempt to achieve something more. I came to see how one style of mid-Victorian

houses would begin in one street and become something quite
different in the next. Studying the outward forms of vast numbers
of living museums (yesterday's homes) in London, I learnt about
the generations of Londoners who had served the needs of the
metropolis, content to remain in just one small community
throughout their lives. These anonymous residents of Georgian,
Victorian, and Edwardian London, skilled to an enviable degree,
all helped to create a London I was just beginning to discover.

Concerts at the Festival Hall aroused mixed emotions, and a
consolation that never failed was to drive around the sleeping city
on my own after a late supper. I passed through deserted streets
taking in the atmosphere and character of each of the many villages
that had, over the centuries, grown together into the City of
Cities. I was able to discover areas that still retained, as testimony
to bygone elegance, some lovely houses south of the Thames,
symbols of a forgotten pattern of life. 18 Holland Villas Road was
such a house. Large, double-fronted, detached, and built on part
of the Holland Estate about 1860, it followed the fashion of the
time by having three large reception rooms on the ground floor, a
semi-basement, two floors allotted to family and an attic for
servants.

At the turn of the nineteenth century Holland House was the
centre of Whig reform and hosted many discussions attended by
the inimitable Sydney Smith. Fifty years later the estate was
developed and our house was designed and built to accommodate
an emerging class of *nouveaux riches.*

Within a month of moving to Holland Villas Road Mother was
told by the Greater London Council that the Cardinal Vaughan
Catholic School needed a playing field. Our house was one of four
that had been selected to accommodate the school's sporting
needs. Percy Cudlipp, editor of the Daily Mirror, was fortunate.
His house was bought and immediately demolished. Our house
was not, and endured planning blight for the next eighteen years.

Nobody would explain why the Compulsory Purchase Order never took effect. Eventually, in 1967, Mother was offered £44,000 as a final settlement. Today the house is owned by a Swiss property company and has a reported value of £8,000,000. Did Mr Cudlipp, a left-wing champion of people's rights, know something Mother was not told in 1950?

'Show me and I see. Tell me and I forget. Involve me and I remember.' When Mother made her first house purchase in 1944 I set about learning how to repair and re-decorate. I found to my surprise that by involving myself completely in the work in hand I was able to forget about some of the self-doubt about my career. As I attempted to re-create the textures and finish of our lovely 19th century family home I found a new joy in pure physical labour. Whatever else man needs, a daily must has to be, in some measure, a search for beauty.

In the London of the early fifties, before the breakdown of social patterns, it was not difficult to find this renewal. Standing on the bridge over the Serpentine in Kensington Gardens, especially on a cold and frosty winter's morning, I had before me a vista that was as beautiful as anything I could wish to see. What is more it was man-made, or at any rate the setting was. It was all there, bequeathed to anyone who had the time and the inclination to enjoy its serenity. In the late afternoon I used to find an escape by simply standing on the bridge, re-living some joy that music had brought into my life that day.

I was introduced at this time to the music-making world of Toscanini and his protégé, Guido Cantelli. When the Philharmonia played at La Scala in 1952 with Karajan, the orchestra had apparently so impressed Toscanini that he agreed to conduct two concerts at the Festival Hall in the same year. At the first concert the opening bar of the Brahms Tragic Overture had been such a shock for Toscanini that he lost himself for a split second. Without hesitation Manoug moved the strings on to the next beat and the danger passed. I was waiting to play the first note, but nothing happened. I looked up and found that he was standing with his hands clasped in front of him. When we finally did start my own view of the fracas of that first bar was that Toscanini had heard on one level a cold string tone, and on another the brittle sound of brass and timpani stretching out horizontally like colourless threads in a cheap tapestry. The mix had so thrown him that he hesitated before giving the second beat.

When he had listened to the Philharmonia's concert from La Scala he had heard a quality of orchestral tone produced in a sympathetic acoustic. What he heard a few months later in the Royal Festival Hall was the banal product that musically illiterate architects had produced as their answer to London's need for a main concert hall. Remedies have since been attempted by installing microphones and loudspeakers, but to little effect. As Raymond used to say every time I complained, 'Give over! You can't make a silk purse out of a sow's ear.'

My response was always that a sow's ear would make a better purse than twentieth-century architects had made of the Festival Hall.

Toscanini's protégé Guido Cantelli, whose talents at that time had yet to be revealed, was also engaged to conduct the orchestra in several concerts, and the prospects for the Philharmonia augured well. London would have the two-fold privilege of experiencing both old and new genius within the space of a year.

As a cellist I always tried to serve the idea of a totality of performance in the best possible way. Sitting next to Raymond (who was again principal after a short spell in the Royal Philharmonic) was a daily ritual that brought its own rewards. What I was beginning to find increasingly disturbing at this time was the unevenness and conflict of standards *within* the orchestra, particularly with regard to intonation. It was not only one's own intonation within the section, but the need for each section to be in tune with the rest of the orchestra. My lessons with Casals had heightened my awareness but for many of my colleagues intonation was just one of the hazards of the profession about which little could be done. Another irritation was what Casals described as 'pear-shaped' notes. These occur when the player changes the speed and point of contact of the bow without regard to the quality and dynamic change that is likely to be produced. Today, with the advent of the fashionable 'authentic performance', there is an apparent preference for what I was taught specifically not to do. I wonder what Casals would have said about this trend, now so heavily backed by recording companies.

It was on a lovely spring morning that I set off to spend the day recording with Cantelli at the EMI studios. The change in the weather was compensation indeed for the dreary months of a winter made worse by my persistent feeling of malaise. I had not taken the trouble to discuss depression with a doctor. It wasn't until I read a biography of the famous Smith of Smiths that I realised that toasted cheese eaten late at night has a disastrous effect on the next morning's enthusiasm for life. The favourite late night snack had been abandoned and everything now seemed to be bursting with new life.

The light was wonderfully clear and it seemed that I had never before noticed the houses and their gardens, even though I had walked along the same road many times. Perhaps the lessons I had learnt as an amateur architect had not been wasted after all. These houses, relics of a bygone age, had been built mostly for rich men's 'fancies', providing scope on the one hand for the rapidly expanding building trade of the late nineteenth century but contributing, on the other, to a dubious service to both public and private morals.

It was sad however to witness, in terms of its architecture, the autumn of an era, even on this lovely spring morning. In post-war England the wealth of yesterday's rich men was in the process of re-distribution. Their 'fancies' had long since withered and the houses that had survived were in their last moments of glory.

When I entered Studio One I was surprised to find that the usual layout had been altered. Instead of the orchestral tiers that gave a clear view of the conductor to both soloist and orchestra, all the players were now placed at floor level. This must have been requested by the record producer but was going to cause problems. Parquet flooring is usually made of hard wood, so spikes are inclined to slip, usually during a quiet section of a recording. The hard surface deadens resonance, particularly in the cello section, and for everyone to be seated on the same level would inevitably create difficulties with ensemble and dynamics.

As there were only a few members of the orchestra present I decided to 'prelude' as it is known in the profession. Putting the spike into a groove I was immediately irritated by the sound I made. It was dead, without any trace of warmth or colour. I put the cello back into its case and went off to seek solace in the canteen, wondering what Raymond was going to say. Sipping my chemical coffee didn't help either. What I was drinking somehow seemed to equate with the quality of sound the orchestra was going to make.

My thoughts turned to acoustic variation, which was much less of a problem in the early part of my career than it is now. Players worked for the most part in halls that had been built of the same basic materials and had also evolved on broadly parallel lines. It was therefore possible to become acclimatised quite easily to the quality of buildings all over the country simply because the echo variation was, broadly speaking, fairly predictable. The majority of post-war buildings, in which there were endless experiments with new materials, the sound was usually lacking in resonance and as dry as a desert. For the player this type of dry acoustic was a form of artistic death. He had no chance to nourish tone, even less to manipulate a phrase. Prior to the completion of the Festival Hall in 1951, Walter Legge's way of tackling the problem had been to rehearse and record at the Kingsway Hall (a Methodist Chapel with an excellent acoustic) a programme that would then be repeated at a public concert in the Albert Hall. This had given the Philharmonia a great advantage over rivals because rehearsals, recordings, and concerts had all taken place in a similar sympathetic acoustic. It had always worked very well, so why was Cantelli recording here at Abbey Road instead of at the Kingsway Hall?

My thoughts went back to a cold, inhospitable Royal Albert Hall at 10am on a Wednesday, held to ransom by a militant, power-hungry union bent on achieving for its members some of the benefits of the post-war rat-race. Most of the players were hunched over their instruments, wrapped in blankets or sitting in their overcoats. All were peering at their music in the dim light considered adequate for rehearsal by the Albert Hall management. Eventually the rehearsal began and Sir Adrian Boult took us through the Overture to Rossini's opera *The Silken Ladder* which begins with a very difficult oboe solo. Sir Adrian, one hand twiddling his beautiful moustache, addressed the oboist Alec Whittaker with mock severity.

'Mr Whittaker, we know it is very cold, and that Christmas will shortly be upon us. But it won't do, you know, it won't do.'

Sir Adrian was referring to Alec's rather feeble attempt to produce the beautiful sound which was still partly hidden in the mists of nocturnal alcoholic exuberance. We began the overture again, but the sound was still thin and raw. I felt that it suited the atmosphere and the conditions perfectly. Sir Adrian decided that enough had been said, and pressed on with the rest of the morning's rehearsal schedule. After the tea-break, we were to rehearse the Schumann Piano Concerto, with its lovely oboe solo near the beginning of the first movement. The cold douche of Alec's playing was splashing in all directions and was so depressing

Sir Adrian Boult in 1962

that even Sir Adrian's monumental good humour deserted him.

'Mr Whittaker, what would Sir Landon say if he heard you play as you have done this morning?'

Alec was born in Manchester and had been a child prodigy. He had been sent to London at the suggestion of Sir Landon Ronald, where he soon captured the hearts of all those who heard him. I know that memory can play tricks, but I believe that Alec Whittaker could, in the right mood, make the oboe sound like the promise of eternal bliss. On this occasion however he was in no mood for criticism, even when offered by a man well-loved for his honest good humour. Without so much as looking up, he snapped back in the broadest of broad North-Country accents.

'I don't know. But I do know what he thought of your conducting, because he told me so himself.'

Sir Adrian wisely decided not to press the point. He knew only too well that Alec would rise to the occasion in the evening.

I was still alone in the Abbey Road canteen after this little reverie, so I decided to return to the studio. On the way I met the recording engineer and told him that I didn't like the new orchestral layout. With an enthusiasm like that of Mr Toad, hypnotised by the sight of his first motorcar, he replied 'Never mind about all that, come and look at this.'

I found myself staring at what looked like a very large Ferrograph tape recorder.

'Just think,' he said, 'this was ready twelve years ago, but Philips have only recently decided to market and distribute it.' He then proceeded to explain how magnetic tape recording had revolutionised the recording industry.

The orchestra soon assembled and Guido Cantelli was ushered into the studio by the producer. I shall never forget how conscious I was, from the very first, of the charisma that surrounded Cantelli. I couldn't be sure whether it was his appearance, his eyes, or his gestures that held my attention. It felt as if he gathered the whole orchestra into the focus of his eyes and then with his hands directed, released and shared new energies.

The music we were to record that morning was La Valse, by

Ravel, a sophisticated exercise in restrained sensuality, or so I understood the young maestro's message to be. It soon became evident that whatever message Cantelli believed he was sending to the orchestra, what we were doing in return gave him little satisfaction no matter how hard we tried.

After much agonizing, he was at last persuaded to risk a test recording. It was, after all, a recording session and not a rehearsal for a concert. There were time limits and commercial targets to achieve. Signor Cantelli would have to recognise that the business side of beauty also has to be respected. He would have to restrict his search for that sound he was apparently hearing in his mind's ear, but failing to create in this arid studio. He knew we were capable of making this sound for he had heard us play at La Scala. I felt sure it was that wretched parquet floor that was chiefly responsible for the distress the Maestro was now exhibiting.

After the 'take' Cantelli was ushered into the balance and control room and through the glass panel I was able to witness a little fragment of the ensuing drama. The gentle, poised young man who had left the studio then rushed back to the rostrum. He immediately stepped down again, and asked Manoug Parikian to give him a cigarette. The somewhat startled leader of the orchestra obliged at once and Cantelli, without wasting a second, inhaled deeply. The next moment he looked as if he were going to be sick and the players at the front of the orchestra backed away for safety. Then, throwing the rest of the cigarette away, he began to cry with despair and frustration. There was nothing anyone could say or do.

We were witnessing Cantelli, the artist, reacting to the sound of a record before the engineers 'doctor' it by adding a richer mix of high and low frequencies. The message Cantelli had just received had come through naked and unadorned, without any 'sales treatment'. The shock had been traumatic.

The producer emerged from the control room and suggested that the orchestra should take an early tea-break. I went outside.

At least the sun was still shining. Raymond was standing under the branches of a large chestnut tree and, to judge from the expression on his face, he looked as if he wanted to be left alone. Respecting each other's wish for time to reflect we both stood there, thinking our thoughts. The principal viola player appeared.

'Well Raymond,' he asked, in his most penetrating Birmingham accent, 'What d'ya *knaow?*'

There was a long pause.

'Not much,' Raymond replied eventually, in the broadest possible Yorkshire equivalent. 'Otherwise I bloody well wouldn't be here.'

During the four years that Cantelli worked with the Philharmonia we witnessed the growth of a formidable rival to Karajan. There was little to choose between the two men as artists. As a political animal Karajan definitely had the advantage, but on the emotional level Cantelli seemed almost to be old before his time.

Cantelli's tragic death on 24th November 1956 in an air accident at the early age of 36 was an irreparable loss for those who loved and respected him and his work. During his short and brilliant career, his recordings, certainly those in which I participated, do not convey the vibrant expression of a sustained and great musical talent that his all too few public performances afforded us.

CHAPTER TWENTY

One Summer of Happiness

Up to the tour of Europe in 1954 Karajan's behaviour to the orchestra had been exemplary. Recording with him, though frequently a challenge, was never dull. Sometimes, if the positions of microphones had to be changed, and since he knew that Manoug was also interested in cars, there was a discussion between the three car enthusiasts at the front of the orchestra. This often irritated Dennis Brain because, sitting in the horn section yards away from the strings, he was unable to join in.

Unlike many conductors, Karajan was willing to learn from his players' specialist knowledge. Aware, for example, that Raymond was a little hard of hearing in his left ear, he would sometimes speak to me about a technical problem concerning the cellos. However he combined artistic endeavour with a ruthless business aptitude. As long as Legge's plans suited his purpose, he was willing to help further them artistically. The foundations for what was to become a very successful Karajan business empire in the late 1960s were already being laid in 1950.

Karajan and Schwarzkopf were often involved in productions at La Scala, Milan and in Vienna, while at the same time she was busy recording extensively in London and Vienna. She sang the Verdi Requiem in Salzburg with de Sabata conducting and gave *Lieder* recitals all over Europe. At Karajan's behest she learnt and performed new operatic roles, and at one point gave sixteen performances of four different operas in five weeks, all conducted by Karajan in various European venues. On another occasion, after a performance at Covent Garden in London, she flew to Milan to give a *Lieder* recital and was back the next day at Covent Garden.

Herbert von Karajan rehearsing in Lucerne 1954

She recorded the complete *Land of Smiles* under Otto Ackermann at the Kingsway Hall, and while Walter Legge was in Milan with Callas recording her first *Tosca*, Schwarzkopf was at the Salzburg Festival giving a recital of Hugo Wolf Songs.

In September and November 1952 she recorded the Bach B minor Mass with Karajan in what Alec Robertson was to describe as 'a landmark in the history of the gramophone record'. Her career was truly on the wing.

The Schwarzkopf-Karajan-Legge trio was now world famous. Two members of the team were at the peak of their respective careers, but the third, based at La Scala, was playing a waiting game.

It was perhaps because he had never been humbled in front of an orchestra as a player that Karajan could be so utterly ruthless. As a conductor can never *sound* wrong, it is always the player who has to bear the brunt of a conductor's mistakes. It is only when a conductor ventures to perform in public on a musical instrument that an audience will sometimes hear that he too is a mere mortal. Listening to Solti and Murray Perahia play piano duets a few years ago in a television programme, Perahia's talent was there for all to hear. Solti on the other hand hammered away in exactly the same way he used to beat the air. I was fortunate enough not to be working in London during the Solti era, but many harrowing tales by colleagues at Covent Garden about his behaviour, made me grateful that his considerable ability to bully rather than to persuade was never directed at me.

During a tea-break while working with Sir Michael Tippett in the 1960s I related an embarrassing incident concerning Karajan that occurred one afternoon at the Kingsway Hall. Because of Dinu Lipatti's illness, Bartók's Music for Strings, Percussion and Celesta was substituted for the Piano Concerto No. 3 that Lipatti was to have recorded. Karajan didn't know the work but, taking a risk, agreed to conduct. We managed to struggle our way through the first three movements, but several failed attempts to follow his beat in the last movement revealed quite clearly that his normally super-efficient stick technique had deserted him. Eventually he asked us to rewrite the time signature and to ignore what Bartók had written. He would then give us four clear crotchet beats per bar. He assured us it would all work out in the end but of course it didn't, and we all had to retire with egg on our faces.

Sir Michael then told me a story of his own. His work, *A Child of Our Time*, was to be conducted by Karajan and broadcast from La Scala. Karajan, who was staying at the same hotel as other members of the cast, was not only late for the performance but, without consulting either the composer or the radio producer, insisted on having an additional interval. I asked Sir Michael if he felt disappointed or annoyed at Karajan's lack of professional behaviour.

'His behaviour was uncalled for and extremely cavalier.'

Sir Michael had a lovely freshness about him and I never once heard him raise his voice at rehearsal. This was the first time I had seen anger in his eyes.

'I was not disappointed,' he added, as an afterthought: 'I was furious.'

This time I laughed and he was curious to know why, so I explained that when conductors become ill mannered I adopt a thick-skinned attitude.

'I wish I could have done the same that night,' he said with a smile.

I went on to say that when Karajan was angry he was colder than usual, but twice as dangerous, so it was vital to be equally cold in return. Because he was so insensitive to other people's emotions, he was, in a way, more vulnerable when his own were challenged, particularly when he wanted a favour. My answer to conductor 'tantrums' has always been to make a stand from the beginning if I considered that they were either threatening me, or trying to blind me with musical science.

Walter Legge could also be irritating, and he could certainly be dismissive, but his irritations were usually a consequence of artistic disappointment. Karajan, as several famous singing stars were to find in 1964 when he had finally achieved his ambition, was ready without a single qualm of conscience to end a working relationship overnight. Sena Jurinac is reported as saying 'When Karajan was through with me, he was through!'

When Karajan decided that Walter Legge was no longer of any use to him, he was cast aside. For years Walter Legge had given priority to Karajan's needs. The orchestra had achieved a standard of playing that had surprised even the Vienna Philharmonic, so much so that the *Gesellschaft der Musikfreunde* agreed to provide its chorus for a new recording in Vienna of Beethoven's Choral Symphony. Although the success of the Philharmonia was in large measure the result of its collaboration with Karajan, it was obvious that this was just part of the Karajan strategy.

Furtwängler died in November 1954. The main impediment to Karajan's desire to become director of the richest orchestras in Europe had been removed. By December he had already received a coded telephone message from Berlin: 'The King is dead. Long live the King!'

The ideals that inspired Walter Legge were doomed because there was insufficient support from both the Arts Council and Society itself, the latter being the tragic legacy of World War One. The flower of English and German youth was savagely removed from Europe's cultural scene, having been sacrificed in an absurd quarrel between the Royal Families of England and Germany. Those Englishmen who died might well have supported him if they had been granted the opportunity to live. Those who survived could perhaps be forgiven for being too cynical to be able to appreciate the spiritual rewards offered by the music of an *ancien régime*.

For several years, tension between EMI and Walter Legge had been building up and in 1963 he finally gave one year's notice to the company. There was no alternative for him but to abandon his dream. The responsibility for the temporary demise of the Philharmonia Orchestra in 1964 must rest squarely on the shoulders of the money-men of London and the Arts Council.

By the middle of 1953 I had taken the decision to leave the Philharmonia. Although the orchestra had given me the opportunity to meet and work with the greatest talents of the twentieth century, I nevertheless felt that I was trapped. I was also totally incapable of tolerating the acoustics of the Festival Hall any longer. If the Queen's Hall had been rebuilt after the war, as had been promised to Sir Henry Wood, things would have been different. Perhaps Karajan might even have been willing to abandon La Scala for a rebuilt Queen's Hall.

I went to see Walter Legge one day in April 1953 between rehearsal and concert. It was a spur-of-the-moment decision with no real plan. I just wanted to talk. I asked him why the Queen's Hall project had been abandoned and why the empty bombsite should eventually have been allocated to an American Hotel syndicate. Legge did indeed know most of the answers, but he said there was no point in fighting shadows. Where had I heard that before?

He must have told Karajan about my doubts because, quite soon after, Karajan asked me to come to the artists' room to have a talk. He had recently been conducting in Tokyo and spoke persuasively about the emerging scope for a single, unattached, musician in Japan. There was a vacancy in the Tokyo Radio Orchestra and the appointment allowed anyone interested plenty of freedom to develop outside hobbies. If I wanted to, he said with a smile, I could even return to Europe every nine months or so and play in some of the Philharmonia concerts.

I was very tempted, but I had reservations. Unfortunately it was many years later that I became aware of the interest that certain western composers had felt towards aspects of Oriental belief and thought. For example awareness of the Hindu Upanishads had influenced both Beethoven and Debussy and helped them in their search for new and wider dimensions in their own work. I am now sure, without any doubt, that I should have gone to Japan. The trouble was that in 1953 Japan was still, as far as I was concerned, the Empire of the Rising Sun. I had been made brutally aware of what that had meant to a cello pupil of mine, awaiting mock-execution while working during World War Two on the Burma Road. Eight years after his release from internment, great weals would still periodically appear on his body whenever some deep-inflicted pain re-surfaced.

I finally left the orchestra in the spring of 1953 and one morning in May I set off once more for Paris to see Madame Loquet and Pierre Fournier. I was determined to try to obtain a work permit in Paris as cellist, dishwasher or anything. After a few weeks of refusals and rebuffs I gave up and decided to go to Heidelberg and stay there until my money ran out.

During the three months in Heidelberg I must have sampled every variety of sausage ever made in Germany. Hot or cold, long or short, white or brown. They were all delicious. In between this rewarding apprenticeship I would either practise, visit local beauty spots, or go for very long walks.

The palace of Swetzingen was not very far away and it was only too easy to while away the hours in this spiritual cradle of mid-eighteenth century music-making, relishing the luxurious sound. There was no comparison whatever with the starved, dehydrated noise produced by architects and builders two hundred years later in London.

Then there was a little round chapel in Heidelberg itself, its Lutheran choir practising choral music every day which, surprisingly, belonged to the great Catholic musical tradition. I was astonished to learn that in the days of the Holy Roman Empire it took fourteen years to train a boy's voice, partly because everything had to be sung from memory. I believe that because Guido d'Arezzo invented a form of notation in the eleventh century, it is now impossible to imagine what added quality the absence of a printed note must have given to daily communion. His initial intention had been to make learning plainsong easier for choirboys and he certainly achieved this aim. His solution proved to be so useful that it was improved over the next six hundred years to become the basis of the written note for composers all over the world. But in making performance easier for the boys, something indefinable must certainly have been lost.

The spring of 1953 brought many new and untried experiences. There were so many lovely places to visit and re-visit, particularly in and around Swetzingen, where the ideals of the patron, the architect, and the music-maker had been fused into one perfect construction.

I left Heidelberg after three months with a keen sense of regret. It was a centre that had contributed so much to the heritage of which I had wished to be part. There was, in particular, the enormous impetus Swetzingen had given to string players. Leopold Mozart wrote his celebrated book on violin playing while he was attached to the orchestra there. But now there was only an unused, deserted palace for tourists to stare at. The eighteenth-century search for beauty had been superseded by the obscene ugliness of post-war Democratic Reconstruction.

Waiting for the train to leave I remembered the delight I had experienced listening to the choir rehearsing in the little round chapel. I wondered whether the beauty of their singing was the *result* of, or *assisted* by, the design of the building and the materials used in its construction.

In 1953 Felix acquired a Chrysler Coupé with an open dickey seat. When tensions ran high it was possible, in this marvellous example of vintage America, to enjoy a completely isolated sulk, free from any obligation to make conversation. In the well-upholstered seat, wrapped in weatherproof garments, I enjoyed the freedom of vision unhindered by the limitations imposed by windows. Trips to Oxford and Cambridge provided me with an interesting insight into the dichotomy with which the emerging poor are always faced. On the one hand Mother, Darrell, Felix and I had been struggling since the end of the war to improve the quality of our lives. On the other, Myron, who was at school with Rothschild, Hussein, McAlpine and many other sons of wealthy parents, was attempting as best he could to conceal his lack of funds and gradually drifting into a comparative isolation at Harrow and Cambridge of which we were not aware. The strange thing was that, while the family took pains not to embarrass Myron by visiting him at Harrow in Felix's ancient high-loader Austin taxi, his friends were thrilled by what they considered to be our eccentricity—and especially by the taxi. They envied what they saw as our freedom from convention. They thought we had a choice.

On one of my visits to South Africa House in 1952 I met Esmé Joubert, niece of Air Vice-Marshal Joubert who, during World War Two, had been seconded to the British War Office. To my surprise Mother invited Esmé to accompany us on a family outing to visit Myron at Cambridge. Esmé and I became good friends over the next twelve months or so, as she was always welcomed into the house by Mother.

One evening I arrived at the official residence of the South African High Commissioner who was acting as Esmé's chaperon. We had planned to have dinner after a Philharmonia concert. The butler informed me in a matter-of-fact tone that Esmé had returned to South Africa that morning. There was no message and no letter of explanation. The butler made it quite obvious that I was *persona non grata* and I thought I detected the suspicion of a sneer on an otherwise bland countenance.

In 1953 relationships were still constrained by conventions that now appear almost comic. My relationship with Esmé had been affectionate, but formal and correct. I was not rich, but neither was I poor. I was a sub-principal in a superb orchestra with an international reputation. She had attended several concerts in which I was performing, so there could have been no reason to doubt my professional status and yet this butler seemed to be saying 'A musician is not welcome in this house'.

Women seem to have loyalties to each other that defy analysis and when necessary they can guard a secret with unshakeable tenacity. It was only shortly before Mother died in 1977, that I learnt what had happened. Esmé had gone to see her early in the morning and had explained that her family was against a relationship with a musician. Possibly hoping that Mother *would* in fact tell me, Esmé made her promise *not* to tell me. She could have had no idea of the degree of integrity with which Mother conducted her affairs. Mother said nothing, even when I told her that I had met Esmé in Capetown on a trip in 1964. She only mentioned the promise to Esmé thirteen years later in 1977.

It is sad to reflect that an anglicised Cape Afrikaner such as Joubert should have descended to such myopic manipulations of essential truth, courtesy and respect. He may well have believed himself to be all the things he was convinced I would never be, but surely this did not entitle him to prevent his niece from making her own decision.

With Esmé I had found something that was different. There was a lovely feeling of companionship and laughter, strange yet compelling. Stranger still, the last film we saw, which had meant so much to us both, was Bergman's One Summer of Happiness.

In 1954 I was asked to play with the Philharmonia Orchestra on another European tour, and was only too happy to test the variation of acoustic properties in the concert halls where we were to play. Walter Legge was amused by the intensity of my continuing dislike of the Festival Hall but asked rather wearily whether I didn't think it was time to accept that I had made my point and make the best of a bad job. I replied that if playing in a dry, featureless hall for the rest of my career was all there was to hope for then, as far as I was concerned, it was time to give up playing the cello.

The tour of Europe included concerts in Hamburg, Berlin, Munich, Vienna and Linz. It was at Linz that the players' collective irritation with Karajan's ruthless manipulation of the orchestra to his own advantage boiled over in one of those unpredictable ways. We had played to a full house in a vast Sports Palace. The concert had gone well and we all knew it. Karajan was inspired that night and every member of the orchestra was alive to the occasion. As the music stopped the applause began. A few members of the audience rose to their feet and within minutes practically everyone else was standing as well.

After many recalls the orchestra began to follow the conductor off the platform at his request. As it was the last concert of the tour, some of us stayed behind to pack our instruments in readiness for the journey the next day back to England. We were happy and relaxed, looking forward to a celebration with some of the local beer. Suddenly the orchestral manager appeared and asked us to vacate the platform as quickly as possible so that Karajan could take more applause, this time on his own. By the time the message had reached every member of the orchestra, the mood had changed to one of a deeply felt resentment. Karajan went off the platform again, making it quite clear to us that we should clear the area and we had no alternative but to comply. But Nemesis was at hand. The only access to the platform was through one door. The audience were treated to the spectacle of members of the orchestra pushing their way out and Karajan fighting his way back on to the platform from the opposite direction. After a frantic struggle he finally had the stage to himself.

Karajan had richly deserved the ovation for his music-making that night but he had destroyed something much more valuable. It had not been only his contribution to the concert that had helped to make it such a memorable event. The contribution of the Philharmonia Orchestra had been of equal importance. It was to be the last time he would receive that respect and co-operation from the players which it had taken him over seven years to achieve.

CHAPTER TWENTY ONE

Les-Baux-en-Provence

The attempt to emulate Montaigne in my self-education circa 1953 proved to be far more costly than I had anticipated. Apart from the difficulty of interpreting any of the subliminal messages being received from this compassionate father figure of the sixteenth century there were other more pressing problems. In one essay my mentor had advised me that '...we must strive every day to create order out of chaos,' but this was something that had eluded me so far.

Experiences accumulated during the eight years in the orchestra had served to achieve a measure of self-discipline, which I should now be able to apply to improving my cello playing. The art of acquiring enough money on which to live, while developing this new discipline, proved somewhat elusive.

The main purpose of my resignation from the Philharmonia was to register a one-man protest against the horrors of the Festival Hall. Secretly I was, of course, hoping against hope that my gesture might elicit some kind of response from an unknown Midas willing to take the place of the Maharajah of Mysore. However, the only practical consequence of this gesture was to deprive me of my income.

Salvation came in the shape of an offer by Peter Gibbs, a violinist friend, to play entr'acte music in a piano trio he had been asked to organise for a new production of *Anastasia* at the St James's Theatre. Yet again I had been prevented from sliding too far down Skid Row.

Peter Gibbs, who was something of a maverick, had spent the war flying Hurricanes and regretted the peace that prevented him from relishing the thrills and challenges of piloting that legendary plane. When we met to discuss the pieces we were to play during theatre breaks, he said that he didn't want to restrict the repertoire to the usual arrangements of Viennese waltzes for piano trio. He had already selected the pieces but they would still have to be properly arranged.

'Only Russian music will do,' he insisted. 'Only Russian music can capture the barbarity of this tragic story of ethnic hatred.' That is what he said, and I am sure he was right in principle. In practice things turned out rather differently. A month passed and I heard nothing. Then one day he rang and asked me to come with him to the theatre to meet Tommy Rajna, a delightful and very competent pianist who would be the third member of the trio. Peter produced a selection of violin solos and we managed to agree without too much trouble on a general strategy as to who played what. Little did Tommy and I know what was in store for us.

The dress rehearsal took place the next day. Like Brahms, Peter was never afraid to pour a quart into a pint pot. He arrived just in time to park his motorbike, rush into the pit and distribute a selection of violin solos, no doubt assuming that Tommy and I would be able to make a convincing contribution to the occasion. Needless to say, we couldn't and I dread to think what impression was created by a solo violin playing deeply moving Russian music, accompanied by a pianist having to cope with cuts in the score and a cellist who didn't know where he was, because he was playing from a piano reduction of a different edition. Throughout the entire run of the play Peter never made clear what he did want me to play, but since I was entirely preoccupied with trying to *ad-lib* the cello part, I didn't really notice the reaction of the audience. They couldn't have been more bewildered than I was.

Peter was an endearing eccentric endowed with enormous but wasted talent. He was fortunate to have been born with the courage to face danger from any quarter without showing the

slightest trace of nervous anticipation, as anyone foolish enough to
fly with him was soon to discover. The great advantage of the
theatre job was that my mornings were free to work on the newly
acquired Alvis Speed Twenty. Occasionally, as agreed with Walter
Legge, I would play as a deputy on the back desk of the
Philharmonia and, less frequently, accompany Felix and Daphne
Ibbott on short UK tours with the Beaufort Piano Trio.

The first months of 1954 passed without too many problems,
apart from my eldest brother's decision to marry in secret and
spend a sabbatical year in America. Felix too was becoming more
than just a little interested in a particular lady. She was part of a set
of friends that he brought home regularly to Holland Villas Road
to act as a kind of smoke screen with which to disguise his real
intentions. This ruse, if it was a ruse, seemed to work, because
Mother appeared to be getting on quite well with all of them. They
were the sort of people who could speak easily on a whole range
of subjects most of which were more or less outside my orbit of
experience.

I had recently worked as a part-time mechanic at the Golders
Green branch of Alvis stripping engines down prior to re-building
them with new parts. It was more of a therapeutic exercise than
anything else and when the Alvis couldn't bridge gaps in my daily
life I would resort to some of my other pet interests: architecture,
conductors, philosophy and teaching methods. My family always
managed to silence me as quickly as possible whenever we had
visitors, so without wishing to embarrass either my relatives or
their guests, I would usually disappear and return to my 1934 Alvis
for real communication. While lying underneath the car in the
drive of our house one afternoon, I noticed a girl standing next to
Felix looking a little perplexed. Later I learned that Felix had told
her I was a cellist. Seeing a grimy car mechanic she found it hard
to envisage how a cellist-cum-car-enthusiast earned a living. Like
many people Felix introduced me to, she assumed that I did a few

gigs at night to keep myself in pocket money and worked during the day as a car mechanic. This, in a sense, was true at that particular time.

After cleaning up as much as possible I went to meet the other members of the party and discovered that the girl's name was Annette Ingold. She had a fresh complexion and a disarming charm about her that, coupled with a refined but genuine modesty, was to put an immediate curb on what had become by this stage in my life a more robust attitude to women. Her mother had a force and vitality of character that completely magnetised me, and I will always remember her with great affection. I do believe that she thought me well intentioned but, as I was later to learn, she and Annette both considered me to be a rather a 'rough diamond'.

Shortly after we met I had to leave London for a tour of America and didn't see Annette again for nearly two months. I often thought about her while I was away, and when I got back home, I asked her whether we could meet for lunch. She said she would, and we agreed that I should call for her at her dress-making shop in Tottenham Street. On the top floor of a dingy terraced house I saw four women sitting at tables sewing and smoking. Annette came into the room, looking as white as a sheet. She said that she had just been talking to the costume manageress at the Windmill Theatre who wanted a new costume yesterday, and seemed surprised that Annette was behind schedule. She sighed and then she asked whether we couldn't possibly go out another day. I put my arm round her shoulder.

'No. I think what you need is a short break and a decent meal. There is a Bertorelli's round the corner and we can walk there in a few minutes.'

She agreed, and while she was fetching her handbag and tidying up, I noticed the very flimsy dancer's costume to which she had just referred and, lying next to it, a very ornate costume which she later told me was destined for an actor at the Old Vic. At lunch she admitted that she was very tired and apologised if she had seemed ungracious. The manageress at the Windmill had just been shouting that she should reduce her prices and yet she always left her orders to the last moment. This meant that whenever there was a deadline there was inevitably a crisis.

I listened with genuine sympathy. Her problems seemed to be very like mine. She had had to cope with a costume manageress who probably had no real knowledge of the art of dressmaking, while I had to play in halls designed by architects who knew little about acoustics.

Within a few days I felt sure that I had at last found someone with whom I could share an enthusiasm for music, theatre, architecture and possibly even Alvis motor cars. I was invited to accompany Annette and her mother to Anthony Besch's production of *Così fan Tutti* at Glyndebourne and although I have always had reservations about opera (which I found it difficult to explain, especially to Walter Legge) I felt grateful for this possibility of a new experience.

It soon became evident that Annette and I faced the same problem. We both needed to earn just enough money to subsidise our respective hobbies. They provided us with a rewarding involvement, and a great deal of pleasure, but it wasn't always easy to balance the books. Those few months of grace were certainly some of the happiest days of my life, but it does seem rather sad to me that because neither of us measured up to the 'success' image that has so much importance for society, we became, in effect, social lepers.

We both found little comfort in the world of the action-packed newly-awakening-but-yet-to-be-liberated youth which was about to lead England into the Swinging Sixties. To us the values that Harold Wilson and Barbara Castle were so very sure about seemed totally incomprehensible.

Near the end of my theatre job in July 1954 I was told that the Philharmonia was to tour France and Switzerland ending with two additional concerts at the Edinburgh Festival. It was a heaven-sent opportunity to test the reliability of the Alvis and far too good to miss, especially as the management was offering a generous travel-allowance. The concerts were to take place at Les Baux and Aix-en-Provence and the remainder as part of the Lucerne Festival.

It was not too difficult to persuade Mother, Felix, Jock Sutcliffe (first oboe) and Jennifer Franklin (assistant to the orchestral manager Jane Withers) to travel with us in the car. The prospect of driving an open tourer in that most beautiful part of France was infinitely appealing. All foreign exchange, petrol coupons and travel expenses were being taken care of by the management and my only responsibility was to ensure that the car would survive the round trip of over two thousand miles. It was too good to be true.

On the last day of rehearsals prior to our departure, Karajan had been unusually friendly towards the orchestra. He seemed genuinely pleased with the playing and gave the impression that, although a period of hard work lay ahead he would do his best to ensure that the tour would be made as pleasant for us as possible. As I was putting my cello into its wooden travelling box I was surprised to hear him ask whether I was looking forward to taking the Alvis on the tour. He assumed that it was still the same car that had won the Edinburgh 'circuit' and was curious, and probably anxious, to know whether it would get to Les Baux in one piece. He had learnt that Jock Sutcliffe was travelling with us and, typical of his attention to detail, he was checking for himself. He wanted to know how long I had allowed for the journey and hearing that we planned to enjoy a leisurely trip over two days, he seemed satisfied. He then asked whether I had ever driven an Austin Healey Hundred. I replied, as diplomatically as I could, that although I admired the shape and general finish of the car, I had never driven what an Australian cellist-friend of mine had once described as Britain's most beautiful 'sin-wagon'.

Karajan seemed amused by the term.

'Don't. There is not enough power in second gear to get you out of trouble in an emergency.' He then went on to describe a near head-on collision he had had in France while driving one of these beautiful but under-powered machines a few months before.

As a matter of interest I asked him if he had ever driven an Alvis. To my astonishment he replied that not only had he never driven one but, until the Edinburgh incident, he had not even heard of one. He then asked if he could drive the car. No Alvis owner could have been happier to oblige.

Abandoning my cello to the care of the instrument carriers I drove him to Regents Park, where he took the wheel. He drove round the Park's inner circle and was polite enough to appear impressed, but then it was always difficult to know what the Maestro ever really thought. When I took over and demonstrated some of the characteristics of the famous Alvis front-wheel suspension design, I sensed that he was more than a little taken aback. He then drove the car back to Friends' House where we said our good-byes. Karajan had been extraordinarily kind to me that afternoon, revealing a side to his character I had failed to recognise in the years we had worked together. I suppose that the 'togetherness' was a result of our both loving cars and he only deserted the brotherhood when pressure of time necessitated the use of a private plane.

'You still need a car to get you to the airport,' commented Dennis Brain wryly.

The next morning Mother, Felix and I packed the car, ready to leave as soon as Jock arrived. We had agreed to set off for Dover at 10am, cross the channel at noon and allow ourselves two days' travel, with more than adequate time for stops *en route*, so as to reach St Rémy for dinner on the second day.

10am came and went. I rang Jock an hour later but received no reply. Finally, at 11.30, he arrived, calm and unflustered but, as can be imagined, I was in a panic. Without waiting for an explanation we set off for Dover. Although I drove faster than I should have done with four up plus luggage, it was useless to try and beat the clock. We arrived in Dover just in time to see the ferry sailing out of the harbour.

Worse was to follow. A strike by airport staff at Le Touquet meant that air passengers had priority over latecomers on ferries to the Continent. The four of us sat in silence in the car imprisoned in gloom and embarrassment. Nobody wanted to be the first to make recriminations. We knew, as did Jock, that his late arrival had been the cause of our predicament but to apportion blame would only exacerbate matters.

I tried to explain our predicament to the Port authorities, to the Shipping Line and to any fellow traveller who might offer us his place in the queue but it was useless. There were no vacancies and any lingering hope that it might still have been possible to enjoy a leisurely drive along French roads was now finally out of the question. At 10pm we were told that there would be no space available from Dover that day, or indeed for the next few days. There was nothing to do but capitulate. Felix, Jock and I would have to travel by train, Mother would return home and the car would have to be left in a local garage.

Just as black despair was beginning to sour the atmosphere a sympathetic music-lover I had spoken to earlier, who was also travelling to the Lucerne Festival, managed to arrange a crossing for us at Felixstowe. We would have to leave at once if we were to get there in time. Although this would mean a night drive, the knowledge that we would soon be able to cross the Channel and be on our way acted like a magic potion. Waiting became a pleasure enhanced by a leisurely meal on the ferry which Jock insisted on paying for as a gesture of atonement.

We disembarked in that depressing and remorseless drizzle that makes everything damp but only provides just enough moisture on the windscreens to make the wipers squeak. By 1.30am we had cleared Customs and set off in high spirits on the first stage of our journey.

It wasn't long before the rear passengers began to complain about a persistent drip through the canvas hood. I suggested that Felix and Jock should seek solace in the bottle of brandy I had bought during the crossing. We were making very good time, and with little traffic on the road I was able to drive faster than I had originally intended over the appalling roads of Northern France, particularly the cobbled surfaces of the towns. In the middle of Beauvais the engine suddenly cut and all the lights went out. I tried the starter but there was absolutely no spark. For a few moments I sat stunned, unable to imagine what could have gone wrong. The battery and coil were new and all the wiring had been checked.

I climbed out into the damp, dark night, asking myself 'Why, oh why?' and a lot else besides. Opening the bonnet released even more water over the engine. It was then I remembered that in the rush I had left the torch at home. I could do nothing. It was about 4am. We were cold, tired and hungry but there was nothing to do but wait for the nearest garage to open, and hope that the problem could be solved.

About two hours later, as dawn was beginning to lighten the sky, I decided to take another look at the engine just to see if there was some loose connection I could now spot. The rain had stopped and it even looked as if the clouds might be clearing. I wiped the bonnet and opened it carefully to prevent more water from splashing on to the plugs. I took out the main ammeter fuse, cleaned it, and put it back again. Immediately, all the lights came on.

Without daring to believe that the remedy could be so simple, I gently closed the bonnet, climbed back into the car, and pressed the starter. The engine fired at once and we were on our way. It had been the French *pavé* that had caused the main fuse to shake loose. For the second time in two successive days we had had to experience near-despair, followed by instant joy. Once more, as if by magic, all traces of irritation and aching limbs suddenly vanished. We were on our way to St Rémy.

That moment of elation may not have lasted very long, but the memory of it will remain with me as long as I live. It is as firmly fixed in my mind as the afternoon in Prades when I had walked back to the Grand Hotel after my first lesson with Casals in 1949.

My passengers did not complain or indulge in dire prophesies of possible disasters. They accepted the fact that there was a long drive ahead, and that there was no point in adding ill-humour to the existing predicament. We agreed on a couple of hours driving before stopping for our first *petit déjeuner* of the tour. After breakfast we had a wash and a change of driver and then set off on the next lap, hoping to arrive at the head of the Rhône Valley on the N.17 in time for lunch.

By 9pm that evening we reached St Rémy. Allowing for stops, we had averaged about 58 mph which, even if we did have to bend a few continental rules about what is permitted on two-lane roads, is very creditable motoring. When I came to check the engine the following morning, oil, hydraulic and water levels were normal. All things considered, it had been a grand start to motoring on the Continent, a real test of camaraderie and, to crown it all, a happy ending.

The first rehearsal for the concert at Les Baux was to take place in the afternoon of the next day, so we were free to wander around St Rémy until it was time to leave after lunch. Walking down a narrow street, I came across the statue of Nostradamus tucked away in a corner. I had just read his predictions for the future of mankind but had forgotten that when he wrote his prophesies of doom and gloom he was living in this beautiful Roman holiday town. In the clear light of the morning and with a forecast of perfect weather for the rest of the day, it seemed rather incongruous to be looking at the statue of man whose mind was so clouded with doubt.

In 1954 Provence was uncluttered by car maniacs like myself, and the population had not yet been swollen by several million refugees from Algeria. Walking round St Rémy that morning, I could savour the clear dry air to the full and began to appreciate just why the area had been so popular in Roman times. It must have been a paradise for some, even if what remains of the amphitheatre today offers an example of the hell it must have been for others.

Seeing Les Baux for the first time was an unforgettable experience. Until then I had never heard of Simon de Montfort or the Albigensians, and had not been aware that the original purpose of the Inquisition had been to give the Roman Catholic Church a powerful instrument with which to root out heresy and destroy the Cathars. I could still sense the feeling of utter desperation that must have guided the Cathars' choice of terrain. They had established a base in Les Baux to defend themselves against the Catholic Knights of Christendom rather than submit to religious persecution. For having thus transgressed, their women would be raped and their houses pillaged and destroyed by soldiers whom the Pope had conscripted from all over Europe.

In 1954 Les Baux was still as peaceful and remote as France had been when I first fell in love with Provence and the Pyrenees in 1949. The view from the southern side of the ridge, looking down over the vast plain towards St Rémy, was as beautiful a sight as I had ever seen. An air of majesty now pervaded the silent and deserted part of the town the Cathars used to occupy.

Many years later I was to read of the power struggle of a Pope, jealous of the prerogative of the established Church and greedy to acquire the assumed wealth of the Templars. Greedy also to possess the secret they had been suspected of sharing with the Cathars since the fall of Jerusalem. His victims were dissidents who, after a lifetime of sober hard work and pleasurable enjoyment, aspired to a state of spiritual perfection in an ascetic old age rather than submit to the concept of fire and brimstone promised by the Pope's God of Wrath. Whatever the rights and wrongs on either side, I experienced a sense of horror at the thought of people being burnt alive in the beautiful setting I saw that day.

I returned to St Rémy again in 1993 and decided to drive to Les Baux just to remind myself of that first visit. The high ridge had the same tinge of russet as I drove towards the hilltop-town in the late afternoon but the mountain stronghold no longer exuded the same sense of isolation. Road safety requirements demanded uniform signals and roads had been enlarged. New hotels had been built and old ones modernised to house spectators interested in the cave homes of yesterday's martyrs. The leisure industry had invaded the sanctuary of a people who had endured hardship and privation in a vain bid for survival. Where there had been peace and serenity there was now noise.

Karajan's choice of music for the concert included the *Symphonie Fantastique* by Berlioz, and the performance was to take place in a great arena carved out of the rock, sheltered on three sides by a high ridge. Imagine for a moment a vast open-air stage, erected for the occasion, looking out over the auditorium. Breathtaking in its simplicity and empty except for three people, Walter Legge, Herr von Karajan, and Mother.

Karajan, worried about the acoustic, had asked Manoug Parikian to conduct the orchestra while he and Walter Legge listened. Manoug, a conductor *manqué*, was happy to oblige and started us off. From time to time I could hear the two men talking, particularly during soft passages. There was one section that seemed to be causing Karajan special concern and when we came to it, the voices of the two men became even more audible. This was, to be sure, no idle chatter but a serious debate about the problems of performing in an open-air theatre. More particularly the problem of playing softly, an absolute essential part of Karajan's conducting credo. String players spend many hours learning how to project a soft tone that will nevertheless carry. Often, however, the quality of the sound is sacrificed in an effort to satisfy the conductor's idea of an effective *pianissimo*. Karajan, determined as ever to achieve that rich velvety orchestral sound for which he was already famous, was becoming more and more agitated.

Mother, sitting bolt upright with her eyes tightly shut, was obviously enthralled by the magic of Jock's *pianissimo* in the section Karajan was trying to balance. As the orchestra pushed the limits of that pianissimo to the extreme the voices of the two men echoed loudly in the emptiness of the auditorium. Suddenly, a most compelling 'Sssh' startled everyone present, especially Karajan and Legge, who stopped talking at once. Manoug turned round and the orchestra stopped playing. Cringing with embarrassment, I nearly dropped my bow. It could only have been Mother!

CHAPTER TWENTY-TWO

Jock's Oboe Reeds

After the concerts at Les Baux and Aix the plan was that Jennifer Franklin would join our party. We would relax in the sun on a Mediterranean beach for a few days and then set off on the long drive to Lucerne, London and Edinburgh for the second half of the tour. On my advice she had bought a new Morris Minor Tourer and although she was rich enough to afford a new Alvis TA 14 the irony was that the deposit alone on her car would have stretched my resources to breaking point. Nevertheless, being Jennifer, she was tactful enough to make me believe that her real love would always be the Alvis.

As luck would have it the weather changed on the first day of our holiday and our hopes for days on the beach had to be abandoned. To pass the time we drove through the persistent drizzle to small seaside resorts around St Tropez, consoling ourselves with eating more delicious meals than perhaps we really needed.

In 1954, before the era of Brigitte Bardot, St Tropez was a quiet, lovely little village rather like Collioure near the Spanish border had been in 1949 when I was studying with Casals. Occasionally, when a change of scene and some exercise were necessary, some of his pupils would hire a car and drive there across beautiful mountain scenery. In as yet unspoilt surroundings, we would lie on the beach basking in the sun, enjoy an inexpensive *Plat du Jour* in the evening, and return to Prades to face another stint of practice. When I returned to Collioure in 1995 it had changed out of all recognition. The fishing boats had gone, the little restaurant had been rebuilt, and the workman's *Plat du Jour* had been replaced by an expensive *à la carte* menu.

At breakfast on the second day Jock mentioned that he wanted to buy a few bundles of locally grown oboe reed-cane that was apparently the answer to an oboist's prayer. Anxious to see as much as possible of Provence I offered to drive him to the other side of St Rémy to call on the supplier. By the time we arrived in the village the sun was out so Jock decided to complete the journey on foot. I was more than happy to wait for him in the shade of the tall plane trees that surrounded the village square. I settled back in the open car to watch the typical French mid-day ritual of bread-buying and apéritif-drinking.

After two hours, as Jock had still not returned, I decided to buy a freshly baked baguette, a bottle of wine, some cheese and tomatoes and a couple of tins of very small Norwegian sardines. More time passed and, as there was still no sign of Jock, I began nibbling at the bread and cheese. The bottle was then opened, to help the digestion, and in no time I had eaten and drunk everything. I managed to restock my *al fresco* larder in case Jock hadn't eaten, and this time, using the valance between the bonnet and the wings as table and the generous front bumper as seat, I sat down to my second meal. All was well without and within, especially within. Nothing clouded the peace and serenity of the moment.

Several hours later I woke to find Jock slumped across the rear seats of the car. Judging by the alcoholic haze that was wafting around in the stillness of the afternoon, he too had participated in the good life. He explained later that his host had offered him a local wine of such exceptional quality that it had somehow taken precedence over the business of the occasion. When he finally left, laden with bottles of this new-found elixir (and of course the reed-cane), he lost his way and was on the point of collapse by the time he found me. He had fallen asleep within seconds of settling down in the car.

A team of *boules* players who had gathered near the Alvis, and were no doubt attracted by the odd couple snoring within, came over to inspect more closely a car that was different from anything seen before in the village. It was soon clear that, for them, the 2CV or the indestructible and basic Citroën Light Fifteen was all that anybody could possibly wish for in the way of a motorcar. Renault had recently begun to re-think its design and marketing policy and the arrival of the Frégate in 1954 was certainly a step in the right direction, but neither the Frégate nor the inimitable Renault 8 could, in my opinion, compare with the Morris Minor. Meanwhile, the Alvis, already twenty years old, represented a totally different range of values to my newfound friends.

I tried to explain in halting French that a car was not necessarily just a car. Why should something on which Society places an increasing commercial value, and upon which social stability has come to depend to such a great extent, simply be regarded as a tool to be discarded and replaced without any kind of bond between the instrument, its maker and its owner? A car, like everything else man has created, remains inanimate until man himself injects the life force by turning a switch (quite often saying at the same time a little prayer). As I droned on my audience appeared to be lost in thought. One onlooker, whose command of English was much better than my French, wanted to know whether I thought that cars represented ethnic qualities. In other words, should France produce a car to suit French needs, while Germans, Swedes, Italians, and so on, followed suit. (At the time, neither the Soviets nor the Far East had yet entered the international car market.) Why, for example, did my car need two large P100 headlamps, four fog lamps, two spare wheels and vast quantities of high-grade chrome? Did this display of grandeur necessarily provide a more reliable, or a safer vehicle?

'So where does that leave my car?' I asked.

His silence, and that of the rest of the group, seemed to imply that rather than risk being impolite to a stranger it would be wiser to say nothing. Returning to more important matters the men drifted away to resume their game of boules. I did get the impression by the time Jock and I finally said our good-byes that one little boy (to judge by the look on his face) had come to accept the idea that a car should be something more than just a mechanical box on wheels.

We arrived back at St Tropez in time to enjoy a delicious farewell dinner at a little restaurant Felix had discovered, and the following morning our party set off on its journey to Lucerne. The weather was beautiful. The scenery was beautiful. The car was behaving even more beautifully. With the hood down we cruised comfortably along empty roads through one of the most glorious parts of France.

The occupants of the back seat of the car were fidgeting like a class of naughty school children. Thinking that the hotel must have presented them with a farewell present of bed bugs I pulled up at the side of the road to investigate. Everyone turned out their pockets, rolled up their trousers, and examined their coat sleeves but nobody could identify the culprits. Just as I was getting back into the driver's seat I saw a movement. A thin line of small black ants was moving between the bonnet and the rear seat of the car. They had that frenetic look which suggested that they were on to something good. I followed the line up to the front bumper and suddenly noticed a sticky patch and remembered the bread and sardines in rich olive oil. Some of the contents must have been spilled during my solitary lunch while I was waiting for Jock the previous day. With the help of a brush and scoop the ants were removed to a new home at the side of the road without too many casualties.

This was to be the last mishap on our journey of over 2,000 miles, apart from a slight over-heating problem halfway up the St Gotthard Pass. We reached Lucerne the next day, in some ways a little sad as the best part of the tour was now over.

While walking back to the hotel on the evening of the last concert in Lucerne I heard, through the open window of a house, a memorable performance of the Schumann Cello Concerto played, I learnt later, by André Navarra. Both he and Tortelier were orchestral players when I had first stayed in Paris in 1947 but had since made enormous strides as soloists in their respective careers. On this occasion, a live broadcast from somewhere in Switzerland, Navarra gave a performance that could not have been bettered. When it was over I continued my walk but by the time I had reached my hotel room memories that had lain dormant since 1949 had been re-awakened. I was to have studied the Schumann with Casals but my illness had made this impossible. Once again I felt uncertain about what lay ahead. If merely hearing a cello well played could be so unsettling was I ready for the responsibilities of marriage? I was unofficially engaged and could not possibly walk out on Annette, but I wondered whether perhaps we would be helping each other by delaying the marriage for a year. Navarra's performance of the Schumann that afternoon was to provide me with a source of inspiration for the rest of my life. At the concert that night Fournier played Strauss's Don Quixote with his usual refined artistry which further unsettled me. Even as I write this, nearly fifty years later, I can again feel the urge to make one more attempt to go back to the cello and try to master its repertoire.

On the return journey we drove through Ronchamp to see Courvoisier's Ark and stopped at Chartres to pay our respects to the Cathedral, a must for me every time I am near enough to make the detour.

Just before leaving Lucerne Felix informed Mother of his intention to marry. Since she had only a short while before received confirmation from Darrell that he too had decided to marry, this additional flight from the nest was very difficult for her to digest. In the space of just a few months her two eldest sons had broken the ties that had held and supported her since the time, in 1938, when she had first decided to move to England. At the time I marvelled at her control on receiving the news. Not once on the journey home did she refer to the uncertainties and loneliness that might possibly await her in the future. I now realise that Felix and I must have been very insensitive to her needs. We could easily have been more supportive in the little things that make life bearable.

The car had proved itself on the European trip and the weather promised to be kind so we decided to travel in style to Edinburgh. This time there would be no boat to catch and no dreamy oboe player oblivious to the imperative of punctuality. Having persuaded our two fiancées Ann and Annette to accompany us, Felix and I set off with the intention of meeting his future parents-in-law in Sheffield. The weather continued to be fine and after lunch with them we made good time up to Newcastle. We found ourselves on a newly constructed dual carriageway with very little traffic. After the roads in pre-autoroute France, driving under these conditions was bliss. There was no pavé to shake fuses out of their sockets and Felix, who was driving, could not resist the temptation of trying to reach the magic 'ton'—100 mph —and for just a few exhilarating seconds we luxuriated in the marvellous sensation that seems peculiar to fast travel in an open car.

Felix was just settling back to a cruising speed when he noticed a Ford Eight saloon ahead on the left. Suddenly without warning, and with no signal of any kind, the driver turned right. Felix hooted frantically and slammed on the brakes. The Ford continued to turn, still with no signal. Just before we hit it an arm appeared out of the window as if, belatedly, to correct any possible misunderstanding. It all happened so quickly and Felix had no time in which to take avoiding action. I saw the long bonnet of the Alvis plough into the side of the Ford, knocking it on its side. Steam rose in a dense cloud from the front of my beautiful car. My first thought was for the instruments: Felix's Guadagnini and my Testore. With a full load of petrol in the tank I was terrified that fire would engulf everything but mercifully nothing happened.

It was only after I had helped Annette out of the wreck and had carried the cello to safety, that I noticed the Ford lying on its side. The legs of one of the passengers were trapped by the running board and the victim must have been in terrible pain. I bent my legs and jammed my shoulders into the top corner of the car roof. Straightening my legs I managed to lever the Ford up far enough for the injured person and the other four occupants to be pulled to safety. The strain on my back must have been much greater than I was conscious of at the time because, very soon after the crash, I realised that my left side had become almost rigid.

The owner of the Ford, covered with blankets, lay on the grass verge waiting for an ambulance. Meanwhile Felix, looking stunned and very white, was trying to calm a very frightened Ann.

Obviously, the driver of the Ford had been in the wrong. If he wanted to make a U-turn at such short notice, he should have moved over to the correct lane when the road was clear after Felix had passed. He must either have had no sense of distance, or else he had just not bothered to look in the mirror. Had Felix swerved, he would certainly have hit the Ford's door area and, instead of the occupants being dazed and shocked, they might well have been killed.

Hugh Bean and several other members of the orchestra arrived on the scene shortly afterwards and took Felix and Ann on to Edinburgh. Annette and I had to stay behind in order to make the necessary statements to the police and to arrange for the car to be taken away. Later that night we were able to hitch a lift in the cramped cabin of a lorry travelling to Edinburgh.

By the next day the pain in my left arm was so bad that I could not play at the concert, and I was advised to return to London by train in order to seek medical advice. For years to come I was in and out of hospital, living on painkillers, unable to drive and walking around each day as if there were sand in my eyes. I was in a state of constant depression and could find no permanent relief however many doctors I consulted. Was this the result of the accident or had the crash merely triggered off an already existing condition?

Annette and I were married at St Luke's Church, Chelsea in 1954 and, inspired by Jerome K. Jerome's book *Three Men in a Boat*, we decided to take our honeymoon on the Thames in a motor cruiser. On the return trip, between Chertsey and Oxford, I was to discover an interest in some of the more improbable aspects of History. Until then I had accepted recorded historical fact as a basis for certainty, but reading some of the books Annette had brought on the trip made me realise just how fact and fiction are paraded as truth by slanting the evidence. She had worked in the War Office for several years and had been a silent witness, bound by the Official Secrets Act, to countless examples of her employers' wilful distortion of fact as part of war propaganda.

We hoped that the rest would restore me to health and vigour but in the months that followed no doctor ever connected the unremitting pain I was suffering with the damage I must have done myself by lifting the car after the accident. The injury was to take many years to heal. If I had known then what I know today about the problems of psyche I feel sure that I would have been able to adapt sufficiently to meet Annette's needs. As things were, the harder I tried to understand what was happening to me the worse matters became. Also the actual physical act of playing the cello was so painful that I was rapidly losing contact with the world of professional music. I began to question other people's values because I could no longer maintain my own. Annette was totally supportive, but like everyone else, she had no solution to offer.

After Darrell, Felix and I had married, the house in Holland Park was altered by common family consent into four flats. Annette and I decided to make a complete break with London by letting our flat and living in the country. We were fortunate, or so we thought, to find an old farm cottage in Wadenhoe in

Northamptonshire, but on arrival we discovered that our dream home was cold, damp and very dirty. By the time we had cleaned, dried and heated it my fibrositis, rheumatism, muscular pain or whatever it was, had worsened to an alarming degree and it began to look as if the whole plan was doomed.

One cold miserable day in February 1955 I again thought about Prades. The warmth and the smell of Spring, the towering, snow-capped peak of Canigou and the beautiful scenery of the Golden Valley between Prades and Perpignan. Should I really accept the fact that I did not want to spend the rest of my life playing in an orchestra without a spiritual home? I remembered my last lesson in 1949 with *Le Maître*. Would he help me again? It was certainly worth trying. In any case it would be cheaper to live in France.

Having for many years sat on the first desk of the Philharmonia, I had initially assumed that the standards demanded of a principal applied, more or less, throughout the whole section. When I began playing on the last desk in 1953, I soon realised that this had been a misconception. It was not until the concerts in Lucerne in the summer of 1955 that I was able, because of the orchestral layout plus the acoustic in the hall, to hear the orchestra from this new perspective. I was very disappointed by what I heard, an undisciplined and ragged quality in the back desks. This was not a consequence of insufficient training and talent but because of the refusal by some players to be serious about the need for discipline during rehearsals, which inevitably led to unnecessary mistakes in the performance.

On the first desk, you are very conscious of the conductor's charisma, assuming of course that the figure in front of you is a Karajan and not just an embarrassing lightweight. There are also conductors who can energise players into a higher degree of attainment. For players at the back of the cello section it is much more difficult to pick up the electric charge without which no 'spark' can be created. In spite of this greater distance I was still able to be inspired even though the energising impulse was less concentrated.

A rather idiosyncratic deputy called Jem Marchant became a good friend during the last three years I played in the Philharmonia. Jem had first met Manoug Parikian soon after the latter's arrival in England from Cyprus in 1947. Like all of us he had been tremendously impressed by Manoug's playing and persuaded him to use the Philharmonia as a stepping stone in his career. Jem was a reasonably competent cellist, but his dreamy, all-forgiving philosophy did have its problematical sides.

On the first rest-day at the 1955 Lucerne Festival members were invited to visit a local beauty spot that could only be reached by funicular railway. We were shepherded into the cabins and I found myself sitting opposite a viola player called Muriel, while Jem ensconced himself in the corner next to her. She was obviously very nervous, and her colleague, an excitable Italian widow called Norina Semino, did her best to allay Muriel's fears. Suddenly the car stopped. Jem chose this moment to light his pipe and his choice of tobacco did not endear him to Norina. Sensing her disapproval he got up, rocking the car slightly in the process, and opened a window. The resulting sway, slight as it was, nevertheless broke down all barriers of self-restraint on the part the ladies. Irritation had almost turned into anger when a mournful pair of eyes appeared at the car window and viewed the occupants with the bovine equivalent of Jem's normal expression. Jem took his pipe out of his mouth.

'Hello Muriel!' he said to the cow, in a tone of genuine delight.

Knowing him as I did I was certain there was no hidden meaning implied in this friendly greeting, but the ladies thought otherwise and verbal abuse almost degenerated into physical assault.

On another occasion in the London Festival Hall Jem and I were dozing through a very boring performance of a choral work. It had been decided that a recitative and aria should be accompanied by only one cello so we were looking forward to a short rest. Maurice Westerby, who was on trial for the position of sub-principal, began the recitative and it was soon evident that he was nervous. My reaction to anxiety in others is to close my eyes, but Jem's was to light up.

'Jem!' I whispered. 'What the hell are you doing?'

He came to with a start and dropped both pipe and tobacco pouch on the floor of the platform. Remembering my first meeting with Klemperer I was determined not to react, but unfortunately Jem started the rot and we both laughed. Maurice must have thought that we were laughing at him and, although Jem was unworried by the situation he had thoughtlessly created, I felt very uncomfortable.

Following this incident Walter Legge asked me to return to the front desk after my days in the wilderness, but I had just agreed with Casals that I should go back to Prades. I simply could not forget the lovely sound of water trickling down from Canigou to feed the rich earth every morning. I remembered the smells of the place - the fresh bread, the new potatoes, asparagus, peaches, the delicious Muscat bought in very persuasive three-litre containers. What had strike-ridden London and its conflicts to offer as a viable alternative?

Annette too was struggling. Greedy people, at the competitive edge of the rag trade, were never satisfied. They expected hand-made clothes to retail at discount prices and always complained if there were delays. She had become interested in natural dyes, and thought that a year or so spent in France would enable her to gather enough information to form the basis of a book she wanted to write. I wrote to Casals to discuss possible dates for my lessons. He gave an encouraging reply, and the decision was made. We would go to France.

For reasons of economy I had wanted to buy a Morris Minor van, but however practical the idea may have seemed, driving

through France in an un-soundproofed buzz-box was not
something to look forward to. Perhaps the fact that I had just
discovered an 11.9 Alvis Firefly Saloon was the reason for a
dissatisfaction with contemporary car design that was now
crystallizing into downright aversion. Or was it rather that one
cost £75 and the other over £500? I bought the Firefly. For once it
proved to be the right decision.

CHAPTER TWENTY-THREE

Herr von Karajan and Peter Gibbs

Standing with Dennis Brain at the bar of a converted Liberator bomber *en route* to Boston in 1955, I was totally captivated by Karajan's enthusiasm for life, music, fast sports cars, flying and sailing. On that memorable night he talked about his hobbies in a way that was to make what followed ten days later doubly sad for Dennis and me, especially after what we believed to have been a new-found rapport.

The following morning, standing at the top of the steps into the aircraft, we heard him handle a hostile press with enormous skill, evidence of another undetected talent. While we were forced to remain in a hot, cramped, smelly, smoke-filled aircraft, longing to get out and stretch stiff and tired joints, Karajan took his time as he faced his adversaries. He seemed to be in his element as he replied carefully and courteously to obviously loaded questions about his future as a possible successor to Furtwängler in Berlin. He used every one of the arts we had come to know, stutter included, to demolish irrelevant and spurious questions.

Officially Karajan had agreed to conduct the Philharmonia on a two-week tour centred round Boston to boost record sales. Unofficially, as we were to learn later, he wanted to impress members of the Berlin Philharmonic Orchestra with the prospect of joining the world-wide recording bandwagon with the help of Walter Legge. It was however strange to hear him dealing with inane questions about his private preferences that apparently interested readers, especially after the hours of delightful, well-informed conversation Dennis and I had just had with him on similar topics. A few reporters had sensible queries, but I couldn't

Philharmonia Orchestra's 10th Anniversary celebrations in New York 1955. Left to right: Herbert von Karajan, Marie Wilson, Jane Withers, Walter Legge.

help thinking how much more insight into his character would have been revealed by a report of our conversation the previous night. Readers would have learnt about Karajan the car enthusiast who had recently test-driven an Austin Atlantic and a Kharmenn Ghia. Karajan who had spoken convincingly about his preference for the VW to the Austin. Karajan the always curious driving enthusiast, anxious to compare Ford's latest sports model, the Mustang, with English and European cars of similar pedigree.

During the flight Dennis and I had been particularly interested to learn how post-war Germany was coping with the rebuilding of its car industry. But Karajan had also mentioned that he intended to see how cars were put together in America, adding that he had

10th Anniversary Celebrations. Front row Left to Right:
J. Edward Merrett, Herbert Downes, Renata Scheffel-Stein,
Gareth Morris, Walter Legge, Jane Withers, Manoug Parikian.

already suggested to the management that those members of the orchestra who were interested, could visit the Ford factory in Detroit. Other topics of conversation had included developments in the quality of fuels, improvements in the design of car suspension relative to tyre safety, better brake and engine reliability and many other aspects of car ownership. To have had the opportunity to talk to a musician of such eminence and then be obliged to hear him waste his time (and ours) dealing with reporters who were intent on trying to trip him up on trivia, irritated us as much as it must have irritated Karajan. He had been amused to hear about the game Dennis and I played—guessing the make of a car by the sound of its engine. Until a few years ago this used to be possible but now, because post-war manufacturers use standardised, inter-changeable engine components to maximise profits, all car engines sound the same.

'In Britain,' he said, 'there have always been many models to choose from, but it was never so in Europe, even before the war. You still have more car manufacturers than we ever had in Germany.'

Dennis and I began to count up the names of England's post-war car manufacturers. We soon realised that the pre-World War Two old-faithfuls such as Singer, Humber, Riley, MG, Hillman, Jowett and Sunbeam had become, by the mid-fifties, nothing more than variations of standard suspension design, engine specification, interior trim and a tawdry badge. Exorbitant taxation by Government and the determination by car manufacturers to rationalise Britain's post-war motor industry as a means of survival, had changed the scenario radically.

'If there were only a few basic models before the war,' I said, 'it would seem to follow that car manufacturers in Germany today would not have to rationalise the industry to the same extent as in England. But you did have the famous 1939 BMW that became a legend, just like my 1934 Alvis Speed Twenty Tourer.'

Karajan had never heard of an Alvis until he had driven my Speed Twenty the year before, but he had been too polite to admit it at the time. He had been sad to learn about the accident but hadn't realised that the car was being re-built.

'Who makes this car?' he asked.

I explained that the car was made in Coventry, and that the factory also manufactured the famous Leonides aircraft engine and the Saracen Scout car.

'But is the owner of the factory called *Alvis*? I have never heard the name Alvis, before.'

'The name *Alvis* comes from two words: *Al* from aluminium and *vis* from the Latin word for strength.'

As professional musicians we had little real knowledge of the mechanics of motorcar manufacture and maintenance. Nevertheless we were very committed to two things: better roads and improved speed and road-holding qualities. Of course both Dennis and Karajan could better afford to indulge their whims. I could only talk.

Neither Dennis nor I could explain our continued preference for pre-war cars. For me a new temptation had appeared just the year before in the shape of the latest Alvis Drop-Head TA14. It was not particularly lovely to look at, by Alvis standards, but its chief virtue was that it was very reliable. It provided passengers with a smooth ride, and above all, was not too large for London's growing traffic problems. These were important considerations since the question I needed to answer in 1955 was whether I should abandon my loyalty to pre-war cars and surrender to contemporary values in the shape of an Alvis drop-head. Dennis was driving a big Citroën and seemed content. For Karajan it was so simple—he just bought whatever he liked, when he liked.

At our first concert in Boston we were performing Strauss's *Don Juan* and had just reached one of those moments in the work where I would have expected Karajan to have his eyes tight shut in concentration, where Nemesis was confronting the seducer. Just for a few seconds he half-opened his eyes and in the fleeting look I saw him give the orchestra he revealed *his* image of an elemental and tortured soul. This was far removed from the players' more passive, extrovert concept of a non-repentant culprit having to confront retribution. Music can mean different things to different people, and that had never been demonstrated to me more clearly.

I was being elevated to a state bordering on hypnosis by the music, by the magic of the occasion, and by Karajan's determination to achieve a sensuous beauty of sound and compelling melodic line. In that fleeting glance, however, I felt that I had caught a look of intense disdain bordering on contempt.

It was a look that had not been there when we were talking for all those hours during the flight from England.

Had he now, from the very first chord in this tone poem, envisaged the role of a man after his own heart, in his mind's eye? A man who would never capitulate, even if he himself, like Don Juan, were compelled to confront the grim menace of the dreaded Commendatore? Was he wondering whether we were on his side or had chosen to side with approaching Nemesis? The look in his eyes that night convinced me that Karajan would never be afraid to stand his ground. A man apparently determined to remain at arm's length from his fellow men. I knew I would capitulate again and again to the magic of his music-making, but the ice cold look in his eyes is what inevitably springs to mind whenever I think back on *Don Juan*.

I had seen a softer version of that same look a year before when, rehearsing for a concert at the Kingsway Hall, he had complained to Raymond Clark about a drop in dynamic at a crucial moment. Trying to help, I had pointed out that only half the cello section was playing while the other half was turning the page. Karajan ignored my contribution. My remark wasn't considered worthy of even a token acknowledgement.

The concerts had gone well so far and there were only two more to do, one in a small town near Boston and the last one in Boston itself. As always, Karajan's behaviour had been scrupulously correct on the tour. There had been no untoward incidents and everyone had been reasonably happy and content.

During the second half of the penultimate concert the Maestro's behaviour suddenly changed. He didn't seem to care. Our performance became slipshod and no better than second rate Sunday Specials at Southend. We were forced to follow him in altered interpretations of the pieces we had rehearsed so methodically. Admittedly everyone was tired, Karajan included, but after the interval he suddenly appeared to be completely lack-lustre. He was unmoved by the spirit of an attentive and gracious audience and rushed from one item to the next in such a way as to embarrass even the players, who were never over-keen to prolong a concert and miss the chance of a drink before closing-time.

After the final item Karajan left the platform. Normally he would return and we would rise at a nod from Manoug. Karajan would then acknowledge our contribution and we would sit down again after he had left the platform, and so on. On this occasion we waited for several minutes but no conductor appeared. Several more minutes passed but still no Karajan. By this time the audience's response was beginning to flag and word was passed round the orchestra that we must leave the platform as quietly and quickly as possible. Apparently Karajan had already left the building. Manoug was justifiably furious and refused to return to the platform without him, so the orchestra had no alternative but to leave as well.

While travelling back to Boston in the coach we discussed the events of the evening in some depth. Clem Relf, the orchestral librarian, told me that Karajan had received a telephone call during the interval. When Clem went to call him for the second half of the concert, Karajan seemed like a man transformed. Most of the players believed that Karajan was merely paying them back in their own coin and had given them tit for tat because of the events in Linz the year before, but having heard what Clem had to say, I suspected that there was much more to this than met the eye.

It was the day of the last concert. I imagined that tempers would have cooled overnight, but when the orchestra assembled for a seating rehearsal in the late afternoon, I realised that the anger of the players had been merely simmering, ready to boil over at any moment. Suddenly, a voice from the back of the second violins made itself heard above the general hum, asking for permission to address a few words to the conductor. Karajan, standing on the podium, was dressed in his usual black outfit, with sleeves pulled back and watch upside down.

'Of course,' he said, in a matter-of-fact tone.

I knew immediately that the voice in the second violins belonged to my friend Peter Gibbs. He was not only a fine violinist but was very well spoken, widely read, and able to converse in several languages on a wide range of subjects. He was a natural loner but could be, when in the mood, a disarmingly engaging companion. On this occasion, however, his mood was not friendly.

'Herr von Karajan, I feel it to be my duty to remind you that conductor and orchestra have a collective obligation to show appreciation to an audience for its applause. This is a question of civilised standards, one might almost say of Right and Wrong. Last night your conduct was not only *wrong*, it was *uncalled for*. Many members of the Philharmonia wish to place on record that someone so blatantly ill-mannered as you were last night, should not be permitted to conduct this orchestra in future.'

I glanced up at Karajan. He stood silent and absolutely motionless, almost as if some well-deserved eulogy was being delivered.

Peter paused for a moment but was possibly encouraged to continue by certain members of the orchestra who began to shuffle their feet, tap bows on stands or murmur agreement. When his lecture began to develop into a political diatribe, with particular reference to World War Two, the mood of the orchestra began to waver. After all there was a job to be done, and Karajan was good for business. Sensing the division, Karajan turned to those who were seated nearest to him.

'Who is this man?' he muttered in a half-tone.

Manoug rose to his feet and asked Peter to let the rehearsal proceed. Peter did not stop speaking at once, but eventually he sat down to a round of uncertain applause, after which there was a moment of silence. Then, as if nothing had happened, Karajan asked us to play a section from *Don Juan* for balance. One way or another the rehearsal was completed and we went back to our hotels and thought no more about the afternoon's events.

At 8pm we assembled on the platform for the last concert of the tour—always an occasion with a special flavour of its own. Manoug Parikian appeared, took the applause and turned to the oboist. The orchestra tuned and he sat down. We waited for the conductor to appear.

Five minutes passed. Out of sheer embarrassment some of the woodwind players began to warm up their instruments again, but there was still no conductor. At a signal from the Orchestral Manager Manoug left his seat and walked off the stage, leaving the rest of us in suspense. A few moments later, word was passed round the cello section that Karajan had insisted that the orchestra should dissociate itself from the remarks made that afternoon by Peter Gibbs. Furthermore, we would be required to sign an individual written apology during the interval. Finally, Peter Gibbs was to be barred from the performance that night and from any future engagements with Karajan. Without these agreements there would be no concert.

By organising the promise of a collective apology so that the concert could proceed, the management succeeded in smoothing things over. We gave the concert and returned to England the next day. This time there was no Karajan to talk to. The document containing the apology was presented to the orchestra shortly afterwards at the Kingsway Hall, but most of the players, myself included, refused to sign.

Thirty-four years after the sad end of that American tour I read a biography of Schwarzkopf and found out that my instinctive feeling had been right, when Clem Relf told me about that telephone call in the interval. It appears that, two days before the end of the tour, Karajan's appointments to Berlin and Vienna had been confirmed. From then on these two orchestras, together with his work in Salzburg and his vast recording commitment, were to become the foundation on which Karajan would build his empire. He had no further use for the Philharmonia.

CHAPTER TWENTY-FOUR

The Second Firefly, the Mercedes and Karajan

Of the twelve Alvis models I was privileged to own while playing in the Philharmonia, my second little Alvis Firefly, with its enormously strong chassis and bumpers, provided more than adequate protection for its occupants.

The dictionary describes a firefly as a 'small luminous winged insect', a definition that somewhat contradicts the car's sturdy appearance. Luminous or not, my latest Alvis acquisition gave me more than two years of safe and untroubled continental motoring, apart from one irritating breakdown.

Without power steering it was admittedly heavy to handle when parking, but once it was moving, the steering was light, responsive and positive. Its Wilson pre-selector gearbox made light work of driving in heavy traffic, and although contemporary car designers would shudder at the power required to propel a vehicle built to such wide margins of safety, its fuel consumption was nevertheless reasonable. Beautifully balanced, with grace and pace and ample boot space it was the easiest of cars to drive.

Annette and I set off in April 1955 on a tour of France, Italy and Switzerland, and by the time we returned, eighteen months later, the Alvis had covered over three thousand miles. We motored in a leisurely way down the west side of France, visiting Rouen and Le Mans with its memories of Stirling Moss, Mike Appleyard, and the famous Jaguar victories of the 1950s. Then we turned South-west to Nantes (the centre of my Huguenot ancestors' 'hope, despair, and ultimate demise as a cultural unit in Europe') and then back again in an easterly direction to Poitiers, at the particular insistence of Annette.

We visited several châteaux, and I learnt about some of the famous people who had lived, plotted and died in these amazing architectural wonders. I learnt with especial interest about Catherine de Medici, Diane de Poitiers, and the saga of Chenonceaux.

Catherine de Medici, Mother, Monarch and Mistress, needed Chenonceaux as the setting for the power struggle on behalf of her sons. In this outwardly enchanting building, with the elegance of French medieval architecture at its best, she planned the assassination of all those who opposed her. Chenonceaux had also been the home of Diane de Poitiers until the early and unexpected death of her husband, one of Catherine's sons. Diane was reputedly the most beautiful woman of her time but, unfortunately for her, the ambitious Catherine had other plans for her son's mistress. She was driven from her home and instructed to spend the rest of her life at Chaumont, further along the Loire.

Annette and I spent the afternoon wandering around Chaumont. To live in such a lovely building, situated in a commanding setting, did not seem to me to be a very great hardship, but the 'philosopher's brow' in Diane's portrait hinted that she would probably have been content wherever she had to live. Diane loved a man but lost him twice. First to another woman and then, either by accident or assassination made to look like an accident. Thereafter she was at the mercy of Catherine and yet, housed in a château of incomparable beauty, she was nevertheless able to live out her days in peace and security.

We visited Orléans and Blois, where Mary Queen of Scots witnessed the execution of Huguenots on her wedding night. It was also where, because nobody was willing to prepare 'the old goat' for her final journey, Catherine de Medici lay for three days unattended on her deathbed.

We motored on to the wonderful Romanesque Church at Angoulême, followed by enchanting towns like Perigueux,

Bergerac, Souillac and Sarlat—home of Etienne de la Boétie, friend of Montaigne. We saw the house where, in the 1550s, the two young men discussed religious prejudice, intolerance, and all forms of bigotry that dictated the murder and mayhem imposed, in Democracy's secular society, at the end of the millennium.

We spent the night near Albi, in an old town nearby called Villefranche. We visited the great red brick monument to a Protestant God at Albi, and then set off for Carcassonne.

At about 11.30 we stopped, and having bought some of the local sausage—a delicious reminder of the *Boerewors* my father used to make—Annette soon had the primus going while I went about the car, tightening up bolts and screws. French roads were still fairly tough on tyres and suspension, and it was better to be safe than sorry.

While looking at the engine, I noticed that the inlet to the SU carburettor was weeping very slightly. I tightened up the large brass nut but stripped the thread in the process, causing petrol to pour down onto the exhaust manifold that was still quite hot. I managed to stop the flow temporarily with a rag, and then I turned off the petrol tap. How was I to replace a hexagonal brass nut turned in England in 1933? Should we abandon the car until I could have a replacement sent out? What was I to do?

Annette suggested we should have breakfast, and then decide. The meal she prepared, savoured in the shade of a gently sighing plane tree, was a great success, then Annette suggested that I should take the entire carburettor assembly to a local garage and ask for help.

I hitched a lift into nearby Réalmont and found a small garage. Using mostly sign language, I explained the problem. The mechanic took the nut and rummaged around in a heap of discarded bits and pieces and found an old Zenith carburettor. The brass inlet nut looked vaguely similar to mine and, after working on it for a few minutes in his vice, he handed it to me.

He wouldn't take any money and more or less told me to get lost. I was a little taken aback but when in later years I began reading Asterix books to my children I recognised at once that gruff generosity that seems so characteristic of the French working class.

I set off on my walk back to the Alvis, a distance of about ten miles, but just a few minutes later a Peugeot 403 stopped and the driver offered me a lift. I accepted gladly but within seconds I wished I hadn't. The man was a Fernandel-type character whose wife had apparently nagged him into accepting a job as a commercial traveller. He had always wanted to be a farmer, but by 1955 there was no more money in farming and so, '*avec les gosses et cette femme acariâtre* ...' He shrugged his shoulders.

Every time we nearly collided with an oncoming vehicle, usually just before a bend in the road, he would throw his hands into the air with a despairing gesture.

'*Eh bien, monsieur, que voulez-vous?*'

He would sigh, and then put his hands back on the wheel just in time to stave off another impending disaster.

Just as we reached a crossroads a lorry suddenly careered past, apparently out of control.

'*Zut alors!*' my driver muttered in surprise.

Braking hard in the middle of the bend, he skidded onto the verge. Fortunately the skid didn't end in the ditch and once back on the road he immediately picked up speed, proceeding in a kind of gentle slalom on our way back to Annette. I was now in something of a panic. I had visions of Annette visiting me in hospital, or having to identify me in the local morgue, still clutching the precious brass nut.

I tried to tell him in broken French of a salutary cartoon I had once seen in *Punch*. Two cars were racing towards each other in thick fog, both drivers concentrating on the cat's eyes in the middle of the road. Both were saying cheerily to their passengers just before the predictable collision, 'What a boon these cat's eyes are!' The point of the story did not seem to sink in. By the time I eventually spotted Annette sitting under a tree, calmly reading a book, I was almost speechless. She suggested we should all have some coffee but my *voyageur de commerce* declined, explaining that he had a very tight schedule that day.

Apart from a few rough edges I had to file down, the brass union was a perfect fit. From then on neither the car nor the carburettor gave any more trouble.

Prades in 1955 was not so very different from what it had been during my first visit in 1949. The town itself had not changed, although what came to be called the Prades Festival was already well on the way to achieving the status of an international institution. Serkin, Horsowski, Wallfisch, Menuhin, Szigeti, Curzon, to name only a few of the international set, were to play in performances of chamber music at venues in the little town, and I was lucky enough to be given the job of either doorman or page-turner. I was warned that so-called friends of *Le Maître* were using his name to gate-crash the concerts. True to type, well-known personalities from London's circle of music lovers had told me that Casals had given them permission to enter at the stage door. When I mentioned this to *Le Maître*, the uncomprehending look on his face told its own story.

Within a few weeks I was outwardly more self-assured than I had ever been, but nevertheless there was still the apparently insoluble problem of my arm and back. I had arrived in Prades in the hope that Casals, Prades itself and driving an old Alvis in the foothills of the Pyrenees would provide a cure for my aches and pains, but it was not to be. They got steadily worse and it was a very distressing period.

To this day I cannot understand the medical mind. When I told my doctor several months before that my back ached, he advised me to take some exercise, preferably a daily swim. When I complained about my shoulder the answer was that the pain was psychosomatic. It would go away once I had sorted out the mental problems that were causing it. When it didn't, I was eventually told to attend at St Stephen's Hospital, Fulham, where for several weeks I was given injections in a physical rehabilitation ward. When this too failed, I was accused of being work-shy, and it was even suggested that I was jealous of Felix.

Normal medical treatment was proving to be a failure but nevertheless, I learnt things from my stay in hospital that were to influence me profoundly over the following few years. Not only did I begin to read books again but there was the salutary effect of watching other patients coping with illness, particularly if that illness proved to be terminal.

Next to me was a young man whose calm acceptance of approaching death terrified me. It was quite obvious that he was in complete control of his life even though his illness had made him so dependent on others. What made it so particularly poignant was that I had just finished reading a biography of Heinrich Heine. The knowledge that both Heine and the young man had the same disease was numbing. It was another turning point for me to meet someone whose life-span was measured only in weeks or months, but who nevertheless still wanted to talk about tyranny, injustice, exploitation. This young man was a captive, but his mind was liberated.

'Live with what is available' he said, 'and try to find answers for what is desirable even if it appears to be out of reach.'

He tried to teach me chess but inevitably he would win and I would be shown, yet again, that one must think unemotionally if one wants to learn what one can be emotional about.

When I went for my first lesson with *Le Maître* in 1955, he was kind and attentive, but it was soon apparent that my condition perplexed him as much as it did the doctors in London. He spent a great deal of time trying to adjust my right arm to what he considered to be the correct angle, but nothing really took away the pain. We then developed a method of working in which he would first go through part of the cello repertoire. I would then play what I could, and finger and bow those parts I couldn't. As a result I was able, during the eighteen months I was in Prades, either to study, or at least to play through, a major part of the solo cello works which up to that time I had found too daunting even to look at. We didn't only study repertoire; Casals was very insistent that I should practise scales and bowing exercises as well.

Pablo Casals

Musically, it was an exhilarating experience, but I lost a great deal of weight and my body ached as if I were having another bout of rheumatic fever. I must have been an appalling companion for Annette. She spent her days gathering and analysing samples of lichen about which she would then make copious notes. We lived separate lives, occasionally meeting in some peripheral involvement, but music certainly did not provide a bridge. There were no obvious links between our various spheres of study. Perhaps she didn't really believe that I was in trouble but merely hoped that I would eventually come to my senses.

One shared experience gave us both a great deal of joy. We were able to rescue a *chien de chasse*, bred to hunt wild boar. We called him Fellagha, although the name didn't go down too well with the local inhabitants, most especially those who had returned from Algeria and whose attitude towards Arabs didn't match our affection for the dog. He must have been a pedigree hound but was apparently gun-shy. For that reason he was, we were told, of no use to amateur hunters in the Aude district. He was unceremoniously abandoned in the street outside the hotel in Prades.

We had been to see the film *Lady Chatterley's Lover* and had stumbled across the dog in the hallway leading to our apartment. I thought he was one of the many hungry dogs that seemed to materialise from nowhere when rubbish was due to be collected. He had an uncanny way of waiting for the bin to be knocked over by the biggest dog and then, while it was rolling around and the big dog was busy defending his patch, Fellagha would dart in and fetch out some juicy morsel.

We made friends and he was smuggled up the stairs that night without the knowledge of the concierge. We had been warned to keep his presence a secret because the lady in charge of the building was very fierce about tenants having pets in their rooms. The first few weeks of his convalescence were therefore fraught with danger. Occasionally we would take him in the Firefly into the hills to help us look for lichens. He loved this and would lay his muzzle on the back of the seat, peering at us with large brown eyes full of interest, his ears flapping all over his face.

Apart from minor involvements, Annette and I were not really benefiting from our stay in Prades. My silences were certainly the result of my physical condition but I began to realise that I had been mistaken in assuming that marriage, of itself, would solve problems of communication. Love and mutual respect were there but the seeds of support and expectation had not taken root. I decided to discontinue the lessons before the Prades Festival started in 1956 and see whether exercising my body in other ways would help my aching back and shoulder.

I worked on the Alvis with a view to softening the suspension a little, and by way of experiment I took a couple of leaves out of the front springs. I did this work in the road that led to the public baths —not to be confused with swimming baths—and it was quite interesting to see who went for a bath, how often and with whom. It soon became obvious that the person in whose company one visited the baths was not always the same person one appeared with at the Festival concerts.

Turning pages for the pianists at rehearsals and performances was a fascinating experience but not one that would help me make progress as a cellist, although I was still seeing Casals every day. Another of my tasks was to act as unofficial chauffeur for some of the artists and I can remember to this day the look on the face of *Le Maître* when he saw the Firefly for the first time. I once asked him if he liked my Firefly, going on to explain that the name was not just an extravagance on my part, it was so called because... I suddenly realised that I had not the least idea why the car was in fact called a Firefly. Casals, courteous and considerate as ever, remained silent for a while, puffing at his pipe.

'Firefly,' he said, and then repeated the word softly.

'Firefly. It is such a big car for so small an insect. But perhaps to you it is just as beautiful?'

He looked at me with a twinkle in his eye.

Walter Legge suggested that I re-join the orchestra, still on the back desk, in time to participate in the 1956 Lucerne Festival.

'Just to ensure we have an engine at either end,' he explained. I thought it an interesting idea at the time and so did British Rail, thirty years later. Walter Legge was always ahead of his time.

Having now spent over a year working on basic technical problems it was going to be very interesting to see what sort of condition I would be in when I returned to the Philharmonia.

Annette, Fellagha and I set off on the journey from Prades, through Languedoc, over the Basses Alpes, crossing northern Italy into Switzerland. The Alvis was no trouble, and our arrival in the car park of the Concert Hall in Lucerne was greeted by my colleagues with the usual amused comments. My appetite for Alvis cars was already something of a joke in the profession but the sight of Fellagha, sitting next to the cello in the back seat, proved to be an unexpected surprise.

He had not been altogether happy at the start of the journey. Because of the many excursions in search of lichens on which he had accompanied us, he must have come to assume that the entire back seat was reserved for his sole occupation, and was rather put out when he realised, on the morning we left for Lucerne, that he had to share his pad with a cello. It took several days for him to accept the presence of this bulky object, and it wasn't until I tried putting the case directly behind me, thus allowing him an unimpeded view of oncoming traffic over Annette's head, that his normal sad-happy nature began to reassert itself. By the time we arrived in Lucerne he was so well-trained that he would automatically sit on his side, even if the cello case wasn't obstructing his view.

Dennis told me that Karajan's latest toy was a gull-winged Mercedes and, sure enough, soon after Annette and I arrived at the Hall in the morning for the first rehearsal, Karajan drove up in this silver car-of-the-future. He very kindly 'walked' the orchestra through the first half of the morning's schedule well ahead of time. We were naturally happy to co-operate, but there had to be a reason; with Karajan, nothing was for nothing. The answer came at the tea-break.

Karajan was overheard asking Dennis if he would like to drive the latest acquisition, and within minutes, most of the orchestra's car enthusiasts emerged from the various cafés around the hall, eager to witness the spectacle. Dennis and Karajan arrived, seemingly unaware that they were being observed, apparently deep in car-speak. They climbed into the Mercedes, and closed what looked like the cockpit covers of a fighter aircraft. Karajan pressed the starter. Nothing happened. He tried again. Still nothing happened.

Soon most of the other players came to join us. We saw before us an animated Karajan, a Karajan nobody had previously been permitted to see. As with most car enthusiasts in those early days, he must have realised that 'The one you love can sometimes be the one you hate!' (until the engine fires of course, and then all is forgiven). Instead of leaving the petrol to evaporate from the carburettor he betrayed an amateur's impatience by keeping his finger on the starter. This sucked an excessive amount of neat fuel into the dormant engine. Dennis was looking very uncomfortable.

The situation was richly ironic. One of the most relaxed and distinguished individuals in the profession was struggling to start a car, and getting very hot under the collar in the process. His distinguished companion, normally equally relaxed was also looking agitated.

Suddenly the cockpit covers were raised and two flushed faces emerged. Karajan leapt out, jerked the bonnet open and stared at the engine with an expression of total incomprehension. I went over and stood beside him and could see immediately why this cool and calculating man was at a loss. Just as the body design was not for the everyday driver, so was this no ordinary engine. It was one of the most sophisticated pieces of machinery I had ever seen. By now most of the players were crowding round the car and advice was being offered from all quarters. Jim Merritt helpfully suggested using a flint and Karajan asked him to explain.

'An English joke,' he mumbled.

Karajan was now not in the best of moods and unable to imagine how a grown man could be so naïve. Dennis meanwhile was reading the instruction manual, which is something even great Maestros have to do as a last resort. He peered over the cockpit rim.

'Herr von Karajan, could you please translate this section? My German isn't up to it.' Karajan took the book.

'It says that when you start the engine from cold during the day you should kick down the accelerator and not use the choke. Perhaps we had better do what the book tells us.'

He climbed back into the cockpit, with the merest suggestion of a smile on his face, closed the cover and prepared once more to start the mighty engine. We waited. We could see Dennis drawing his attention to something else in the manual but the Maestro was too impatient.

Unused fuel had obviously evaporated during the few minutes that had elapsed and suddenly the engine sprang into life. An enormous cloud of black smoke billowed from the two exhausts, completely enveloping the onlookers. The machine shot forward without warning and I had a fleeting glimpse of Karajan grappling with an unexpected G force as he took the right turn out of the square on two wheels. He must have jabbed the accelerator a little too aggressively, and the car, now fully alive to the demands and character of its driver, had responded generously. Twenty minutes later Dennis, white-faced and silent returned to take his seat in the orchestra. Neill Sanders leant over and said something to Dennis who just shook his head. At that moment Karajan appeared exactly as he always did; suave and aloof as if nothing had occurred.

Dennis told me later that Karajan had driven so fast that he had almost been car-sick. This was the first time he had seen him behind the wheel of the most powerful piece of machinery that Germany had yet produced for public road-transport. The Mercedes was made for the Autobahn, but the roads in and around the city of Lucerne were something else.

In the excitement I had forgotten about Fellagha in the car, parked in the shade of a tree, but I needn't have worried. The noise of an over-primed, powerful engine coming to life with such exuberance had produced a noise much like a gunshot. I found him, curled up and pretending to be asleep, deep down in the well of the car. He was trying hard not to be noticed, just as he had been when we first found him.

The concerts were a great success and Walter Legge was no doubt pleased with the outcome. In his private war with contemporary entrepreneurs in England, who saw his one-man system of orchestral management and artistic flair as a challenge to their own manipulation of the bureaucratic system, he had achieved yet another success. He had managed to bring the orchestra to Lucerne again despite the crippling restrictions imposed by the MU on anything and everything.

His aims for the orchestra were completely at odds with the street market values being introduced into England as 'culture for the people' by the new bosses of EMI. Over the next ten years Legge would gradually become disillusioned with life in an England that he felt had already begun to lose its way before World War Two. By the time we met for the last time in 1963 he was forced to contemplate abandoning his Philharmonia dream.

I too would only know in time whether I could ever achieve any of my dreams. The thing I did learn that year in Lucerne was that I could never be happy on the back desk of any orchestra. It is impossible to hear what is going on at the front and that is where the real action takes place and where nerves are tested.

It would be foolish to pretend that my orchestral experience has not been of enormous benefit to me. To begin with there is the repertoire of fine music that has introduced me to the talents of great composers throughout the ages, and to the dedicated mind of Beethoven in particular. I have had the privilege of being associated, in however subordinate a role, with most of the great interpretive musical minds of the orchestral and concerto repertoire of the century. Last but by no means least, orchestral work has enabled me to travel widely and see many architectural wonders that otherwise would have been no more than mere travellers' tales or pictures in a book. For all this I will always remain indebted to Walter Legge.

Fellagha, Annette and I returned to Prades. I practised, my wife gathered lichens, and Fellagha dozed away the hours between meals. On the days we spent in the hills he would rush from one imagined certainty to another, eager to find that elusive trail to an even better scent.

I began to spend more and more time just sitting and thinking, until one day, walking around an old fort on a hilltop called Bourg-Madame, it began to dawn on me that I was simply avoiding the real issue. I no longer wanted to be an orchestral player. So what did I want? Peace of mind would be a good start, I thought, but how does one achieve it? One of Montaigne's Latin poets tells us that 'Ease and tranquillity of mind are due to plain good sense, not to the grand sea view.' Blessings, I was beginning to realise, with which I was not over-endowed.

I thought of Walter Legge and I knew that he had been right—I should not have gone to Prades the second time. I ought to get back to London. But surely that would be a bit feeble, I thought, with a stirring of rebellious irritation. Is there no more to life than just plain good sense?' Don't we need a bit of Sturm und Drang as well?

'I love those who love the impossible,' says a German poet.

That's more my line, I thought, but I could not simply dream my life away. If I wanted to play the cello, I had to get to grips with my irresolution, and make a decision one way or the other. Regular trips abroad were certainly very educational, but they brought no solutions.

I decided that Prades would not, and could not, be the answer to my problems. I had to train my mind to an acceptance of disciplined thinking and set myself limited goals, only moving on to Stage B when Stage A had been mastered. I could go on forever philosophising about life and chasing my tail, but enough was enough. I would go back to London and ask Walter Legge for a job in the Philharmonia.

The first problem that needed to be tackled was that of my shoulder and hand, both of them as painful as ever. Somehow a cure must be found. Annette agreed that we should return to England. She made the necessary arrangements to import a dog, we said goodbye to our friends, and I paid my respects to *Le Maître* for the last time. No doubt he was by now as irritated with me as everyone else, but when I called on him in his little house, he was his usual courteous, kind self.

On the way home we paid a second visit to Chartres and, at Annette's insistence, stopped briefly at Fontainebleau and Versailles before heading for Calais where we were to catch the boat for England.

As we were waiting in the queue an opulently dressed man emerged from a brand new Silver Shadow just in front of us. He gave what looked like a five pound note to one of the ship's crew, obviously trying to organise a 'last-one-on-first-one-off' arrangement, or so we thought.

'The advantages of being rich,' I murmured to Annette. 'Distributing a little largesse here and there makes life so much easier.'

Eventually we were all aboard, and as this was the last time we were to see Fellagha for six months Annette and I stayed with him for the entire voyage. On our arrival at Dover we were asked to

wait until all the passengers had disembarked before handing
Fellagha over to the RSPCA who would transport him to the
kennels. I shall never forget the look of betrayal on Fellagha's face
as the wooden crate into which he had been coaxed was finally
nailed together. The official seal of the Department of Immigration
was stamped on the lid and he was swung overboard in the net of
a large crane. He was gone.

Annette and I drove over to the Customs shed where I was then
asked if I had anything to declare. We had a Voigtlander camera in
the boot and I had to rummage around looking for it, with the
Customs officer in close attendance. The boot was crammed with
Fellagha's personal belongings including some bones in an
advanced state of decay. The smell was not particularly inviting and
the customs official stepped back discreetly and waved us on
having apparently lost interest in the camera.

In the next shed was the Rolls Royce. The opulent man, with his
opulent family, were watching as three officials took the car apart.
The door furniture and seats were lying on the ground alongside
carpets and body panels. Everything that could be removed, had
been. Perhaps the recipient of the fiver had had the same reaction
as I about there being one law for the rich and another for the not
so rich. He had certainly pocketed the money, but must have
decided, just to be on the safe side, to tip off the Customs. It was
quite evident that the searchers were enjoying themselves,
whereas those being searched were certainly not. Annette and I
exchanged glances as we drove out of the Customs shed. Our eyes
seemed to be saying 'There, but for the grace of an Alvis Firefly,
go we!'

CHAPTER TWENTY-FIVE

The Alexander Technique and Dartington

When we finally returned to London after our eighteen-month stay abroad Annette and I felt out on a limb. Although we had been through many strange and sometimes trying experiences, we both felt that our horizons had been enlarged. Living in the City of Cities was certainly as interesting as ever, but something had changed. It seemed as if the wartime atmosphere of fellowship and benign good humour was no longer to be found in day-to-day existence.

There was already evidence of conflict and confrontation between a fast-growing immigrant population from India and the West Indies that was more than willing, but as yet unable, to focus on its own needs and quality of life in a new country. There was also the sadness and isolation of the recently displaced poor of London's slums, now housed in monstrously ugly tower blocks, designed by well meaning but mistaken political philanthropists.

We missed Fellagha much more than we had anticipated during his period of quarantine. We persuaded ourselves that it would be better for him if we were to move out of London after he had been cleared, and that perhaps Bristol might be less depressing. Re-united with Fellagha in the late summer of 1956, we rented a rather damp flat in Leigh Woods, south of the Clifton Suspension Bridge. It couldn't have been a better choice for Fellagha. Getting lost in the woods every day, whatever the weather, was absolute heaven for him, but it was a real pain for us.

We soon found that the dry warmth of the South of France had been a far greater boon than we had realised. We spent a small fortune on heating and painkillers as my aching limbs and swollen joints worsened. On some days I could barely walk. Even when I was driving to and from London for sessions and concerts with the Philharmonia, working on the Alvis Crested Eagle I had bought to replace the Firefly, or taking Fellagha for a walk, I had to battle with an aching body. Because nothing I swallowed eased the pain, the doctors said the symptoms were psychosomatic.

During the winter of 1956 I had the great good fortune to meet the cellist Niso Ticciati. From both Niso and Walter Carrington I learnt about the work of F. M. Alexander. I began to study posture, balance, mental control, breathing. Gradually, very gradually, light began to filter through the dark regions of despair that had become seemingly entrenched forever. Step by cautious step I was taught how to differentiate between psychological and physiological depression. How to assess their effect on my health, my life and my work. Niso made me abandon all medical treatment and start again from the beginning. I had to re-think everything I did each day, study every physical action, from lifting a teaspoon to picking up the heaviest object. He showed me how to sit down, how to stand up, how to hold myself when I was seated, how to balance my head and never allow it to sink into its socket. At several fixed intervals during the course of each day I had to reflect on every movement made in the preceding hours and try to understand what it was that was causing the pain. As we laboriously charted every possible variation, I gradually built up a picture of myself. A picture of someone who was always over-anxious and consciously or unconsciously over-emphasising everything he did. By holding my head in a fixed position for hours on end, I was limiting the blood supply to the rest of the system, adding immeasurably to the strain on the back muscles. It seemed so obvious. Niso also insisted that I think much more seriously about diet.

My eldest brother, being an orthodox medic, had never shown much interest in my continuing malaise. He viewed the saga of my ill-health with a benign scepticism and would never admit that diet was or could be anything else but of secondary importance. He has, rather belatedly, been obliged to change these views but in 1956 he was still sceptical, almost to the point of being hostile, about my new found approach to body-care.

It was my mother-in-law who first connected aching joints and jaundiced appearance with problems of diet, and she began to make me eat non-greasy food. Within six months I was able to treat most of the pain resulting from incorrect posture. I experimented with the angle at which I was holding the arm, elbow, or finger and changed the emphasis of what I was doing until the muscle stopped hurting.

Niso suspected that the trouble had originally been caused by tearing some of the muscles in my back and shoulders in the car crash of 1954. By lifting the Ford Saloon I had strained most of the back muscles and probably the heart muscles as well. In the months that followed I had tried to carry on as before instead of resting and allowing the muscles to heal.

After several months of instruction in the Alexander Technique I began to feel so much better that I started work on the Crested Eagle. Although the gearbox was a dream, the brakes were anything but. Talking one day to an Alvis enthusiast in Manchester I learnt that it was possible to fit the Crested Eagle with a servo-box from a Lanchester Light 15 saloon without too much difficulty. The servo-unit was an instant success and I was able to drive many thousands of miles knowing that I could stop in a hurry if I had to.

The car was no sooner going well than I happened to come across a rebuilt Charlesworth Speed 25 Saloon. I had just bought a 1939 Speed 25 Drop-Head from *Performance Cars* in 1954, so knew what mechanical delights were in store for me. However, on closer examination, the bodywork proved to be in very bad shape, and as I did not have the money to do any work on it, I had to sell it to a restorer.

The Charlesworth Saloon was a dream. It had been lovingly restored by an Alvis enthusiast and was just too good an opportunity to miss. Up to 1959, while I was still able to drive comfortably from Totnes to Holland Park in less than two hours, I remained totally loyal to Alvis.

From the time that I began to earn a living as a professional cellist it was imperative for me to be at a given place at a given time. Flat tyres, engine trouble, train derailments, strikes, cancellations etcetera may, in the normal course of events, be perfectly valid excuses for being late for an appointment. None of these excuses, however, make the slightest impression on the sort of person who runs a freelance agency. It is a simple case of 'First come first served' or 'Late come—no serve'. As a self-employed musician I could not afford the risk of relying on either Public Transport or a twenty-year old car, however well loved. Very reluctantly I was eventually compelled to 'go modern'.

In 1957 through the good offices of Colin Sauer I was offered a post at Dartington Hall in Devon. The warden, Peter Cox, was a little vague about the exact nature of my duties but basically I was to give lessons in cello playing and lectures on the History of Music. The students were mostly trainee-teachers and apart from providing a fairly generalised historical course I would also have to play in the student orchestra and coach chamber-music groups. The salary was to be £16 per week which was not a princely sum, but the work at Dartington did offer other very real advantages. There was peace and quiet, the countryside was idyllic, and there was a superb library.

I accepted the post immediately and threw myself into the task of preparing the first lectures on the History of Music, a subject about which I had only scant knowledge at the time. I used Laing's *History of Music in Western Civilisation* as a main guide and found to my surprise that the art of music-making was considerably older than I had realised. The book raised questions that had never before crossed my mind. As a boy I was always made to feel that I was a 'sissy' because I played the cello and sang in a church choir. I thought it was something out of the ordinary to love the sounds and challenges of music. It certainly never occurred to me to ask what music had meant to people throughout the ages.

Who were these musicians of the past and how and where did they play? Who made the instruments on which they played? What influenced the design of the instrument, and what were its origins? Who listened to the music, and who paid for the privilege? The cultures of Greek and Arab provided the basis of what has been taken for granted by musicians in Renaissance and post-Renaissance Europe for over five hundred years, especially those musicians who played instruments used in bands and orchestras. Furthermore the subtleties of this inheritance, intellectual and spiritual, are also evident in much of Modern Europe's influence on musicians from the Middle and Far East who have absorbed Western styles by study in the West and also by listening to recordings of Western music. All this was completely new to me in 1957. I was immensely happy in my work and was entranced by the buildings, the gardens, and the quiet dignity of Dartington Hall.

Annette and I had been promised a suite of beautifully panelled rooms in one of the wings of the main building. I could imagine no greater delight than living in these rooms, preparing my lectures there, studying, practising and teaching. It seemed too good to be true. Annette was more cautious. She listened politely to Peter Cox expounding on the virtues of the 'artist in the rural community', but said nothing. However, because of her interest in hand printing and natural dyes, she was much more in sympathy with the aims of the owners, Dorothy and Leonard Elmhirst.

Elmhirst had worked with Rabindranath Tagore in India prior to meeting and subsequently marrying Dorothy Straight, at the time known as 'poor Dorothy'. She had inherited a mere £8,000,000 of the Whitney-Straight fortune at a time when American and English banks were starting to implement their stranglehold on the assets of the nations of the world. It was doubly fortunate for Leonard that his wife should have inherited a dowry of such magnitude when the dust-bowl was claiming victims in America, many parts of the world were in thrall to grinding poverty, and large sections of the working class in Britain and Southern Africa were existing respectively on a diet of nettle soup or maize.

Elmhirst returned to Europe convinced that lessons he had learnt in India could be applied to England. He and his wife devoted a major part of their vast fortune to creating a European-style working model of a concept, defined as that of the 'artist in the rural community'. According to the Elmhirsts the needs of a rural community were to be encouraged to reflect arts and crafts, rooted in local culture. With this end in view they purchased an abandoned castle that had at one time belonged to the Black Prince. In the first flush of my enthusiasm for the Elmhirsts' experiment, I visualised Dartington Hall as a possible future English equivalent of Swetzingen in Germany, or of the Juilliard School of Music in New York. I tried to share this enthusiasm with Mrs Elmhirst but she exhibited no more than polite interest.

The first winter term began well enough. The misty autumnal evenings were an intoxicating mixture of things past and of promise for the future. There was a smell of apple wood burning in open grates, and long walks over the moors with Fellagha. There were visits to Mothecombe Bay where Annette's godfather, Major John Mildmay-White, introduced me to A. L. Rowse, whose love of Cornwall and knowledge of English literature opened my eyes to even more avenues for investigation.

The Mildmay family, owners of Mothecombe and the beautiful grounds leading to the small estuary, were kind and generous, and I have many happy memories of weekends spent in that exquisite house. Over the next two years I was also to learn from John

Mildmay-White about the activities of Baring Bank and about the investments of nominee clients, my first insight into the world of secret financial deals.

The bliss of the surroundings, however, could not disguise the fact that, as a teaching centre, Dartington Hall left a great deal to be desired. Apart from myself only three other members of the staff had ever held a position outside the school. Peter Cox certainly professed a great admiration for the ideals of the Elmhirsts and by tact, diplomacy, and unwavering perseverance over a period of many years, he had managed to assure for himself the guardianship of these ideals. To me, however, he seemed to be singularly incapable of suiting the deed to the word. As the months passed his style of administration began to remind me of a musician who, though playing more or less correctly, displays little or no understanding of the composer's true intentions.

The first term was drawing to a close and I was asked to participate in the Christmas show. At some stage or other of the proceedings there was to be a procession through the Great Hall of adults and small children pretending to be large and small horses. Noises-off were to be provided by bells, recorders and drums. All this was intended, if I remember rightly, to conjure up visions of times so distant and remote that they seemed to belong to another world, and possibly to another solar system as well. Try as I might I could not enter into the spirit of the thing and before the evening was over I saw, from the look in the Warden's eyes, that he was mortally offended.

At the end of the Lent term members of staff were asked to participate in a concert, so I decided to play Boccherini's Sonata in A major with Richard Hall, Head of Music, accompanying. Unfortunately his performance was, to put it mildly, far from accurate. I was by this time making good progress with the Alexander Technique and my muscular pains were to a large extent a thing of the past. I was also reaping the reward of eighteen months' hard work in Prades and managed to play the sonata with a fluency the pianist couldn't match. Colin Sauer said afterwards that Richard had formed the impression that I intended to embarrass him. Once again I saw that hostile glint in the Warden's eye.

My initial reaction was one of enormous irritation. What had been the use of all those years of hard work if it did no more than cause my employer's resentment? Having slept on the problem I realised next morning that I had perhaps over-reacted. After all, the choice had been my own. I had wanted to go to Casals to work at solutions for technical problems associated with my chosen profession. I had obviously benefited far more than I had realised and that was my reward. This did not alter the fact that I now felt myself to be in a vacuum at Dartington. There was no competition, or at any rate no challenge for me as a cellist.

For a time old frustrations began to re-assert themselves, but I soon began to see that the academic side of my post gave me a wonderful opportunity to learn about new areas of music and its evolution. I found Laing's book stimulating and tried to synthesise what I was reading into a formula that would encourage the students to contribute to a team effort of discussion and analysis. For example if we decided to study the use of modes and their origins, every member of the class, myself included, would undertake to study a particular example in detail. Each individual would gather as much information as possible and present it as a written paper the following week. Very soon some of the students began to respond with enormous enthusiasm, particularly a young man called Robert Spencer, whose work on the sixteenth and seventeenth century lute, viol and ballad repertoire was to lead to an international career. Many of the more senior class members were also willing to teach me skills they themselves were learning or had already mastered elsewhere.

This method of collective study occupied the entire first year at Dartington. I like to think that it helped several outstanding young people to overcome most of the barriers that are often so easily created between teacher and pupil. At the same time the clash of views and conflicting opinions gave flesh to the somewhat skeletal knowledge I had brought to the appointment described by Peter Cox as 'Lecturer in Music'. Things were going too well. There had to be a catch.

There was. Peter Cox had changed his mind about the accommodation for Annette and myself. One room was now deemed sufficient for us, and we were told to move. My teaching was henceforth to take place in a shed opposite the garage and workshops. It was clear that Mr Cox did not approve of me or my wish to establish a 'professional' standard which he considered to be inappropriate to the needs of Dartington. It was quite clear that when the Warden waxed lyrical about the 'Artist in the rural community' he had no intention of including me in his concept.

Annette had already begun to accept that I was not right for the job. This concerned and depressed me profoundly and for a while I gave my resentment more or less free rein. Luckily, the Philharmonia and the Beaufort Piano Trio kept me busy at the professional level, and of course there was always the Alvis Speed 25 Charlesworth Saloon. Cleaning and polishing this beautiful car became an obsession until I realised that it was merely diverting me from a feeling of failure and not really helping me to come to terms with my work at Dartington.

The car which was already a source of unending pleasure and solace, became more so when I made the acquaintance of a mechanical and engineering wizard called Raymond Bowles. Raymond had a garage about five miles from Elstree Film Studios where I did the occasional session, and whenever I had a free moment I would call on him. I revelled in the joy of watching his technical skill, trying to follow and understand the mental processes whereby he could analyse and put right mechanical faults, all of it done with impeccable ease and elegance. Raymond would have been an artist in any community. All he wanted from life was a decent living with a satisfied clientèle. It is a sad reflection on post-war society that both artist and clientele were denied the fulfilment of this modest ambition. Raymond's skills attracted the attention of so many classic and vintage car thieves that insurance premiums rose beyond the reach of most of his clients. Raymond was eventually put out of business and finally reduced to earning a living as a petrol station supervisor.

Both Jane Withers, the orchestral manager, and Walter Legge were still keen to have 'an engine at both ends' and so, even after I resigned as sub-principal of the cello section in 1953, they very kindly continued to pay me the same fee that I would have received had I been sitting next to Raymond Clark on the first desk.

Sitting on the last desk proved to be highly educational. I was better placed to bridge any awkward gap that might occur between the last desk of cellos and the first desk of the basses. Because it takes the bass player longer to articulate the sound of a note on the instrument, the player has to anticipate the movement of the bow if the resulting sound is to coincide with the conductor's beat. For this reason Karajan always insisted that the upper strings had to wait until they heard the sound of the double-bass. This is crucial when the orchestra has to play a *tutti* chord that often occurs at the beginning of a work or at some point after a grand climax.

In 1954 Furtwängler recorded Wagner's *Tristan and Isolde* with the Philharmonia at the Kingsway Hall. He didn't work with the orchestra as often as Karajan did but by the end of the recording session (four continuous weeks in a hall with a resonant and workable acoustic and the equivalent of 82 miles of recording tape) I began to think that I had a somewhat better understanding of the conducting techniques of Furtwängler and Karajan. Furtwängler achieved wonderful results as players, despite or because of his uncertain stick technique, gradually came to rely on each other as much as on the Maestro. He was prepared to expose himself to criticism on his stick technique because he trusted the professionalism of his players. Karajan with his excellent and reliable stick technique also achieved wonderful results, but he relied primarily on himself and made it crystal clear how and when he wanted you to play.

In 1957 at Elstree Film Studios Dennis, by this time an aspiring conductor himself, listened with amusement to the Bobby Kok Theory of Conducting Technique. We talked about Furtwängler's growing impatience with the limitations of the Festival Hall, and Dennis told me that shortly before his death in November 1954, Furtwängler had offered to give two performances for the price of one just to help the orchestra's finances. It is a lasting sadness that I was never to have the opportunity of sharing in Dennis's vision of music-making as a conductor.

CHAPTER TWENTY-SIX

Dennis and the Dartington String Quartet

It was in the summer of 1957 while listening to the car radio that I heard the dreadful news that Dennis Brain had been killed in a car crash early that morning. My thoughts went out immediately to Yvonne his widow, to Walter Legge, Manoug, Neill Sanders and to the orchestra. It was inconceivable. Barely ten days before we had been talking about restoring a Stanley Steam Car and about Cantelli and Karajan as possible contenders in a conductors' version of the 'Edinburgh Circuit.'

The news of his death was given to the orchestra that morning. They had been booked to record Capriccio by Richard Strauss with Wolfgang Sawallisch at the Kingsway Hall. The members of the orchestra were deeply shocked and so was Sawallisch. He kept shrugging his shoulders despairingly and saying 'What can we do? We must go on.' Alan Civil, the third horn, stepped into the breach and it is a tribute to the musicianship and professionalism of all concerned that the recording achieved a considerable success. Alan Civil was appointed principal a few days later and proved to be a worthy successor, but Dennis's death cut the ground right out from under my feet.

In 1944 I had played in Dennis's recording of Benjamin Britten's *Serenade* for tenor, horn and strings. It was the first time I had heard the wonderful range of sounds he could produce. His playing enchanted me as much then as it did, nearly twenty-five years later at Elstree Film Studios, when I was to hear him play for the last time.

I will never accept that he fell asleep at the wheel of his car. I know the road and the place where he crashed. If he managed the

Wolfgang Sawallisch recording Capriccio at Kingsway Hall on the morning after Dennis Brain's death.

roundabout, why should he fall asleep a few seconds later? The crash had to be due to mechanical failure. Without doubt Dennis had been one of the star contributors to the success of the Philharmonia. His playing of solo passages in the orchestral repertoire could create something rare and beautiful out of what seemed to be nothing.

When talking to Dennis and Manoug in the summer of 1955 after Karajan's bad manners in Boston we all hoped that Cantelli and Giulini would be willing to help Walter Legge maintain the musical integrity and professionalism that the orchestra had achieved. Since Cantelli had already contributed greatly to the quality of our work and Giulini could not fail to bring further credit to our prestige concerts, the future had looked promising. Now that Furtwängler and Cantelli were dead only Giulini and Klemperer remained.

Supposing Furtwängler had not died and had been permitted to live out his full three score years and ten. I couldn't help wondering how this would have affected Karajan's career when he was no longer a crucial part of the Philharmonia's workload. I was convinced that Klemperer was too cynical to consider helping to train the next generation of young players. Considering the physical affliction he had to contended with this is understandable. I knew that I would have found it difficult to take on board his particular musical fingerprints. I knew for sure that I could not happily work with a man like Klemperer who, although willing to exploit the standards achieved by other conductors with the Philharmonia, seemed to have little regard for the aims of the orchestra itself.

It was to a large extent the deaths of Cantelli and Dennis that had made me decide to accept the post at Dartington Hall rather than return to the orchestra as a full-time member. I wanted to try to teach the next generation what had been revealed to me so generously by those who managed to achieve international eminence. As I have already described, the first academic year was a disaster and the second went on to be a catastrophe.

I was convinced that a string quartet at Dartington would be a step in the right direction and suggested the idea to Colin Sauer. We were greatly encouraged when William Glock (then Music Controller of the BBC) agreed to back the idea, but I had reckoned without Peter Cox. When I told him that Colin and I wanted to form a string quartet to provide the basis of a string department, he listened politely. I told him that Pierre Fournier had promised to help as a coach if a few of his peers were prepared to do likewise.

'If the word "Dartington" is to be used in the name,' he said 'it must be made absolutely clear that the proposed quartet will not be connected, in any way, with the image of the artist in the rural community I have spent years trying to create. If establishing a string quartet were to happen at all, and this is unlikely, it would have to be an offshoot of the Music Department, nothing more.'

When I then asked him if I could call the group the *Dartington String Quartet*, he immediately said no. We discussed other variations of the name and finally he suggested that we should call ourselves the *Dartington Hall Music School String Quartet*. As the Music Department was run at the time by Richard Hall, I couldn't resist asking whether we shouldn't call the quartet The Dartington *Music Hall* String Quartet. Mr Cox was not amused.

When I heard what he was prepared to offer as a salary I was not amused. He refused to contribute a penny towards a salary for the other two string players, but was prepared to offer board and lodging for Peter Carter and Keith Lovell, the violinist and viola player. Annette agreed with typical generosity that we should share half of my salary of £16 a week with Keith and Peter for a period of six months. This meant that the Koks had to live on £8 a week while Carter and Lovell would each have £4. Not a princely amount but a start had been made.

I was soon to discover for myself the truth of the old saying that a string quartet has all the disadvantages of marriage but none of the compensations. Colin was an extremely capable violinist but seemed to be more amused than concerned by my continual plea for the fire and imagination a first violin must bring to performance. This constant need to be 'amused' is possibly the reason why I have come to believe that England, as Matthew Arnold once said of France, is 'Famed in the Arts, Supreme in none'.

The qualities of dynamic enthusiasm lacking in Colin were certainly present in the playing of Peter Carter, but doting parents and his respect for Colin were good enough reasons for Peter not to exert himself unduly. Like Colin, he was a keen tennis enthusiast and both men were seldom over-anxious to rehearse. Keith Lovell was kind, co-operative and reserved in his manner. Because he really wanted to learn he was always asking questions and his quiet determination augured well for the future. In spite of the usual ups and downs rehearsals were a great joy and I was certainly hoping for the best.

We made our début at the 1958 summer concert. As things turned out we might just as well have sight-read the programme, so great was the confusion and uncertainty of style and tempo particularly in the slow movement of Beethoven Opus 59 No. 1, where Colin's tempo differed completely from that of the rest of us. William Glock and Hans Keller, who had come down to hear us, were certainly not amused by the name of the quartet and, however sympathetic they may have been about first-night nerves, they both criticised my choice of programme.

'The Beethoven was too ambitious,' said Hans Keller. 'You should have played something less demanding.'

I felt that Colin had let me down and in a moment of temper and embarrassment I resigned.

That summer Annette and I had been invited by Keith Lovell and Peter Carter to spend a couple of weeks in a villa on the shores of Lake Como. I certainly needed the holiday but the real reason for jumping at the suggestion was that, ever since our return from France, Annette and I had drifted apart. She was never overtly critical when I tried to report on the content of Peter Cox's daily moots (Old English for 'democracy') and I was never able to explain to her what exactly had been achieved by so many hours of talk. Occasionally she would whisper a word of caution about alienating Peter Cox but in principle she believed that it was I who should accept the Dartington Hobby-Horse ethic. If I couldn't then the only honest thing for me to do would be to resign.

We had never found it necessary to talk merely for the sake of talking, but in that first year at Dartington the silences had become almost unbearable. About a mile away, on the Dartington Hall Estate, was Dartington Hall School, founded in the 1930s by O'Neill, the liberal educational reformer. Matters between Annette and I were not helped by Julia Child, the current headmaster's daughter.

Julia was a member of the string orchestra that Colin had started. It was obvious from the start that she was rigid with anxiety even before she played a note. I soon learnt that she was left-handed and was finding it very difficult to adapt to playing the violin as if she were right-handed. Her parents, who had only recently been appointed as joint heads, appeared to pay lip service to the ideals of progressive education, but it is quite possible that in their heart of hearts they were as sceptical as I was about the whole experiment. Evidence for this view was their attitude to their daughter and to her very real problems. When I suggested that she should be allowed to have the instrument adapted to her special needs the suggestion was dismissed out of hand.

'With proper training' they made certain I understood the innuendo 'it should be possible for her to become right-handed without much trouble.'

I have come to loathe the phrase 'with proper training' especially in the mouth of an educational 'specialist' when he or she feels obliged to allege poor teaching by another staff member.

I also failed dismally to produce the least spark of interest in the daughter of Dylan Thomas. She managed to stall her way through each lesson with an adroit mixture of non-and-wrong-knowledge. As she did not practise from one lesson to the next she made no progress at all. Mr and Mrs Child considered that I was to blame, but as the girl later obtained a post in Switzerland as a linguist perhaps the real message was that she didn't like playing the cello. However, I did manage to do something for Julia, and she responded sufficiently to be able to win a place at the Guildhall School of Music in London.

Julia and I saw each other regularly at my lectures every Thursday on the *History of Music in Western Civilization*, and also at orchestral rehearsals on Tuesday evenings. She was eighteen and very lovely and, because of the nature of the work in which we were involved, we had a great deal to talk about. As our work progressed so did the range of shared interests bring us closer together.

Annette and I were unable to bridge those awkward silences but we still loved each other enough to want our marriage to continue. We agreed that a holiday in Italy, playing quartets with Carlo van Este, Peter's teacher, would be a good way to find common ground again and rebuild our friendship

While I was standing at the window of the Italian Consulate, waiting for a visa, the son of the Chairman of Guardian Assurance elected to drive his Rolls Royce into a Jaguar at the crossroads outside the Embassy. I saw my brand new Standard 10 Estate telescoped by nearly two feet as the Rolls cannoned into it.

The owner was charmingly apologetic, assuring me that there would be no difficulty in arranging transport for my holiday the following day, so on his advice I hired a Ford. We only found out later that what he meant, and what I had *assumed* he meant, were two completely different things. Hiring a car was, as he had rightly advised, no problem. Paying for it cost me nearly half a term's wages.

Apart from this initial setback, we had great hopes as we crossed France that summer of 1958. By the time we found the villa and had established contact with Keith, Peter and our new friends, it had become possible to bridge at least some of the silences between us, but we still found ourselves out of touch, despite the beauty of the setting, the inspiring playing of Carlo van Este and the wonders of the chamber-music repertoire we played.

As soon as we returned to Totnes, Julia's presence re-asserted itself. The more we met, the more we needed to meet. Matters came to a head one appalling Tuesday evening after a particularly long and dreary rehearsal with the orchestra. It was raining and as I had used the Speed 25 that night I offered to drive Julia home to the Old Postern where she lived with her parents. As we drove through the dark wetness my mind was in a turmoil. I was throwing my life away in this rural retreat. I wasn't practising. I was married to a lovely woman I couldn't talk to and I was beginning to suspect that I was in love with a beautiful girl whom I was afraid of offending by talking too much.

Then in one of those moments when all judgement is suspended I selected second gear on a forty-five degree left turn and accelerated up to peak revs. With wet leaves adding further hazards to an already dangerous surface the Alvis didn't have a chance. I hit the right side of the bank and everything went blank. When I regained consciousness I saw Julia slumped forward in her seat and for one horrible moment I thought that she had broken her neck. Almost blind with panic I grabbed her by the shoulders. She stirred ever so slightly and I kissed her pale, silent little face, grateful to a benign providence.

From that moment I was lost. It was an impossible situation. Either Julia would have to leave, or I would. In the end, it was Julia. She went to London and I stayed behind, filled with feelings of remorse and guilt vis à vis Annette, but powerless to stop myself thinking about Julia.

Dartington without her was bleak. Annette and I remained as uncommunicative as before, the only difference being that she was now deeply hurt. She knew that I had a sense of duty and obligation and that I was very fond of her, but obviously did not love her as a husband should. She also realised since hearing me play late Beethoven quartets in the romantic surroundings of Lake Como, that a sharp edge had been added to a numbing unhappiness that had already become apparent to her and to everyone who knew me.

Those musical evenings had aggravated my feelings of inner dissatisfaction even more, making them impossible to conceal from Annette. Having played such divine music in such an ideal setting, how could I even think of returning to orchestral playing for the rest of my life? Dreams I thought had gone for ever were returning to haunt me. I felt trapped at Dartington, but I did not want to go back to the orchestra. Might it not be possible to try once again to study cello technique in depth?

At Lake Como after the others had gone to bed, Carlo and I would sit and talk about Beethoven and the unique insight into sentiment his music provides. It was the first time I had ever had the chance to hear or play the seventeen quartets within the space of a single week. Sadly it was also the last, but I was so inspired that I decided that, whatever else I did, I would make a thorough study of the works this incomparable man has bequeathed to posterity. I remained true to this resolve and, in the years that followed, spent many hours studying his scores with awe and dedication.

During those Italian summer evenings, there were moments when the music was so profoundly moving that nothing more could be said. There was no strain, no rhetoric, no dramatic distortion but a quiet overwhelming message that was unambiguous. Then I would look up and see only bewilderment in Annette's eyes.

How many kind and generous people are there, I wonder, who are unable to accept that music at its highest emotional and intellectual level is incomprehensible, that it has to be felt before it can begin to be understood? Where did Annette find her inner serenity? The question had never crossed my mind before. Was she simply blinkered as we all are in our different ways? It was hard to believe that she could be unaware of the inner meaning of the music.

The *Adagio* of Opus 127 encouraged me to hope that there might be room for me in the mansion of Beethoven's mind, provided I was prepared to submit to the impersonal companionship that his music offered. Then when we played the *Cavatina* from Opus 130 it was like the revelation of Truth untarnished at the source. In this work personal suffering is transfigured through artistic expression. Nothing is omitted that can be felt or imagined.

In earlier works, suffering born of isolation through deafness had driven Beethoven to represent various aspects of life in strong and often violent contrasts. In the late works, which can be said to constitute Beethoven's Last Will and Testament, all former conflicts have been resolved. The many experiences life affords still pass before the mind's eye, but now the diversity is contained and disciplined by the iron will and determination of the composer to survive as a dedicated servant of Art.

My introduction to the late quartets gave me the impression that at last I was hearing the real 'language' of music. It seemed that Beethoven was describing an attitude to events and experiences that, to a greater or lesser degree, are shared by everyone on earth. The difference is that Beethoven's experiences seem to have been larger than life itself, and the scope of his mind infinitely more varied than ours could ever be.

The holiday on the shores of Lake Como taught me a great deal about Beethoven but it failed to drive Julia out of my thoughts. It was like being in love with a shadow, or was she the bright sun burning down mercilessly out of a clear blue sky while I, a traveller trying to escape from the same sun's rays, was unable to find any shade?

Torn by the conflicting emotions of love for the unattainable Julia, and guilt because of an inadequate love for the long-suffering

Annette, I was determined to seek salvation in the training of the newly formed string quartet. Colin Sauer had demonstrated beyond all shadow of doubt at the Summer School concert that he lacked the necessary dedication to lead a team of players at international level. Before we left for Italy Colin and I had discussed the possibility of his allowing Peter Carter to lead the quartet for a trial period and he seemed quite happy with the suggestion. I mentioned the idea to the other two members of the quartet at Lake Como and they too seemed agreeable. It was therefore something of a shock to be informed, on my return to Dartington, that my resignation was now to have immediate effect, although it had been initially rejected. Peter Cox summoned me to his office, and told me in the nicest possible way, that I was to vacate as soon as possible the position I held and the premises I occupied.

I did not know until many years later that Colin had changed his mind soon after we had spoken. He was not willing to play second fiddle to Peter Carter, and told him so in the presence of Keith Lovell before they left for Italy. Not a word of this was mentioned at Lake Como, but at the start of the Autumn Term it appears that the other three members of the quartet had asked Peter Cox to reverse his decision and accept my resignation. I was the architect of my own misfortune and cannot expect too much sympathy. The really sad aspect of this little saga is that I threw away the chance to develop the centre for string players I had planned and set up, and for which Annette and I had sacrificed so much.

Mr Elmhirst told me on the day I left that I was not what Dartington wanted, and that I would be better suited to the cut and thrust of London.

'You need a larger canvas,' he said.

This brief interview was the most numbing experience I had yet encountered in my career, but the die was cast and I had to go.

Despite my reservations about the concept of 'the artist in the rural community' I had been truly fascinated by the romance of Dartington, by the smell of the building and of apple wood burning in open grates in the winter. I had loved listening to tales of the Black Prince that might well have been told over the centuries in front of the same great open hearths. Where was I to go now? It had to be back to the hell that London had become since we returned from Prades.

CHAPTER TWENTY-SEVEN

Maggie

During the two years at Dartington Annette had gradually established a niche for herself in the Arts and Crafts Department. Rather than endure further uncertainty over accommodation we decided to buy a property in Totnes called Little Meadow House. This meant that, although I had to leave the Music Department in the Autumn of 1959, there was no immediate compulsion for me to leave Totnes, except to work. The only work I could find was in London of course, so to London I had to go. To rub salt into the wound, steam locomotives were replaced by diesel-electric trains in the months that followed, so even this innocent pleasure was denied me.

As time passed so too did my depression deepen. Perhaps I am over-dramatizing the situation, but I think I can now begin to understand the feeling of isolation that must have influenced some of the students at Dartington when, in desperation, they were driven to take the final, irrevocable step.

My real nightmare began one day in 1959. I had felt very ill all morning. By the afternoon I could hardly walk and was unable to breathe properly. I was hyperventilating but somehow managed to drive to the doctor in Totnes and knocked on the door, not aware that the surgery wasn't supposed to open for another ten minutes. In my agitation I knocked again because there was no immediate response. Eventually the door opened and a grim-faced woman in her thirties, whom I initially took to be the receptionist, asked me what I wanted. I explained that I had been advised to consult Dr Dunwoody by my neighbour, Margaret Isherwood, who was also one of her patients—or so I understood.

'*I* am Dr Dunwoody,' the woman said brusquely.

From the look on her face it was clear that I had transgressed gravely. She told me to sit in the waiting room until the official opening time, adding that I had been very inconsiderate. When I was finally admitted into the presence of this would-be rival of Harold Wilson in the next decade, she spent the first few minutes of the interview reminding me that illness has to accommodate itself to the opening hours of a surgery. But since I was by this time unable to appreciate either the merits or demerits of her lecture, I could only launch into a garbled account of what I assumed were the first symptoms of a heart attack. I couldn't help noticing that she was writing notes the whole time I was speaking.

Without any clinical examination whatsoever she handed me a prescription and motioned me to the door. Apart from the initial tirade Dr Dunwoody had said nothing. It was evident that she did not believe that I was going to have a heart attack, nor did she consider that I required medical attention. What she did make absolutely clear was that I had wasted her time. Perhaps it had for her just been one of those days, but I desperately needed help. I needed to talk to someone and she failed to recognise that need.

I collected a bottle of pills from a chemist and went home. Finding that Annette had still not returned from a walk on the moor with a party of friends, I lay down in the bedroom and closed my eyes, trying to shut out the world around me. It was no use. The events of the past few years kept intruding.

I remembered the afternoon in 1954 when Ann, Annette, Felix and I had been travelling to Edinburgh. I remembered seeing the bonnet of my beautiful Speed Twenty crashing into the car Felix had hit at seventy-five miles an hour. I remembered my Speed Twenty Five, wrecked that fateful night four years later in an instant of folly. I remembered Julia, pale and lifeless, slumped across the dashboard. Above all I remembered the pain in Annette's eyes.

I remembered Peter Cox, creeping around the courtyard at Dartington where most of the teaching took place, spying on everything and everybody with his 'you-can't-see-me-looking' stoop. I remembered Colin, always cheerful, never at a loss for words and capable, in spite of his religious beliefs, of sticking a knife into someone's back.

I tried to get up, thinking that perhaps a cup of tea might rid me of thoughts that had become a tangle of unrelated regrets, and help me concentrate on what to do now. Sleep, I decided, was priority number one so I took the prescribed dose of pills and closed my eyes. After about an hour, feeling no change, I took some more. As I was still awake an hour later, I took two more. Nothing. A little later still I swallowed a whole mouthful in one gulp, feeling slightly amused at the awe with which I had until then regarded this passport to oblivion.

When I opened my eyes again I gradually became aware of several people standing around the bed. There was a nurse, holding a stomach pump, a young doctor with the buttons of the ubiquitous white coat undone and the equally ubiquitous stethoscope dangling from the breast pocket next to a large black fountain pen. Beside him I saw a police officer, notebook at the ready, waiting to ask me some questions.

Apart from talking to Dr Dunwoody I have yet to experience anything more depressing than talking to a police psychiatrist. He asked me who I was, whether I was married and had any children. He then asked me whether I masturbated.

'Why the question on masturbation?' I asked irritably.

He told me that it was a well-known factor in mental ill-health and was commonly practised. It was not in itself important, he explained, but it helped him to build up a picture. By this time I'd had enough. I told them all to go to hell, rolled over on my side, and fell asleep. It was the sleep I had been craving for the previous four months.

I stayed in bed for nearly a week. Great spasms of despair, the like of which I had never before known, overwhelmed me several times a day and left me utterly exhausted. It was total physical and mental collapse.

One afternoon after one of these attacks, and for no reason I can remember, I got up and, still in my pyjamas, took a bucket of soap and water and scrubbed the kitchen floor. I then collapsed on the bed physically drained and immediately sank into a deep sleep. Thereafter, every time despair threatened to engulf me again, I would get up and do any menial job that needed physical effort. This self-help gradually built up my resistance. Slowly day by day I began to free myself from a form of mental tyranny that had, one way or another, affected my life since that first attack of jaundice in 1936 in Johannesburg.

During the whole period of my convalescence confused thoughts of Dartington kept going through my mind. Cox had never provided a proper syllabus. There were just endless 'moots', producing endless variations on the recurring theme of 'the artist in the rural community'. My means of escape from boredom was to drift off into my own dream world. I would try to lose myself in the dark recesses of a window seat and conjure up images of cars seen in the most recent issue of *Motor Sport*. While Peter Cox and other members of staff wrestled with problems of national educational requirements and their relation to the hobby-horse concept, I would sit and dream about wonderfully exotic cars that I wanted to drive. It must be indicative of something that at one time during my two years at Dartington Hall I owned a 1934 Austin 7, a Standard 10 Estate, two Morris Minors (a convertible and a saloon), an Alvis Crested Eagle and Alvis Charlesworth Speed Twenty-five, an Alvis TC 2100 and finally, the most beautiful of all post-war models, an Alvis Grey Lady Drop-Head. All were purchased and used, as the mood dictated, on a basic salary of £16 a week.

As the maintenance of my private fleet of yesterday's cars took place mostly in a vast barn of a building near Colin Sauer's studio, I could not help noticing the traffic flow of his many pupils. One in particular, a lovely young girl called Maggie, was undoubtedly the toast of the college during my second year at Dartington. She professed to love the violin enough, it would seem, to merit a lesson almost every other day from Colin. She managed to keep a circle of ardent admirers at bay with an air of reserve that was quite enchanting, and although it would be inaccurate to suggest that she was unapproachable, she certainly did not encourage familiarity.

Although Maggie was a constant visitor to Colin's studio, only rarely did I hear sounds of violin playing when I was attending my fleet of cars nearby.

When I teased Colin about his *dolce* approach to teaching Maggie and his technique of long silences, he was not at all reticent.

'Maggie is wonderful,' was the ingenuous, stock response to every query.

Alvis TC21 / 100 Grey Lady

I needed no assurance on that point but I became increasingly interested to learn how it is possible to teach a stringed instrument with such insistence and enthusiasm, but without actually making any sound.

'In what way is she wonderful?' I asked.

'Maggie never tires of telling me stories about her background. About her adoption as a baby, and how she spent most of her childhood on a post-war housing estate. She talks about the schools she attended, and how she survived the battery of supposedly stimulating new teaching techniques based on the 'learning-must-always-be-fun' principle. Although she must have had her fair share of fun by the time she came to Dartington,' he went on with a wry smile, 'she certainly had very little learning.'

Being conscientious, intelligent, and also receptive to the atmosphere of elegance and beauty at Dartington, she had soon tired of returning home during the holidays, Colin told me. Life in her new surroundings was infinitely preferable. This much emerged in her first year at Dartington. For most of 1957 Maggie continued to spend her lessons talking to Colin. Although the

Alvis Speed 25 Charlesworth Saloon

lessons were interspersed with occasional outbursts of temper, they were immediately followed by inconsolable tears of contrition.

'It's extremely difficult to know how to react,' said Colin, serious concern clouding his usually cheerful countenance. 'After every holiday it takes me several weeks to re-establish a contact I had struggled to build up in the previous term. I just don't understand why.'

The explanation came half way through the summer term of 1959. Maggie was found in a coma in her room. She had taken an overdose, and if it had not been for the timely visit of a friend, she would probably have died.

I was cleaning the Alvis Charlesworth Speed 25 when I saw the ambulance arrive in the courtyard and only found out later that evening that it was Maggie who had been taken to hospital.

After her recovery an investigation by the local authorities established that she had been the victim of intolerable circumstances at home, particularly in respect of her foster father. He had always been very fond of her and right from the beginning he had helped to bath and dress her. This easy familiarity continued as she passed through puberty and was accepted as part of parent-child interaction. By the time she was in her early teens she had become a very attractive young girl indeed and the foster father saw himself less and less in the role of a father and guardian, and more in that of a man. Eventually the inevitable occurred and became part of a pattern of daily life. A feeling of revulsion grew in Maggie until she could not cope any longer with her own feelings of self-disgust. Colin told me that she had hinted at the situation on several occasions, but he had not understood what was being implied.

She was, on the face of it, a healthy, lively girl who appeared to be perfectly capable of coping with unwanted attentions. He was therefore very surprised when the investigating officer told him that sexual demands by foster parents are much more prevalent than is generally admitted. In Maggie's case an unexpected development had been that the foster mother refused to admit that there was any truth in Maggie's allegations. Even when her husband admitted the offences, and was sent for trial and sentenced, she still refused to accept the implications behind his misconduct.

'To have done so would have been tantamount to committing suicide,' Colin told me. An instance, perhaps, where the need to love is greater than the need to receive love.

Maggie's was not the only case of attempted suicide that occurred at Dartington in the two years I was on the staff. Only one, however, failed to respond to first-aid treatment and died before reaching hospital. There was drug abuse, a symptom, one must assume, of a certain malaise within the little community, but the reasons for this were difficult to analyse. As I understood it, the experiment that Leonard Elmhirst and Dorothy Straight had committed themselves to was to restore to a rural society the arts, crafts, and quality of life which are determined by the needs of that society. Is it really possible to transplant the hopes and ambitions of a mixed bag of adults and students into a remote country estate? Most of the students I taught were from urban areas, refugees from the stresses of city life who found themselves suddenly transported into another world.

What was required from us teachers was to make life bearable in the desert of a society dedicated to material needs. The ethic of the twentieth century's obsession with what Socrates called the 'tyranny of one' meant little to the student starved of affection and tied to repetitious and meaningless routine in soul-less housing estates. I decided that Mr and Mrs Elmhirst's endeavour, though founded with the best of intentions, was doomed to failure. They had indeed tried 'to have by letting go'. The tragedy was that others, on whom they relied, had not.

CHAPTER TWENTY-EIGHT

Tom Bowling

One day I was returning to Dartington after a concert with the piano trio. Suddenly I saw it again. A maroon and silver Alvis drop-head. The same model I had first seen, way back in 1955, driving up the hill towards the Lascaux Caves in France. In my heart of hearts, I must have known at the time that one day I, too, would have to own just such a car. And here, parked on the forecourt of a garage just outside Newton Abbot near Totnes, was the long-awaited opportunity to do just that. Decorated with the usual signs and telling the usual story: Alvis TC 2100 – One owner – Only 14,000 miles on the clock – Original condition – As new etcetera etcetera. It was too good to be true.

Somehow I raised the money and, of course, it was too good to be true. The car's performance was lamentable. Something was definitely wrong. Why had I been so blind when I tested it?

'There are none so blind as those who will not see,' sighed Annette.

I took the car back and complained, but the dealer was dismissive. However he made the mistake of implying that I was looking for trouble where no trouble existed.

'You're a musician,' he said, pointing to my cello in the back of the car. 'You should stick to your own trade and leave car maintenance to people who know about cars.'

This annoyed me, and eventually I threatened to take legal action if he didn't co-operate. After an initial show of resistance he agreed that I could take the Alvis to a main dealer of top-quality cars in Exeter. I made an appointment with the chief mechanic as soon as possible and we drove it around Exeter for a while.

'For a car of this age,' he said after we got back to the garage, 'and with 14,000 miles on the clock, the engine is in average condition.'

But since I had by now been driving Alvis cars all over Europe for eight years, I knew that either the chief engineer was a fool, or that he was lying. In due course, with Raymond Bowles from Elstree in close attendance, the engine was dismantled and it was immediately obvious to him that wear in the bores indicated a mileage nearer 140,000 than the advertised 14,000 miles.

The dealer, anxious to avoid unpleasant publicity, wanted to make some kind of compromise, but I was determined to press my advantage and prosecute.

On the day of the hearing I was interviewed for a few minutes by my barrister, a tired-looking middle-aged man who had obviously not even read my Statement of Claim. After scanning the pages he was clearly sceptical about my insistence that the car's mileage was not genuine. This was a bad start. Later, in Court, the Defence made me out to be a prize idiot, which is only to be expected in the insane practice of adversarial law. But my lawyer, in the replies he gave to the other side's defence, made me look even sillier.

When I eventually appeared in the witness box I was subjected to a vigorous cross examination seemingly with the intention of demonstrating that I was simply a neurotic musician with too much time on his hands. All his questions were directed at me personally, as a musician. No mention was made of my interest in, and experience of, Alvis cars, or indeed of the real nature of my complaint.

My chance came when counsel for the defence started cross-questioning me about my query as to the sound of the engine. He first asked what sound I expected to hear from an engine.

'Music,' I replied.

'What sort of music?' he asked with amused tolerance.

'I expect to hear the music of balanced composition, true to form,' I replied (inwardly acknowledging my gratitude to Laing). 'Music is a series of sounds produced in isolation or in groups. Performance suffers when there is distortion, irregular rhythm, poor tone quality or insecure intonation. The engine, which is the cause of my dispute with the dealer, is weak in all four areas described.'

The judge was beginning to look slightly bewildered but for some reason my lawyer suddenly began to take an interest. He led me through a series of questions that enabled me to make it quite clear to the Court that the car had been bought because it looked in good condition which, I assumed, would mean that it had been well looked after.

Counsel for the Defence now tried to adapt his questions to a musical idiom. He suggested that to buy an expensive car, and then quibble about the cost because of a few minor defects, was to behave like someone who wanted to acquire a Stradivarius violin at a fraction of the true cost, merely because there were signs of normal wear and tear.

'The wear and tear of a Stradivarius is not in any way comparable to wear and tear in the bore of a car engine,' I retorted. 'The report states quite clearly that engine wear is generally agreed to be roughly one thousandth of an inch per 1,000 miles. The engine wear in the bore of the Alvis revealed a margin that implied either exceedingly negligent after-sales service, or else a far greater mileage than the milometer indicated.' The point at issue was, quite simply, whether the salesman had set out to deceive me and altered the mileage on the milometer.

At this moment a key witness for the Defence asked if he could make a second statement.

'Your Honour, I wish to retract my original statement. The car was used for more than a year by my firm as a hire-car for special occasions. It has probably already been twice round the clock. I am very sorry for having misled the Court.'

With that, he left the box. What made him change his mind I shall never know, because by the time I was free to leave he had vanished.

It was the late autumn of 1959. I was in London, and had just had tea with Mother. With her share from the sale of 18 Holland Villas Road she had bought a house in Kensington, in Marloes Road. After refurbishing it most beautifully (I was never able to discover how she financed it) she sold it with enough profit to buy a beautiful house in Addison Avenue. This broad avenue leads into the famous St James' Square and is probably one of the most elegant nineteenth century developments in that part of London. Because she had bought the house in 1956 with a sitting tenant who occupied the basement and also had sole use of the garden, it was not completely outside the limitations of her purse.

The tenant was willing to give up her rights to the garden as she herself had no actual interest in gardening. When the vendor had informed her that the house was to be sold, she had asked that the garden should be assigned to her flat in case 'some undesirable' should buy the property.

'I wanted my privacy in the garden,' she added with a laugh. 'But of course I am quite happy for you to have it.' Mother was delighted. She was so entranced by the house and its possibilities that she agreed to this verbal arrangement without any qualms.

The garden had been neglected for many years, and was no more than a piece of wasteland. Coal had been dumped in one corner and refuse in another. Mother with her all-or-nothing philosophy transformed it within a few months, but it was this transformation that created problems for her.

The cause of the trouble was the tenant's cat. Mother hated cats, especially those that dug up her cherished flowerbeds. For want of a better solution Mother would spray the offending animal with either a hose or her watering can whenever she caught it substituting some of its own droppings for the flowers she had so lovingly planted.

Naturally, the old lady protested. Mother retaliated by suggesting that she should discipline her pet. As this was impossible, the pet continued to dig up Mother's flowers and Mother continued to turn the hose on it. The old lady became angry and forbade Mother the use of what she now referred to as 'her' garden. Naturally Mother ignored this 'impertinence' and was duly summoned to appear in court to defend her rights as the owner of a freehold property whose garden had been assigned to a tenant in the original purchase, albeit verbally.

The law being what it is, the Judge was bound on the basis of the assignment to uphold the tenant's claim that Mother should henceforth be excluded from the garden, on top of which she also had to pay the costs of the proceedings. The Court case made Mother extremely bitter but she decided to act on her favourite maxim 'Where there's a will there's a way'. She simply ignored the ruling and tended her plants whenever the tenant was out. She also developed a system of nocturnal gardening that led the tenant, a lady of Irish extraction, to remark somewhat whimsically that the leprechauns appeared to have been busy again.

Mother and I began to walk back to Addison Avenue and I noticed a terraced house with a For Sale board in the front garden. While she was busy preparing supper I established that the price of the house was £1800 and that it had four floors, three of which were occupied by statutory tenants. One of the tenants had been offered alternative accommodation by the council, and a closing order had been placed on the basement.

I asked Mother to look at the house next day. Her only comment was 'Nothing ventured, nothing gained'. I decided that same afternoon to take a gamble and proceed with the purchase. With that decision life took on a new sense of purpose. The closing order had been issued in the belief that there was no damp course, but when I began clearing the rubble, I discovered that the cause of the damp was nothing more than a fractured main water pipe.

The subsequent lifting of the closing order on the basement raised the value of the house considerably and this enabled me to increase my borrowing. Within three months I had a home to live and work in.

I now felt encouraged to practise again, so to give myself some sort of an aim I gave a recital at the Wigmore Hall in January 1960. My playing didn't appear to have suffered too much as a result of the manual labour I had been doing in my new home, but since the overdraft was mounting up, more regular work had to be found. I entered the lists for the position of principal cello of the BBC Symphony Orchestra and was lucky enough to be offered the post, starting in June 1960. The BBC management welcomed me into the fold and my name was duly slotted into the pigeon hole marked 'orchestral player' as distinct from chamber-music player, soloist or in exceptional circumstances, musician.

With a heavy heart I attended the first Promenade Concert rehearsals at an ex-cinema near Kilburn. Ahead lay several weeks of rehearsal. While Colin, Peter and Keith would be playing tennis, swimming, and sunning themselves in the splendour of Dartington at its best, I was back in the orchestral rut.

By the end of the first week I was already at war with the system, and by the second I was cursing Colin and myself. They were now safely established as the Dartington String Quartet while it was I who was trapped and forced to endure six hours of rehearsal a day, five days a week, for concerts that were only due to take place eight weeks later. It appeared that the main function of the orchestra was to provide a platform for music that was not heard very often in public, if indeed at all. The most soul-destroying aspect of the job was having to rehearse in Studio One, Maida Vale, which had a colour scheme that would have done credit to a run-down wartime Nissen hut.

After an absence of several years, including trips to Europe where the Philharmonia had given concerts in many fine halls, it was hard to accept that there was to be nothing to delight the senses or to help make an *occasion* of the twice-weekly broadcasts. You rehearsed. The red light went on. You played and then you went straight to the bar and had a few stiff drinks to deaden the pain.

Some individuals in the orchestra managed to survive by using the job more or less as part-time employment. Paul Marinari, for example had talents that extended over wide areas. These not only brought in the odd pound or two but also served to keep him sane. He could paint, was a wonderful photographer and could mend almost anything mechanical. He was a fine cellist, did his job well and was fluent in French and Italian, but asking him to enthuse over his job in the BBC Symphony Orchestra was like trying to make water flow uphill. Alex Nifosi was another gifted man in the cello section and there was my sub-principal, Alan Ford, a man of sweet temper and of unfailing good humour.

The reality of Dartington was by now almost totally obscured in a haze of poignant memories, whose rosy hue became increasingly unreal. When I wasn't romanticising about Dartington, I found myself thinking back on the superb concerts the Philharmonia had given while I was a member. With the appointment of Klemperer as its chief conductor, the orchestra was very much in the news and was attracting great acclaim.

What had I achieved with all this soul-searching since leaving the first desk in 1953? I was Principal Cellist of the BBC Symphony Orchestra, but had the struggle been worth it? It would have been more satisfying from every point of view to have stayed next to Raymond Clark in the Philharmonia.

But memories have to be managed, and I was being weak. Every move I had made since 1953 had been undertaken for a good reason, whether it was for the sake of the Philharmonia or of the BBC. As a principal I had now a position of some authority. There must always be something to learn from each new situation.

The Promenade Series went quite well and thanks to the loyalty and support of the cello section my task was made much easier than I had expected. On the last day I arrived for the morning rehearsal with a very bad head indeed. The night before I had witnessed the Beethoven Ninth Symphony ritual, the Promenaders encouraging Sir Malcolm with the usual badinage and Sir Malcolm responding with a kind of crash course on Beethoven Culture Made Easy. On this particular night, Sir Malcolm gave the audience a résumé of a recently published book on Beethoven and an analysis of the Ninth Symphony as well. Although I agreed that the book deserved the praise he gave it, when we came to the actual performance all feeling of compatibility vanished. Sargent's idea of Beethoven's music was not mine.

In the artists' bar afterwards I found myself in the company of Paul Beard and the orchestral manager, both also in need of spiritual hygiene. After a few drinks we began to exchange comments about the musical desecration in which we had just been obliged to participate. Paul was quite sure that in all the years he had played the Ninth Symphony no performance had been quite so banal. The orchestral manager agreed. I had only played the work with Karajan and Furtwängler, so couldn't contribute to the evaluation.

The next morning I was still suffering the effects of the previous night's alcoholic consolation and was quite unable to cope with the bustle around me. Sir Malcolm barking orders at the TV crew so as to perfect arrangements for the 'Sargent-TV-Stagewalk-Spectacular' was agonising. His objective was to achieve maximum TV coverage, which meant that the violins had to have new seating positions. Apparently he had been irritated by a recent TV broadcast in which he had only been heard to conduct the orchestra, so had planned the longest approach to the rostrum on record, causing the TV crews to spend much precious time repositioning and realigning their equipment.

The climax of the last night of the Proms is traditionally Sir Henry Wood's *Fantasia on British Sea-Songs*, ending with *Rule Britannia*. Although I had been playing in orchestras for fifteen years or more I didn't know the work. Consequently I was unaware that every movement features a particular instrument. When the time came for the tuba to be featured, Sir Malcolm brought proceedings to an abrupt halt. He spoke sharply to the tuba player, asking him to do the solo phrase in one breath. We tried the passage a second time, and again the soloist failed to achieve the breath control necessary to play the phrase in the way demanded. By now Sir Malcolm was definitely angry but before he could say anything, Paul Beard got up from his seat and whispered in his ear that the tuba player had recently undergone a severe stomach operation and had only just begun to play again.

'Then he shouldn't be here. I haven't got time to be a wet nurse.'

We started again and this time the gallant tuba player got through the solo as directed, albeit at enormous cost to himself. He was ashen when he finally put his instrument down. Together with the rest of the orchestra, I was fuming. How could anyone be quite so callous? Then Frank Ford turned the page and I was suddenly confronted with the solo cello part of *Tom Bowling*. I was faced with one of the chief hazards of orchestral playing—that of being heard.

It was certainly negligent of me not to have checked whether there was anything I needed to practise before the rehearsal, but the events of the morning had proved to be so distracting that somehow neither Frank nor I had given the Fantasia on British Sea-Songs much thought. The solo is not difficult in itself, but deciphering at sight the attempts of three earlier principals to work out a suitable fingering was well nigh impossible. Added to which, the lighting was bad. As a result I played several wrong notes and, not knowing anything about the mood of the piece, gave a less than adequate performance.

Sir Malcolm was now not only irritated but also slightly worried. What sort of a principal cellist had he been landed with? He couldn't even play Tom Bowling.

'Play it again.'

This was no request, it was an order. My second attempt was not much better than the first, but before Sir Malcolm had time to say anything I stood up and held out the offending sheet of manuscript.

'I'm sorry,' I said, 'but the light is atrocious and these notes are almost illegible.'

Sir Malcolm peered at it in some surprise and was momentarily taken aback. I decided to press home the attack.

'If the orchestra is to give a reasonable performance then it has to have reasonable conditions in which to work. How can anyone be expected to read a manuscript as messy as this while most of the main lighting is directed at you?'

The orchestral manager steered his way unsteadily through the maze of cables to point out that it was now too late to rehearse the solo again. In any case he was certain that everything would be fine on the night. It always was, he said, as any professional worth his salt knows very well.

This belief that everything will be 'all right on the night' is one of the enduring and on occasion very touching manifestations of why the professional musician does not despair to the point of total resignation. Concerts can, and mostly do, pull a little something out of the bag. However, the other equally enduring belief is that it can only be as good as it is going to be.

'Why not call a halt and have a drink?' suggested the manager.

The chorus of approval from the orchestra was too immediate and vociferous for Sir Malcolm to ignore.

George Willoughby, the manager, had a real talent for distinguishing between real battles, and skirmishes that were just part of over-reaction. In the latter event he was firm. The only satisfactory remedy was the bar. On this particular morning, he had obviously already made up his mind into which category, battle or skirmish, the confrontation between Sir Malcolm and myself fitted.   Sir Malcolm was very angry, but I was more angry with myself than anybody else. I regretted my decision to accept the post and, in consequence, my attitude to the job was cavalier. There would have been no argument that morning if I had practised the solo. I was in the wrong and had learned the lesson the hard way.

I put my cello away and slowly climbed up the steps of the band room. Paul Beard met me and suggested we had a drink. When we got to the bar the manager was already there, looking rather unhappy. I apologised for the fracas and, pretending not to notice the general gloom, began talking about the performance of the Ninth Symphony the previous evening.

'How is it possible,' I asked, 'that a man can be such a gifted speaker, make such penetrating observations about all kinds of things, be so obviously gifted as a musician and yet be such a crashing bore as a conductor?' Nobody ventured an opinion. 'Sir Malcolm is a fine pianist, he can compose and arrange, he has a big, clear beat. Why is he unable to share the magic of music with the performer?'

Paul was guarded in his choice of words, but he agreed that the previous evening's offering had been amongst the worst that he had ever had to take part in.

'Flash (the orchestral players' nickname for Sir Malcolm) never manages to sustain a musical line,' he said. 'He seems to have no idea of tempo and even less of dynamic contrast.'

We finished our drinks and went our separate ways. I practised my solo and, as Mr Willoughby had predicted, the concert was a great success. After it was all over I was told that Sir Malcolm wanted to see me. As I entered the room Paul was speaking and there was a twinkle in his eye.

'In all the years I've been leader of the orchestra, I've never heard such a marvellous performance of the Ninth Symphony. It seems to get better every year.'

Sir Malcolm flushed with pleasure and then turned to greet me.

'Ah, Mr Kok! And what did *you* think of the Beethoven?'

For a moment I stood speechless, my mind racing. I recalled Paul's words in the bar 'A tidal wave of synthetic emotion…' Paul was watching me carefully, his eyes seeming to ask 'How is he going to cope with this?'

Montaigne came to my rescue once again.

'He knows not what it is to burn,' I quoted a little uncertainly, 'whose flame in words he can express.'

Mr Willoughby choked over his gin and tonic. Paul looked startled. Sir Malcolm seemed impressed.

'Who said that?' he asked.

'I read it in one of Montaigne's essays,' I replied. 'But I can't remember whom he was quoting. It may have been Petrarch.'

'You must come round tonight. Just a few friends, you know.'

He could not have been more insistent.

Sir Malcolm's intrusive vanity could cause intense dislike, and he had a callous side, as shown in the episode with the tuba player that morning. During the 1930s he had said that orchestral players needed the threat of unemployment to keep them on their toes, a remark that he was never to live down. It was made at a time when fellow musicians had contributed to the cost of his convalescence in Switzerland after an attack of tuberculosis.

There must have been a fair amount of genuine shyness in his make-up however, and I believe it created an almost insuperable barrier between himself and the players. His mental brilliance made him quick to lose patience, and when people were slow on the uptake he could be decidedly testy. Perhaps it was the very intensity of his inner feelings that made it so difficult for him to communicate effectively with the orchestra. Over the next five years, Sir Malcolm and I had many discussions about music and its influence on life, and the better I got to know him the more I realised that there was also a very attractive side to his nature.

About this time I was moving away from the established church and was trying to experience belief rather than formulate or comprehend it intellectually. Sir Malcolm, on the other hand, was happy to remain within the fold, although he read widely and in depth about the whole question of faith. He gave me *The Hundred Religions of Man*, a book I shall always treasure.

Underneath his glossy exterior there was a restless spirit as well as a brilliant and enquiring mind. There was also a benign humanity that was, I am convinced, the real Sir Malcolm, but all this lay in the future. On that first evening at Sir Malcolm's home after the Proms, I only saw a rather shallow man basking in the afterglow of audience appreciation.

I awoke the next morning knowing that I had a few days' break from orchestral playing. I had played Tom Bowling for the first time and had learnt a little more about human vanity, my own included. More to the point the Grey Lady, cause of so much trouble the previous year, was now ready for collection. The engine had been rebuilt and the bodywork resprayed. What better test could there be than to drive down to Dartington, see a few friends—and possibly talk to Julia as well.

When I reached Totnes Annette told me that her life had changed drastically. Her friendships were attaining new and absorbing depths because, as she added with obvious amusement, there were several interesting 'relationships' going on at the same time.

'Living apart isn't all gloom and doom,' she said. 'It is in fact quite enjoyable, provided there are not too many "relations" around!'

It appeared that various suitors had not been slow to express an interest in a beautiful grass widow abandoned by a lunatic cellist in search of a dream. Furthermore she had recognised how much easier it is to work consistently when there is day-to-day financial security, and enough time to appreciate it. Her many friends noticed very quickly that Annette married to me was not the same person as the Annette now living on her own. She had survived unhappiness, and had re-surfaced stronger and with greater self-reliance. She was now free to direct all her energy into her work at Dartington Hall and into the society in which she had begun to establish a safe niche.

Bobby with Alvis Grey Lady in 1954

Even prior to our marriage her life had never been easy. Her father had returned from the Great War shell-shocked and it was her mother, Mrs Ingold, who had held family and business together. After the death of her husband, Mrs Ingold retained control of the company in the belief that her son would take over, but he wanted to be a farmer. When her daughter decided to marry a musician rather than someone who could have helped her manage the factory, Mrs Ingold must have had many sleepless nights. A further worry for her was my poor state of health after the car accident.

During the two years I was at Dartington Mrs Ingold never interfered but was always willing to help whenever she could. She had only begun to express doubts when Annette and I moved into a staff bungalow outside Totnes in January 1959. Our neighbour was Margaret Isherwood, aunt of Christopher Isherwood. I was unwittingly adding insult to injury by being able to talk endlessly on many subjects with Margaret although I was apparently totally incapable of communicating with Annette. The world-view clearly expressed in Margaret's book *Faith without Dogma*, seemed to parallel my love of music. She understood my disappointment with Peter Cox and with the paradox of a lovely setting filled with examples of non-artistic endeavour. These further hurts to Annette were too much for Mrs Ingold, and we agreed that it would be better if Annette and I were to separate for a while.

In the two years prior to our divorce in 1962, Annette not only learnt to talk freely to Margaret Isherwood but she also formed close relationships with two men, each offering her a depth of shared experience that she and I only touched once, and that was on the day before I finally left Totnes for London. We had gone to hear the Amadeus Quartet playing an all-Beethoven programme at Exeter University. One of the works had been the Opus 135, Beethoven's last quartet. It was this piece, written in the language of the purest art form yet devised, that broke down the barriers of her restraint. A cauldron of conflicting emotions erupted that evening, the last we were to spend together under the same roof. There were tears in her eyes for the first and only time in the years we had known each other.

'Why does this music hurt so much? Could you not have warned me, helped me to understand?'

I could say nothing. She had helped me to create the Dartington String Quartet precisely because she had known that I was so drawn to the repertoire of the string quartet and to the late quartets of Beethoven in particular. The quartet had been established with a concert platform in the Great Hall that was always available. Yet on the evening after the Amadeus concert I could find no words to comfort her.

CHAPTER TWENTY-NINE

The Seventh Symphony

Sir Malcolm Sargent's relationship with the BBC Symphony Orchestra frequently tested the goodwill of the players. As a consequence, most of the players had to develop a defence strategy of some sort or other. By the time I joined the BBC in 1960 I had already played in various orchestras for over fifteen years, working and watching the man at work, so I knew what to expect.

Off the rostrum I remember him as a lonely man, unsure of his public image but rarely able to resist adulation. On the rostrum his behaviour could often be a little unreal. If challenged he was very quick off the mark, forgetting that even if conductors never sound wrong, not even conductors can always be right. At some point during rehearsal, and nearly always during a concert, he deliberately chose to hide from us players a feeling for poetry that was certainly present in his makeup.

He could sometimes be very generous, but confronted by a hostile group of players he was eminently capable of holding his own. In front of a large group of singers, especially a ladies' choir, he could be charm itself and the bigger the choir the better. When he wanted information from the orchestra he became unpredictable, often illogical and impulsive and sometimes embarrassingly emotional. In private he was the perfect host. Never in all the years of our relationship did he once make me feel uncomfortable or ill at ease when we met for a meal and a talk. Once 'on the box' however his behaviour towards me was often so contradictory that I never knew what to expect or how to respond.

Having played Beethoven's Seventh Symphony so often, my

reaction at the prospect of a rehearsal and performance with Sir Malcolm in Studio One, Maida Vale was one of despair.

In the performance conducted by Furtwängler at the Albert Hall in 1947 the tempo he chose in the very first bar made the long melodic line of the woodwind melody immediately convincing. He controlled the two opposing themes with a logical insistence while, for those of us who have to play on the first beat of every bar, the energy required by the chord did not detract from the sustained sound of the solo woodwind.

Under Sargent we began with the customary hiccup on the first chord.

'The timpanist, brass, woodwind, and strings, were not together,' he said in his 'I told you so' tone of voice. This was the traditional and predictable Sargent broadside at the start of this particular symphony. Every time we rehearsed it we laid bets that he would stop us during the first bar. We would then be given a lecture on the need for concentration before proceeding any further. A technique tried and tested in amateur orchestras all over England.

I think that Sargent was unlucky. His work with the Liverpool Philharmonic had been his only opportunity to work in a hall with a satisfactory acoustic which was the same for both rehearsal and concert. Sir John Barbirolli told me in the early 1940s that his reason for accepting the Hallé appointment was so that he could rehearse and perform in a hall with a good acoustic.

The opening of this symphony presents problems of tempo and dynamic that benefit from a resonant hall, but will never convince the listener in a recording studio, or in the dry acoustic of the Festival Hall. This suits BBC engineers because they need a dry, dead sound, devoid of any sensual quality. But the dead sound does not suit the player, who must then manipulate it in order to give it life.

Flash gave a clear directive to his players, but if anything went wrong it was always their fault. The players, in turn, blamed the BBC engineers for making working conditions so difficult. At the same time they blamed Flash for being Flash, and Government for its perennial lack of interest.

This continuing collective disagreement created a hostile atmosphere. Even if the first chord was together and the woodwind passage flowed as it should (this did occur occasionally) Sir Malcolm would immediately make us play the section again 'just to make sure'.

He had many other hang-ups in the orchestral and choral repertoire, all manifested in the same manner and all rehearsed on the same 'I told you so' principle. One such was Nimrod in Elgar's *Enigma Variations*. Even if all the notes were played correctly the first time, the variation would have to be repeated 'just to make sure'. The players, being the well-trained household-pets Sir Malcolm thought they were, developed a tactic to cope with these Sargent blind spots. For example in the Elgar someone in the viola section would deliberately anticipate the beat or play a very audible wrong note.

'You see?'

Flash would be in his element. He would direct a broad, toothy smile at the wooden faces in front of him, and once again we would be subjected to a lecture on the need for concentration. We sat still, at peace with our thoughts, finding that this was less trouble than playing the section again and again.

Another source of irritation was the enthusiasm with which Sir Malcolm tried out new ideas without really understanding their inherent problems. During the lunch-break I was practising some of the sections we had rehearsed that morning, trying to find out what had made Sir Malcolm stop at these passages and what he had hoped to achieve. He came over and picked up the part.

'How do you play this? You appear to be playing the short note in different parts of the bow. Why don't you remain in the same part of the bow?'

'Because the short note would then have to carry the speed of the re-take. If the whole cello section were to do the same thing, you would hear an accent just where there shouldn't be one.' I played him the bars in question.

'The insistent rhythm, coupled with this rather exuberant dynamic marking, can easily become tiring,' I explained. 'To avoid this, and especially if the stroke has to be loud and insistent, the player has to have a relaxed bow arm.'

To illustrate this I played a few bars of the Allemande of Bach's G major Suite where the same bowing problem occurs.

After the break Sir Malcolm asked me to demonstrate to the cello section the bowing I had used in the Bach.

'Now look at the semiquaver section after the opening. Try to let the bow travel in the same way that Mr Kok's does.' This was easily one of the most embarrassing experiences I have ever had. Imagine my horror when he turned to Paul Beard and asked him to do the same thing for the violins and violas. Not surprisingly, he was greeted with a stony silence. I was given dark and, in some cases, venomous looks.

String players do not take kindly to being given dos and don'ts by a conductor who is not a string player. Sir Malcolm had not realised that although 'staggered bowing' solves a problem in the first section of the phrase, it can create another in the second. Also it takes practice to acquire this little trick and it was definitely not something to be trotted out in the middle of a rehearsal. The long and the short of it was that the rehearsal became a total shambles. Sir Malcolm was angry, the players were sullen and rebellious and I was left feeling responsible for it all. Sir Malcolm's talents as a musician could not compensate for his abrupt manner on the rostrum, but as professional musicians, we were obliged to consider the overall quality of his work, not his ability, or inability, to handle players. What irritated the players most was that he failed to share in concerts the poetry we knew he certainly possessed. He lacked an awareness of what music can mean, that might have compensated for its absence at rehearsal. He was a disciplinarian, egotist and driven by ambition and could not manage to balance that 'poetry in his heart' against his love of public display on the rostrum. On the whole, his performances lacked an inner grace that could convince and soothe. He found it hard not to interfere and did not trust the player enough to allow his or her talent the essential freedom required to breathe life into dead notes.

Furtwängler and Karajan, Cantelli and Giulini possessed a quality of poetry that was never in doubt, but they also had the courage to trust a player, where only trust can achieve the highest level of performance. I recall vividly concerts and recordings with Furtwängler. When I was still sub-principal in the Philharmonia I was able to watch this tall, gangling figure of a man at close quarters as he coerced and cajoled the orchestra, first into compliance and then into enthusiastic co-operation. This was never an easy task even at a distance of five feet, but when, later on, I played as an extra on the last desk I had to follow his extraordinary beat at a distance of about twenty-five feet.

Life had obviously left its mark on Furtwängler, and although he was consistently courteous in his requests to the players, he became noticeably remote and introvert with the passing years. He was always deeply concerned that the orchestra should give of its best and was particularly aware of the acoustic properties of the Albert Hall in which we were to perform the Seventh Symphony.

Where, in this particular Beethoven symphony, Sir Malcolm had an inflexible approach that left the listener uninvolved, Furtwängler would, almost imperceptibly, contrive to deceive the ear by moving the tempo along during slower sections and then holding it back in the quicker ones. He guided his players through the slow and impressive opening with a light touch. Sir Malcolm's progress through the same passage always appeared to be impeded by a load of heavy and unnecessary accents. When music is over-accentuated, the point and speed of contact between bow and string can be lost, and this inevitably changes the quality of the sound.

Because of the lively motif that emerges in the Allegro immediately after the transition from the slow introduction, the first movement of the symphony is particularly tiring to play evenly. The transition can, like the opening, also be a problem for conductors and it is one that Sir Malcolm never really solved. Furtwängler moved the orchestra from this passage to the next with an effortless ease that liberated the fresh and engaging first subject from the solemnity of the introduction without dissociating one from the other. It was always a wonderful experience to work with Furtwängler, although the air of constrained sadness with which he sometimes looked at us in moments of great emotional intensity was very disconcerting. When he was still a young man, he had wanted to achieve the highest possible standards, but I sometimes had the feeling during the recording of Tristan that, as far as his life experience was concerned, he was simply marking time.

Both Furtwängler and Karajan allowed players to help them to achieve their best, not merely in order to give a fine performance but for the sake of the work itself. Sir Malcolm, on the other hand, always had to be *in charge*, even when the work was greater than both conductor and orchestra.

CHAPTER THIRTY

Rome

One hot summer afternoon in May 1962 the BBC Symphony Orchestra was rehearsing the slow movement of a Haydn Symphony that has as its main theme a solo for the cello. Rudolf Schwarz, the orchestra's principal conductor at the time, wanted to alter the dynamics in the woodwind before moving on to the next movement. I wasn't sure whether we would be repeating the slow movement so sat waiting, happy to be given the opportunity to repeat my little contribution.

The argument waxed and waned and I must have dozed off for a few minutes. I had just finished reading H V Morton's book *In the Steps of the Master* and was revelling in the memory of sights and sounds of a Europe I had come to love during the few years I studied with Fournier and Casals.

Frank Ford nudged my knee with his bow before I began to snore. I started awake and on the spur of the moment made a decision. Why not go to Rome? The annual holiday was due at the end of the month and I needed an intellectual stimulus. In Rome I might find evidence of values that for centuries had given men and women of talent the strength to excel. Through their work I might find it possible to renew the faith in people that I once had.

A few weeks later I set off for Dover alone in my Rover 95 determined to head straight for the Fontana di Trevi and throw my coin into the fountain of love, hope and forgiveness. As I drove into the outskirts of the port I was stopped for speeding. I took the car-ferry ticket out of my pocket and pointed at my watch, looking pleadingly at the two policemen—and prayed.

'Don't do it again,' said the elder motioning me on my way.

I heaved a sigh of gratitude to St Peter. The holiday had begun.

An Italian friend of mine had arranged for me to stay in the semi-basement of a large house within walking distance of Trastevere, and it was there that I would return each night for the next three weeks, laden with post-cards, Chianti and pasta. The plan to abandon the car and to walk everywhere was fine to begin with, but as I extended my exploration of Rome, I had to rely more and more on public transport or taxis. I would usually end up in a piazza drinking 'Est, Est, Est'—a delicious example of Italian wine at its best and called 'Est' because no better name has yet been found.

Rome seemed, at first sight, to be a city within cities - ancient, old and contemporary. I planned to see St Peter's at daybreak, at noon and at night in order to see how the great basilica was built in relation to the sun and the moon. When I found myself facing its enormous doors, late in the afternoon of the second day, I felt vaguely disappointed. I had expected to find a warren of old streets shielding, until the last moment, the magnificent spectacle of the Christian Church's answer to the Colosseum. One built to consecrate Life, the other to extinguish it. It will never again be possible to emerge suddenly onto the Piazza and approach the great basilica with a thrill of surprise. Even the house in which Raphael had his studio had to be demolished to make the broad new Via della Concilazione.

My reaction at the sight of the Colosseum was one of unequivocal amazement. The Venerable Bede had called it a monstrous circle of savagery. It is built on marshland and its stupendous weight has been resting for nearly 2,000 years on artificial foundations set in water. To have built a structure of such size on such marshy soil is surely one of the great wonders of engineering.

The arena was a suntrap from which there was little respite. I settled down in a cool spot with the intention of practising my DIY eye-camera technique: shutting and opening my eyes until I could remember as many details as possible. I imagined Caesar seated in the Imperial box and the senators and their wives near the rails. Above them the Aristocracy would have sat, with the Vestal Virgins just below the top of the giant circle. All were separated from the mob, but all gathered to witness the effect on humans and animals of terror, pain and the fear of death. I was sickened by the thought of the living and the persecuted put to death simply to please or appease.

The next day I made my way along the Via Appia, through the desolate Campagna and found myself standing in front of the Church of St Sebastian. Entering the cool interior I remembered a concert at the Festival Hall with Cantelli in 1954 that included Debussy's *The Martyrdom of St Sebastian*. It is always difficult to listen objectively to beautiful playing, in this instance the oboe phrase near the end of the work. Jock Sutcliffe had played it with such exquisite timing in spite of the poverty of the acoustic.

I could still remember the sound of that concert, so by the time I reached the catacomb of St Calixtus, where I wanted to pay my respects to St Cecilia the patron saint of music, I was already in a state of supercharged emotion. It was therefore with feelings of awe that I looked at what must have been one of the earliest paintings of the Madonna, Child and Magi. My whole life and everything I had ever worked and stood for seemed to be so trivial by comparison.

Legend has it that St Cecilia was obliged to invent a musical instrument in order to express the heavenly sounds that she alone heard and, presumably that is why she was chosen as the patron saint of musicians. She was a very rich patrician, living in a palatial house on the site of which St Cecilia's Church in Trastevere now stands; one of the loveliest churches in Rome. She was to be put to death for turning to the new Christian faith but, because of her position in society, it was decided that she should be spared the shame of a public execution and die by asphyxiation. She was locked in the bathroom of her home with the heat vent fully opened, but the following morning she was found unharmed, kneeling in prayer.

Once again she had to face the executioner, but this time she would be beheaded. She died from the blow, but the executioner was unable to sever the head completely. Placed in a coffin made of cypress wood St Cecilia lay undisturbed until 817. When the coffin was then opened, the body was found to be intact. It remained so until 1599 when, after it was opened for the second time, Stephen Maderna (a local sculptor) made a plaster cast of the body, still intact, lying as if in a deep sleep. In the catacomb of St Calixtus was a replica of the plaster cast, with an inscription written by the sculptor himself.

'Behold the body of the most holy virgin Cecilia, whom I myself saw lying incorrupt in her tomb. In this marble I have made for you the image of that saint in the very posture in which I saw her.'

I made up my mind to go to Tivoli next, to see the Villa d'Este and Hadrian's villa, so the next morning I set off in the direction of the Sabine Hills. Tivoli is about 700 feet above sea level and while Rome lay sweltering, the weather was perfect in the little town. No wonder that so many of the men of ancient Rome spent as much time as possible here during the hot summer months.

When Hadrian was a small boy Nero inaugurated the first persecution of the Christians in AD 65. He would possibly have seen some of the early members of this new sect, whose teacher was a man called Peter. After his crucifixion St Peter's body was buried in a nearby hillside cemetery and it was in this very graveyard that the victorious Christian Church erected the first buildings of the great basilica that was later to bear his name.

Nothing is left of Hadrian's tomb except for an immense brick core, every scrap of marble having long since been stripped away. Even his ashes have been lost, and all that now remains is the urn and a tablet on which are inscribed the words of Hadrian's famous address to his soul. I do not know Latin but this translation appears in Jerome's book 'Roman Memories':

> Genial, little vagrant sprite,
> Long my body's friend and guest,
> To what place is now thy flight?
> Pallid, stark and naked quite,
> Stripped henceforth of joke and jest.

It is difficult to understand how such a man could write something as simple and unaffected as this, having in the formative years of his life witnessed the horrors attributed to Nero and Caligula. Then I remembered Gibbons' cautious words:

> 'After the Church had triumphed over her enemies, the interest as well as vanity of the captives prompted them to magnify the merit of their respective suffering... A convenient distance of time or place gave an ample scope to the progress of fiction; and the frequent instances which might be alleged of holy martyrs whose wounds had been instantly healed, whose strength had been renewed, and whose lost members had miraculously been restored, were extremely convenient for the purpose of removing every difficulty, and of silencing every objection...'

I must have dozed off in the middle of these thoughts and, on awakening, found myself being stared at by a young woman. I asked her if she would care to share a pot of fresh coffee with me and we exchanged backgrounds. As we waited for the coffee to arrive, she asked me why I looked so worried. I explained that I seemed to have reached some sort of crossroads in my life. I couldn't go back to an imagined existence in the past, and if I stood still in the present-day traffic-jam occasioned by the multi-media and multi-national invasions of my privacy and individuality, I should simply be flattened. I went on to talk at some length about the rival claims of Religion and Science and the seeming failure of either to bring that 'peace that passeth all understanding'.

'Why should we assume that it is necessary to be continually trying to advance our knowledge?' she asked. 'We imagine that we are looking for solutions when, perhaps, we are not even asking the right questions. You spoke just now about the need for belief and acceptance before Religion can bestow its blessings. How then do you reconcile this need for acceptance with the questing spirit? Life is a continuous process and if we remained inert and static we should soon cease to exist. We are always in the process of *becoming* whatever we have it in us to be.'

We finished our coffee and then walked along to the famous cascades where the River Anio takes its impressive leap into the valley below. We climbed up to the little circular temple of the Sybils, hiding beneath its low roof. Of all the relics of antiquity left to us, this was the one most frequently reproduced in English county estates during the period of Georgian grace, when the search for meaning was demonstrated by a unique blend of architecture, music and philosophy.

It was at the nearby Villa d'Este that Liszt had lived because he considered his trills to be in need of 'maintenance'. He spent over three months practising them for several hours a day. When I got back to England, I listened to a recording of the *Fountains of the Villa d'Este* played by Horowitz, and could easily imagine the old abbé Liszt, sitting on a terrace, looking out over the avenues of laurel and ilex and listening to the ceaseless symphony of the waters.

Late in the afternoon my young companion and I parted company and I set out for Hadrian's Villa. It stands on 180 acres of land and I must have walked over most of it, trying to imagine what it must have looked like when the Master of the Roman

World came there to spend the last days of his life, devoting his time exclusively to painting, music, poetry and literature.

He had travelled all over the world of his time, and in his declining years brought together replicas of famous buildings that had impressed him on his imperial tours. I walked round the foundations of the Lyceum, the Academy, the Prytaneum, the Stoa Poecile, the Egyptian sanctuary of Canopus and enormous domed libraries. There were swimming pools large and small, and a large beach for sunbathing, the sands of which were artificially heated in the winter. In the centre of all this stood the imperial palace on a small island, surrounded by a high wall and dotted with the remains of marble-faced rooms. It was separated from the mainland by a bridge on rollers and once the bridge was withdrawn nobody could reach the island. What a place for a studio!

The next day two friends were to join me. Charles Chase, the architect, and Daphne Ibbott, whose husband had recently died after a long illness. We had all agreed to meet in Rome so that we could throw our three coins into the famous fountain. Charles was due to arrive in the late afternoon so I decided to visit St John in Lateran (the 'Mother Church of Christendom') and the church of St Paul in the morning. The original Church of St John had been destroyed by Pope Sixtus V. An old man, and in a hurry, he swept away the whole cluster of Byzantine and medieval buildings, thereby severing all direct links with the first great Christian church ever built, and one that contained a mosaic of the first picture of Christ to be shown in a public place.

Time passed unnoticed and I had to drive as fast as the Italians to reach the airport in time to meet Charles. He had already arrived, and I was delighted to see that tall figure and the bearded Castro-like face. It was nearly four years since we had last met and then parted, having agreed to differ. He had taken Annette's side during the break-up of our marriage and I suppose I felt in my

heart of hearts that he was right, although I had very much needed
his support at the time.

As we drove back I pointed out the ruins of the aqueduct
covering the flat, featureless landscape.

'Wouldn't it be marvellous if that aqueduct could be made to
bring water down from the hills again!'

'Why?' he asked, and his voice was dry and devoid of any
interest. As we entered the outer suburbs, where stark concrete
blocks of flats stood impenitently amid piles of Roman rubble, I
tried again.

'I wonder how much of that rubble came from the ruins of great
palaces?'

'There ought to be fewer palaces and more rubble,' was his
reply. 'One should live in the present,' he said icily, 'and work for
the future, and on no account allow oneself to he restricted by the
past.'

I said nothing more. Daphne would be meeting us that evening
at my favourite restaurant by the Fontana di Trevi. I was sure they
would enjoy what the little taverna had to offer and then we could
drive to various vantage points on the Seven Hills and let the
Eternal City weave its magic spell around my unhappy old friend.

The meal was excellent and Charles was polite to Daphne, but
remained stiff and formal, and at the first reasonable opportunity
he went off to bed.

The next morning the three of us set out to walk along the
Great Wall of Rome. It didn't take long to reach the Palazzo
Borghese, to cross the Tiber and then walk up the Via della
Concilazione to St Peter's. I wanted Charles to see the Bernini
Baldacchino, but although it made no visible impression on him I
had my reward. The sun was beating down on the magnificent
entrance, and as we stood watching the great doors began to open.
Long searching shafts of light thrust into the interior of the
building and touched the Bernini Baldacchino. I felt as if I were

looking into the very womb of Christian belief and I stood transfixed, speaking somewhat incoherently about memories, dreams and visions.

This was all too much for Charles.

'Why do you always want to live in someone else's shadow? You want Rome to be something it never was and never can be. Learn whatever you wish, but for heaven's sake learn also to let go. You've often said yourself that growth is indispensible for life. You are simply bogged down in your own static world and, in such a world, how can there can be any growth?'

Charles once told me that the happiest period of his life had been in Germany after the war had ended. For several months he had found love and happiness in the friendship of a young girl - happiness he had never known before or since. His frequent visits to a certain block of flats were eventually reported to the military police. He was put on a charge for fraternisation with the enemy and sentenced to a term of imprisonment. When he had served his time he went to look for his girl but found that she had gone. He tried at first not to believe that she had simply walked out on him, but this is what he was told by all those who professed to have known her. Perhaps the Military Police had been right after all. Perhaps she was just one of the many 'plants' that were used after the war to exploit the loneliness of young soldiers to transmit information - any information - back to the secret services of governments that wanted to be informed about the true intentions of their loyal and gallant allies.

After this experience his reaction was to throw himself into the pursuit of material gain and then, after the death of his wife, he sank into an unhappy agnosticism.

'What I consider to be important,' I said, 'is not necessarily my religious belief as expressed as a label of itself. The quality of my life must surely be affected when I see around me evidence of the quality that existed for all to see 2000 years ago and what we are able to achieve today. Compare the White City Stadium at Shepherd's Bush with the Colosseum. Which is the more impressive?'

'Don't be a fool,' he snapped.

'You're denying everything I say exists because either you don't believe it or you don't understand it. I want to experience the quality of my daily life and each day enables me to search for an understanding of what matters.'

'How can you discuss the quality of your life when two thirds of the population of this world are starving?'

'What can anyone actually do about someone else's pain?' I asked. 'It is an appalling indictment of our planet that people can apparently enjoy witnessing the systematic killing of other people, but it happened and still happens. What I have been trying to understand, especially during the last three weeks, is whether my belief in God would have been strong enough to withstand the onslaught of torture and the fear of death.'

'How can your levels of belief and understanding apply to everybody?' said Charles dismissively. 'How can a race of people living in the Amazon rain forest know anything about our idea of God and Reality? There are no answers, just face it and accept it.'

Daphne had not yet said a word, but now she joined in the conversation.

'My husband wasn't very old when he died,' she said quietly, 'and he didn't have a very easy death, either. We were always short of money and we lived in a rather dreary part of London, but I doubt whether it would ever have occurred to him to suggest that the under-privileged could be helped by stripping the world of its beauty. It is not the indulgence of artistic creativity that causes poverty. On the contrary it encourages crafts and craftsmanship, which in turn benefit the spirit. It is war, and the fruits of war, that create conditions that lead to hunger and disease. Apart from the spiritual uplift, the building of all these churches and palaces must have provided food and clothing for generations of workers. The Glorious October Revolution, which you appear to admire, has done little more than spread disease and famine on an unprecedented scale.'

'I'm sorry,' said Charles gruffly, 'I didn't know about your husband's illness. There may be practical benefits that workers derive from the extravagance of their rulers, but I'm not particularly impressed by the so-called spiritual needs that you seem to think can be satisfied by one man breaking his back in the hot sun so that someone else can live in the lap of luxury.'

'Charles,' I said. 'You are advocating a purely materialistic approach to life to the exclusion of all spiritual values. Could you explain what it is you love about Alvis motor cars that make them special for you?'

I knew for certain that I had touched on a raw nerve. He was obviously trying to marshal his thoughts, but how was he going to define those qualities which make an Alvis different from other cars, without climbing down and admitting that there was at least some validity in Daphne's argument.

'Alvis was a good car when it first appeared on the roads because it was well made, according to the standards of the time. Today it is, strictly speaking, an anachronism. By modern standards it is uneconomic and inefficient. A materialist like myself can also be sentimental from time to time, but that is a purely personal matter. An Alvis has no inner core of valuable existence, it is just a collection of particles that have been arranged in a way that happens to suit me. When I disappear, the value disappears.'

'But you didn't arrange those particles,' said Daphne. 'Someone else did—a whole team of people in fact. What is the common bond between the arrangers of the particles and the observer of them? Quite a number of individuals, besides yourself, seem to find that bond stronger than the bond of economic necessity about which you speak.'

'Surely,' I said before Daphne could continue, 'a bond of this kind is created by a common purpose, uniting the efforts of the team in order to achieve something of value. Even though the thing of value is in this case material, the quality that gives it its true value is immaterial. We are inspired by something that is outside us, unseen and unknown, but it must be there because we are moved by it. It is therefore valuable in itself and, because of its essence, it imparts value. Call it what you will, but I call this something, God.'

'Rubbish,' said Charles. 'The difference between us is that I have struggled to be myself, whereas you have tried, or pretended to be, somebody else.'

This really hurt. I knew that many of the things I had hoped to achieve had eluded my grasp. There were certainly many contradictions in my character, but this did not make me a pseud - which is what Charles seemed to be implying.

Suddenly I felt relieved that the holiday was almost over and that I had to get back to work in London.

On the return journey to England we visited the church at Ronchamp and I was interested to know what Charles would make of this experiment in concrete. Not surprisingly he told me that this was the way ahead for architecture. We noticed that there was about a six second echo, so I suggested that we should sing Three Blind Mice in celebration of his vindication. By the time I joined in as the third mouse the echo had almost obliterated any clarity of sound and we were forced to stop. Daphne and I were laughing at our attempt to sing in a 'concrete' context, but Charles was not amused. We had stayed quite long enough for each of us to confirm our thoughts about Courvoisier's use of concrete to enclose consecrated space. Charles offered to drive from Besançon to Boulogne and I leaned back on the rear seat of the car and went to sleep. When I awoke, we were only a few miles from Boulogne and boarded the boat with a few minutes to spare and reached London at 3am.

The next day I decided to spend the day quietly in an attempt to unwind a little. After breakfast I walked down the street to Mother's house, just around the corner. I made her some tea and then we sat down in her favourite spot under a Japanese cherry tree.

She listened in silence while I spoke of my disappointment at having lost the ability to communicate with a man whom I had come to love, but with whom I was unable to share the many reactions my holiday had awakened in me.

'It seems to me,' Mother said in a matter-of-fact tone of voice, 'that although Charles is obviously capable of surviving in this world, his refusal even to consider the next must cause him more problems than he is willing to admit.'

'Charles appears to think that if a man's basic needs have been satisfied, with food to eat, water to drink, sanitation and medication to keep him more or less healthy, then it is superfluous to direct his energies into the vague areas of metaphysical speculation.'

'Poor fool he,' said Mother.

The dismissive tone in which she spoke these three words made me rise involuntarily to the defence of my friend.

'Isn't that a little unfair?' I said. 'After all, he has had quite a tough life, you know. There was the hardship he suffered as a boy, then the war, and now the death of his wife.'

'Hardship never does anyone any harm,' said Mother. 'As for war, do you imagine I don't know something about war? And about the loss of people who are near and dear to you? We were ten children in our family. My father died before I saw him and two of my sisters and two brothers died young of illnesses that today could be cured quite easily. Life must go on. It's no use complaining when things go wrong. Challenges are there to be met and overcome. To suggest that there is no meaning in the things men do, or in the gifts that Life offers, is merely part of the mass neurosis of the world today.'

I knew that there was no point in my trying to defend Charles against Mother. If he spoke of the need for simple, basic doctrines that all members of society could use as a term of reference, Mother would inevitably ask him what was wrong with the lessons of the Christian Gospel.

'It is inert and static,' he would reply. 'It preaches a 'once-for-all' doctrine and that is not good enough for me.'

'What the Gospel teaches, is a matter for study and speculation,' Mother would say. 'The fact that its message has been interpreted in so many ways is proof that it is possible to believe in matters of the spirit, or God if you like, and yet be able to retain independence of thinking. The Gospel deals with the immaterial world and the State is concerned with the material. Parents should strive to give their children security, but the time comes when children are faced with needs that can no longer be sustained by the thought patterns of their childhood. They become insecure once more, but should by then have learnt to live securely with insecurity and to continue to grow as human beings.'

As I sat with her under the cherry tree I realised that the hours of toil in the many gardens she had made must have been an ideal time for speculation which formed the basis for her positive attitude to life.

I mentioned my question to Charles about Alvis motor cars, asked in the effort to shake his belief in the materialistic approach to life.

'Unless he is prepared to re-examine his Marxist concepts and widen his horizons he will shrivel up like a dried apple,' said Mother. 'You know, old Charles really is a *pampoen* (pumpkin z/nitwit). He is intelligent and yet he swallows the simplistic jargon of atheism. Just look at those flowers over there. The whole cycle of growth, death and rebirth is plain for all to see, if people only want to look. As for Ronchamp,' Mother had a mischievous glint in her eye, 'perhaps Courvoisier wasn't altogether wrong.

One should always be willing to test new materials to see if they are in any way compatible with the task in hand.' Then, with an air of finality, 'but that does not mean that one has the right to disregard form.'

CHAPTER THIRTY ONE

Dorati and the Mendelssohn Octet

In those dream-moments of rehearsal time, when neither the composer's intentions nor his messenger's beat have been understood, and protracted arguments about detail can so easily turn into a vendetta, my last resource was to drift away into a land of 'suppose'. In one such dream-moment an idea I had been toying with for some months past began to take shape.

Suppose we were to enable members of the orchestra to balance the prescribed menu of public-duty music with programmes of chamber music? Suppose we were to form a group consisting of principals, and do what Berlin and Vienna have done. We could call ourselves 'The London Octet' and, with luck, be invited to play in the Musikvereinsaal.

The BBC orchestra had been rehearsing the second movement of the Schumann Symphony in D minor and because it is such a sublime work I wanted the performance to be equally sublime. It occurred to me that if the violins were to have the 'space' that a particular phrase in their beautiful solo warranted, the bowing in the cello part would have to be altered.

I noticed that the part had already been marked with a blue pencil, so rather than waste time rubbing it out, I added mine underneath the notes instead of above, as is usual. We had reached the most expressive section of the long sustained phrase when Sir Malcolm stopped conducting. With obvious irritation he asked me why I was not playing the bowing marked in blue pencil. These markings were his personal trademarks, he said, and *were not to be altered under any circumstances.*

Obviously Sir Malcolm had right on his side, but his tone of voice was so unpleasant that I immediately took umbrage and reasonably civil disagreement soon developed into a fairly acrimonious exchange. However the conductor's word is final, it is a battle the player must inevitably lose, and I was obliged to yield.

Turning to the cello section I apologised for my mistake and for having wasted everybody's time. Sir Malcolm's *blue-pencilled* bowings were re-instated and, still feeling annoyed about the whole stupid incident, I turned to Frank Ford (my sub-principal) who was busy altering the part.

'Chateaubriand says that every nation gets the Government it deserves.'

Frank, slightly deaf in his left ear, asked me to repeat what I had said. I obliged, but Sir Malcolm, anxious to get on with the rehearsal, had already started the movement again, and I was still only halfway through the quote when a sudden pianissimo gave my illustration of the Politics of Power an unexpected prominence. Normally, this would have passed without comment but a distinctly audible voice from the back of the cello section said, with obvious feeling and perfect timing, 'Yes, and every cello section gets the Leader it deserves.'

Some of the players, although initially amused at my discomfiture, were now becoming irritated. Others began to laugh. Sir Malcolm, anticipating trouble, pretended he hadn't heard the repartee and started the movement yet again, with only half the cellos playing. By this time there was so much laughter in the section that the rest of the orchestra joined in. Sir Malcolm had to give up the struggle and call an early break.

I was putting my cello in its case when I heard the leader of the second violins, whose manner and appearance had earned him the nick-name of The Iron Duke, say to Sir Malcolm, 'This sort of thing always happens when you get chamber musicians trying to be orchestral players.'

Having overheard the remark I couldn't resist asking The Iron Duke what he meant, but since no reply was forthcoming, I suggested that I should play the disputed phrase in two styles, first under the Iron Duke's direction as an orchestral player and then as a chamber music player. Or, I added as an afterthought, would the Iron Duke care to demonstrate his point on the violin and permit Sir Malcolm to arbitrate?

Sir Malcolm muttered something about my not having to take the matter so personally.

'On the contrary,' I said, 'why should I be publicly rebuked for trying to improve the commitment of my section? If we are to be fully involved in the performance we must be allowed to contribute some of our individual and collective experience. With all due respect, bowing the cello part as you did creates an accent on every bar line. To me, this spoils the shape of the phrase.'

'You see!' The Iron Duke could not conceal his triumph. 'You see! Exactly what I was I saying!'

Then with heavy condescension he explained that orchestral playing requires 'a much broader spectrum'.

'You have to learn,' he said, 'to forget what you think the music means and simply play as directed by the conductor.'

Having played for nearly twenty years in a famous orchestra I was a little surprised to be written off in so cavalier a fashion, but made no comment. Instead, I asked a question.

'Tell me, how do you avoid misplacing the accent in a phrase if the decision isn't consciously recognised before you make the mistake?'

'It will all come out in the wash,' was the Iron Duke's reply.

'Perhaps,' I replied, 'but since the washing has been soiled for so long, can't we at least try and get some clean linen for a change? I'm sure none of us would want to be caught wearing dirty underwear.' Fortunately the break was nearly over and we had to abandon the argument.

As luck would have it the next item in the schedule was the Brahms B Flat major Piano Concerto with Claudio Arrau as soloist. I had played the solo cello part in the slow movement on several occasions, and the second cello part even more often. It is therefore quite possible that I approached the third movement of the concerto with my own version of a 'blue-pencilled' interpretation.

Arrau was as magnificent as always, weaving the piano filigree with consummate skill and sensitivity in contrast to the broad, typically Brahmsian melody played by the cello. As we neared the chord leading to the resolution in the last bar of the cello solo, I was already anticipating my little bit of heaven. By lengthening the top note of the descending arpeggio (just as Raymond Clark had done on so many occasions, particularly in the superb recording with Solomon and the Philharmonia). I could enjoy an extended *rubato* over the whole section before the piano enters. For this to succeed, it would be absolutely essential for me to keep an eye on the soloist up to his final entry.

I looked at Arrau, played the first note, and held on to it, making a slight *crescendo*. Arrau nodded his agreement. I released the tension in my bow arm and began the downward flow of the arpeggio. It was a lovely moment.

Sir Malcolm brought the baton down on his stand with a sharp tap.

'Mr Kok,' he barked. 'What are you doing?'

I was not prepared to have my moment spoiled, least of all after the contretemps earlier that morning.

'I would have thought it was clear that I am playing the cello,' I replied.

Sir Malcolm ignored the sarcasm.

'Play on my beat,' he said.

I had no choice, so we repeated the section that leads to the piano entry, but by this time the magic had gone. I glanced at Arrau and was cheered to see that he was definitely winking at me as if to say, 'Never mind. Let it pass for the moment, but play it your way at the concert.'

That evening Arrau was as good as his wink. Just before I started the descending phrase I looked at him, and for the remaining bars of the movement we joined forces in mutual defiance of an extremely irate conductor, vainly trying to attract my attention by making increasingly large and vicious cuts in the empty air.

I was duly reported to the management and was informed of Sir Malcolm's displeasure at my lack of professional discipline. At the end of the broadcast I saw the Iron Duke making his way to the Artists' Room and was certain that my position in the orchestra was being reviewed. Imagine therefore my surprise when, the next day, Sir Malcolm walked over to me during the break and invited me to lunch.

We discussed the Schumann symphony, my reasons for altering his bowings, and above all, what I felt I had learnt from Raymond Clark about the disciplines of orchestral playing. I tried to explain my belief that an orchestral player needs to react to the music and that he must be given the opportunity to 'feel' the occasion, not only as part of a group but also as an individual. I added, with special reference to the Brahms, that he should also be given the opportunity of contributing to the magic of the music *around* the beat as well as *on* the beat.

Sir Malcolm seemed genuinely interested in what I had to say and when we finished our meal he asked me round to his flat to go over the score of the Schumann with him.

I don't know whether I ever converted him to my point of view, but I do know that I came away feeling an overwhelming need to play some chamber music. I felt a need to revitalise myself, especially after my visit to Rome, and went to see Sir William Glock. I had heard the Berlin Octet play at Cape Town University in 1961 and since then had cherished the idea of following their example. I could already picture *The London Octet*. Why should we too not achieve recognition *via* broadcasting, or even concert status at home and abroad?

Sir William was enthusiastic and gave me the green light. I spoke to the other principals and a series of concerts was planned which was to include a performance of the Mendelssohn Octet at one of the 1963 Promenade Concerts.

Many hours were devoted to rehearsing the string sextet version of Schoenberg's *Verklärte Nacht*, a work of infinite subtlety and enormous sensitivity. I prefer a small group for this work, mainly because, in the context of his musical imagery, Schoenberg arouses emotions that are far too intimate for the sixty or so string-players of a symphony orchestra. Our recording of *Verklärte Nacht* was the one piece of chamber music in which a standard of performance was achieved that would be accepted and adopted by the orchestra as a whole.

I believed that, to have a healthy orchestra it is essential to provide as wide a range of involvement with music-making as possible. I therefore conceived the plan of introducing into each section a rota system that would enable players to devote themselves at regular intervals to specialist areas of teaching, to solo and chamber music performance, instrument repair, and even instrument making. Players could also build up a programme of teaching at schools in their neighbourhoods and so help promote the excellent work initiated by Jenny Lee after World War Two. (It is not generally known that the Act she brought before the Commons stipulated provision by the State of both teacher and instrument even if the pupil wanted to learn a Chinese gong.)

The more ambitious members of the orchestra could give concerts within the Home Counties' seventy-five mile radius, a limit the BBC had to observe in order to guarantee autonomy to regional broadcasting. They could also play, for expenses plus a minimum fee, at the many Music Clubs that were being threatened with closure all over the country because of the Arts Council's withdrawal of support after 1945.

I still consider my project to have been eminently reasonable and yet, when I proposed it to the BBC authorities in 1963, their reaction was immediate and negative.

'Far too radical,' was the official and final verdict. A verdict that was not only discouraging but also extremely shortsighted because it inevitably condemned players to work solely within the confines of the administration. It deprived them of the challenge of playing as individuals and also of hearing themselves play in varying acoustic conditions.

I was still nursing the grievance caused by the rejection of my rota system for principals, when Hans Keller phoned me one evening to ask whether I knew that Antál Dorati was to replace Rudolf Schwarz as Permanent Conductor. Also Hugh Maguire and Paul Huband were taking over from Paul Beard and George Willoughby, who were retiring. Up to that moment I was unaware that anyone had even been approached, so news of the three appointments came as a complete surprise.

For two years, in anticipation of the retirement of these key figures, Sir William and I had been discussing various essential appointments that would bring the BBC into line with London's four other top-line orchestras. I had suggested that the advice of eminent outsiders such as Manoug Parikian or Walter Legge should be sought before final choices were made, and Sir William had appeared to be in agreement. Now it seemed that everything had already been arranged without any consultation and I was faced with an entirely unexpected situation.

Maguire and Huband were, like myself, ex-Academy students, but Dorati was no more than a name to me. It would be useless to pretend that I did not feel slighted by the way in which my suggestions had been ignored and I did not look forward with any great enthusiasm to making the acquaintance of the new conductor. However I soon realised that in spite of his idiosyncratic music-making, Dorati was a very gifted and lovable man.

On his very first day at the BBC the orchestra was treated to an electrifying display of Dorati's temper. Mr Huband had hardly completed the introduction of the orchestra's new Permanent Conductor when Dorati announced that we would all get to know each other much better if we were to rehearse the Eroica Symphony of Beethoven.

He gave the first down beat. The orchestra responded. Then came the second down beat for the second bar. Finally, on the third down beat, the cellos are supposed to set off on the exposition of a work that is surely Beethoven's finest symphony. Dorati stopped the orchestra. Looking in my direction, and without attempting to disguise his displeasure, he barked, 'Play on my beat!'

The orchestra started again from the beginning. Again he stopped. This time he was really angry. A profusion of remarks about lack of attention to rhythmic discipline was directed at me and we had to start again. I was at a loss to understand why the cellos were being singled out when quite obviously *all* the players in the orchestra had come in late.

'Not bad for ten minutes' work,' I said to Kenneth Heath, my recently appointed co-principal. I looked across at Hugh Maguire who, touching his right ear, grinned in mock sympathy.

For some reason the third bar is usually played slightly behind the pulse beat; it has become a tradition. Perhaps Dorati was right. Perhaps we had got into the habit of taking too much time to get back to the heel of the bow after the first two chords. Turning to the cello section sitting in embarrassed silence behind me, I suggested that we all count six beats from the beginning and then come in firmly on the seventh.

Dorati tried once more. He turned his head slightly so that his left ear was almost in line with the cello section. It was then that the meaning of Hugh's sign language became clear: Dorati was deaf in his right ear. Since the cellos were on the right side of the rostrum, he would hear the upper register of the orchestral sound before the lower one. It was now too late to warn the section, so having religiously counted our six beats we all arrived in the next bar way ahead of the rest of the orchestra and, of course, way ahead of the new conductor. This was too much for Dorati.

He slammed down his baton, stormed off the rostrum and retired into his dressing room where through the window we could see a silent-film charade of anger and placation as conductor and orchestral manager tried to reach common ground. Visibly shouting at Mr Huband he changed out of his work tunic, put on his shirt, tie and jacket and obviously intended to leave.

Those of us who were able to watch this pantomime were beginning to think that this might be for the best. There had been endless stories about Dorati and his tantrums when he conducted the LSO, and although Hugh had learnt to live with them, the rest of us had still to be educated. After such a silly reaction was he really the right man for the job? Unquestionably he had many exceptional gifts. It was his particular misfortune that he heard the upper frequencies of sounds ahead of the lower.

Most people hear sounds grouped in a form and sequence that may or may not be called music. They are absorbing a range of independent tones linked together in combinations, which they define as melodies or chords. One of the central problems arising from the acoustic properties of the varied halls in which music is performed, is the way in which the human brain sorts out and organises an extremely complex set of tonal stimuli into such combinations as determined by the composer. Judging from the extreme reaction displayed by Dorati on that memorable afternoon, there had to be more to his behaviour than mere petulance. I was convinced that there was something that could be investigated to our mutual benefit.

Eventually Dorati returned and somehow we survived the first encounter. As time went by I began to discuss with him the damaging effect the acoustic of Studio One, Maida Vale had on the hearing of the musicians who were compelled to work there. I began by re-reading various texts on the mechanisms by which the listener links successive tones into a musical sequence. In 1950, when acoustic tests were being carried out at the Festival Hall, I had been interested to discover that right-handed and left-handed listeners to music hear sounds in different ways. Right-handed listeners hear the high tone in their right ear, the low tone in their left ear, and they maintain this preference even when earphones are reversed. Left-handed subjects, on the other hand, are just as likely to localise the high tone in their left ear as in their right. So, whereas in *right*-handed people the left hemisphere of the brain is dominant and its primary auditory input comes from the *right* ear, in *left*-handed people either hemisphere may dominate.

In the case of Dorati, who was left-handed, his right-side hemisphere acted on a sound input from the cello section that did not exactly tally with the left-ear input. During the next few months Dorati became as interested as I did in the baffling problem of acoustics. In the end it was the bridge that helped us to become extremely good friends.

The practical consequence of all this was that I began to experiment with sound, particularly with tone-production in Maida Vale Studio One. I constructed a platform of softwood that held the cello spike a few inches above the floor, which was made of hard wood glued to concrete. It was easy to convince Dorati that the platform really did make the cello sound and also feel better, which is of great psychological importance. Dorati then agitated at the very highest level. I was eventually asked to appear before a group of boffins from the BBC research centre in Surrey. I played on my homemade platform. They listened. I then played on the floor, with my spike going straight into the teak blocks on their concrete base and finally on a carpeted section of the studio. Recordings were made of the variables, and comparisons made.

Several months later I arrived at Studio One and was astonished to see a beautifully constructed platform made especially for the cello section. The boffins had turned up trumps. Not only was there an elegant platform, but specially designed chairs and music stands had been included as a bonus.

I immediately went to thank Dorati, who was only too happy to try out there and then the promise of our joys to come. I produced my cello, adjusted my chair exactly to fit my generous size and began to tune. Total disaster. The new platform had been made of *hardwood*.

I suppose it was inevitable that engineers would decide to build what suited their recording criteria. Musicians would still be forced, like the damned standing before the entrance to Dante's Inferno, to raise their voices in anguish and cry out 'Abandon hope all ye who enter here'.

There was of course another major problem. Supposing, for example, there were to be three days of rehearsal at Maida Vale. For 18 hours players would be adjusting to the acoustic of Studio One, and the orchestral parts would be marked in accordance with that acoustic. On the day of the concert the final rehearsal would take place in an empty hall in the morning with a changed acoustic. In the evening the sound would again be different because of the lack of depth to the sound and also because there was now an audience to deaden the brittle effect of the hall's acoustic.

This arrangement was one that neither the management nor the programme planners were prepared to discuss. The BBC was understandably proud of its in-house orchestras, particularly its Symphony Orchestra, committed as it was to the provision of 27 hours of live and recorded music per week. It was nevertheless not prepared to recognise that music-making is either a sentient living thing or it is nothing. Perhaps it was a consequence of a bureaucracy that had 'grown upon what it had fed'. Whatever the reason, the cold stifling hand of the mediocrat misdirected and finally killed any hope of maintaining the artistic standards that Sir Adrian Boult had achieved before World War Two.

Casals had taken great pains to make me understand that when I had learnt to make a beautiful sound on one note, I then needed to ensure that the *next* note sounded equally beautiful, and the next one after that, and so on. Beauty of sound for the BBC boffins is definitely an irrelevance.

Meanwhile there were many matters of daily routine to think about. What had I actually achieved so far in my three years at the BBC? I had done the usual orchestral grind like everyone else, but apart from that I seemed to have spent most of my time at meetings and on the telephone, trying to establish for the players financial parity with members of the London Symphony Orchestra, the Philharmonia, the London Philharmonic and the Royal Philharmonic. The one bright patch in all this dreary routine had been the formation of the London Octet and the opportunity to play chamber music as part of our contract. Together with the sextet version of Schoenberg's *Verklärte Nacht* we had recorded the Spohr Octet. We were working on the Mendelssohn Octet which we were to perform later that summer at the Proms—the first time that a piece of chamber music would ever be heard at a Prom series. We were soon to broadcast the Schoenberg String Trio and the Brahms A minor Clarinet Trio. A promising start had been made and Sir William Glock had certainly kept his word. If I could organise the players, he would do his best to provide us with a public platform. At least the need for chamber music was being acknowledged.

My suggestion that orchestral players should be encouraged to teach in the areas in which they lived had been dismissed by the BBC administration as being far too radical. I had been told that

Sir Adrian Boult rehearsing, Manoug Parikian leading
Walthamstow Town Hall 1957

the West of England Players were to be disbanded because of
insufficient funds, or so it was alleged. However, the BBC, the
Musicians' Union and the regional branch of BBC Bristol had
agreed to set up a training orchestra, with visiting teaching staff
from London and a permanent conductor. An international string
quartet was to coach the string players, and other departments
were also to receive help at the highest level.

However, the MU insisted that the orchestral trainees should be paid a salary so that their concerts could not be said to violate the Union's stand on exploiting young players. My idea of providing a pool of London trained players, attached to the BBC by bonds of loyalty to, and friendship with, orchestral members who had taught them, had been rejected as being radical and too costly. What had been put into operation was far more costly and did not help the players in the BBC orchestra. The training orchestra, based in Bristol, replaced Peter Martin's West of England Orchestra, an existing group that had to be destroyed in order to make funds available. In its place, students drawn from all over the country were to be exposed to embryo conductors, not so much concerned with helping young students on problems of technique, as determined to catch the public eye. The much-vaunted wage they were to be paid would, of course, be fixed at the minimum level and in consequence the recipients could not receive any real practical benefit.

I did not know at the time all the details of the demise of the West of England Orchestra, and fairly soon the hoped-for saving to the Corporation was proving deceptive, although anyone with an elementary knowledge of human nature could have foreseen the consequences. The visiting coaches were offered first class train tickets to Bristol, expense accounts were opened for meals, taxis, and so on. As might have been predicted, some of the teachers would travel third class, take sandwiches, stay overnight with friends and then submit agreed expenses.

To make matters worse it was gradually becoming apparent in the months that followed that the Octet too was creaking at the joints. I had been so busy trying to organise the way ahead that I had not paid enough attention to warning signals from several of the players who had come to the orchestra with Maguire and Dorati. Right from the beginning it was obvious that the younger talent would not be able to cope with the boredom of the job. The result was that within a year most of the new members had left.

The effect of this dissatisfaction within the ranks inevitably spilled over into the activities of the Octet. Since neither Hugh Maguire nor Harry Danks, the principal viola, cared overmuch for each other's company it required endless patience and conciliatory manoeuvres on my part to maintain tempers at rehearsals. I redoubled my efforts to make a go of things but the result was almost complete nervous and physical collapse.

A specialist advised that the rheumatic fever of my youth had left me with a slow vascular reaction and that one of the after-effects was a vertigo that made getting up at the end of the rehearsal or concert unpredictable. Bad lighting combined with inadequate ventilation didn't help either. The moment I entered the cavern in which the orchestra was supposed to have its spiritual home I felt an immediate physical change in my body. Once I was involved in the rehearsal the feeling would not be so dominant, but it would only disappear completely when I could get into the fresh air.

My doctor advised a radical change of activity and as much fresh air as possible, so the BBC granted me three months leave on full pay. I decided to visit my younger brother Myron, who had returned to South Africa in 1960 and was now living in Johannesburg. He was writing long and turgid political letters to Mother, very little of which I understood since they were written in Afrikaans. Nevertheless, they made me curious and so one cold, blustery day in February 1964, I left Southampton by boat, *en route* for Cape Town.

I was determined to enjoy the sea trip to the full, and yet, as I looked at the passengers on deck, waving to friends and family on the quayside, I had my first sense of misgiving. They were either flashy, opulent looking East-Enders from London, going on a month's cruise to escape the dreariness of an English winter, or £10 assisted-fare emigrants sailing, they hoped, to a better future in a new land of promise in the Southern Hemisphere. All were leaving England just at the time when tens of thousands of former colonial subjects were beginning to quit their homes in India, Africa, or the West Indies to move to England.

Sitting next to me at dinner that evening was a gentleman from Manchester. He told me that he had invested all his savings in an enterprise that would produce various drugs for export to Switzerland and the world market. He was on his way to the borders of Basutoland (a British protectorate surrounded on three sides by the Transkei, the Free State and the Cape Province) to set up in business as a manufacturer of pharmaceutical products. He explained with ingenuous candour 'my factory will be built on the South African side of the border although I shall be able to recruit labour from the Protectorate.'

'Why?' I asked.

'More profit,' he replied. 'I build my factory in the Republic and benefit from financial help given to entrepreneurs by the South African Government. I do the Colonial Office a favour by creating work for the unemployed in Basutoland, and I make a lot of money for myself in the process.'

'But why should that be so profitable?' I asked.

'I get a good grant from the South Africans,' he said cheerfully, 'and I pay low wages in the British Protectorate so I score on both counts. Since the Swiss don't ask any unnecessary questions I sell to them at normal world-market prices. You see,' he said, 'I score again.'

It was all too clear. Nothing changes.

CHAPTER THIRTY-TWO

Definitely no Musikvereinsaal

Sir Hugh Carleton Greene, near neighbour and great admirer of Mother's garden, had apparently been upset by remarks I had made to her about the current Winter Concert Series the BBC orchestra was giving at the Festival Hall. I did not realise that she would repeat them to him.

'Sir Hugh would like to talk to you about the Festival Hall's acoustic problems, assuming he agrees that there are problems,' Mother said at breakfast one morning.

She knew that I had strong reservations about the use of the studio at Maida Vale as the next best thing to a spiritual home for the orchestra, and as Controller of the BBC during my five years with the Symphony Orchestra, he had naturally reacted.

An avid listener to Radio Three, Mother would occasionally spice up her chats with Sir Hugh by commenting on the poor quality of the orchestra's tone in their weekly broadcasts. Of the concert of contemporary music which had attracted only three hundred to the Festival Hall she asked with sweet reasonableness whether the music being performed hadn't left a great deal to be desired. 'Don't you agree, Sir Hugh?' Was it the fault of the BBC engineers, the acoustic of the hall, the players, or a combination of all three, she had asked.

'Sir Hugh insists that the BBC's Maida Vale Studios are as good as any in the world,' continued Mother.

'Tell him to ask Sir William Glock if he agrees,' I replied.

I was talking to Mother in her front garden a few days later when Sir Hugh stopped to have their usual gardeners' chat. Mother introduced me and suggested we had a cup of tea. I felt a little embarrassed to begin with, but as he was friendly and seemed willing to listen I explained that I had been on a one-man crusade since 1953, agitating for better facilities for orchestral players. What was disheartening, I explained, was that however well an orchestra plays at the Festival Hall our performances would never be an improvement on rehearsals. A point made by Karajan in a comment on the 'limitations' of the Philharmonia when forced to play under similar conditions.

I tried to make Sir Hugh understand why a fine orchestra requires a hall that allows both player and audience to share in the mystery of sound, rhythm and pitch by contributing a quality of its own. If the performance is to have life, this can only be revealed if the acoustic of the hall is worthy of the occasion and contributes its quota of magic. For an excellent rehearsal in the morning to achieve that 'extra' spark that will produce a wonderful concert, encouragement from both audience and hall is essential.

'Surely that is not too difficult to understand?' I said. 'Why then does London's privileged oligarchy care so little about music that all the London orchestras, but especially the Philharmonia which has been described as "second to none", are obliged to give concerts in a hall whose drab and lack-lustre acoustic matches its drab and lack-lustre appearance? Believe me, Sir Hugh, playing in the Festival Hall, but with vivid memories of performances given in the Musikvereinsaal is both depressing and dishonest. What is more, to accept a compromise of such magnitude betrays a level of awareness that is even more worrying.'

I then had to leave for an appointment, so added a bit more as a parting shot.

'The Festival Hall is a complete disaster—and the studio at Maida Vale is just as bad.'

I was still a relatively new boy when I spoke to Sir Hugh that morning and had yet to become acquainted with the BBC's Tortuous Corridors of Internal Power Politics. So, even though I

A VOICE IN THE DARK

felt sure there was little he could do to improve matters, I asked Sir William Glock (the BBC's Music Controller) if he and Sir Hugh would agree to meet Walter Legge. I wanted to know what they thought about the acoustic properties of the Festival Hall and Studio One and whether they agreed with me that London's orchestras needed a more cultured acoustic. The possibility of also acquiring a spiritual home for the BBC Symphony Orchestra would be a bonus. In 1933 it was realised that the concert hall at Portland Place was too small, so as a temporary measure an empty roller skating rink was leased and adapted for use as the BBC's main rehearsal and concert hall.

I realised that if existing concert venues had to be retained for economic reasons, perhaps Sir Hugh could elaborate on his famous 'fresh air' quotient and what that quotient needed to be. I was convinced that if anybody could do this Walter Legge could.

Sir William agreed with me and said that I could certainly discuss these problems with Walter Legge. However, for political reasons he thought it best not to involve Sir Hugh for the moment. So a few weeks later, in the late spring of 1963, I arranged to meet Walter Legge for lunch at EMI Studios.

Early blossoms were particularly beautiful that year, even though the fragile pink flowers were already being blown into untidy heaps, to become this year's nutrient for next year's growth. The brief miracle had been accomplished ready for the next stage in the cycle of regeneration.

I felt extremely moved when I talked to Walter Legge again. I hadn't seen him for over two years and was glad to find that he had weathered several well-publicised storms without losing his sense of humour.

We spoke about many old friends and colleagues, and about some whose friendship had been found wanting in the balance. I sensed that Karajan was the one who had really disappointed him. I wanted him to know that I shared his disappointment and that I too had felt slighted on occasion by Karajan.

'In the ten years I played under him, Karajan would look right through me both during and after the performance. Sometimes this lack of warmth, or gratitude for a job well done, could be devastating.'

'You didn't find that with Cantelli, did you?' said Walter Legge, lighting a cigarette. 'Quite apart from the warmth of his manner, his death was an even greater loss because he was more interested in performing than in recording music, which would have benefited not only the orchestra but music lovers all over the world.'

'With Karajan committed in Europe, Cantelli dead and no prestigious conductor (apart from Klemperer who I find I cannot take seriously and Giulini, who is never available), what options are there for you?' I asked.

'From the time Karajan began his gigantic recording schedule with the Berlin and Vienna Philharmonic Orchestras in the 1960s, every record he completed abroad inevitably disadvantaged the Philharmonia,' Walter Legge replied. 'I don't have to tell you' (referring to various newspaper articles about the future of the orchestra) 'about the difficulties I am having to cope with at the moment.'

I then related my little drama with Flash and the Iron Duke as an example of how dull music-making was at the BBC. He agreed that there was a lack of artistic flair in most of the programme planning for London's orchestral concert series, but pointed out that it was difficult enough to plan interesting schedules even when one had complete control, as he had. I should not under-estimate Sir William's considerable achievements, considering the circumstances in which he had to work. His problems at the BBC had arisen well before the war when members of the orchestra were forbidden to accept outside engagements.

'There were two main reasons for this,' he said. 'First, there was a binding and enforceable contract of which the BBC and the

Musicians' Union were very proud. Second, there was the "pigeon-hole" mentality adopted by producers. For example, you, Alexander Kok, are an orchestral player. You are *not* a chamber music player, a soloist, a light music player or a jazz musician. This not only deprives you of some extra income but it also restricts your chances of developing any versatility you may possess as a player.'

He told me how, long before the war, Sir Adrian Boult had set out to echo Lord Reith's ideals in terms of music.

'Initially Sir Adrian's hands were not tied by dogma imposed either by the Union or by petty administration. Sir Adrian insisted that the conductor of the orchestra should also be the artistic director and as such, he had to have the right to hire and fire. These conditions no longer obtained after the war, and still do not I might add!'

I gave Walter Legge an example from my own experience. A few weeks after I had joined the BBC in 1960 we were to play *Don Juan* at the Proms. Sir Malcolm had cancelled the second half of the morning rehearsal and we were to meet again at 2.30pm. I suggested that as we had several hours to kill, the cello section might just as well take a short break for coffee and then get together to practise some rather tricky tutti celli passages. All the members of the section were willing, but a few minutes after we had started the orchestral steward appeared. He had phoned the Musicians' Union, reported the situation and had asked for a ruling. To use the favourite MU phrase, the answer came back 'loud and clear' that our little get-together had to stop at once.

Walter Legge sighed.

'You have just described exactly what will always prevent any attempt to make music live in the Corporation,' he said. 'If you want my advice, stop fighting shadows and leave the BBC.'

I told him that as the BBC's 'Man at the top', Sir Hugh, wanted to 'open the windows of the corridors at the BBC and let in fresh air.' I described what I thought would be the benefits if the BBC's orchestral players could be integrated into the educational system of the communities in which they live. I also outlined the benefits of having co-principals so that a combination of teaching, orchestral playing and chamber music could help to maintain equilibrium in a demanding profession.

'Both disciplines are essential as a basis for the musician's role in society,' I continued. 'Playing the orchestral repertoire alone can be very damaging, particularly for string players.'

Walter Legge still remained silent.

Beginning to feel a little discouraged by what appeared to be lack of interest, I then tried to give a typical example of the problems Sir William faced when dealing with entrenched BBC bureaucracy.

'Take the Winter Concert Series,' I said. 'When Sir William was planning the programmes two years ago, key performers had already been contracted elsewhere by the time in-house departments had worked out rehearsal schedules, booked soloists and the venue.'

Walter Legge sighed audibly.

'Another extraordinary facet of BBC administration,' he said, 'is the blend of suspicion and condescension with which programme suggestions are treated by producers. They make you feel that it is an honour for you to be employed at all and, because your performance is broadcast and you benefit from their so-called free advertising, you must accept a fee that takes this advantage into account. What is so strange is that these producers are obviously unaware that radio audiences are in fact almost non-existent. If you point out that it is the BBC that will benefit from a performance that has achieved worldwide acclaim, you are told that this is irrelevant. Their stock answer is always that the BBC has to provide for the public in general and not just for an élite few, seeking perfection. You have to work within the mean average of what is available, they say, or words to that effect.'

Walter Legge seemed to have lost confidence in the future of the orchestra, and possibly even in his own future as a record producer. He still had the same enthusiasm and love for music, but the failure of others to acknowledge his and the orchestra's outstanding achievements had begun to sap some of his vitality. What he was in fact telling me was that in spite of years of hard work he had failed to achieve proper status in London for the Philharmonia.

After he lost the connection with EMI, Walter Legge no longer had a base from which to operate and even less chance of winning support for a permanent home for the orchestra. Because the orchestra's prestigious achievements had been ignored it was going to be easier for Lew Grade to succeed in his pop record-producing venture via EMI and HMV. This would inevitably squeeze Walter Legge and the Philharmonia out into the cold and apparently indifferent world.

On the purely artistic level Sir William did achieve some of his objectives. He was often obliged to accept compromises that made nonsense of what had been intended but because he was an exceptionally talented musician and a kind friend, his social conscience and insight made those five years I spent in the BBC an extremely interesting challenge.

Competing with Sir William's hopes for the orchestra were *avant garde* musicians whose ideas on promoting contemporary music and its performance had become a *cause célèbre* in music as it has done in education and science. Only the motorcar seems to have escaped the discerning minds of these miracle men of the twentieth century. As far as the BBC music programme department was concerned, popular arrangements for solo cello (but written for other instruments) were banned for at least three generations. The explanation Hans Keller gave me was that there was no intellectual validity in playing a piece that had not been written specifically for the cello by the composer. What did attract attention and financial investment on an unprecedented scale however, were the promoters of Aldous Huxley's LSD counter-culture.

Competition within EMI, based on the profit motive, derived from the 'bottom-line' approach to popular entertainment, really took off in the 1950s and this boded ill for the Philharmonia. Karajan's defection in 1959 deprived the orchestra of its most prestigious conductor, a body blow that must have hurt Legge for the rest of his life. Had Karajan remained loyal, out of gratitude to Legge, if for no other reason, and prepared to allocate just a few months of every year to the Philharmonia, it might still have been possible to find a permanent home for the orchestra in London.

There could have been an interchange of opera productions (with their casts) between London and the four major opera houses in Europe controlled by Karajan; there could have been concert performances and recordings of the orchestral repertoire in all five centres. This is, after all, not so very far removed from what Karajan intended to do in Europe, so why could he not have included London in the equation? For that to happen Karajan's heart, for once, would have had to rule his head.

All these speculations would pale into insignificance in 1956 and 1957 when Cantelli and Dennis Brain died within a year of each other. The number of recording sessions offered by EMI to the Philharmonia were restricted even further and by 1964 it had been made clear that EMI and Walter Legge would now be going their separate ways.

Legge was thus forced to accept that there would be no further interest and support for the Philharmonia and faced the onslaught of the expanding drug-based counter-culture. The main record-producing companies in England and America were poised to play leading parts in the pop-music industry, and had little or no interest in the music Walter Legge wanted to be associated with.

There certainly was a market for classical music, clearly

demonstrated by The Academy of St Martin in the Fields, which has sold more records than Karajan. Their outstanding recording of the *Four Seasons* with Alan Loveday as soloist put both Vivaldi and the Academy on the map. Unfortunately the recording quickly became fashionable with people who had never before heard of either the composer or the orchestra, and soon would listen to nothing else. Legge certainly valued the solid benefits of good sales but he did not wish to make records merely to make money. Grade's favourite sales pitch, 'Art for art's sake but money for Christ's sake' attacked the very essence of an art form Walter Legge had for over thirty years brought to millions of people all over the world.

According to Lord Peter Carrington, Grade's adventures into film and TV culture nearly torpedoed Britain's oil-money-interdependency with Saudi-Arabia when *Death of a Princess* angered the Arab world. Exactly how Lord Carrington managed to save the British treasury from collapse remains a mystery to me, since he was, at the time (and remains) a director of Kissinger Associates with, presumably, a conflict of interest.

Acting on the principle that it is always the next all-absorbing interest that needs to be addressed, Walter Legge and I found ourselves discussing the future of the BBC Symphony Orchestra, which had of course been the main reason for my wanting to meet him in the first place.

Although we doubted whether Sir William was ever likely to succeed in recreating the orchestra as he would wish, given the dubious qualities at Maida Vale Studios, I couldn't help noticing that Walter Legge seemed saddened that even that very tenuous lifeline was more than had ever been offered to the Philharmonia. Nevertheless, he wished me every success with my mission, while warning me at the same time that if I were to challenge BBC administrators, I would be fighting shadows for the rest of my career. I should also bear in mind that those members of the orchestra who would inevitably fail the auditions being planned, would present another danger. They would certainly blame me for the loss of their positions, suspecting that I had wanted to curry favour with Sir William. The fact that I too had had to compete for my position would mean absolutely nothing.

'Without discipline, you can have no freedom.' These words reflect an ethos that relies on an ineluctable truth. They were first said to me by Casals, speaking about their particular relevance to the study and performance of Bach's unaccompanied cello suites. According to the educational policies of the new intelligentsia learning had to be fun, and it was fun that provided freedom, not discipline. What then are the values associated with the 1960s? Have they ever been identified or defined? I shall attempt to examine the process by which these values are established.

Drug-dependent young music-lovers are encouraged by record producers to accept a drug-dependent music scenario. The rapid growth of the pop-music industry garners immediate cash returns for media controllers and unlimited opportunities for drug-pushers and suppliers. LSD and a host of other 'fixes' of one brand or another are firmly associated with a mindless noise. Finally, the *latest sound* of a drug-dependent *hit* song, solemnly described as *great* in endless radio repeats on every available channel, twenty-four hours a day, completes the cycle.

How could Walter Legge hope to compete? Popular entertainment is bound by definition to have an advantage over more serious forms of art. This Walter Legge would not dispute or complain about. But if he were here to continue the struggle he would not merely be competing with popular entertainment. In the opposing camp he would have to face successive controllers of the popular media like Alan Yentob, Michael Grade, Michael Green, Lew Grade and the Saatchi brothers—all powerful, immensely wealthy advocates of—what? Nothing that merits the wealth they control.

Lew Grade's interest in the record business, for the sole benefit of his entertainment empire, earned him a peerage. Walter Legge's creation of an orchestra of world stature brought him nothing. His love of music had aroused in me a fierce desire to raise my own inner awareness. No concert in future would be considered to have achieved its purpose without several 'tingle factors'.

CHAPTER THIRTY-THREE

Where now?

I am told that Walter Legge was a difficult man to work with, that his reactions could be unpredictable and sometimes dismissive. If your ideas about aesthetics differed from his, collaboration was never easy and he could make unkind remarks. However, when I *did* once hear such a remark, I felt that the outburst was more the result of exasperation born of frustration.

When we were preparing to make a record, it was sometimes possible to hear why he thought one 'take' was unacceptable, and it was therefore necessary to do another. His sense of pitch was astonishingly acute and quite often it proved to be bad intonation that had spoilt a phrase rather than a misconceived accent or nuance. The artistic integrity of the music performer, and the music infrastructure on which both depended, ruled out easy options, and I have no doubt that he found it difficult to reconcile himself with compromise.

Post-war London was not, until 1949, the easiest environment in which to record on wax masters. Europe, cooling and shrinking away from Hot War, had not yet been coerced into contemplating the need for Cold War. The effect of 'the workers' consensus' sometimes made a mockery of Walter Legge's efforts to plan and execute a series of recordings with foreign nationals, especially if they happened to have German connections. Consequently, there were many post-war strikes.

The Musicians' Union, ostensibly intended to serve the needs of the working musician, seemed unable to comprehend that artistic achievement must sometimes come into conflict with parameters set by agreed fees and recording-time-per-session-plus-overtime, when the duration of tea-breaks etc. etc. become a matter of constant dispute. Those early years must have required the patience of Job, yet Walter Legge still found time to listen to my requests for guidance and advice.

His granting of 'leave of absence' to study abroad was one of the many tokens of kindness shown to me by a man with a conscience and a sense of social obligation. I learnt many years later that two other cellists in the orchestra deeply resented that he allowed me to return to my position on the first desk after each sojourn abroad. Not once did he mention to me the letters of envy, malice and protest he received because of his generous gesture towards the youngest member of the orchestra.

After World War Two he faced more problems, when German music and its significance to the German psyche were being examined world wide by intellectuals. Politicians and City men who had rejoiced to see Germany humiliated by the Treaty of Versailles in 1919, were by 1945 little inclined to look kindly on a man who was still so openly attracted to a country which had represented the sine qua non of his musical horizons before the war. For him there was only one objective: the need to find and encourage new talent. He wanted to get on with music-making. Arguing and preaching about the role of musicians in society he regarded as a waste of time. His hobby, career and obsession was music, and only music.

Born at the turn of the century into a loving and safe family environment near Shepherd's Bush, London, Walter Legge was encouraged in his love for music by his father. This love, nurtured through adolescence almost to the point of obsession, enabled him in 1931 to establish his authority with his first album of Hugo Wolf songs. Joan Ingpen devoted eight years of her life to managing first the Classical Music Section of ENSA from 1942 to 1945 and then the Philharmonia's daily affairs from 1945 to 1950. In the first five years of the orchestra's existence, with no grants and no promise of government support, it was not possible for the management of the Philharmonia to offer key players a reasonable minimum wage. Nevertheless, her role in helping Walter Legge to provide work for the orchestra was crucial to the success of the venture.

As early as 1953 Walter Legge had to contend with entrenched practices of money barons indifferent to the expectations of minorities or to society's spiritual needs. It was therefore not surprising that ten years later he felt disinclined to tangle with the Swinging Sixties and the threatening political shadows of Mr Wilson and his friends, and help me fight a rear-guard action at the BBC.

It was being mooted at this time that for parents to want the best education for their children was damaging to new concepts of social justice. Legge's insistence that only the best was good enough, would no doubt have had to be rejected as anti-social, but he and others of his generation never abandoned their belief in the need for excellence. People like Sir Victor Schuster, who had helped create ENSA when the country was at war, made it absolutely clear that the formation and establishment of the Classical Music Division was to foster high standards of performance as an essential part of music-making.

At the BBC I had tried to help Sir William Glock because I wanted to give something back to society, stirred by the memory of the many wonderful concerts in which I had been involved in the early days of my career.

In 1971 I established the Cheltenham Music Centre in the hope that I would be able to influence others as I had been influenced. The Music Centre must have fulfilled a local need because from very modest beginnings it expanded so well that by 1983 I was obliged to look for larger premises.

I was lucky enough to find an empty bakery in which to house, in addition to the Music School, a small concert hall that I intended to be a tribute to Walter Legge. His widow Dr Elisabeth

Schwarzkopf and his sister Marie Tobin came to look at the charming Edwardian building and both agreed that a Memorial Hall dedicated to Walter Legge would be a project that would be worth supporting.

Unknown to me it had already attracted a ransom site value and by the time I entered the market most of Cheltenham's heavyweight property speculators were involved in secret deals. Not surprisingly, the project eventually failed.

Two more failures were to follow. The first was a TV series that I devised to present England's unique domestic architecture in the context of the English Monarchy from Edward I to Elizabeth II, and was to be called *The Sound of History*. Each episode would depict the reign of an English Monarch and it would adduce music that was being played in the buildings of each particular period, show what sort of clothes were being worn, and what sort of furniture was being evolved, in keeping with ever-changing architectural styles. Above all, there would be no 'Voice over', and no intrusive face to confuse the picture image being presented. Only the eye and the ear would be the immediate source that would stimulate the mind.

Dr Schwarzkopf agreed to help me oversee music that was to link each episode, and the response from everyone I approached was encouraging. Amoco contributed time and money and John Ritchie of Colletts, Dickinson and Pearce obtained the promise of funds from Silk Cut, if either the BBC or Channel Four made a commitment. As Channel Four had already started on a vaguely similar project, they declined the opportunity to participate. Alan Yentob, Head of BBC Television, also declined for reasons I have yet to understand.

Because of a prolonged strike in the American recording industry, most of the drug-based commercial pop music of the Western World was recorded in England during those fat years from about 1955 to 1980. After I resigned from the BBC in 1965

I participated in that unlovely experience. Apart from working with a few talented composers, film and television producers, this period of my life reminds me of soiled linen. For the few hundred session-players in London's never-before-has-so-much-money-been-earned-by-playing-the-same-few-chord-sequences-so-often world, working nine hours a day, seven days a week, was a good illustration of the French proverb: 'A runaway horse runs many more miles for its freedom than for its master.'

Discussions with Sir William and problems relating to the Legal Department, the Inland Revenue, and pension related schemes took up an immense amount of time. At last, in 1967 the BBC Management capitulated, and a co-principal status was officially recognised.

I had resigned in 1965 because of the lack of support for my plans to widen the scope of the work, so didn't benefit from this new arrangement. Because so many performers were required for the 'pop-industry,' the principals and their newly created co-principals considered the BBC's belated concession to be a licence to participate in the Pop Music bonanza in their free time. My plan for the BBC Symphony Orchestra to serve the teaching needs of the local community and the wider public at all levels, based at Maida Vale in Studio One but with an improved acoustic was forgotten. The wealth of classical training for several generations of English orchestral players was rapidly being dissipated in the rapidly expanding drug-based commercial counter-culture.

For the BBC Symphony Orchestra to achieve an equivalent status as that of the NBC in New York or the Hamburg Radio Orchestra it became clear to me that there must be other factors I had overlooked. Did London's music audience really want an orchestra of international stature? Most players simply avoided the question and its implications, content to settle for more money.

Raising the standards of performance had been relegated to improving the quality of all the orchestras employed by the BBC, not just that of the BBC Symphony Orchestra. Pay awards negotiated for the benefit of the symphony orchestra were therefore used as a lever by the Musicians' Union to raise salaries in the other BBC in-house orchestras. Proposals Sir William Glock suggested for artistic reasons, but that threatened the status quo of some obscure BBC administrator, were automatically opposed, using every conceivable tactic by time-servers inside and outside the Corporation.

Sir William had supported, with his usual energy, all the options he could to attract young players and to encourage members of the orchestra to give solo and chamber-music recitals. We were thwarted, and in the end defeated, by a combination of entrenched attitudes on the part of the BBC time-servers, by the Musicians' Union, and by the temptation of easy session-money for the players offered by the pop music explosion.

By 1963, with no Walter Legge to turn to, I felt isolated. Each day was a trial of will against a moribund management that had learnt nothing. Trying to cope with Sir William's conscience-programme planning had been a nightmare in itself – he believed that he had a moral obligation to perform music in Maida Vale Studios that was unlikely to be heard anywhere else.

Consequently, programmes of *avant garde* music were presented by what sounded to me like a bewildering assortment of half-inch nails being rattled in empty jam jars or the sound of a loaded tea-tray being dropped in contra-rhythm. (We never got the timing right. Perhaps the composer had misunderstood Newton's calculations regarding acceleration ratios of tea-leaves in cheap expendable porcelain.) Stringed instruments were chastised by cheap replacement bows in places where it pained the chastisers, never over-keen to damage their costly tools of trade. The concentrated energies of Monsieur Boulez, afraid to stand in wonder at a flower or humbled by the sound of beauty, were directed towards extracting noises from instruments that were not designed to be mere sound-boxes for the starved imagination of contemporary atonal composers in search of rootless wonderment.

Intended to placate the new-music lobby, these concerts at Maida Vale, the Festival Hall, and the Roundhouse came and went—for most of the players not soon enough. While in the process of being interpreted by what one must assume to have been honest endeavour on the part of the conductor and/or soloist, they were nevertheless doggedly supported by a determined assortment of misguided/misdirected/opportunist cranks. It had all become unendurable.

Sir William Glock told me, many years after I had left the BBC in 1965, that he had been disappointed to learn from my father-in-law that I had only left the orchestra because there was more money to be earned as a session player. He knew that I had struggled hard in those early years in the Philharmonia Orchestra to improve my cello playing. He helped me to establish a string quartet at Dartington Hall and yet, despite our many talks about the need for self-improvement, Sir William had nevertheless become so indoctrinated by the BBC system that he believed the fable instead of enquiring as to its source. The five years I had devoted to an attempt to create some magic in the BBC had apparently been forgotten.

I was disappointed with Sir William for not attempting to establish the facts concerning my dispute with the orchestral manager, and he had been disappointed that I had not invited him to mediate.

While I had been working in the Philharmonia I had obviously been living in a dreamland, created to a large extent by Walter Legge. In the BBC, the orchestral works I was obliged to play, because nothing had changed, had become a nightmare of contradictions and unfulfilled aspirations, never, as far as I can recall attaining any degree of 'tingle quotient'.

One day, in a moment of total incomprehension at the monumental stupidity of the orchestral manager, I resigned from the BBC without any thought for the future. My second wife Ysobel (daughter of Harry Danks), who was soon to be the mother of our first son, was understanding, but blamed my predicament on my involvement with Sir William's hopes and his promise of an artistic renaissance.

'It's all Walter Legge's fault,' she said, with typical feminine logic.

Despite this instinctive reaction she was nevertheless convinced that the root cause of my unhappiness in the BBC was a lack of standards by the administration in the Corporation, particularly that which related to the orchestra. I had been led to expect that the BBC Symphony Orchestra could emulate what the Philharmonia had achieved. But without the driving force of a Walter Legge it had been more than stupid to expect the BBC to become the Philharmonia Orchestra by another name.

'Do you mean Sir William Glock's or Walter Legge's or both?' I asked, because both of them demanded nothing but the best from themselves as much as from society. 'Surely to want the best cannot be considered a fault?'

That morning, in the orchestral manager's office, I had looked into the eyes of a man who had no idea of what had prompted my support of Sir William and what had nurtured my enthusiasm for his plans. I could see nothing that could persuade me that he had even begun to understand the contradictions of hope and fear a player has to confront and overcome, before he or she plays a note: A conductor never sounds wrong. A player is only as good as his last performance.

My inability to stomach the condescension of this desktop time-server had nothing to do with Walter Legge's artistic integrity. I left the BBC in the way I suppose most of us do when the crunch comes, because of an emotional impasse.

Paul Huband, an ex-Academy colleague who had been tempted into orchestral management, had a job he had failed to live up to. I had failed to overcome my dislike of his lack of artistic awareness and because it would have been dishonest to remain for that reason alone I had to leave. As I sat listening to him I realised that I was never going to be a useful candidate in the field of contractual artistic organization. I recalled the endless staff meetings at Dartington, meetings with Sir William and representatives of the BBC orchestra and its administrators, talks with players in the orchestra itself and with hostile and enthusiastic programme producers all relying on so many and varied human traits of self-interest.

I woke from my reverie to hear Huband say 'If you are to survive in the atmosphere of the BBC and in the codes of conduct we expect from the members in the orchestra, etc. you will have to be a good boy in future.'

Suddenly the vacuous mediocrity of the man in front of me resolved my uncertainty. Everything he was saying pointed to misconceptions by me. I was the one who had to go. Montaigne was right: 'The lover who leaves is the one who has made the decision.'

My life and career have slipped past too quickly for my taste. The ideals I set myself in my student days may not have been achieved, but the privilege of participating in the best of music-making provided opportunities I would never have been able to experience without the help of the mentors in my life.

In the unhappy years that followed my departure from the BBC, I was so busy trying to find answers that it was not until the establishment of my small music-teaching centre in Cheltenham that I fully realised how Walter Legge's achievements had been ignored. I began to realise how much I owed him for the opportunities he provided for me to look, at the very least, at the stars in the heaven his energy had created.

During my very last meeting with Walter Legge I had told him about my experience at the ENSA audition in 1943 at the cold, dark Theatre Royal in Drury Lane.

'I had intended to start with a short solo, but a voice from the auditorium asked for the Brahms. To my horror I found that I had forgotten to bring my part so started playing from memory, expecting to break down at any moment. To my surprise we were stopped after only a few bars and I was then asked if I played the Haydn Concerto. It's strange, you think you've been let off lightly at the time only to realise later that perhaps you hadn't been so fortunate after all.'

'Why?'

'I said I could play the Haydn, but felt guilty because I hadn't actually played it in public and may have given the wrong impression. Then the voice asked me to come back in a week's time and play it to the panel. You can imagine how hard I worked! Then when I turned up I was told that the query had only been a test. Nothing more than a simple question as to whether or not I knew the concerto. I can't honestly say I was sorry I didn't have to play the Haydn, but I have always wondered what would have happened if I *had* played it, and then been turned down.'

'But you weren't turned down,' Walter Legge said with a smile, searching for another ashtray. 'I only asked the question for the reason you have already explained.'

I sat back speechless. Twenty years had passed and I had never known that the 'voice in the dark' at the audition had been that of Walter Legge. My entire career as an orchestral player in London since 1943 had been based on his evaluation of the way I had played the first thirty-two bars of the Brahms E minor Cello Sonata.

Chronology

1926   Born in Brakpan, near Johannesburg, Transvaal.

1931   Moved to Johannesburg.

1932   Myron Kok born.

1935   Given a cello made by a local carpenter which was too big. Auditioned for the choir of St Mary's Cathedral Johannesburg. Head Chorister.

1936   Began studying cello with Mr Leftwich, later with Betty Pack. Played in local competitions with Darrell and Felix.

1938   Moved to England.

1939–41   Attended Haberdasher Aske's School. Lower School Captain 1940–41

1942   Awarded the Ada Lewis Scholarship to the Royal Academy of Music.

1943   Loaned a Betts cello by the Royal Academy. Formed a duo with Joyce Hedges. Joined ENSA.

1945   Began teaching at the London Violoncello School. Monthly BBC broadcast to South Africa with piano trio. Played in Jacques String Orchestra and Boyd Neel Orchestra. Heard Dennis Brain.

1945   Joined the Philharmonia Orchestra. Formed the Beaufort Trio; successful BBC audition.

1947   Lessons in Paris with Pierre Fournier. Met Schnabel. Accepted as soloist by Ibbs and Tillett.

1949   Lessons with Pablo Casals. Met Suggia.

1951   Opening of the Royal Festival Hall.

1952   Toscanini and Cantelli.

1953   Resigned from Philharmonia. Heidelberg.

1954   Married Annette Ingold.

1955   Further lessons with Casals.

1957–59   Taught at Dartington Hall. Founded the Dartington String Quartet.

1960   Principal Cellist BBC Symphony Orchestra.

1962   Divorced Annette Ingold.

1962–63   Formed the London Octet and London Ensemble. Performed Mendelssohn Octet at Promenade Concert.

1964   Married Ysobel Danks, daughter of viola player Harry Danks. Three sons: Simon (1965) Darrell (1967) and Matthew (1971).

1965   Left the BBC Symphony Orchestra. Began working as a 'commercial cellist' for pop and television sessions.

1968   Tour of Europe with Menuhin (Bath Festival Orchestra). Covered a six-month sabbatical for Roy Carter at Cape Town University.

1971   Founded the Cheltenham Music Centre. Recital tour of South Africa with Virginia Fortescue.

1976   Divorced Ysobel Danks

1977   Fellowship of the Royal Academy of Music

1981   Married Marian Hardy. Rebuilt Steanbridge Mill at Slad in Gloucestershire.

1983   Devised television series *Sound of History*. Attempted to buy the Old Bakery in Cheltenham to rehouse the music school and create a small concert hall, to be dedicated to the memory of Walter Legge. Plans confounded by local politics.

1986   Car-crash in Gloucestershire, all material for autobiography and *The Sound of History* burnt, as were two cellos and bows.

1987   Placed in receivership on false evidence.

1988   Receivership rescinded. Next fifteen years spent trying to recover losses and to prove fraud.

1998   Moved to France. Created a building with a perfect acoustic for use by talented young performers.

Index